THE STORM PROPHET

Hector Macdonald's first experience of the sea was Mombasa Harbour, where he lived on a yacht for six months. He didn't pick up much nautical wisdom, being only one year old at the time, but a childhood on the Kenyan coast brought him many happy hours in sailing dinghies, as well as the mixed joys of being taken to school in a boat.

He first came to Australia at the end of 2002, for a two-month stay in Sydney. During that time he watched his first Sydney Hobart race, developed a healthy admiration for the Australian way of life, and fell in love with Pittwater.

He lives in London, but spends most of each winter wondering why he hasn't yet moved to Sydney. He is already at work on a new Petra Woods novel.

For more information, visit **hectormacdonald.com**

Praise for *The Mind Game*:

'A splendidly engineered tale of deceit and illusion, this is undoubtedly heading for the bestseller lists.'
Maxim Jakubowski, *The Guardian*

'An intelligent, provocative novel – a stylish re-interpretation of *The Magus* for the MTV generation.'
Peter Whittaker, *The Independent*

'A stunning debut . . . A vital new voice in storytelling, Hector Macdonald washes away *The Beach*.'
Aly Burt, *The List*

The Hummingbird Saint:

'John Fowles crossed with Conrad.'
The Guardian

'A chilling thriller that taps the surface of moral idealism in an imperfect world.'
The List

'Does Macdonald write thrillers? Well, yes, although there is far more style and invention here than is often found in the genre.'
Crime Time

THE
STORM
PROPHET

HECTOR MACDONALD

VIKING
an imprint of
PENGUIN BOOKS

for all those who put to sea in storms to help others

VIKING

Published by the Penguin Group
Penguin Group (Australia)
250 Camberwell Road, Camberwell, Victoria 3124, Australia
(a division of Pearson Australia Group Pty Ltd)
Penguin Group (USA) Inc.
375 Hudson Street, New York, New York 10014, USA
Penguin Group (Canada)
90 Eglinton Avenue East, Suite 700, Toronto, ON M4P 2Y3, Canada
(a division of Pearson Penguin Canada Inc.)
Penguin Books Ltd
80 Strand, London WC2R 0RL England
Penguin Ireland
25 St Stephen's Green, Dublin 2, Ireland
(a division of Penguin Books Ltd)
Penguin Books India Pvt Ltd
11 Community Centre, Panchsheel Park, New Delhi – 110 017, India
Penguin Group (NZ)
67 Apollo Drive, Rosedale, North Shore 0632, New Zealand
(a division of Pearson New Zealand Ltd)
Penguin Books (South Africa) (Pty) Ltd
24 Sturdee Avenue, Rosebank, Johannesburg 2196, South Africa

Penguin Books Ltd, Registered Offices: 80 Strand, London, WC2R 0RL, England

First published by Penguin Group (Australia), 2007

10 9 8 7 6 5 4 3 2 1

Text copyright © Hector Macdonald 2007

The moral right of the author has been asserted

Cover and text design by David Altheim © Penguin Group (Australia)
Cover photographs by Rob Homer/Fairfax photos (boat image); John Lund/Getty Images (wave image)
Typeset in 11.5/18pt Adobe Garamond by Post Pre-Press Group, Brisbane, Queensland
Printed and bound in Australia by McPherson's Printing Group, Maryborough, Victoria

National Library of Australia
Cataloguing-in-Publication data:

Macdonald, Hector.
The storm prophet.
ISBN 9780670071012.
1. Yacht racing - Australia - Fiction. I. Title.
823.92

penguin.com.au

CHAPTER 1

In the time I knew the boy called Moses, he made three terrible predictions. The first was his own death; the last was something personal to me. But the prediction everyone still talks about is the Sydney Hobart storm.

So much garbage has been written: that he named the boats, the casualties, that he gave the precise meteorological conditions and wave patterns. This from a boy who'd never been to sea. But I was the only person present when Moses made his storm prediction, the night Kirsten launched *Sentinel*. I was the only witness to his actual words. And I was sure, right from the start, that Moses couldn't see the future.

•

It's about eight o'clock when I leave my office at Spring Cove and head up to the showers. Through the broad windows behind my desk, I've been watching the last Inshore crews docking. There's a new captain in *Melina*, and it's great to see how well he's doing.

Coming in to dock, he has the fenders out and the mooring lines rigged well in advance, and he takes a wide circle into the mild westerly wind for

1

greater control during the stern swing. In training, I had some difficulty persuading him to unlearn his amateur boat-handling techniques – guys often find it hard when a woman tells them they've been doing it wrong all these years. But now he's bringing the stern neatly round, allowing for a measure of wind-driven lateral drift, correctly compensating for the reverse steering peculiarities of SilverBird waterjets as he backs into the slip, and touching the forward throttle just enough to halt *Melina* half a metre from the dock. A model procedure. The sight lifts my heart as I call a provisional end to my working day.

For Kirsten's big night, I actually went to Bondi Junction and bought an outfit. The new dress is already hidden in my shower-room locker, wrapped in a plastic sleeve to protect it from the inevitable residues of sunscreen, engine oil and salt. The matching shoes are tucked away in the forelocker of *Giselle*. No way am I tottering out of here in heels. My plan is to slip down the fire stairs to the basement workshops, then come up the loading ramp onto the dock. Stuart, my patrol partner, might see me from a distance, but at least I won't have to deal with the gags face to face.

The make-up is a lot harder than I remember. I'm rushing the mascara and blusher because any moment one of the dispatchers might wander into the shower rooms and catch me at it. They all know about the party, but that doesn't mean they get to share in the humiliation. The results are hopeless: Kirsten's going to laugh at me. Washing it all off again, I throw on some lipstick, pinch my cheeks, slick my eyebrows with Vaseline and leave it at that. It's going to be dark, after all.

At least the dress is easy enough to get into. It's green silk. The shop girl, who's got to know more than I do, said it brought out my eyes, and that green and my shade of blonde go well together. Still, it feels indecent. Not that it's showing too much, but the material is unnervingly weightless, like some kind of flimsy nightdress – although I'm no expert on those either. I sleep in a T-shirt, work in tennis shorts and my yellow Coastguard polo shirt, and hang out in jeans. It's going to be hard walking out of here in nothing more than a few grams of silk.

An odd thing: looking at myself in the mirror, this alien elegance, I catch a glimpse of Kirsten there.

A nervous laugh, and the impression is gone.

Out of the shower room, down the stairs, and I'm wondering if anyone will pick me up later for walking barefoot through the basement – against regs because of all the engine parts and scraps of sharp metal down there – when there's a blast on the incident alarm and Stuart's voice comes over the speakers.

'All staff! Mayday, tug on fire. All fire-rated crew to Ops.'

I'm already running as my heart goes flat. It's the worst emergency in the book. Most of what we do is picking up launches that have run out of fuel, or sailing dinghies blown out to sea. Sometimes we save people from drowning; occasionally it gets hairy. But fire is a whole different matter. And trying to get people off a burning ship at night – well, we train for it, but we all hope it'll never happen.

'Update,' comes Stuart's steady voice as I pelt along the corridor to Ops. 'Fire spread to cargo vessel, Darling Harbour. All fire-rated crew to Ops.'

Besides Stuart, there's maybe fifteen staff assembled in the Ops room, most of them Inshore crew just come off the 16:00–20:00 watch. A couple of engineers, the Night Duty Officer, and Carole from Admin make up the rest.

'We need crew numbers and types of vessel,' I'm already telling the

Duty Officer. 'Call in Donald and all ALB crews. Alert AMSA, Marine Area Command and Fire Brigades. Stuart, check if the Navy have a team available. And warn Royal North Shore to expect severe burns victims.' Still speaking at a furious rate, I switch my attention to the three Inshore skippers present: 'Take two extra fire R&A kits per boat, and . . .'

It's slowly dawning on me that they're arrayed in a semi-circle around the doorway. That no one's making any effort to respond to my orders. That they're all grinning.

Unable to help myself, I glance down at my dress. Which is when they start clapping.

'Oh, that's low,' I whisper. 'That's brutal.'

A flash goes off. Moment captured forever. 'Petra, I never thought I'd say this,' declares Stuart, 'but you look like an angel.'

'Not to mention irresponsible and completely against regulations.'

'Talk less and you might even pass for a lady.'

'You should all be on a charge for this. False alarms fall under Section 81.3. Instant dismissal, even a police report.'

'Admit it, you'd be cracking up if some other lemon was standing there in the frock.'

They're all still laughing. 'Billy's in for a surprise,' one of them says. 'Does he know he's marrying a girl?'

Carole steps forward with concerned eyes. 'You want some help with your make-up, Petra?'

There's no way to salvage my authority in this dress. I grab Stuart's arm and march him through to Comms. Everything feels more normal here. The two dispatchers have missed out on the fun to stay at their posts, always alert, always listening. But their screens are blank, the radios all silent. No maydays, no urgent signals. The Harbour cameras show nothing out of the ordinary. The weather prognosis is for calm seas and minimal wind.

All the same, the question has to be asked. 'Confirm, please, before I go off to this ridiculous party: there's no cause for concern that we know of tonight?'

'It's not a ridiculous party,' replies Stuart. 'Our sponsor is having her big night. Go and make sure she enjoys it.'

'There's nothing happening?'

'In fact, get her drunk and squeeze some more cash out of her for a new all-weather boat. Donald says ALB-3 is falling ap—'

'Stuart! Answer the question.'

Stuart straightens, a half smile creasing his sharp little face. 'Nothing to report, Captain. All quiet. Recommend immediate departure to CYCA for fun night with best friend.'

'That was a cruel trick.'

But there's a smile on my face as I slip the lines on *Giselle* and head out of Spring Cove.

•

This last Friday before Christmas has fireworks erupting over the city, and tinsel-festooned cruise boats hosting extravagant corporate parties all around the Harbour. I'm keeping my speed right down to protect the green silk from spray – never thought I'd be afraid of saltwater. A dozen balconies on Point Piper hold euphoric crowds of revellers. Shark Island has been transformed into a classical music paradise, with full symphony orchestra and an audience of five hundred picnickers. But none of this beats the intoxicating energy surrounding the Cruising Yacht Club of

Australia in Rushcutters Bay. Here, Sentinel Bank logos drawn in shimmering pink and blue light rotate in the sky above. The thud of music reaches right out into the dark Harbour. This party's going to be intense. Part of me just wants to steer out to the comforting black ocean, rip off the dress and swim – cold, alone.

But Billy's promised to come, and the few hours since I last saw him seem like years. And Stuart's right: it does no harm for Sydney New Coastguard to be represented at Sentinel Bank events. Five years ago, the only people looking out for boats around Sydney were the water police and a couple of under-resourced volunteer groups. If Kirsten hadn't persuaded her board – one of her first acts on inheriting the presidency of her family's bank – to put up the funds for a new, professional organisation, we wouldn't even exist. I'm not entirely happy with the situation – it's uncomfortable knowing how much rests on our friendship – but at least there are now regular inshore and offshore patrols. A safety net for all those sailors and fishermen and thrill-seekers who get themselves in trouble beyond the reach or training of the Surf Lifesaving Clubs.

Mooring *Giselle* at CYCA is awkward work: I can't hop up onto the foredeck like I'm used to. Just climbing over the gunwale means lifting the dress indecently high. It's constricting, paralysing. Why do women do this to themselves? Securing the lines, I spot a tiny smear of oil on the silk. It doesn't matter, no one will notice, but it's frustrating.

The glamour of the party would intimidate me if I let it. It is a stupid waste of time and money and effort, and there's no way it comes close in importance to my job, but all the same a little bit of me does envy those shining, smiling beauties who float about all day in salons and spas. It's not like I want to spend even a second in a seaweed wrap, but there's this little voice that sometimes whispers how great it would be to have people stare

6

at you like they can't even blink. The way the world stares at Kirsten.

She's standing on the prow of *Sentinel*, the most beautiful yacht I have ever seen. In a silver-slashed ice-blue dress, her dark hair hanging loose over bare shoulders, Kirsten has that poise I always envied when we were kids: a straight back that seems to require no effort at all, a chin that lifts just high enough to lend strength to her whole face.

'It's true we've won before,' she's announcing through a microphone. 'It's true this yacht is a triumph of engineering, perhaps one of the finest sea craft ever constructed.' Enthusiastic applause brings a smile to her lips. 'But that doesn't mean we're complacent. Bass Strait is usually good for some shocking weather, and there are plenty of strong crews out there reckoning to offer us some competition. Ladies and gentlemen, let's drink to the world's greatest ocean race, to Australia's most dynamic bank — and to this magnificent yacht, *Sentinel*!'

Kirsten's a different species to the colourless Sentinel Bank directors clustered limply about her, probably unsure which parts of the deck are safe to step on. But she's also quite distinct from the sailors, tempering their rugged physicality with a grace not often seen around CYCA. Even the celebs and racer chasers seem outclassed beside her, lacking the drive and determination that have always defined Kirsten McKenzie for me.

She looks on top of the world, and I'm one of the few people who know otherwise. Kirsten has always confided in me first, even about business. Especially about business. She likes the fact I know nothing about it, that I would never think to act on any privileged information she might reveal. She is surrounded by directors, consultants, lawyers. But sometimes Kirsten just wants to get in a dinghy with me, paddle out into the Spring Cove night, and say all the things she doesn't dare in front of the professionals. So it's possible the Sentinel suits still don't realise how much trouble their bank could soon be in. How low its liquidity has fallen. How desperately Kirsten needs her new stock issue to succeed. Certainly the ratings agencies and regulators have no idea. But as Kirsten always likes to say, it's perception that matters, and right now she couldn't look better.

Sentinel is thirty metres long – 98 feet – CYCA's limit for the Sydney Hobart race. In the violent seas commonly encountered, longer yachts are more likely to break up, so the rule is essential to prevent competitors seeking extra speed with an ever-longer waterline. There's also the more prosaic problem of finding mooring space for these great beasts. *Sentinel* has been allocated the entire end of one of the docks. Her 44-metre mast soars far above the regular yachts. Her clean, uncluttered deck can accommodate eighty guests with ease, but that's a fraction of the total attendance: the rest of the party is spread out over two barges moored in the adjacent pens.

A dozen waitresses, every one of them model material, swarm about the barges in clinging skirts and men's tailcoats. Kirsten's crew, in handsome pink and blue Oxford shirts and pressed white slacks, are struggling to find common ground with the bankers. Those who know me call out their congratulations. I get the same from a few of the other race skippers, most of whom look a little intimidated by the scale of Sentinel Bank's hospitality. No other sponsor is waving their boat off to Tasmania with quite so much style.

The yacht itself is roped off as a VIP area. Kirsten's most valued investment banking clients are all here, along with the biggest fund managers in Sydney and her richest private clients – the UHNWIs, or Ultra High Net Worth Individuals. This moneyed crowd is interspersed with a dozen Grade-A celebrities and the cream of Australia's financial and gossip media.

For a moment I hardly dare approach. I totter slowly past the barges and hesitate at the dock steps.

But now Kirsten's seen me, and she's turning her back on Michael Walters, of all people, and calling down so sweetly, so pleased to find me there. And her security guys are helping me over the rail onto the special matting they've laid across *Sentinel's* deck, and I'm being hugged by Kirsten and I'm hugging her back. It's like we're in the Palm Beach tree house, or out in Kirsten's first skiff, and everything else is just our dreaming aloud.

'Can you believe, I've got two First Citizen candidates on my little boat,' she whispers. 'Michael Walters *right* here, and Rodrigo Valance down below. They're trying to avoid each other. It's quite childish, really,' she laughs.

But she can see my eye's been caught by someone else, because now she says, 'I wondered how long it would take you to spot him.'

'It's really him?' I knew Kirsten had met Daran Sacs a few times in the usual celeb hang-outs, but I hadn't ever expected to see him like this, right here, out in the open.

'It really is. You want to meet him?' Not waiting for an answer, Kirsten snatches up my hand and leads me over to RTV's very own god, calling out, 'Daran, remember I was telling you about Petra? The coastguard, my best friend – the only one of us doing anything useful.'

And I'm in front of Daran Sacs, wondering what the hell to say to him.

'Big pleasure,' he declares. His hands are pressed deep in the pockets of a burgundy jacket. 'Big, big pleasure. Big.'

'Thanks,' I mutter. 'For me too. I'm a huge fan of —'

'Honey, don't embarrass yourself,' laughs Kirsten. She cups a palm around my chin and draws my cheek in as if for a kiss. 'Is that oil on your dress?' she whispers.

Flushing, I turn back to Daran, who says, 'A coastguard, huh? We could really use you on the show.' Smile lines crease his deep fake tan. That wonderful, iconic hair is so close I could reach out and run my fingers through it.

'Me? Oh, uh, no, I'd be terrible on TV.'

'No one's terrible on RTV. We're all real people making Real TeleVision.' You can hear the capitals in his voice. 'You'd be tremendous. Can you swim?'

'Well – yeah, of course. I'm a —'

'That's fabulous,' he says, lovingly. 'You know it's the most rewarding part of my job, discovering I've inspired good smart Australian kids to make something of their lives. Coastguard, right?'

'Right.'

'Next time I'm drowning, I'll demand they send you to the rescue!'

'. . . OK.'

He gives me his TV wink, only it doesn't look so good in the flesh. 'That's a promise, Pennie.' Then it's like I've disappeared, and he's deep in conversation with the girl off *ChatChatChat*.

Kirsten has both arms wrapped around Michael Walters's elbow. She calls, 'Help me convince Michael to have a drink with Rodrigo.'

The one-time schoolteacher is looking embarrassed. 'Really, I'm not sure it's appropriate for First Citizen candidates to fraternise.'

I'm not paying much attention. There's so much to look at. The smooth sleek lines of the cockpit, the instrument panels above each wheel, equipped with the very latest gear, the communications equipment on the mast, just visible through the sparkle of party lights. And then – something disturbing. An unsteady guest has dislodged the yellow cover on a storage locker, revealing a line of trigger-operated parachute rocket flares, each twice the size of anything in civilian circulation and tipped with a sinister metal cap.

'Kirsten,' I say, bending to get a closer look. 'Are those Stellar flares?'

She's beside me in a flash, snapping the cover back in place. 'Let's not start drawing attention. Petra, do you really not possess any make-up?'

'Where the hell did you get them? I'm supposed to report prohibited pyrotechnics. You know the charge is powerful enough to kill someone?'

'I was planning to fire them at the sky,' Kirsten says with a wry laugh. 'Billy, darling, there you are.'

He's right behind me. The Stellars are already forgotten. His broad arms encircle my waist, and now I'm twisting in his embrace to get my lips to his because suddenly nothing else is even registering on my radar.

'Missed you,' he whispers between kisses. His words are soft currents of air on my cheek.

'So sweet,' sighs Kirsten. I'm allowed three seconds more before she has him by the arm and is pulling him towards the stern. 'We have to talk about your job, babe. You're OK to start Monday?'

Throwing a resigned smile at me, Billy lets himself be dragged away. He's barefoot, I notice, and I can't help envying his carefree disregard for life's rules.

Somewhere around three sips of wine later, a man comes over and introduces himself as Sam Drauston, of the *Sydney Business Times*. He's thin in face and body, his black hair close cropped, clothes a little too neat, but he has a relaxed air of wisdom that's unusual in young professionals.

'You're Petra Woods, aren't you? I did a story on corporate sponsorship a couple of years ago. You gave me a quote.'

'I remember. You need another?'

'Help me out with a rumour. You were on this trip Kirsten took to South Africa?'

'Not much of a rumour. We're old friends.'

'Is it true she's brought back some kind of seer?'

My surprise must be painted across my face. 'How do you know?'

'I have sources,' he says with a smile. 'So it's true?'

'She's giving a troubled African kid an education in Australia. That much is true.'

'And it just happens that the boy can see the future?'

'That a serious question? Come on! Maybe a few rural villagers in Africa believe he can.'

'But Kirsten doesn't?'

'Why on earth do you imagine she would?'

'It's a seductive idea for anyone in the investment business. A kid who could spot the next iPod or Google? Who wouldn't be tempted by that kind of stock advice?'

Somehow his smile has shifted from charming to predatory. It's a tiny physical change, but the effect is unsettling. 'Sam Drauston,' I say. 'Weren't you the guy who broke the Corinth story?'

'That's right.'

'Then I don't know why Kirsten lets you on this boat.'

'She'll always need the *Business Times*, whatever we've written in the past. She's too smart to hold a grudge.'

'You just suggested she was gullible.'

The journalist turns to look at her. She's standing on the flat lip of the stern with Billy. As we watch, she reaches out and takes his cheek in her hand. It's a moment of intimacy that vaguely bothers me. Kirsten senses our gaze, smiles at us, and lets her hand fall. A quick word to Billy, and he wanders our way.

'She's a curious mixture, isn't she?' Sam says. 'Highly intelligent, driven, yet somehow out of her depth. Twenty-nine is still very young. Those private equity deals she made last year were rash – how much of the bank's balance sheet is now tied up for a decade in South American fuel depots and Eastern European motorways? And this new issue is over-ambitious. Too much, too soon after Corinth. You can almost see the ghostly hand of her father on her shoulder – clutching so hard she'll do anything, try anything, to keep his bank growing.'

'You don't like her.'

'It's not my job to like or dislike people.' He pauses. 'I feel nervous seeing her at the helm of such an important financial institution, that's the truth.'

'It's easy to criticise from the sidelines,' I say flatly. But my irritation fades as Billy reaches us. His universal friendliness to every stranger still delights and occasionally shames me. He's one of life's believers, is Billy – in the stars, in happy endings, but more importantly in people. His easy acceptance of everything used to bother me until one day I realised I loved him and suddenly it didn't bother me at all. At last I understood that what two people believe is irrelevant to how they feel about each other. And I never stood a chance against someone able to love so unconditionally.

'Billy, this is Sam Drauston from the *Business Times*.' Then, at a loss for some way to explain our intense, slightly frosty atmosphere, I stupidly add, 'He was asking about Moses.'

Billy's easy smile vanishes and his eyes widen. 'That kid is supernatural!

Did Petra tell you about the crash?'

•

Billy's crazy; I rescue people. Put the two together and that's how we met.

A distress call is passed to me one day off Port Hacking Point. Stuart's gone on board a troubled yacht to help her novice crew sail home; on my own, I'm not going to be able to haul this idiot out of the crevice he's got himself into. The other SilverBirds are all galaxies away, which means we've got a forty-minute wait before back-up arrives. *Giselle's* bobbing around in choppy waters at the base of the cliff, and all I can see is a leg sticking into the air. Not a good sign.

'How're you doing up there?' I call.

'Just fine,' comes back the reply.

'Bleeding? Concussion?'

'Nope.'

'Anything broken?'

'Coupla little things. A finger. Wrist. Rib, maybe.'

'OK, hang on.' I drop anchor and shut down the engines. 'I'm bringing you some Entonox for the pain.'

'Don't need it. Just give us a hand out of here, will ya?'

'Can't move you. Another crew will be here soon. The helo's grounded, so we've got to winch you down to a boat.'

'No need,' comes this voice, all amused. 'Just hop up here and help us out – if you're not scared of heights?'

I give him the silent treatment while I secure the anchor, buckle the medpack to my waist, and radio my intentions in to Spring Cove.

'You coming, then? I'm in a hurry, see, and I'll call someone else if you're not up to the climb.'

The nerve of the guy! Still I don't say anything, but he probably hears me dive into the sea and swim to the cliff. It's not bad going, and I'm past the worst part, the slimy, barnacled wet rock, without too much difficulty. The cliff is steep, but there's a few handholds and I get up it quick enough to surprise him anyway. Only, just as I'm reaching that sticking-out leg, I go and nick my elbow on the rock, and I make my grand appearance with blood dripping all over my shorts and legs, so that he says, 'Bloody hell, you're . . . bloody . . .'

I'm annoyed at myself, and say, 'It's nothing,' but he's looking up from that contorted, upside-down position in the crevice and shaking his great curly blond head.

'No, I'm saying you're bloody gorgeous – for a coastie.'

Which, as if I'm not red enough from the blood, sets my cheeks burning, because the guy wedged arse-high in that crevice, with one arm pinned beneath him, is beautiful. Well, not beautiful exactly, but he has this wildness of spirit in him that I recognise in a flash. There are straggly curls going haywire over his forehead, and he's got this stupid little tuft of beard that I know already I'm going to make him shave off. Not that I'm planning to see him again. But yeah, that tiny thought does flash through my head.

'We have rules about harassment,' I say stiffly. 'I don't have to assist you if you're abusive.'

'Fair enough,' he says, like nothing's ever going to bother him. 'Rescue time then. Got a pack under me that's caught on the rock. Can't reach the clip myself. If it's not harassment or abuse, how's about you stick your hand behind my back and let me out?'

It's easy enough once he's explained. There's the strap pulling at his waist, with the clip well out of the reach of his one free arm. Squatting down, I slip my hand into the narrow gap beneath him.

'What are you doing here? Coasteering?'

'Bit of a race, y'know? Made a right balls of that last jump. Buzz'll be catching up any second.'

I've handled a thousand people in my work, but still I feel a moment's shiver as the back of my forearm brushes his side. Then it's done, and he's heaving himself out of the crevice, not waiting for me to help him, even though the movement in his wrist makes him bellow with pain.

'Stay still!' I cry angrily. 'We've got people coming to get you down.'

'Thanks. Like I said, no need.' Already he's yanked the pack free of the crevice and clipped it back on. 'Got to go. You're a star, gorgeous.'

And with that he steps up onto the lip of the crevice and leaps into the sea.

The maniac. What that broken wrist must have felt like on impact with the water. Bad enough for me – I fluffed the jump and smacked myself a red-hot sting on my back and legs. Billy, by this stage, is whipping through the water, his one good arm doing the work of three. That man knows how to swim all right. He looks round at the guy who's just appeared on the cliff top above, and he roars with laughter and ploughs on to the next beach.

I could have caught up with him. I'm a pretty strong swimmer myself. But then what? Wrestle in the ocean? Hardly the professional solution. So it's back to the boat, medpack off and anchor up, then cruise on over to him.

He hears the engines and flips onto his back – still swimming, with

16

one eye on Buzz scrambling down the cliff behind – and he says, 'Now, gorgeous, aren't there rules about coasties stalking? Harassment, isn't it?'

'Get in the boat.'

'Can't. Wrist's bust.'

I set the hydrosparks idling and lean over the side, but Billy's already eight metres away, beating surf like he's got a great white after him.

'Get back here! You could fall unconscious any second!'

'Been going four hours and twenty minutes, ahead all the way,' he calls back. 'Just two cliffs to go. Not handing the race to Buzz now.'

Behind us, Buzz plummets into the waves. Billy sees it and steps up a gear.

He's only twenty metres from the beach when I bring *Giselle* along-side him a second time and use a skiff hook to clip the tow line onto his backpack. He gets what's happened once I have *Giselle* moving again, but now the line's taut and his yanking and shaking and swearing do nothing to free him. He tries with his good arm to undo the backpack, but he quickly finds himself too busy keeping his head above water to manage.

'Come on! Let me go!' he yells, when he gets enough air. 'I'm winning!'

'No way you're climbing a cliff with a broken wrist.' I toss him a lifebuoy to make the ride a little more comfortable for him.

'You don't understand. Buzz'll crow about this for months!'

But he knows I'm not going to free him, and by now I've hauled him so far out to sea, he stops his yelling and struggling. Even he's got to admit there's no way he's swimming all the way back to shore in that condition.

'Jeez, you're some strict coastie,' he grumbles as we come to a halt. He's hugging the lifebuoy to his chest now, like he can barely keep afloat without it. His mood is dead.

We don't speak much on the way in. He's seriously pissed at me, and there's no more 'gorgeous' from him. I hand him over to the medics at Cronulla, and probably would never have seen him again if I hadn't felt bad about his race. A part of me knew even as I was hauling him out to sea that Billy wasn't one to faint on a cliff face, busted wrist or no. He would have made it. He would have won his race.

So let's say it was guilt that had me stop by the hospital that evening. He's lying there in this starch-stiff white bed, looking so out of place and uncomfortable, and the first thing I say is, 'You really have to shave that goatee off.'

And he looks at me with this surprised smile, and says, 'How about you do it for me, gorgeous?'

It's a while before it happens. At first we just chat. He guilts me out by telling how Buzz has been in all day, yanking his chain for being shanghaied by a girl. And I tell him crossly how irresponsible he is, and he pretends to take that as a compliment. I ask him what his ideal water temperature is, and try not to react when he says he reckons it's 23ºC, exactly the same as me. And eventually he comes back to the shaving, but there's no razor in the room, so that's how the dare comes about.

It's what he would have done, after all. Still, sneaking into the nurses' station and pinching a scalpel? I'm meant to be a responsible coastguard. But Billy loves it, he just loves it when I return with my prize, and he sticks his strokeable jaw high in the air and laughs all the time I'm scraping the hairs off his chin.

Our first kiss is peppered with his bristles.

•

A couple of happy hours spin by on the deck of *Sentinel*. I'm almost starting to get used to the dress, almost enjoying it. Billy and I catch up with the small handful of our friends that made it onto the Sentinel Bank guest list. We swap Africa memories with Kirsten's mastman and latest boyfriend, Dermott. We listen politely to the mournful old sailor on the dock predicting disaster for this 'flimsy featherweight of a boat'. We dream aloud about a holiday in the Cook Islands. Then Billy says, 'How's about we see what's up down below?' I get my brain around that one, and we climb down the wide steps of the companionway and join the party in the main cabin.

Sentinel has the kind of interior sailors fantasise about. Everything is made from the lightest materials possible; it would feel flimsy if the workmanship weren't so meticulous. Beneath the cockpit, the senior crew quarters are fitted with enclosed bunks for Kirsten, her sailing master and her two watch captains. The rest of the crew will share the foldaway bunks in the main cabin which, cleared of its usual cargo of long, cumbersome sailbags, feels spacious and airy. The great engine block that powers the hull and keel hydraulics, and generates the electricity for the winches, is currently serving as an untidy drinks table. Forward is another, smaller cabin, a dry refuge containing the crew's lockers, food stores, back-up charts, and medical station. For tonight, the whole interior has been laid with thick pile carpet.

The crowd in the main cabin is looking pretty far gone. Daran Sacs is pressed together with Dahlia Damson from RTV's *instant gratification* show. The three remaining waitresses have given up working. One has lost her tailcoat, a second is just about to. A few of the guests, blaming the heat, are stripping off to match them, including a couple of older UHNWI wives who really shouldn't. Rodrigo Valance, hairier and heavier than he looks on TV, runs his hand between the legs of the youngest waitress and scoops her back onto his knee.

Billy gets caught up in conversation with a couple of surfing idols, but I can't quite let go of my Daran fixation. He is such a disappointment, so not the sexy older man I imagined him to be, and yet I can't deny my fascination. He catches me watching him, looks me up and down. His eyes are bloodshot.

'Who the fuck are you?'

From some uncharted recess of my wounded pride comes a response that bewilders me: 'I'm Rodrigo's personal stripper. Didn't you catch my show earlier?'

Daran stares up at me in shock. His hands twitch in his jacket pockets.

'Is that engine oil?' says Dahlia, eyeing my dress.

I manage a scornful laugh. 'Lube from the pole.'

Daran recovers himself enough to say, 'Would you, uh, like to join . . .?'

'No, thanks,' I reply, coolly dismissive. I've turned on my heel, ready to walk off with great panache, when Kirsten says, 'This is the kid I was telling you about, Daran. You're going to love him. His name's Moses.'

•

Now, I hadn't seen Moses at all since the flight back from South Africa. He was staying with Kirsten for a few days, that much I knew, until her PA could fix up some homely family to take him on for the next two years. I imagined she might have someone take him to the beach, or maybe the zoo. If she found the time in the run-up to her stock issue, I half expected her to arrange a get-together with Dermott and Billy and me, familiar faces for Moses. A barbecue perhaps, or a trip to Luna Park. But I never guessed she would bring him into this vodka-sodden den.

She must have had him waiting in the forward cabin. As Moses comes trustingly into the midst of that crowd, his eyes crinkle with bemusement at the state of Kirsten's guests. He steps with neat precision over the legs of a passed-out hedge fund manager. A young crew girlfriend fumbling groggily with the strap on her jewelled sandal attracts his momentary concern.

'Hi, Moses!' calls Billy. Then Dermott is beside him and giving him a hearty slap on the back.

'How d'you like the party, eh?' he demands.

Moses treats the question with his usual seriousness, looking all around before committing to an answer. By now his young face, his skin colour and his sobriety are starting to attract attention. He is dressed in smart new clothes: a patterned red shirt that hugs his bony frame well, and grey-black trousers hitched up with a shiny-buckled belt. The black leather shoes look expensive. His hair has been tidied up as well, the slightly comic bushiness that met us in South Africa trimmed down to a skull-hugging sheen of disciplined curls.

The stares are becoming more pronounced. Two diminutive soap actresses have climbed onto a bunk to get a better view. It's more than just his appearance: there's a sense of difference about Moses which even the drunkest guests are registering. No one, once they've noticed him, seems interested in returning to whatever they were doing a minute earlier. Conversations and flirtations fade into silence. A mood of expectancy spreads through the cabin.

Daran pulls his hands out of his pockets. He holds up a shiny dollar to Moses. 'This is heads, right? This is tails.' He spins the coin and lands it on the back of his wrist. 'So which is it?'

Moses stares at the hand covering the coin, then at the curious faces on all sides of him. Unquestionably, he is more interested in the crowd than the coin.

'What is he *doing* here?' I whisper.

Kirsten shrugs lightly. 'He saw Daran on TV. Wanted to meet him, same as you.'

'Come on, heads or tails?'

'Daran, he's not a conjuror,' objects Kirsten.

'I'm about to show him the result. He can look into the future and tell me what it's going to be. Isn't that right, buck? Heads or tails?'

Moses gives him an indulgent smile. 'Heads,' he says.

It is tails.

Daran snorts. He snaps the coin into his palm. 'Got yourself a con artist, Kirsten.' His hands go back in his pockets.

'Magic tricks don't interest me,' Kirsten says, settling back on the bunk opposite. 'It's the darker things he comes out with that I find fascinating – and eerie. Tabitha, what was it he said about my hand the other day?'

Her PA seems reluctant to answer. 'He saw blood on it.'

'Nasty,' says one of the fund managers, slugging vodka from the bottle.

'Kirsten, that boy shouldn't be here,' I whisper in her ear. Moses's smile has faded at Daran's dismissal and he now wears a puzzled expression, as if he wants to ask for directions but does not trust anyone to give them. His faintly drawn, permanently arched eyebrows have risen a millimetre higher. 'He's too young for all this.'

'Disturbing, huh?' says Kirsten, ignoring me. 'We're not sure if he means it literally, or if he's saying I'm going to cause the death of someone.'

'That's horrible,' shudders the *ChatChatChat* girl. 'You shouldn't talk like that.'

A couple of others nod in superstitious agreement, although most eyes are still on Moses.

'Oh, come on, sweetie,' laughs Kirsten. 'It's not real.'

'Then why are you taking him into the bank every day?'

Until now, I haven't been aware of Sam Drauston's presence in the cabin. Suddenly he's right beside me, staring at Kirsten with an expression completely at odds with the general mood of drunken entertainment.

Kirsten locates him, focuses on him, even smiles quizzically at him. 'How on earth do you know about that?'

'Aren't you a little busy to be playing the tour guide just now?'

Reaching for Moses's hand, I say, 'I'm taking him to the Club. He shouldn't be exposed to all this.'

'No! Leave him.' Kirsten turns back to the journalist. 'As it happens, I'm hopeful Moses will want to join the Lester McKenzie Global Internship Programme when he's older. And, Sam, if one of my employees is spying for you –'

'Two weeks before Sentinel Bank's biggest-ever stock issue, this is your focus?' Sam Drauston frowns apologetically.

'What are you suggesting?' Kirsten's smile has disappeared. A tension darkens her voice.

'I'm not suggesting anything. I just observe. I see a bank that's been holding a conservative investment position after a bad year of trading suddenly acquire controlling interests in three unknown small-caps, same time the President's hanging out with a . . .' He nods towards Moses.

'That's an outrageous notion! You're insinuating I'm gambling Sentinel Bank funds on a spiritualist's prediction?'

'Kirsten, take it easy,' says Dermott.

'I don't think for a moment you believe in this stuff,' says the journalist calmly. 'Which is why I can't understand what you're doing with a fortune teller. It's bizarre.'

'He is not a fortune teller!' Kirsten's angrier than I've seen her in a long time. Hands pressed down to push herself off the bunk, she says, 'He's just a boy who needs a break, and if you write a single word that implies I'm – *shit!*'

With a flicker of astonishment, she raises her hand and stares at the palm. A thin row of crimson beads runs from the base of her thumb to the centre of her hand. Not a single word is spoken throughout the cabin. Everyone is fixed on that tiny injury, watching in awe as the drops of blood swell into one continuous line. The stillness makes me aware for the first time that there is music playing in the cabin.

Kirsten looks down at the bunk. The jagged head of a steel screw protrudes five millimetres from the frame. 'Tabitha,' she says absently. 'Make a note, will you? Get the whole interior checked again. Can't have this during the race.'

Still no one moves. That scrap of blood has paralysed us all.

'It's . . . That's the second time,' Billy says, uncertainly.

'Let me fix that,' I say, pulling one of the First Aid packs off the cabin wall. But Kirsten seems to want to keep the wound open, let the blood flow.

'Sam, I think you should go now,' she decides, not meeting his gaze.

'He's said other stuff?' someone ventures, eyes still locked on that wound. But no one answers him, and several people seem distressed by the idea.

Daran spins Moses around, points him towards Rodrigo Valance and Michael Walters, and asks, 'Which of these guys do you reckon is going to be our First Citizen?'

'How many children am I going to have?' demands Kirsten's navigator.

'Is *Sentinel* going to take line honours?'

'What's the trick?'

'Is there some African spirit telling you this stuff?'

'Why did you get that coin toss wrong?'

There's a general surge of fund managers, UHNWI wives, and gossip journos towards Moses. But, intimidated by the barrage of questions, he has retreated into a shell of silence. It's becoming obscene, the pressure, the booze and bodies around this kid. I can't let it go on any more. While Kirsten turns to exhibit her bleeding hand to another banker, I put my mouth to Moses's ear and whisper, 'Count to three hundred, then come outside and go to the front of the boat.'

I really don't know how he's going to react, don't even know if he can count. He simply looks at me and says, 'Yes.'

•

There's all kinds of carnage on the docks, where CYCA's security guys are doing their best to keep the drinkers on the barges, and amorous couples off other people's yachts. No one takes much notice of me on the way back to *Giselle*. I feel bad for leaving without telling Billy, but right now I need to move fast.

Dropping into the SilverBird, I jettison those painful shoes and start the port engine. The lone hydrospark is muffled by the noise of the party. The remaining guests on *Sentinel* are all down below, and no one notices as I draw up beneath the chisel-sharp bow. Moses appears in the companionway a half-minute later. I find myself holding my breath as he makes his way along the deck towards me. He gives a little wave which I return, although I'm struggling not to yell at him to hurry up. Then Kirsten comes out on deck.

She spots the SilverBird first.

'Honey, are you leaving? I'm trying to find Moses – have you . . . ?'

Already, she can tell something's wrong. She looks up.

'Moses?'

He stops by the forward hatch.

'Come on, Moses,' I whisper. 'Let's get out of here.'

'Petra? What's going on?'

'Let's go, Moses,' I call louder, starting up the starboard engine and switching on the nav lights.

Kirsten climbs out of the cockpit. 'You're not trying to take him, Petra?'

Her heels slow her down, and she's got a lot of super-maxi deck to cover. But Moses is still not moving, still uncertain.

'Moses, hurry!'

Finally, he moves. Kirsten has paused to kick off her shoes by the mast, but now she dashes towards him. Moses climbs awkwardly over the rail, then hesitates. A SilverBird has a fully open deck, like a dinghy, so all he has to do is jump. But it's a fair drop, and he doesn't like it. Kirsten is level with the first deck hatch. As gently as I can, I steer *Giselle* up against *Sentinel* until my fenders brush the hull. Throwing the engines into neutral I move forward to help him.

'Jump!' I cry, just as Kirsten reaches him.

She snatches for his arm, missing by a millimetre. *Giselle* rocks beneath us, but I manage to catch Moses. His feet scramble for a hold on the gunwale.

A look of anxiety flashes across Kirsten's face. Then the cool, controlling gaze is back. 'Unlike you to make children leap between boats at night,' she laughs. There's a brittle edge to her humour that I find unsettling.

'He shouldn't have been here, Kirsten.'

'He wants to be here, remember? He chose to come.'

I strap a lifejacket on Moses and throw *Giselle* into gear.

'Take him if you want, Petra. I could do with a night off from baby-sitting. But get him back to me in the morning, OK?'

Already she's turned away from us, heading back to her party as if my removal of Moses was exactly what she'd planned. And yet that anxiety, that inexplicable worry in her face, told for the briefest moment a contradictory story.

It makes me uneasy, and I don't know why.

•

The journey home is always beautiful at night. The ocean is calm, allowing us a good fast ride. I've given up worrying about the dress: let the spray do its worst. Moses stands in the centre of the boat, rocking to keep his balance, gazing out at the nothingness to starboard.

'Like it?'

He nods.

'Better than that party, huh?'

He turns to me, tilting his head as if amused.

'I mean, I'm guessing you didn't much like all that noise and those people and that stupid heads-tails stuff.'

'It was no problem.'

'No, sure, no drama, but you didn't like it, did you?'

'Yes. It was fun.'

'Well, but then . . . Moses, why did you come with me?'

He thinks about this for a while, and answers, 'That's what I saw will happen.'

I smile. 'Right.'

He turns back to gaze at the ocean, lifting slightly off the deck from time to time as the SilverBird bounces on the gentlest of waves. He's so still, so contented, that it doesn't seem right to talk to him. Any temptation to give him the guided tour – Manly, Dee Why, Narrabeen – is overcome by his deep serenity. It's like he's praying – standing upright, balancing, getting wet from the spray, but all the time silently praying.

That's why, when he screams, I'm not prepared for it at all.

•

The scream rolls across the sea. It won't stop. It turns jagged. It undulates. It tears out the heart of me.

I kill the engines and rush forward to grab him.

'What is it? What is it?'

He's shivering all over. At my touch, his legs give way, and he collapses in my arms. I lower him to the deck and loosen his lifejacket. He lies there breathing hard and furious while I try to calm him.

'Are you sick? Are you hurt?'

His eyes have gone strange. All loose, like they're rattling around in his head. There's this hot acrid smell coming off him.

'Moses, talk to me. What's *wrong*?'

The last word comes out hard and loud because he's frightening me: I don't understand this thing, this fit. Lacerations, broken bones, lungs full of seawater, these are manageable problems. But when someone just freaks out, that's a different squall altogether. That's why I say it so hard and loud, 'What's *wrong*?'

And that seems to reach him, because his breathing quiets down and his eyes settle, and he looks up at me with this face split apart by worry and says, 'Her ship, out there – lots of ships – dying.'

He points with such certainty out to sea as he says this dreadful thing that it's like it's happening right now, and I even scan eastwards before I remember what a quiet and windless night it is.

'"Her ship"? Whose ship? What are you talking about, Moses? Who's dying?'

'The ships are dying. Her ship – your friend.'

Suddenly I know exactly what he's trying to say.

'The race yachts,' I whisper. 'You mean Kirsten's boat.'

He's nodding vigorously now. 'With water up high, like a house. Like a hill. And so much wind. Wind that sings and shouts.'

I grip his shoulders hard. 'You're telling me you can see this? You see this in the future?'

I want to believe it's some kind of joke, some really bad taste line that maybe Kirsten set him up to deliver. But she had no idea I would take him out to sea. And even as the accusation hovers on my tongue, I remember the scream and the fear in his eyes.

To Moses, this thing is real.

•

So that's the truth of the famous Storm Prophecy. That's what he said. That's *all* he said.

I didn't think for a moment he could see the future. I really didn't. Despite the blood on Kirsten's hand, despite the thing in South Africa. But I have to admit, that night he scared the life out of me.

CHAPTER 2

When Kirsten first raised the idea of a South African holiday, back in August, I hadn't had a break in four years. Not since we set up the Sydney New Coastguard. Kirsten took holidays all the time – that was part of her job, the way she saw it, being the glamorous face of Sentinel Bank. A lot of people thought that's all she was, that the real work was done by her directors. But those people didn't know her father, or his exhaustive efforts to set her up as his successor.

Kirsten veered off his script briefly at sixteen – that thing with the chauffeur which got into all the sleaze papers – and again the next year when she 'borrowed' a bundle of cash and ran off to Mexico. After that, right through university and her early work experience on the trading floor, Lester McKenzie rotated her across every department and had her complete every task imaginable in a financial services company, from reconciling accounts and analysing economic forecasts to laying out the coffee and biscuits for those precious UHNWIs. By the time the throat cancer got the better of him, she'd done it all. She's worked seriously hard, Kirsten, no one can say she hasn't. But she's also managed to fit in a lot of visits to European ski resorts and fancy horse events where everyone's taking her picture. Good publicity, that's why. Success, wealth, international popularity – it all plays well back home.

Foreign holidays don't interest me. Sydney and the ocean are enough. I've no urge to get on a crowded airliner and go chatter with French playboys in the Alps. I'd miss the salt, the rock pools, the unexpected slap of a tailfin against my ankle. When Kirsten and I were learning to sail on Pittwater, struggling to follow my father's bellowed instructions, I remember once we stopped all of a sudden, let go of the mainsheet and sank down into the bottom of the Pacer. Lying there, listening to the flapping of the sail and the trickle of water along the hull, Kirsten said, 'Why doesn't the whole world come here? It's so beautiful.' Pressed against her, feeling water we should have bailed out soaking through my shorts, I said nothing because I'd been thinking exactly the same thing.

Sometimes I wonder about those people who've never seen the sea. Never stood on the shore and stared out over empty reaches of sunny blue or stern cold grey. Never felt the lift and tumble of a hull beneath their feet. Where do they go when they need to be alone? Where do they think? How do they breathe?

My father always wanted to climb Uluru. That was before it was frowned upon, and before the accident stopped him climbing anything higher than an armchair. He had this whole patriotic thing – it's our rock, it represents Australia, it's a part of who we are.

It's not part of me. Too far from the coast, too dry. I can't imagine standing on that great red rock and feeling anything but stress. They say you see waves in the sand. They say it's like standing in the middle of an ocean.

Funny kind of ocean.

So when Kirsten suggested taking off in early December to some dusty inland corner of Africa, just us and our guys, I didn't exactly erupt with excitement. But Kirsten's persuasive – really persuasive. The day her father died, she walked into the President's suite, called an extraordinary board meeting, and talked with such informed passion about the future of each department of the bank that not one director dared contest Lester McKenzie's succession plan. She was twenty-four. I had to hold back her hair that night while she threw up, then cradle her head until dawn to calm her shivering.

I agreed to go to Africa. I refused to let her pay for the trip.

'Come on, honey,' she laughed. 'I know how much you make, and you can't afford this.'

The lodge she'd chosen was exclusive. Just six rooms – actually individual cottages. We all had personal butlers, as well as our own guides to take us around the private reserve whenever we felt like it. Champagne, the French stuff, flowed unchecked every evening. It was true, I couldn't afford it and nor could Billy.

'We've got plenty tucked away,' I told her. 'Book it. And make sure you send me the full bill.'

•

For the first two days, Kirsten was unusually tense, even allowing for the pressures of the upcoming stock issue. She couldn't relax, kept activating her satellite link to check Sentinel Bank's daily results and fire off orders to her senior management. It was clear that Dermott, a Brisbane property developer with more bucks than brain cells, wasn't up to the job of distracting her from the work she should have left behind. Sincere and light-hearted, he was nevertheless typical of the kind of guy Kirsten too often settled for: self-absorbed, simplistic, self-satisfied. He was so used to eliminating his own problems with large injections of cash that he tended to overlook more complicated worries in others. Most of the time he was too busy messing in the pool or tossing rugby balls around the lawns with Billy to notice the strain in the face of his perfect girlfriend.

Every morning and evening she'd be on several calls at once: to her finance director, debating memorised spreadsheets of acquired companies; to petulant traders, offering measured praise or cool chastisement; to Australia's most powerful fund managers, extolling the growth prospects of the bank and promoting the new issue; to Nolan, her sailing master, interrogating him on crew development and the progress of rig and steering modifications on her new boat. Four times a day, she'd throw herself into a fitness programme, precisely designed to have her at peak strength for 26 December. She might as well not have been in Africa. Kirsten's ideal water temperature is 29ºC, and that kind of personality always finds it difficult to switch off. But there was more to it than that. It baffled me to see her so stressed, her mind thousands of miles away, while we watched mild-tempered giraffe stoop and sway over the waterhole.

'They'll survive without you for a week,' I tell her when it's just the two of us sat in the game hide, binoculars concealing our eyes. 'Let go a little.'

She doesn't reply to that, but after a while says, 'You know, this isn't far from where Pa grew up. I always hoped to see it. It's not what I imagined.'

'Don't you want to look for his house?' I knew Lester McKenzie had emigrated from South Africa – a brave eighteen-year-old rejecting the apartheid regime, throwing away every family privilege for a fairer society in Australia – but I hadn't realised Kirsten had brought us so close to his

34

roots. 'Maybe we can find some relatives.'

'I don't think I can face my predecessor right now.' There's a frailty, even dread, in her voice that startles me.

'The bank's doing fine, right?' I say, searching for an explanation. 'Apart from the Corinth thing?'

'Yeah, "apart from the Corinth thing". And the collapse in investment banking revenues that caused. And the money we're incinerating to get the brand back in shape.' Once she's started, the catalogue – buttoned up, hidden away until now – is unstoppable: 'Oh, and the horrendous exposure we've had to copper, not to mention too many wrong calls by the traders this year, and too much capital tied up in private equity. Then there's the debt we've got spread all over the place, and the liquidity problems we're having now that the bond market's up the creek. So yeah, we're doing fine *apart* from the small matter of maybe running out of cash.'

Her composure holds a second longer. 'God, what Pa must think of me,' she stutters. Then the binoculars fall to the ground, and Kirsten is crying as I haven't seen her cry in years. Her thin body is shuddering and it's from this, not her words, that I learn how serious the situation is. I never did understand much about Kirsten's business.

But I understand the tears. We've been through a lot together. 'I had no idea. I'm sorry.' She takes the tissue I find for her and blows her nose. 'You always seem so sure of everything.'

It takes her a while to respond. Two black wildebeest join the giraffes at the waterhole, their heads turning our way in vague suspicion. When Kirsten speaks, her voice is muffled and I have difficulty catching every word.

'Have to look confident, especially with this new issue coming up in January,' she says, blinking at the wildlife. 'Three billion's a lot to ask for, a big gamble. If we get it, the cash problem goes away. But if the markets don't buy . . .' She coughs weakly, closes her eyes. 'We've managed to persuade the auditors the profits are there, but now we have to convince stock analysts and investors that Sentinel Bank is in great shape, reassure them the share dilution will lead to an overall increase in value. Big, bold assertions of success like the *Sentinel* launch party and winning the Sydney Hobart.' Her reddened eyes open, find me. 'Markets have got to believe in the bank or we're finished.'

'No way. Sentinel's too big for that.'

'Bigger companies have collapsed overnight. Look, Petra, this stuff is utterly confidential. You get that, right? Far as the outside world is concerned, everything's rosy for us. So rosy the President feels relaxed enough to go on holiday just one month before the biggest stock issue of her life.'

I stare at her. 'That's why we're here?'

'Perception is everything,' she mutters, stooping for her binoculars.

Kirsten's always had a fairly flexible attitude to the truth. When I was thirteen, she covered for me when I entered a dirtbike race, terrified my father would find out. She ascribed my bruises to a tumble down the slope behind her Palm Beach house and cheerfully took the blame – and her father's punishment – for leading me into that forbidden sector of the McKenzie property. Overcome by guilt, I ended up confessing all, getting us both into still more trouble. Kirsten didn't get mad at me: she told me I was right to be honest, and that was that.

She's stood by me so often. She's been there for me most of my life: seeing me through an early pregnancy scare; bailing me out financially; knocking sense into me during a prolonged depression; even standing up to my father when he's come down too hard on me. So instead of getting angry that there was a Sentinel Bank agenda even to our African holiday,

I just felt sad that Kirsten couldn't simply enjoy it.

It was Billy who finally pulled her out of herself. Stuart said, when he met my new boyfriend, that by helping me relax Billy brought out the sun in me. Now, his easy exuberance worked its magic on Kirsten, and gradually over the week her face lightened and her laughter developed a more genuine, spontaneous ring. It was odd seeing another woman benefit from Billy's simple therapy, but it also made me really proud of him, this fount of happiness, of plain untroubled warmth.

Then, on the fifth day, the lodge manager asked if we'd like to meet the local witchdoctor.

•

He's a fraud, out and out. Like some Vendaland tourism official has been watching all those old adventure movies, and has rigged together every bit of costume and ritual going. The guy is dressed in a lion skin, with teeth on a string around his forehead. He has this long stick which he likes to wave around, with some kind of animal's foot on the end.

And the sounds he makes!

Our landcruiser rolls up outside this hut in the middle of nowhere, and the others all manage to be just a little way behind me as we walk in. Kirsten's on the phone to a Dutch pension fund manager, Dermott's trying to shake the dust off his immaculate city clothes, and Billy's caught up in an animated discussion of local dance traditions with the driver. The witchdoctor's assistant, a kid with a street gambler's cunning, insistently beckons me in, and being first I have to sit right in front of the witchdoctor. The hut's dark and grimy, smells foul. Go into a place like that and you can't help wondering what you're about to sit on, how clean the mat is, what kind of animals are living in there with this freaky guy. It isn't only me: Kirsten's face, when she turns off her mobile and joins us, is all puckered and over-controlled. Billy's not bothered, of course, and Dermott just looks bemused, like he can't believe the poor standards of African residential property.

The witchdoctor waves his animal foot in my face, and says, 'What is your name?'

'Petra Woods.'

'How old are you?'

'Twenty-eight.'

Glancing sideways at Billy and Dermott, he asks, 'Who is your husband?'

'I don't have one,' I answer, and now when he asks, 'What is your job?' I say, 'Aren't you supposed to know all this?'

The bits of dead animal wobble, and he tells me crossly, 'I have not begun communication with the spirits yet!'

Anyway, he lets the job thing slide, and decides to start communicating. We get some chanting, then eye-rolling, then he flexes his biceps over and over until there's this throaty gasp like someone's grabbed a hold of his balls, and his eyes just disappear.

Neat trick.

It's unnerving, facing off two blank white eyes. Voice is good too: upper register, but strained – just the way an old woman should sound after she's been knocking around the afterlife a few hundred years.

'Peter Wood,' screams The Voice. 'I am Muelelwa, priestess of Fundudzi. I have journeyed into your soul. Weh!'

That last word is more of a shriek. Really makes me jump. Billy leans over and whispers, 'He got ya, P.'

'Peter Wood,' says The Voice, 'you are not satisfied with your life, is this true?'

'Well . . . not all of it, I suppose.'

'You work hard, but things do not go the way you want, is this true?'

'Sometimes.'

'You work hard but people do not give you the respect you deserve, is this true?'

I feel Billy's fingers pinch me, and I say, 'Oh yes, that's true,' as a way of pinching him back.

The witchdoctor smiles then, like I'm another fool hooked.

'And there is one more reason you are not satisfied. You long for a husband. Is this true?'

Now that makes me uneasy. Billy and I have got along fine for two years, eyes for no one else, souls wrapped up in each other, without any worrying about the longer term. I've always understood the truth of him – that he lives for the moment – and it was his wild, uncalculating heart that captured me just as surely as I once hooked his backpack. Talk of husbands and marriage is not going to be helpful to our relationship.

'Someone else's turn,' I say abruptly, standing up.

The witchdoctor howls, and cries, 'Peter Wood, do not despair. I see a happy future for you. You will marry a rich man and have many children, and you will have much respect and satisfaction. But you must be patient, and you must wear on your arms the medicine the witchdoctor will give you. Be happy, Peter Wood!'

I didn't buy the witchdoctor's magic potion.

•

Probably we were all being a bit offensive in the landcruiser afterwards. Unnecessarily cynical. We knew the guy was going to be a fake, and the whole thing was only supposed to be a bit of theatre. The witchdoctor was included along with the python dance and the pottery workshop in the fancy package Kirsten booked so it's not like we'd been ripped off. But still, you feel robbed when someone is so obviously a bullshit artist. The vaguest insights, and happy-ever-after predictions. Like I even wanted a rich husband or ankle biters.

We were just griping, that's all.

And then the driver, a sweet guy named Daniel who's sorry to hear us bugged, puts his job on the line and whispers to Kirsten, 'I can show you a real sangoma.'

•

He almost seems to be waiting for us.

We roll into a tiny village on the top of a hill, and there's a teenage boy standing alone in front of a small brick and corrugated iron house. He looks like a schoolboy – pressed white shirt, cheap black trousers – and maybe that's what he is. We're craning our necks, looking for the hut where the guy in the lion skin hangs out, but the landcruiser is stopping right there in front of this regular house, and the boy is stepping forward with a solemn smile and curious eyes that make you worry just what he's going to ask you.

But he doesn't ask anything. All that time, I never did hear Moses ask one question. How does a kid become that self-assured?

'*Ndaa*,' he says. 'Welcome.' And he shakes us each by the hand and leads us round the back of the little brick house to a yard where a woman is sweeping. 'My mother,' he says, and smiles patiently while we all coo our nice-to-meet-yous before telling us that she doesn't understand. Despite the language barrier, it is clear she is not pleased to see us. She abandons her sweeping and leaves us alone with Moses, who squats and invites us to do the same.

That's when I notice how beautiful his gold-grey eyes are. There's something so very ordinary about the rest of him – his ordinary chin and rounded cheeks, his ordinary stubby fingers and ordinary sloping forehead. Those eyes carry everything.

Be a shame, I'm thinking, if he flips his eyes like the other witchdoctor when it comes to fortune-telling time. But strangely that time never seems to arrive. At least, we don't notice when it does. Moses is just chatting about this and that, saying stuff like, 'Tell me about your country,' which I suppose is a sort of question, and it isn't until later that we realise he's not asking this out of politeness. Not until he says, 'Yes, that is where I am going to die.'

It's confusing, that's all. Nothing eerie yet, no reason to get disturbed. But still.

'In Australia?' queries Dermott.

'Yes.'

'Sorry,' Kirsten breaks in. 'You're going to Australia?'

'Yes. With you.'

A smile curls into place. 'Don't get your hopes up. You're not getting a plane ticket out of me.'

'Hang on, Kirsten,' says Billy, 'he doesn't even know where Australia is.'

Kirsten tilts her head. 'Do you know?'

'By the sea,' says the kid, straight off.

It hasn't yet occurred to me that he's never seen the sea. But I get a buzz hearing my country defined like that. Screw the big red rock, everything important is right there on the coast.

'You know how far it is from here?' asks Kirsten.

The question of distance is not interesting to Moses. Instead of answering, he says to her, 'Your father worked very hard for you.'

Those words, though innocent and theoretically banal, are in some indefinable way disconcerting to us all. But in Kirsten they produce a sudden choking cough.

'OK?' I whisper, patting her back until her watering eyes clear and she smiles me away.

Billy breaks the spell with a step back to the previous point. 'Mate, if you're going to die in Australia, perhaps best not go after all,' he says with that generous smile which makes my heart crumble.

And Moses just shrugs the way he always did, and says, 'God has shown me this' – the way he always did.

It's hard to believe how different those same words would sound a few weeks on.

'So,' says Kirsten, recovering her poise. 'What about some predictions for us then? What's the future hold for Dermott here?'

Our great property magnate, it transpires, is going to buy a house. Kirsten has an important meeting in store, and Billy will be visiting a friend. We learn nothing more enlightening before the session is brought to an abrupt halt by the arrival of Moses's father. A gruff, humourless type with a spade in his hand and dirt on his worn trousers, he clucks something at his son, and that's it – reading, or whatever this is, over. He doesn't speak English, but it's clear enough he wants us off his property without delay.

Moses won't take the money we offer him. Under the steely glare of his father he walks us back to the landcruiser, shakes hands with our driver Daniel, then says to me, 'I will see you soon.'

When I reply, 'That's unlikely,' he only smiles patiently. Smiles – and stares.

'What?' I say. 'What is it?' Something about those eyes of his. They've lost focus.

'It is not good,' he mutters.

'What?' asks Billy, drawing close and wrapping an arm around my waist.

'An accident,' says Moses, eyes still glazed. 'Today.'

The sudden tightening of Billy's arm takes me by surprise. Anxiety is not an emotion I'm used to seeing in him. 'Like a car accident?' he says.

'Jesus, Billy,' laughs Kirsten.

'Yes, a car. This car.' Then Moses is staring at me, eyes back to normal, if a little clouded with sympathy. 'Don't be frightened. You will not die.'

'Good to know,' I smile tightly. Billy's arm is a rigid girdle about my waist. My lips to his ear, I whisper, 'It's not real, you know that, right?'

The arm loosens. 'Yeah, sure. Of course.'

A fleck of doubt lingers in his voice. A suggestion of unease. But Billy has by choice done too many reckless and terrifying things in his life to let this nonsense bother him for long. By the time he's clambered into the landcruiser, he's moved on to debating with Dermott the prospects of getting close to a lion tomorrow.

But as I say goodbye to Moses and turn towards the landcruiser, I notice the stricken face of our driver – who has heard every word – and a hazy intuition of my own takes form.

•

43

I take the front passenger seat, perhaps because I want to keep an eye on the road. It's a meandering mess of potholes and collapsing edges, but there's hardly any traffic and Daniel has already demonstrated his competence and comfort with these conditions. This shouldn't be difficult.

'No rush,' I say breezily. 'Take it slow.'

'No rush,' agrees Daniel, gripping the wheel still tighter. A tyre catches the side of a pothole and he swerves unnecessarily hard.

'You think the lodge could get us a different brand of beer?' asks Dermott, behind us. 'The stuff they have tastes woody.'

'Woody, mate?'

'Yeah, you know . . . woody.'

'What I love about you,' sighs Kirsten. 'Such a sophisticated palate.'

'Hey, I'm a builder. I have simple tastes.'

A couple of trucks force us half off the road, and by the time we're past them Daniel has beads of sweat dripping from his forehead. None of the others notice our erratic course. The conversation has moved on to sailing.

'You all right?' I ask Daniel.

His frozen nod is not encouraging.

'You're not worrying about that thing he said?'

No reply.

In a boat, I would use all kinds of distraction techniques to calm a frightened casualty or over-tense crew. But this vehicle is Daniel's turf; my intercession feels clumsy and counter-productive. After a couple of lame attempts to take his mind off Moses, I give up and let him drive in silence.

'Of course you're coming, Billy,' Kirsten says. 'This is my big party.

How could you not?'

'Bankers and journos?' Billy laughs. 'No thanks.'

'But Petra will be there, won't you, Petra?'

'Huh?'

'The launch party. For *Sentinel*. Tell Billy he has to come.'

The track into the private reserve is drawing near. Two more bends in the road, a small hill, and we'll be fine. Aside from a couple of bicycles, there's no traffic in sight. It might be my imagination, but I sense a slight easing in Daniel's taut face.

'Billy's never obeyed a command in his life,' I say, eyes still locked on the road.

'You'll have to find another way to persuade him,' says Dermott suggestively.

A lone saloon car appears on the ridge of the hill. It is moving fast – not speeding, but coming down the slope at a healthy clip. Apprehension floods across Daniel's face.

'That's our turn-off up there, isn't it?' I say with all the casual ease I can muster.

'Yes.' A taut, vacant response.

We reach the first bend, but Daniel's eyes are still on the saloon, and he seems to turn the corner without seeing it.

'At least come and keep Dermott company. Otherwise he'll spend the whole night flirting with the waitresses, who by the way will be dressed in . . .'

It's such a straightforward bend in the road. A broad stretch of relatively good tarmac, clear white line down the middle, fine visibility. We can see the saloon coming, can see the course it must follow. There's no possible cause for concern in these sunny, dry conditions. Even if we meet it on the bend, there's plenty of room for both vehicles. Possibly the other car's speed has increased a fraction, but it's bound to slow down for the corner.

We've got nothing to worry about.

'Steady . . .' I say, as Daniel clenches his big hands tight around the wheel and edges his dripping face towards the windscreen. My fingers tug at my seatbelt, subconsciously testing its strength.

'Yeah, mate, have some pity. Save me from the waitresses.'

As if determined to clear the bend before the saloon reaches it, Daniel squeezes the accelerator. 'Take it easy,' I say with alarm, but Daniel doesn't hear me. He's crouched right forward, chest almost against the wheel, staring frantically at the oncoming saloon.

'Daniel! Slow down!'

I try to shout these words, but only a strained whisper comes out. Still, the chatter behind us continues, unaware. The saloon has slowed less than expected. Both vehicles reach the bend at the same time.

Gripping my seat, I brace myself and watch stupidly as Daniel skids around the bend, yanking the wheel, missing the saloon car by miles but sending us swerving off the road.

Our front left wheel catches a rock, and we turn over.

The lower chassis strikes a tree, sending us ricocheting upside down across a gully. The landcruiser skids on its roof through scrub and maize until its bonnet disintegrates against a boulder in a savage screech of torn metal.

Throughout it all, I am mute, sensing the violent impacts and bruising of my seatbelt but not registering any particular pain, so focused am I on the outcome. Will this kill us? Will we lose limbs, suffer terrible paralysis? What is the correct procedure for dealing with each potential outcome?

Even as I'm brought to a bone-wrenching stop, hanging upside down in my seatbelt, I'm so engulfed in contingencies that I don't immediately understand I've lived through the crash.

I can't move. It takes me a while to acknowledge that I'm suffering from some kind of immobilising shock. Recognising in myself a condition I've often seen in others is a bizarre experience. There is movement behind me, though I can't turn my head to see who's hurt, who might be dead. Voices collide in a roar of confusion. The smell of petrol grows alarmingly strong.

At the edge of my dazed vision, Daniel lies crumpled against the roof. Fragments of windscreen glass glitter around his bleeding head. His neck looks dangerously crooked. His left hand, sprawled towards me, is motionless.

'Daniel . . .' I croak. My ears pick up no trace of my voice. Instead, other voices become clearer. Kirsten's urgent repetition of my name, Dermott's slow groan. But from Billy, nothing.

'Billy?' I say. 'Billy, where are you?' Straining to turn my head, I feel my eyelids flutter and I wonder absently if I am breathing properly.

'Petra!' Kirsten cries again. 'Are you all right?' Her voice seems to be coming from the far side of the planet. The engine gives out a caustic whine.

Then a new noise, close beside my face: the creak of metal under tension. A squealing, wrenching sound before —

'Petra? *Petra!*'

The door is almost torn from its hinges. Billy's hands reach in. Then I'm lifting, scraping, bumping, but coming out into the sunlight in his strong arms.

'Billy . . .'

'I'm here, P, I'm here.'

'Daniel,' I say, weakly. 'The driver.'

'I got him,' promises Billy, laying me down on crumbling earth, a good safe distance from the landcruiser. 'You OK?'

'I'm OK.' My eyes close.

'Poor thing,' he whispers. Then he's gone.

•

Two doctors have been summoned from the nearby town of Louis Trichardt. They take their time examining us, insisting we all lie down on our beds, then checking every millimetre of our bodies for injury.

Their fees, I would guess from the attention we're receiving, must be high. Really, there's no need for anything more than a little disinfectant, a couple of stitches and a tub of analgesics. Kirsten has bruises about her hip and lower back, Dermott took a knock on the head, and Billy suffered a minor laceration to his shoulder. There isn't a scratch on me.

Daniel was not so lucky. In need of urgent medical attention, he was rushed straight from the scene of the accident to hospital. The driver of the saloon saw us spin out of control in his rear-view mirror, turned around and came straight back. He called for an ambulance on his mobile, then set about checking Daniel's breathing and pulse, and staunching the bleeding – all the things I should have been doing.

'He's going to be fine,' promises the lodge manager. 'He's regained consciousness and nothing's broken. Should have been wearing a seatbelt, of course, but his driving is normally perfectly . . .' He stops himself. 'I'm so sorry. A terrible accident. Anything I can do, please let me know.'

When they have all left us alone, we take ourselves to the pool and sit silently for a few minutes, getting used to the fact that we have survived.

'Wow,' says Dermott. 'Spooky.'

'Surreal,' says Billy.

'Remember that British bloke who drew a picture of the planes crashing into the World Trade Center two years before it happened?'

'You hear stories,' agrees Billy, 'but until you see it . . .'

'Well, we don't know what we saw, mate, but . . .'

'No, sure, accidents do happen.'

'Wait a minute,' I interrupt. 'You don't actually think that boy was real?'

Both men look round in surprise. 'Real, P?'

'Forget it. I'm being stupid. It just sounded for a moment like you believed this prophecy thing.' Already I'm starting to laugh. I stop pretty quickly when I see their faces.

'He predicted we'd have an accident,' says Dermott.

'Go easy.' Billy puts out a hand. 'She had a nasty shock. We're all a bit dazed.' He looks back at me. 'How are you feeling, P?'

'I'm fine, thank you very much, except I'm getting worried you guys maybe left a chunk of your sense back in that wreck.'

'How do you explain what happened, then?' insists Dermott.

'You saw what that prediction did to the driver. He believed it, so he drove us off the road.'

'That's harsh,' says Billy. 'The guy's been seriously hurt. We don't have to blame anyone here.'

'But you saw the state he was in!'

'What state?' asks Dermott.

Billy looks similarly confused. I turn to Kirsten, but she answers,

'Honey, to be honest, I wasn't watching the driver. He seemed OK to me, and it was a tough corner, right? Didn't the other car crowd him off the road?'

'You were all in the back,' I say angrily. 'You didn't see.'

'Well, whatever. That Moses boy predicted we would have a crash,' says Dermott. 'And we did. Of course, it doesn't prove anything . . .'

'No, absolutely,' agrees Billy. 'Could have been a coincidence.'

'No!' I say. I can't believe I'm hearing this. These supposedly rational people are seriously entertaining the possibility of clairvoyance? 'No coincidence, no prophecy. I told you: the driver heard the prediction, freaked out, made it happen.'

'You're saying he deliberately drove off the road?'

'Not deliberately, obviously not. He was spooked into bad driving.'

There's a punishing silence.

'Well . . . maybe,' says Billy eventually.

'Not likely though,' says Dermott.

'It's more likely this kid has some mystical connection with the future? Come on! You never heard of a self-fulfilling prophecy? Kirsten, you don't believe in this stuff, do you?'

She's been unusually quiet throughout this, watching Dermott and Billy with a speculative look. 'Of course not,' she agrees, slightly late.

•

Dinner that evening begins on an ugly note.

'Daniel's family have been to see me,' the manager tells us as we enter the dining room. 'I hear he took you to meet the Lukoto boy?'

There's an anger just visible in his face. The tray of champagne glasses in his hands looks momentarily at risk.

'Well, sure, the fortune teller?' I take a glass quickly.

'He shouldn't have done that. We have a contracted sangoma. A Tourist Board *certified* sangoma.'

'Ah, yeah, we went there too. Daniel was just giving us a little freebie,' says Billy quickly, sensing the danger. 'No harm done, mate.'

'I'm afraid there is, and not only to his head or my vehicle. Daniel's family are after that boy's blood, and they're not the only ones.'

'Why? What's he done?'

'The blacks around here,' sighs the manager, 'they blame him when bad things happen.'

'That's ridiculous,' objects Dermott. 'They think he made the crash happen?'

Billy looks at me, eyebrows raised.

'Always it's something bad he predicts. They forget the times nothing happens, but everyone remembers the fights and the illnesses he gets right.' The manager shakes his head at the madness of the world, then pulls out his notepad. 'Well, anyway. It's not your problem. What would you like to eat tonight?'

After he's seated us and gone off to the kitchens with our order, Kirsten says, 'That poor kid.'

'We should do something,' says Billy.

'Yeah,' agrees Dermott.

'Hang on. Do what?'

'I don't know, P. Just – help him. Feels like our fault he's in trouble. If we hadn't gone there —'

'What can we do? This isn't our country. We don't know anything about the people here.'

'Petra's right,' says Kirsten. 'It's a tough situation, but there's nothing we can do for him.'

'That sucks,' mutters Dermott.

'Look, his parents will take care of him,' I say. 'Remember his dad, right? He's not going to let anyone hassle his son.'

'I guess,' says Billy.

'And at least it should teach him not to scare people with stories of disasters.'

We're all a bit subdued for the rest of the meal, worrying about Moses, feeling bruised and still a little shocked from the crash. The food looks excellent as always, but is completely tasteless to me. Billy is particularly silent. It's not like him: usually he's the first to shrug off any pain or setback. He'd normally be drinking harder, talking louder, cracking jokes and generally getting everyone's spirits into orbit. In fact I'm slightly freaked out that he's just sitting beside me, stroking my arm, smiling thoughtfully. I love his closeness, the scent of him around me, and I love the gentleness of his fingertips on my wrist. But this isn't Billy.

So when he stands and raps the table, I don't know what to think. The only other guests, two Chinese men and a Canadian couple, look up in expectation.

Billy fixes his gaze on the tablecloth and says, 'We got lucky today, guys. That crash was pretty scary, especially for me, seeing Petra like that.' He looks up at me. 'I never thought what it'd be like to lose you before.'

Only now am I struck by the realisation of what he's about to say. Something electric sparks inside me.

'Look, I'm not one for buying pension plans and graveyard plots. Too far off. And I guess I've always seen marriage the same way. But when you weren't moving, Petra . . . that was the worst moment of my life. Ever since, just knowing you're OK, I've had this singing in my head, like there are angels dancing there or something. And if this isn't what it feels like when you chuck everything out the fridge and ask someone to marry you, then . . .'

'Mate, are you . . .?' starts Dermott.

'Petra, honey,' cries Kirsten.

Billy's dried up. He just looks at me.

'Yes, I will,' I whisper. 'I will!'

And then I'm in Billy's arms, and the Chinese men are clapping politely, and the Canadians are cheering. I'm so excited, so tearful, so terrified, that I'm gripping him hard enough to brand him, and my dear Billy is caressing my face with such gentle strokes of his big callused fingers.

I have everything, it seems in that charmed moment, that I could ever want.

•

There's a lot of toasting and celebrating that night, and Kirsten makes me promise she can organise the wedding. She's running off a million ideas from fancy European parties she's attended, and I let her expensive imagination play out. Dermott keeps whacking Billy on the back and pouring him another one. All the staff gather around the table, big toothy smiles at our obvious joy.

Soon enough, we move back out to the pool where they've rigged up some wildlife-friendly music for us. Billy's back on form now, leading the celebratory stunts that have to follow, beginning with a mouthful of flaming spirits and heading towards God knows what mayhem, until Kirsten casually says, 'What are you going to do about a job, Billy?'

It's a surprise that Billy's sober enough to hear her, let alone take in the words. But he does. He's on the tip of the diving board, poised to plunge in fully clothed. Somehow he keeps his balance and looks across at her, all smiles.

'How d'you mean, Kirsten?'

'You're not planning to keep working at Wango's when you get married, right?'

Billy takes a step back and settles his weight more solidly on the diving board. That little part of me that's always on duty around water relaxes a fraction. 'Wango's is just temporary while I'm raising the capital for the new canyoning business.'

'How's that going?'

He grimaces and squats down on the diving board. 'It's not easy, seeing as the last one had that . . . difficulty.'

'I can imagine,' she says, tactfully not mentioning the investment she put up and subsequently lost when Billy's Kiwi partner disappeared to Europe with the start-up funds.

'It's a good business,' insists Billy. 'Next time I'll pick my friends better.'

'But until then, you're going to support your wife on casual work? On tips?'

'Hang on.' It's time to interrupt. 'I don't need a husband to support me.'

She looks round. 'How about when you get pregnant?'

'You know I don't want children.'

Kirsten turns back to Billy. 'And what if she gets sick? She is my friend, babe, I have to think about this stuff.'

Billy's trying not to let his dampened spirits show. 'Well, sure, you're right, I could get a proper job until the company's up and running.' But I know he's thinking of all the spontaneous joy that will be stripped from his life when he can no longer drop everything to ride a great wave or catch the perfect updraft.

'You don't need to,' I say quickly. 'Not for me.'

'I want to. For *us*.'

Kirsten hasn't finished. 'What kind of proper job do you have in mind?'

By now, Billy has turned and walked off the diving board, and he answers with a vague shrug. 'Whatever. I guess . . . a desk job.' He says the words the way he feels them – *desk job* – all splintered-glass consonants and alienation.

Kirsten looks thoughtful. 'Could be tricky. You don't have much of a résumé.'

'OK, that's enough,' I say. I know Kirsten's trying to be helpful, but right now I'd rather she minded her own business and let us enjoy our engagement night to the full.

'Come on, Petra, you and I know Billy's a star, but it's going to be hard for an employer to see it on paper. One failed tourism venture, a couple of low-paid jobs teaching kids to surf, part-time work in a bar . . .'

'What are you saying, Kirsten?' asks Billy. 'I'm not good enough to marry Petra?'

Kirsten laughs her charming laugh. The one that gets waiters and bouncers and shareholders laying themselves across puddles for her. 'Don't be silly. Of course you must marry Petra. I'm saying I want to help make it work. Billy, I'm going to give you a job.'

'Oh, Kirsten, you can't,' I say immediately. The thought of Billy in her bank – any bank – is just wrong. 'I mean, that's an incredibly kind offer, but . . .'

'But nothing. Billy has a great way with people and solid common sense. I've got too many maths freaks and cynical money men – I need more human beings, particularly on the marketing side. Billy would be a real asset to Sentinel Bank.'

'Yes, but —'

'How about it, Billy? Reckon you could handle the hours?'

Billy is staring at her in amazement. 'You're really offering me a job?'

'Starting as soon as possible.'

'That's . . . that's amazing, Kirz.'

'Billy,' I say quietly, 'you should look around first. There's a thousand good companies you could work for.'

'So you'll take the job?'

'Something in tourism perhaps,' I whisper desperately.

But Billy is too drunk and too blown away by the offer to hear me. 'I won't let you down, Kirsten,' he promises.

And that's when we all notice the small dark figure in the dusty white school shirt standing at the edge of the lawn.

'*Moses?*'

The two waiters still on duty are quick to apprehend the intruder. They rush from their posts on either side of the pool to seize him by the arms.

'Hey, now, wait, he's OK,' cries Billy.

'We know him! He's a friend.' Dermott starts towards them, arms waving, as if to shoo the waiters away.

'How did he get here?' muses Kirsten. 'Did he walk through the reserve? What about the animals?'

Not to mention the fences and gates, I think, drawing closer. Moses looks tired, dirty, but otherwise untroubled by his journey. He smiles kindly at each waiter as they release him, suspicion in their faces.

'There was no danger,' he says, apparently in answer to Kirsten. 'I've seen this.'

'Moses, it's the middle of the night,' I say. 'Your parents must be worried sick!'

He waits until we've all drawn close around him, fully attentive. 'My father sent me away,' he announces.

'What do you mean? Sent you where?'

'He told me I have to leave.' He looks vaguely ashamed. 'Because of the trouble.'

We stare at each other in shocked silence.

'He *threw* you *out*?'

'Moses, what about your mother?'

'She is angry with me. Very angry. She told me to go a long way from here.'

The thought of it makes me seethe. 'We've got to sort this out.'

'Too right,' says Billy. 'Let's go round there right now and have words with those bastards.'

'In the morning,' I say firmly. 'When we're sober and calm.'

'All right,' says Dermott. 'Still give them a bloody big piece of my —'

'What if they won't take him back?'

It's Kirsten. Standing a little apart from us, considering Moses with a cool detachment.

'They have to.'

'And if they don't? Do we just get on our plane and wash our hands of him?'

'No!' I answer. But I'm not ready to take the logical next step. It's Dermott, secure in his millions and his complacency, who says it first.

'We could take him with us. It's what he said would happen.'

'Come on, Dermott,' I say irritably, 'this is serious.'

'I reckon it's pretty serious when a mum and dad kick their boy out of the house.'

'They'll have cooled down in the morning. We take him back there, have a few words —'

'No.' Moses says it firmly, bluntly. He pulls away, demonstrably afraid. 'I'm not going back there.'

Drawing close to him, I soften my voice: 'Moses, they've been right out of order, but they're your family – you've got to go home eventually.'

'I'm not going back.' He pauses before his punchline: 'It's dangerous for me there.'

'They *threatened* you?' demands Billy.

'It happened before. The old woman who made devil dances.' With wide eyes, Moses wraps his thumb and forefinger around his neck, then jerks his elbow up, a vividly-drawn hangman's rope.

A hush falls over us, the momentary confusion of holidaying Westerners suddenly confronted with the darker side of Africa.

'Right, that's it,' storms Dermott. 'He's coming with us.'

Billy turns to me. 'We can't leave him to these people. Suppose they take him back, who's to say they won't lynch him a week later?'

'We'll ask the lodge to look after him.'

'You think they're going to bother?' says Dermott. 'They'll send him away the moment we're gone. The only moral option is to take him with us.'

A pressure of confusion and anxiety is building behind my eyes. This crazy idea, late at night on a lot of alcohol. I squeeze the bridge of my nose to counter it. 'The logistics are impossible. He'd need a passport, a visa – you know what Canberra's like about immigrants. And who's going to look after him? The responsibility, the organisation, the cost?'

Dermott doesn't even blink. 'Easy. I'll sort it out, fix him with a school, little apartment in Brisbane. There's tax breaks I can use, and —'

'I want to do it.'

We all look round. Kirsten, separated from our fierce little debate, has been having a silent argument of her own. Her face bears the traces of a tough emotional struggle.

'This is exactly why my father set up the Global Internship Programme. Helping gifted disadvantaged young people, just the way George Berryman helped him.' Berryman was the Parramatta condensed milk manufacturer who, impressed by Lester McKenzie's principled rejection of his own home, gave him a new one, put him through university, and got him his first job with the Bank of New South Wales. And when Lester was ready to make his bid for the small, stalled Sentinel Bank – as was frequently recounted at the Palm Beach dinner table – it was George Berryman who lent him the money. Lester McKenzie was never one to forget his debts. Nor did he stop short of passing them on to his heir.

'I want to do it,' she whispers. 'For Pa. This is his country. Moses is one of his people. He would have expected me to do it. The programme's almost made for this boy.'

'Kirsten, think about what you're saying.' I find myself wondering how drunk she is exactly, whether she's still in shock from the accident. She's always been generous, but this determination baffles me. What is this boy to her? What does she hope to get from him? Respite from the impossible expectations of her dead father? A photogenic embodiment of the bank's social responsibility? Or is there something more? 'The commitment, it's huge. Forget the money; you'd be responsible for his welfare for years. Can you honestly tie yourself down like that?'

'I run a public company, Petra. Responsibility is what I do.'

'But where would he live? With you?'

'At first. Until we find a nice family to look after him.'

'This is . . .' I'm struggling for words. Too many life-changing decisions are being made tonight, what with Billy's job and our engagement. Yet another, and we might wake up tomorrow in some kind of alternate reality. 'It's such a generous thing to do, but . . . You can't be there all the time. What happens to him while you're sailing to Hobart?'

'There are ten reliable people I can call in a second to take care of him.'

'Even if his parents agreed to this, it would still be —'

'His parents have forfeited any right to decide his future.'

'Exactly,' growls Dermott.

I stare at them. 'No! They had a fight, but they're still his parents.'

Kirsten crouches, facing Moses. 'You said you wanted to go to Australia. Now I'm offering you that ticket. Do you want to come with me?'

There's not a second of hesitation in his answer. Kirsten looks round at me. 'It's what he wants, Petra. If we go to his parents they'll probably try to extort money. Jesus, they threw him out!' She smiles tightly. 'Well, so, I'm taking him in.'

•

'That's it,' I tell him, pointing out the pale stretch of beach beneath the silent black wilderness. 'Home.'

As *Giselle* drifts onto the mooring, I hook the buoy and fasten the lines, then shut down the engines, lock the console cover, and disconnect the fuel. My extravagant dress is probably ruined, but I'm not going swimming in it all the same. I tell Moses to turn around, to not look, but the moment I've got the dress off, he does exactly that. He stares at my body like he's interested – not turned on or anything, just interested.

'Moses!'

A little smile appears. It's a relief to have pulled him out of himself, even if at some cost to my self-esteem.

'It's rude to stare at a woman in her underwear.'

He considers this, then turns to face Palm Beach.

'Stay here. I'll be back in a sec.'

Pittwater used to be famous for its sharks, back in the days of the rum smugglers and the timber extractors. There are still a few around, but so far they've left me alone. It's fifteen metres from mooring to beach, and in warm weather I always look forward to that swim too much to bother with dinghies or canoes. Groceries get loaded onto a surf rescue board, as do those rare visitors who don't appreciate getting wet. Like the scattering of homes at Mackerel Beach and the Basin, my house has never been reachable by road. Lester McKenzie was horrified the first time he brought his daughter over to visit. That was two months after he had enrolled her in the Newport sailing school where my father taught: eight weekends of tentative bonding between the rich kid and the instructor's girl. He wanted to know how we would get out in an emergency. But we never saw the sea as a barrier – there was always a way out. We didn't want a road.

A few years later, when the wildfires that ravaged Ku-ring-gai Chase nearly destroyed our little house, Lester sent his launch to evacuate us. Six other boats turned up on the same mission – water taxis, friends in tinnies, even a police launch. My mother thanked them all with the relaxed good cheer she was famous for, added that one of our three dinghies would suffice if the worst came to the worst, then went back to helping my father and me with the back burning.

Kirsten used to envy me being taken to school in a boat. To me that was nothing – as everyday and ordinary as swimming, and certainly not to be compared with the limousine that delivered her each morning to Pittwater House. What I loved most was hearing the radio come to life at the weekend, and seeing Dad run out to his rubber duck, leaving me to imagine the brave rescues he was performing up the Hawkesbury or along the Northern Beaches. When I was old enough to go with him, and discovered the more mundane reality of coastguard work – the launch that needs fuel, or the yacht becalmed in a cove – I wasn't disappointed. By then, I was also old enough to fear the sea and be thankful when its victims were merely inconvenienced.

Then Dad had the accident and everything got a whole lot more difficult. When he resigned himself to moving, shortly after my nineteenth birthday, he wanted me to go too. But I had to stay. It was the only home I'd ever known. And it was the last connection I had with my mother. The one place I could conjure a memory of what she looked like without churning seas and white-capped breakers obliterating every detail of her face.

In the house, I switch on the generator, then search for a one-piece swimming costume. Somehow it seems inappropriate to be wearing a bikini around Moses. When I swim back out with the surf rescue board and show him how to place his weight, he readily climbs out of the

SilverBird. He sits very still, clutching my dishevelled dress against his lifejacket, as I tow him ashore.

My phone is ringing when we reach the house. It's the journalist, Sam Drauston.

'How did you get my number?'

'I have ways,' he says. 'It's not too late?'

'It's very late.'

'I'm sorry. I've got a deadline for this piece. Did Moses pull off any more tricks after I left?'

'Come on, you know Kirsten doesn't want you writing about Moses.'

'Maybe,' he answers.

'What does that mean?'

'Petra, was there anything else? Did he predict anything more?'

'Why are you writing about this? You don't believe this prophecy stuff any more than I do.'

'I'm starting to wonder. Look, I hate to ask you, but has Kirsten mentioned any unusual investments she's made recently? Possibly connected with Moses?'

'You think I'd answer that?'

'What we witnessed tonight, it's very hard to put in words. I need something concrete. What is Kirsten really up to?'

'Goodnight, Sam.'

I park Moses at the kitchen table and go to shower. Already, I'm worried about looking after this boy – having to feed him, entertain him, stop him electrocuting himself. I don't know if I can do it. He'll need a toothbrush, pyjamas, clean clothes – what else? What if he has allergies? My impulsive action on *Sentinel* is starting to feel very rash.

At least he seems content for the time being, fiddling with the spark-plugs and carburettor from a dismantled engine, lining them up in particular ways, examining the pattern from different angles, moving them around again.

'Don't lose any of those,' I warn him after my shower. 'The parts are hard to get.' I sit down beside him and move a washer from the edge of the table to a saucer. 'It's my father's old outboard. I'm trying to get it working.'

He plays with the parts a while longer, but it's clear he's still not feeling right. I'm going to have to confront this sooner or later.

'You saw something out there,' I begin guardedly. 'You had some kind of episode, and you got this idea of boats in trouble.'

'The ships dying,' he nods. 'Going under the water.'

The way he's staring at me, almost challenging me, sets me off balance: 'Look, if this is a joke . . .'

Moses blinks, confused. 'It is very serious,' he says, like I'm stupid not to see it.

'All right, yes. But, Moses, you really shouldn't go about saying stuff like that. It's an awful thing to drop on someone.'

He straightens up. It's a completely deliberate movement that suggests a mental rearrangement. The vague sense of reproach has left his eyes. Sympathy takes its place. 'Perhaps your friend won't die,' he offers, folding one hand limply over the other. 'I didn't see what happened to her.'

•

The cockatoos and lyre-birds of Ku-ring-gai Chase like to screech and howl extra loud at first light, so my mornings always kick off early. This one has me on the firmer sand by the waterline, doing my sit-ups and star jumps as the sun creeps above the Palm Beach peninsula and briefly paints gold a strip of blue Pittwater. A long swim and thirty short sprints follow, then, when I'm tiring, some underwater breath-holding exercises. People assume coastguards have a physically active life, but most of the time we're just cruising in the SilverBird, not a whole lot different from the slobs with their stubbies and fishing rods. We have to work out like anyone else.

I take every new Inshore Coastguard recruit to Pittwater for a week and have him (they're mostly hims) work out with me for an hour at dawn. It always bugs them that I can outlast them, and that's the nerve I'm looking to hit. That way, when I send them off with strict instructions to keep up the training, there's a good chance they will.

Moses ambles out of the house around seven o'clock. The tips of his ears, noticeably protruding now that Kirsten's sorted out his hair, glow in the new sun. He's wearing the shorts and faded blue shirt I left out for him. Both belong to Dad. Somewhat on the large side, there's a fair bit of lightweight cotton flapping about, but Moses doesn't look so bad in them.

He turns his eyes to the steep slope of eucalypts and sandstone boulders behind the house. 'You have a big plot, but it's not good for farming.'

'Not mine,' I tell him. 'That's National Park land.' My grandfather worked for the Ku-ring-gai Chase Trust, and he built the house as temporary accommodation. The timber came from an old Estonian schooner wreck that was parked on the beach. The only word still readable was its place of origin, 'Saaremaa', so that's what he named the house. When he died, the Parks Service let our family stay on. They made my father an honorary ranger, and eight years ago they did the same for me. My only duty is to prevent people camping or lighting fires on the beach, prohibitions that suit me well. Of course, I've chosen to assume that, as a responsible ranger, I'm exempt from these rules, and no one has been around at night to tell me otherwise. Sleeping out on the beach beside a good fire, waking from time to time to the reassuring tumble of the surf, is one of the private delights of life at Saaremaa.

'Occasionally the Parks guys suggest I might like to sell the house to them so they can knock it down and make everything pristine again. But I love it too much to leave. Where else around Sydney could you get a beach all to yourself?'

Moses seems to consider this quite seriously until I say, 'That's a rhetorical question – I mean, you're not supposed to answer it. Um, look, are you hungry?'

It turns out that Moses doesn't like breakfast cereal or coffee, or even toast and strawberry jam, but I'm saved from making a special shopping trip to Palm Beach when he spots the packet of spaghetti by the cooker. It's a special new bacon-flavoured spaghetti, and Moses loves it. He says it's almost as good as mopane worms, which I don't even want to know about. His breakfast is spaghetti with tomato sauce, and I cook enough so he can help himself to more at lunchtime.

While he eats, I take the chair opposite him. 'I have to go to work, but I don't want to take you back to Kirsten until I've had a chat with her. Are you going to be all right here, on your own for the day?'

'Yes.'

'It's not as fancy as Kirsten's place, I'm afraid. But it's a much nicer area, isn't it?'

'It's the same to me.'

'Oh . . . Well, there's the TV, some books, you can play music.'

'I like to think,' he says.

'Right. OK.' I don't get kids, but at least he's not going to be the troublesome type. 'I'll try to get back around five.'

My mobile rings then. Kirsten's already left four messages; she's not in the best of moods after last night. But this is an unknown caller number.

I tap the screen. A familiar face appears.

'Hello, Petra? Daran Sacs. We met last night.'

'Yes, we did.'

'I'm guessing I was pissed as a blue whale in a shot glass, right? Sorry, darling, always happens. Please forgive. Big, big apology.'

'Big,' I mutter.

'Yeah, big. I loved meeting you, by the way. Such a gorgeous person you are. Full of beans. Lovely. And, completely unrelated, word is you're hosting our little prophet friend just now. I'm calling to invite him onto the show.'

I look at Moses, sitting there in Dad's old shirt, staring into space as he chomps through the spaghetti. 'He's not real.'

'Of course he isn't, darling,' Daran burbles. 'But that thing with the blood was intriguing, no? And Kirsten's bloke was telling me about your accident in South Africa. Probably all just big, big coincidence but you never know. That's the fun of it for the viewers. Who can ever be sure? I certainly wouldn't bet my life against it. Would you?'

Moses is eating, eating, pumping spaghetti into his mouth like an automaton. A car crash, and blood on Kirsten's hand. Ships dying. Betting lives. I feel a stabbing unease.

'He's not available,' I say, cutting the call.

Moses glances at me, sauce trickling down his chin, sympathy in his big round eyes like he's a mind-reader as well now.

This is ridiculous. I don't believe in psychic bullshit. Seeing the future doesn't happen. It just doesn't.

The phone rings again: Carole, calling from Spring Cove. 'Petra, where are you?' She looks worried.

'I'm late, I know. Is Stuart getting restless? Tell him I'm on my way.'

'It's the police – the dry police. They want to see you.'

•

One of the most important decisions we had to make in setting up the Sydney New Coastguard was where to locate our headquarters. From an operational point of view, we couldn't have found a better site than Spring Cove. On the eastern side of North Harbour, it's well protected from all northerly, southerly and easterly winds, yet it's just a few hundred metres from the Heads. Nowhere else could give us such fast access to the ocean beaches, while also offering the accessibility and shelter of Sydney Harbour. The proximity of Manly Hospital, only a couple of minutes up the hill, clinched it.

The site, on the south-eastern edge of Little Manly Point Park, used to be a gasworks, with deepwater berthing for the coal ships. It already had the foundations we needed for our headquarters, workshops, boat crane and helipad, and constructing a floating dock out from the existing seawall was straightforward. The municipal park that replaced the gasworks was never the most beautiful of amenities, and few people complain about the small corner we've requisitioned.

The police are waiting in my office. Most of the water police are mates; the dry force I don't know at all, which means I want to have some more clothes on before I see them. Matthew meets me in the corridor with a pair of trackie daks, my Coastguard jacket, and a couple of *urgent-call-me-now* messages from Kirsten that I shove in a pocket. Dressed and ready for business, I walk in coolly and shake hands with the two Senior Constables and the plain-clothes woman, then sit down at my desk like I'm a principal. Very strong show so far.

'What can I do for you?' Nicely calm and collected.

'Captain Woods, this is Grace Cadey, the South African Deputy Consul. She's trying to trace a missing South African national.'

Noting my reaction without comment, Grace Cadey lays a school photograph on the desk and points out the face. 'His name is Moses Lukoto. His father reported his disappearance to the South African Police. He claims his son was – the word he used was "abducted" – by a group of Australian visitors staying at the Mimosa Lodge near Louis Trichardt. Yours is the first name on the register,' she adds with an apologetic smile.

She waits for me to speak, but I'm completely at a loss, still trying to piece together the accusation behind her words and understand how I've come to be implicated in this mess.

'There's probably just been a misunderstanding,' says Grace gently. 'But we do need to find the boy.'

'We didn't *abduct* him. His family threw him out!'

The Senior Constables exchange looks. Grace gazes at me intently.

'Did his father sign an adoption agreement with you? If so, you would need to prove he understood the terms of the arrangement in full.'

'No, it wasn't like that. But Moses was in trouble, and we wanted to help him, put him in school . . .'

'Was there a verbal agreement? Did either parent invite you to take Moses?'

'Look, we didn't see the parents, not at that stage, but —'

'Then what makes you think they threw him out?'

I hesitate, sensing the muddy ground even as I stumble onto it. 'Moses told us,' I say weakly.

She sits back, brow furrowed. 'Children say all kinds of things, Captain.'

Scrambling for legitimacy, I snatch at Kirsten's argument. 'He wanted to come! It was his idea. We didn't force him onto the plane.'

'He's fourteen. A minor. It's not his decision.'

I look at the policemen in a kind of daze. 'Are you arresting me?'

They laugh at that. 'We're not here in any official capacity. Just providing a courtesy escort to Mrs Cadey.'

'Which is much appreciated,' says Grace.

'You're very welcome.'

Matthew knocks on the door. 'Sorry,' he mumbles to the police. 'Petra, an alert's come in and all the other boats are tied up.'

A way out. 'Lives at risk?' I ask, rising fast and grabbing my mobile.

'Not exactly.' He hesitates. 'It's a . . . um, it's a sheep.'

I try to ignore the police grins. 'Right,' I mutter.

'So, but you've got the kid, then?' says one of the Senior Constables with almost casual curiosity.

Grace interjects quickly. 'You're very busy, Captain, I can see that. I can also see you're a responsible and sympathetic person, and I'm reassured by that. Could we have a chat later on? For the moment it's enough to let the family know we've found Moses and he's safe, but we will need to arrange for his return as soon as possible.' She puts a card in front of me. 'Give me a call when you have a moment?'

'Of course,' I whisper.

'Thank you.' She shakes my hand. 'By the way, my husband sails dinghies every weekend. He doesn't swim well. I'm really glad you guys are out there.'

'Oh. Yeah. Thanks.'

The policemen hold the door open for her. As they leave they give me a friendly wave. 'Good luck with the sheep,' one of them calls back.

•

It's standing at the bottom of a cliff, south of Rush Point, bleating louder than a foghorn, with waves breaking over its legs. The tide's rising, the rock it's landed on is just about under water, but neither Stuart nor I can find much enthusiasm for saving the fat lump of wool. It's not going to be a simple job. Can sheep swim? How heavy's it going to be when it's soaking wet? Will it bite?

I'm still on the phone as we draw close. 'She brought the *police*, Kirsten. This isn't a game. We did something illegal.'

'Petra, honey, don't sweat it. *You* didn't do anything. I take full responsibility. Bring Moses over, and I'll deal with the police.'

'He's fourteen and his parents want him back. He has to go home.'

'I promised to put him through school here, and that's exactly what I'm going to do.'

'Yeah, that and hawk him around your social set as the in-house entertainment.'

'Listen, I understand why you did what you did last night. Very commendable. I'm contrite. Won't happen again. You needn't worry yourself any further.'

'He's going home, Kirsten. We can't keep him against his parents' will.'

'Sure we can if he's going to be persecuted in South Africa. There are international laws that protect people like Moses from repatriation. Once they've heard his evidence, the Court is bound to rule in our favour.'

'*What* Court? Look, you're getting way too heavy. We all wanted to help Moses, but it's not going to work, OK?'

'Come on, you know me better than that. I made a *commitment*, Petra. You think I'm going to let him down? When have I ever given up on something at the first hurdle?'

'This isn't about you, it's —'

'I've got to go. Bring him over soon as you can, babe.'

She's already cut the call.

'Are we going to get on with this?' complains Stuart, tossing a thumb towards the sheep. 'We're under observation.'

It's true: this is no ordinary sheep. It looks to be a family pet, and its owner is anxiously watching from the cliff top. We have to get a move on. One of us is going swimming and clambering over barnacle-covered sandstone for the sake of a piece of mutton.

We toss a coin.

I lose.

'You owe me,' I mutter. I pull on tough rubber boots and gloves, and Stuart clips the tow cable onto my waist harness and bleats hilariously in my ear. The SilverBird rocks: a wild old wind is building and we're likely to see a bunch of dinghy casualties today. We need to get this done quickly.

'I get first cut,' Stuart yells as I grab a spare lifejacket and dive in. Loud enough for Madame on the cliff to hear. I'm going to have to be seriously gentle with her big fat darling to make up for that.

Pulling myself onto the rocks, feeling the usual sting as a new scratch fills with seawater, I crouch beside the sheep. Amazingly, it seems unhurt from its fall. It has an evil scowl. For show, I reach forward to stroke the sheep's ears. It tries to bite me. The woman on the cliff is screaming something I can't make out. Savage little gusts are tugging at the waves. I stand up and unclip the cable from my waist. The woman is still screaming. I make an effort, and hear 'Her name is Augusta!'

I look at the sheep. 'Augusta,' I try.

Those evil eyes light up. Seeing my raised thumb, Madame quietens down a touch. Looking back at Augusta, I wonder again if she can swim. Probably better not to ask Madame: unlikely she's ever put it to the test. It's only ten metres to *Giselle* – Stuart could even bring her closer still without risking the hull – but it would look so awful if the sheep disappeared underwater and we had to haul her up like an anchor. Augusta is going in a lifejacket.

This is more complicated than it sounds, especially with an uncooperative animal. No one teaches you the best way to float a sheep. I decide to place the spare jacket under her chest, ease her forelegs through the armholes, and tie the straps around her back. Augusta, throughout this, does her best to knock me off the rocks. Finally, the tow cable gets wound three times around her body and secured between her shoulders.

I bend my knees, wrap my arms around her body and heave.

I can't move her. Augusta has a serious weight problem. She's also getting dangerously stroppy with me. I could swear she growls.

'She's too heavy,' I call out. 'You'll have to pull her.'

Stuart works *Giselle* with efficient precision. Easing the throttle forward a fraction, he generates just enough power to bring the cable tight. Augusta feels the cable tug at her belly and shoulders, and she strains against it. A minute adjustment by Stuart on the throttle, and she loses her footing. With a lumpy splash, Augusta plunges forward into the choppy water.

Despite her outraged bleating and frantic paddling, it's straightaway clear that she's not going to drown. The lifejacket has set her at a comical angle, but her head is well above water, and already Stuart is reeling her in. I follow with a lazy stroke and pull myself aboard as Stuart reaches over the transom to grip Augusta's nape.

'Weighs a bloody ton,' he complains.

He's a great partner, Stuart, and smart too. He used to work for Kirsten as some kind of top equities analyst until we made our presentation to the bank on Sydney New Coastguard's first year of operations. Stuart handed in his resignation that day and came to join us at the end of the month. We pay him about a sixth of what he used to make.

Somehow we get the harness around the sheep and haul her up over the side. She kicks and struggles like a demon. When we let go, Augusta slides around the deck a bit, but manages to stand up without too much trouble. Not a bad achievement in that chop. I undo the cable, give her a grudging pat on the head, and get on my mobile to comfort Madame.

We're heading north to return sheep to owner, and I've got a firm hold on Augusta to steady her against the pummel of the waves, when something in one of those little inlets in the cliffs catches my eye.

'Stuart, slow up.'

He steers us round to take a look. At first, it's pretty hard to see into the inlet, what with all the waves building up around the neck. But Stuart spots it soon enough – a scrap of bright red, which we both know has to be a Sparrow sail. It's not upright, which isn't good because the masts on those dinghies are fixed in place. As far as we can tell, it's draped over some rocks on the far wall of the inlet.

'What do you reckon?' says Stuart. He knows what the answer has to be. We've been working that coastline long enough to recognise every cluster of rocks, remember every detail. This inlet doesn't have an official name, but we call it Snapper 3 because it's the third in a row of seriously unpleasant holes in the coastal wall. Snapper 3 has a tiny, inaccessible beach at low tide. Otherwise, it's nothing but a choppy, rock-strewn pool enclosed by the kind of cliffs only Buzz and Billy would try to climb. When the wind's up and the water's rising, the neck of the inlet turns vicious. The whole ocean's trying to fit through that little gap and it coughs and chokes and throws a tantrum in the process. It's not a nice place to go.

And we've got to assume the Sparrow was skippered by a kid.

Stuart's looking a bit white, I have to say.

I catch his eye. 'Shall I take the helm?'

Stuart nods gratefully. He comes forward and grabs hold of Augusta. Calling in position and intention, I move aft and slip into place behind the wheel. The touch of the throttle under my left palm and the solid pressure of the wheelhouse against my knee are reassuring. All the same, Snapper 3 isn't looking good: it's going to be a hellish ride in over those waves.

At this stage, I can't let myself think what it's going to be like getting out again.

I bring *Giselle* round in a circle, speeding, slowing – settling myself. This kind of approach, I want to have an escape route, so we're going in backwards. Reversing slowly into the neck, I cut the power the moment we're picked up by a wave, and get the engines quickly back into forward gear.

The neck of Snapper 3 is perhaps nine metres across; a SilverBird is 2.4 metres wide. Easy margins in calm conditions, but when you're riding a tumbling wave backwards between boat-crunching boulders, you need a hell of a lot more room to manoeuvre. Already, seconds into the approach, our wave is collapsing to the side, rolling us towards the rocks. With no time to think about it, I spin the wheel and open the throttle, whipping *Giselle* down into the trough and up the next wave.

And now we're getting a clear look at the situation: the bows of the dinghy are still visible, the mast is tilted against the cliff, but the rest of the boat is below water. Up close to the cliff, with water already above his waist, a man in a white and red shirt under a yellow buoyancy vest is clutching a child with big scared eyes, maybe eight years old. The man looks too elderly to be the boy's father; his face is a grey-blue colour, and he's just about ready to fall over. His white and red shirt is becoming redder.

Once we're clear of the neck, the power goes back on and we spin around and surf down the front of the wave. Crossing the inlet, we glide to a stop beside them.

'Oh shit,' says Stuart as he clocks the old guy's blood.

The water's calmer back here, but there's still enough wash to cause us problems, and I don't remember exactly where all the rocks are. We've no time to hang about. I grab hold of the kid and pull him out of the man's arms. Poor boy is covered in blood, but it's clear enough it isn't his. That's all the attention he gets from me. I've rescued a million children over the years, but I've never been one to waste time mollycoddling them once I've checked they're OK. Stuart takes care of the soft stuff.

'Where are you hurt?' I ask the old guy once I've set the kid down beside Augusta.

The man's voice is weak. 'I tried to climb for help,' he says gruffly. 'Fell.'

'Where?' I say again, harshly now because we haven't the time for this.

The man lifts his shirt and shows us the wide gash across his side. He's managed to staunch it with his hat, bound in place with a sheet from the dinghy, but the blood's still flowing freely. My guess is he's already lost more than he can spare. And there's no way of knowing what damage he's done to his organs.

'Any broken bones?'

He shakes his head and lets the shirt fall back.

'Better use the steps to protect that wound.'

I guide him round the other side of the boat, watching his face as the deeper water gets to the gash. He's a tough one – doesn't flinch any more than my father would. We could have shifted the steps across the boat, but I want that wound cleaned as much as possible. He seems to understand this, even stooping a little to submerge the rest of it before he climbs aboard.

It's encouraging to see a good dose of surprise in his eyes on first sight of the sheep. A healthy sign of life. As for the kid, he's completely focused on Augusta. All trace of fear has just disappeared. It's like the boy's forgotten he was about to drown in a miserable rocky hole. Only thing he's interested in is the cuddly animal.

He reaches out a hand. 'Careful, she bites,' I start to say, but he's already got his fingertips on her nose and she's letting him pet her.

'Thank you,' wheezes the man as he slumps down beside the boy. 'I don't know how you found us, but thank you.'

'Did you make a distress call?'

He looks up at me with such an embarrassed smile it's like he's twelve years old. 'Batteries in the radio were dead. I didn't check them. No spares.'

'That's a basic rule of seamanship,' I tell him.

'Yes, yes,' he says, clutching his side, 'I'm aware of that.'

'How bad is the pain?' asks Stuart, throwing me a warning look. We're not supposed to lecture idiot sailors until after they're fixed up. 'Do you need Entonox?'

'No. Thank you. Perhaps you could give my grandson some water.'

'In a moment,' I say. 'We need to get out of here before the waves build any higher. Stuart, I want you on the —'

'Now?' says the man, like I'm some kind of lunatic. He looks back at the neck, where the waves are crashing towards us with punishing fury. 'We can't get through there. Obviously, we must wait until it's calmer.'

'That could be hours. You'll have bled to death.'

'Me? We can strap this up. You must have a medical kit.'

'That won't help if you're bleeding internally. We need to get you to hospital, right now.'

'Young lady, I have to advise you: those waves are far too —'

'Thank you, Sir, I don't need advice from a man who takes a dinghy into hazardous conditions with a small child and no radio!'

'Petra,' hisses Stuart.

But the man has slumped back and my anger quickly cools.

'I don't want to endanger Jamie any more than I have,' he whispers. 'I'm telling you to wait. It's my life. I'm prepared to risk it.'

But I'm already swinging us round and steadying my hand on the throttle as I face up to the maelstrom ahead of us. 'You may not know this, Sir, but the only person who gets to give orders like that in a boat is the captain.'

Stuart gets the message; he's already clipping safety lines to the deck rings. With the power cut back, we hold our position in the centre of the inlet, at the point where the energy of the waves has more or less dispersed.

'Now, I'm going to give you an order, which I'd be grateful if you'd obey. We need maximum weight up front. If you can manage it with that wound, I'd like you on the bow.'

A look of resignation has come over the man, but also a look of reassurance. Like now he's decided he can trust me. He nods quietly and turns to his grandson.

'Jamie, slide up front there, would you? That's it – right up against the forehatch.'

Stuart helps the boy and his grandfather into harnesses. When everyone is clipped on, and Stuart has guided the old guy onto the foredeck, I call out to him, 'Take the sheep as well.'

Stuart turns to stare at me. 'You're kidding.'

'We're going to need all the ballast we've got.'

'Petra . . . I mean, seriously?' Shaking his head in disbelief, Stuart bends down and hoists Augusta in his arms. He's a lot stronger than he looks or acts, is Stuart. 'You want a line on her too?'

'Just don't let go of her.'

'Aye, aye,' he mutters, and dumps Augusta on the foredeck. She bleats furiously, struggling to break free, but Stuart and granddad get her pinned down between them. The bow sinks comfortingly low in the water.

The best way to get through waves is to avoid them completely. You count the sets, then shoot for the gates between breakers. As much as is possible, you stick to the troughs, weaving around the waves. In principle, it's all about timing.

Trouble is, the neck of Snapper 3 is too constricted for nimble boat-work. There are no gaps between sets. It's one continuous onslaught. And where in the open sea one might aim for the shoulder of the wave to avoid the worst, here that would take *Giselle* straight into the rocks. We have no choice but to fight our way through the breakers.

We've got our bow as low as possible, so the waves can't push us up and over. Now it's all down to approach and very careful power management. A SilverBird has two 525hp inboard hydrospark waterjet engines. Each one could take the vessel up to 35 knots on calm water. Working together, they provide a lot of punch when you're facing a blockade of furious water. But too much power at the wrong moment could get us killed.

Letting *Giselle* drift back a little in the wash, I wait for the least destructive set of waves we can reasonably expect, and kiss the wheel.

Then I take her in.

She climbs halfway up the first wave, cuts through the upper water, and immediately I power back to avoid flying off the top into the trough beyond. Seawater crashes over the decks. The fear is back in little Jamie's face, water swirling around him, but he's clinging to the straps by the forehatch, and I think I can count on him to hold on. I ease off the power still further as we slip down the back of the wave. Now is not the time for speed. Stability and control are everything.

The second wave is a whole lot bigger.

This time I estimate *Giselle* will need fifty per cent more power to get through. The water smashes into us with enough brute force to crack Stuart's head against the deck and knock the air out of my lungs. We're submerged just a couple of seconds, but the blow has us all gasping when we make it out the other side.

Ahead of us are eight metres of open trough before the next, huge wave. We're well into the neck now, where the compressed force of the waves is greatest, and already I can see a whole lot of trouble wrapped up in the menacing bulk of water roaring towards us.

The old guy looks back at me and yells, 'Go for it, girl!' and I swear there's a spark in his eye like he's loving this wild ride. He turns back, takes a firm hold of Augusta, and flattens himself against the deck. Stuart's got blood on his forehead, but he gives a thumbs-up to show he's OK and then locks onto the handrail once more.

I take a deep breath, and power us into the wave.

This is way different. All control vanishes. I keep hold of the wheel, even while I'm fully underwater and straining every muscle to stay in my seat, but *Giselle* has been seized by a force that would overwhelm any boat. It lifts us and spins us and sends us flying to the side, and I have to throw on full astern throttle to stop us careering into the rocks. As it is, we hit something – I feel the sickening scrape near the bows, and rage at the damage I've done to poor *Giselle*.

The water clears. We can breathe again, but now we're broadside on, horribly vulnerable, stuck in the neck of the inlet, with another monster of a wave about to lift us and flip us over. Our power's right down from the white water in the jet drive. Stuart's turned towards me, eyes urging me to try I don't know what, and all I can do is keep us in reverse and throw the wheel around to give us some chance against –

The wave reaches us while we're still at a 45° angle. We ride up, up, the deck turning vertical, and time stops as we hang in the balance – nearly toppling backwards, nearly losing everything. The starboard waterjet whines as it comes out of the sea. Little Jamie screams, slips, slides down the boat towards me.

'Grab hold!' I yell, lunging a hand I can't spare towards him.

Giselle falls the right way. At the crest of the wave, she slumps forwards, and one-handed I switch gears and take us down the back of the wave with furious determination.

We punch through the next wave like a bulldozer through brick. Poor *Giselle* staggers in her tracks. Her whole frame heaves a ripple with the impact. But the engines recover their thrust and we're out a second later, barely able to believe that what we're seeing is clear ocean.

The last, small waves, *Giselle* roars up and over with ease.

When we come to a stop, no one moves or speaks for a few moments. I let go of Jamie's shivering hand.

Our silence is broken by a timid bleat.

'Stuart, have a look at that port-side bow damage, would you?'

He hauls the sheep back into the boat, then leans over the side. Jamie pops up like a sprung bunny, stares back at Snapper 3, and shouts, 'Awesome!' I don't get kids.

'Just lost a little paint,' says Stuart. 'Nothing structural.'

All of us look like drowned rats. Coughing up seawater. Soaked. Augusta peeing all over the deck. Blood still dribbling out from under the old guy's buoyancy vest.

But everyone's smiling.

•

As we're heading in to the Harbour, and the ambulance is waiting at Spring Cove, we pass three super-maxis practising their race drills outside the Heads. *Sentinel* is among them, scarlet asymmetric spinnaker blossoming out ahead of her, and I can't help but gaze at her for a while. She's just too beautiful to have eighteen sailors running about her decks – crabs scuttling across the back of a dolphin. I've heard all about her revolutionary stretch-keel and canting hull, how together they're going to put two knots on her average speed and win Kirsten her third Sydney Hobart, guaranteed. But it's hard to care what's under the water when that perfect being glides past. *Sentinel*, unleashed to a good wind, looks like she was sculpted by a god. Like she was meant to fly.

'Glad I'm not riding that one to Hobart,' says the old guy faintly. 'Too delicate for our seas.' I don't bother to respond. This is one man whose opinion on nautical matters I can definitely live without.

Kirsten spots us and blows a kiss. We're close enough for her to see our sodden clothes and the scrape along *Giselle*'s bow. She yells something we can't hear, but her amusement is obvious.

There's no point responding. She's already turned away and barked an order to her crew. The scarlet spinnaker is doused, and in the same moment a larger, snow-white spinnaker takes its place, woollen ties snapping away in rapid succession as the wind fills the sail.

They gybe soon after. Very flash.

CHAPTER 4

Daran Sacs is waiting on the beach at Saaremaa that afternoon, an enormous bunch of long-stemmed pink roses in one hand, a bottle of champagne in the other. His launch, a gorgeous creamy grey Kestrel, is rammed up on the sand. He waves when I reach the mooring; he pops the bottle when I dive in. By the time I come out of the sea, he's holding a glass and a towel.

'Not looking,' he says.

'Yeah, you are.' I take the towel, ignore the glass.

'You told me you were a stripper.'

'You remember that, huh?'

In the late afternoon sunshine, his face has a healthier glow. His clothes are better than the night before, too. Not so flashy – more manly. His hair is divine, as always.

'I don't remember it all,' he says. 'Did I try to kiss you?'

'No.'

'Oh, good. Big relief. Not that I wouldn't want to, of course.' He gives up trying to offer me the champagne glass, screws it into the sand beside the roses, and jams his hands into his pockets. He looks a whole lot more comfortable now. 'Lovely place, lovely,' he says. 'So original.' He glances back at the house, already in the shadow of the sandstone escarpment that is the backbone of Ku-ring-gai Chase. I've seen his mansion in Palm Beach – smoked-glass and fluted columns – a very different affair to my tin-roofed, salt-soaked timber home. But I no longer blush for modest Saaremaa. When I first met Kirsten, she lived in a grand house just a hundred metres up the hill from where Daran now rests his perfectly coiffured head. And for all her father's garages and bedrooms and rooftop terraces, I learnt pretty quickly that Kirsten envied my home even more than I did hers. The simple adventure of Saaremaa, with its pockmarked boulders, visiting wallabies, primeval bird screams and absence of asphalt, has always been worth more than two types of sauna and an infinity pool.

'A suggestion of the settler about it,' Daran is burbling. 'Big, big charm. Been feasting my eyes on that delicious rough paint effect.' He coughs. 'Thought I might catch sight of the Moses kid.'

I've been glancing around myself, perplexed by Moses's absence. 'Did you, Daran?' The door to the house is open. He's had a good search inside.

'Not here, huh?' He snaps a heavy grin in place. 'Then it's just you and me, baby.'

It's an awful line, an awful tone, and I give him a look and head off to the house to get changed. Wisely, he doesn't follow. When I come out again, dressed in my oldest jeans and a crumpled shirt, he looks embarrassed.

'Kirsten said you were hot for me.'

'I was.'

'Teen crush?' He's got this stupid dog smile. 'So,' he says, picking up the roses and tossing them in the sea. 'Apology, right?'

'No drama.'

He sighs. 'I've been in this business too long. That's the trouble. No perspective. No understanding of real people.'

'It's "Real TV",' I point out.

'Real, my backside,' he snorts. 'Even that's not real. Had four silicon implants on each cheek to firm them up.'

'You're kidding,' I stutter.

'Yeah,' he grins. 'I am. Got you though.'

I have to give him that. For a moment, in his unprompted gaiety, he looks almost regular.

'Well. Nice meeting you, Petra. For what it's worth, I really do think you're gorgeous. Natural beauty, sunny, those little freckles, sense of energy. Don't see the type enough in TV studios any more. I'm not just soaping you for the kid. Although now that we're talking about him, I do have a minor scheduling disaster for tomorrow's show, last-minute illness, Mark Teeley, major problem, looking at a lot of empty airwaves unless your friend . . . ?'

I shake my head and he turns regretfully away.

The tide's heading out, and his launch is pretty stranded now. When he struggles to heave it back into the water, I walk over and give him a hand.

'It's a lovely boat and you're wrecking the hull, dragging it over sand like this,' I tell him.

'Ah, that's kind,' he says, as we get the launch afloat. 'Big, big kindness.' He looks down at my jeans, wet from the knee down. 'You shouldn't have. I don't deserve it.'

I hold the boat steady while he gets in. 'Look, Daran, he's fourteen years old, and completely unused to all this. He doesn't know anything about this country. It wouldn't be good for him to go on your show.'

'Your call, your call. But I've seen young people blossom with a little television stardust. I've seen stammering introverts grow confident, kids with no ambition find the energy to become something. It's not evil, Petra, it's an opportunity.' He presses a card into my hand. 'That Moses is a strong buck. He can handle it.'

As he speeds off, I turn and scan the slope behind the house. The sun's in my eyes, but I'm relieved to spot a scrap of faded blue by the water tank.

•

Moses and I sit on the rocks above the house and eat the chicken quiche I've brought from town. The beach is completely in shade now, but up here we're still warmed by the sun filtering through the stand of grey ironbark behind us. Across Pittwater, a seaplane bound for Rose Bay momentarily shatters the quiet, building up speed for take-off. A couple of Legend 41s head for Church Point, tacking against a gentle southerly, their genoas perfectly curved over their bows. These two graceful creatures put to shame those forests of bare masts that never move from Careel Bay and Newport, those graveyards of expensive toys. Something about a well-constructed boat left permanently moored really bugs me. It seems as cruel as keeping a stallion fenced in all day long. Boats need to breathe and stretch their legs; they need to live.

I wonder if Moses feels at home here; the gum trees and seascape must seem alien, but some of the dry brush around us isn't so different from the sparse vegetation outside his village. Certainly Lester McKenzie saw a resemblance to his homeland. He came for a barbie, one rare free Sunday, and let himself be dragged around the slopes above Saaremaa by two over-excited girls with a wealth of Ku-ring-gai Chase stories to impart. My mother was the first to notice the change in his mood.

'Are you all right, Lester?' she said when we tumbled back down to the beach.

'I'm fine. These two terrors only tried to break my leg, but I'm still standing.' His South African accent came out stronger than usual.

'I mean . . . Are you *all right*?'

He looked at her then and saw what she had seen in him. 'Hannah, I'm good, really. This place just took me back, is all. Spend so much time in the CBD, I forget what the wild feels like.' He blinked awkwardly. 'What Africa felt like.'

And my mother threw her arms around him, surprising him with another sensation he'd lost touch of in his glass and steel world. 'Lester, love, how much you must miss.'

Later, while our two fathers jokingly quarrelled over the relative merits of South African and Australian barbecue methods – Dad had quite a sense of humour back then – Kirsten said to me, very gravely, 'I think Pa loves your mother.'

And although Mum was at that moment crouched over a bowl of salad, with sand stuck to her bare legs and vinaigrette spattered down her T-shirt, I suspected in my nine-year-old wisdom that Kirsten was probably right.

'But that's OK,' she added with a reassuring hand on my arm, 'because I love your father.'

The hum of cicadas, the wildness, the weather-sculpted honeycomb sandstone. I hope Moses is happier here than in Kirsten's Darling Point high-rise. He seems happy. Content enough, anyway, to see out his last couple of days in Australia.

'We've had a message from your parents,' I say at last.

Moses flinches slightly.

'They want you to come home. They're worried about you. I'm going to make arrangements with the South African Consulate on Monday. You'll have to fly on your own, but the airline will take good care of you and there'll be someone to meet you in Johannesburg and drive you home.'

He turns to look at me. 'I told you. I'm going to die here.'

'Excuse me?'

'I'm not going back to South Africa. I will die here. God has shown me this.'

'Well, if I was you, I wouldn't pay too much attention. Look, I know you think you can see the future, and I'm sure that's a nice feeling, but maybe you should ask yourself whether it's all that likely – I mean we've kind of moved on from that stuff, y'know?'

Moses's unblinking gaze is damning.

'Look, mate, I just don't reckon you should go around thinking you're about to die,' I say uncomfortably. 'It's not healthy.'

'It's my Fate,' he says. 'It must happen. There is no other way.'

•

It's rare for me to spend Saturday night at home. I like to be somewhere bright and loud, in close proximity to a bar, even if I'm down for the Sunday morning watch. Sometimes I'll go to Wango's with Billy, sometimes we'll shake the sand out of our hair and hit the plush bars in the city. If Billy's away, climbing or surfing up the coast, I'll ride over to the Harbour Hazard Bar and let the water police boys buy me a few drinks and twist my arm onto the dance floor. Not that I'd ever let it go any further. I just enjoy a little attention from time to time, and I like to have fun on Saturday night.

Except this Saturday I'm spending the evening in front of the TV, trying to explain the First Citizen contest to Moses.

'Look, it's not a regular election,' I'm saying. 'The First Citizen's not going to have any political power. He or she has to act as spokesperson for the nation. Congratulate rugby teams, open hospitals, schmooze foreign leaders, that kind of thing. Like a king, but without all the crowns and palaces and stuff.'

'They have a king in Swaziland,' observes Moses. 'And Britain.'

'Right, yeah, and that's the reason, because at the moment the British king is our symbolic Head of State, and we had a referendum . . . we voted to say we'd like to have our own Head of State. And no one wanted a president with real political power, not after what's been happening in America, so we reckoned a popular figurehead would be the best option.'

For a long time, we didn't have a TV at Saaremaa. Dad took the swagman's attitude that nature provided everything we needed bar fuel, tea and sugar, two-speed winches and schooling. My mother came from a suburban paradise east of Melbourne where televisions were plentiful, but on a Pittwater break from the University of Sydney she was easily seduced by the simple ways of the unemployed sailor she met in a Newport pub. It took the first six years of my life for me to work out what I was missing, and another six before Mum agreed to buy a small portable, whatever my father had to say on the subject. By then, Daran Sacs had burst into glorious existence, and Kirsten and I could not be torn away from the Palm Beach set for the fifty-four mesmerising minutes he was on air. If she ever wanted to see either of us at Saaremaa between five and six o'clock,

Mum realised, a rival television would have to be introduced.

Moses's attention is captured by Rodrigo Valance, who has just walked into the RTV studio to cascades of applause from the audience. Rodrigo's looking great: open-neck black shirt with a bit of chest hair showing, taut waist, cowboy boots. He's holding his hands up in the air, blowing kisses to the audience, working them well. Moses is entranced.

'You met Rodrigo, remember? He's the favourite. He doesn't do so well in the quizzes, especially the historical and cultural ones where Michael Walters cleans up, but he's definitely got more charisma. And he won the golf tournament and the outback survival round.'

Suzie Marchdale comes on next. She's expected to do well tonight, as it's the singing round and she's a karaoke enthusiast. Then again, the RTV organisers come up with all kinds of tricks to catch the candidates out, so who knows what they're going to have to sing. Stuart's always saying how the First Citizen Selection Board shouldn't have allowed RTV anywhere near the contest. He reckons there should have just been regular campaigning, that people like Daran Sacs and Caz Teto turn it into a joke. But the whole point was to make it different from regular politics: no commercials, rosettes, rallies, speeches. *A First Citizen of the people, for the people, chosen by the people.* As the most popular channel, RTV was the obvious vehicle for the contest.

Nathan Partridge comes on after Suzie, a little slumped like he knows he's basically out of the running and doesn't get why they still want him to hang around. I can't take Nathan seriously since the candidates had to spend the morning with a group of pre-schoolers and Nathan ended up with fingerpaint all over his cheeks. He did pretty well in the science and technology quiz, I guess, but that was early on and no one really remembers it. Not the way they remember Michael Walters memorising every name in an audience of five hundred, or Elize Price dancing a Viennese waltz like her feet didn't need to touch the ground.

Funny thing – Kirsten seriously considered becoming a candidate. She dropped the idea the moment she heard about the selection process and realised what she'd be expected to do on live TV. She even told me I should enter, and when I asked why, she said because you can, because anyone can. I don't know: seemed a pretty stupid reason to me.

The seven remaining candidates are lined up in the studio, getting ready for the singing contest. Caz Teto has just told them they're going to be singing the British national anthem, so they're all trying to decide whether they'll score better if they belt it out with passion or refuse on principle. And now Moses tears his eyes away from the screen and says, 'Soon, I will be on TV.'

The statement, after Daran's pleas, unnerves me.

'You mean that's what you want, or you see it in the future?'

But that's as much time as Moses is willing to take out from the singing contest. He even hums along to the anthem with Michael Walters. By the time the phone rings, he's on his feet cheering with the studio audience.

'Hi.' The video link shows Kirsten in a restaurant somewhere, the back of a waiter's white jacket just visible behind her shoulder.

'Petra, honey, is this a good time? Have you recovered from your adventures this afternoon?'

'Just about. *Sentinel* was looking good.'

'Wasn't she?' Her voice purrs with pride. 'I need a quick chat with Moses.'

I kill the speaker, and put the phone to my ear. 'About what?'

'What a guard dog you are!' she laughs. 'Don't forget I'm his sponsor.

I need some info from him – it'll only take a couple of minutes.'

Reluctantly, I hand the phone to Moses.

He takes it, fully serious now, and presses it to his ear. He doesn't say anything. At some point Kirsten starts talking, because he nods once, says yes once, then bursts into an enormous smile.

The one-sided conversation lasts another few seconds before Moses lowers the phone and tells me, thrilled to the core, 'I'm going on TV!'

I snatch the phone from him and walk outside.

'I told Daran no.'

'Petra, lighten up, it's only TV.'

'He's not doing it.'

'Well, *Moses* thinks he is. You want to go tell him he can't?'

Glancing back through the door, I see Moses standing on a chair, waving his arms elatedly in time to the tuneless singing of Nathan Partridge.

'That was really irresponsible!'

'I know, hon,' she laughs again. 'Shall I take him, or can you get him to the studios by three?'

•

Moses is asleep when Billy arrives. He's spent the day buying a suit and black leather shoes, and generally preparing himself for his new job. Kirsten's PA, Tabitha, has been showing him around the bank, getting him settled so he's ready for work on Monday morning. I hear the splash of his paddle from my seat on the veranda, and I go down the beach to meet him. Sometimes I hear his motorbike across the water on the Palm Beach sand spit – hear it cut out, then imagine him pulling the kayak from its hiding place in the brush, imagine his powerful shoulders making quick work of the 1500 metres between us. Sometimes my imagination has such perfect timing that just as I'm expecting it he comes skimming out of the darkness.

But the wind's in the wrong direction tonight. I don't hear the bike.

I walk into the water and kiss him while he still has one leg in the kayak. He kisses me back, keeps kissing me back all the time he's disengaging himself – and it takes him a whole lot longer than it should do. When he finally has both feet in the sea, he tosses the kayak up the beach and then lifts me up so I can lock my legs around his waist. I feel loved, open, luxuriously indulged.

'I was hoping you'd be wearing your new suit, Mr Businessman,' I whisper in his ear.

'Mhmm, roleplay,' he laughs.

'Was it strange, dressing like that? Did it make you feel . . . different?'

He hears the anxiety and silently kisses me again. The best answer he could give.

We lie on the old veranda couch together, watching the tiniest of waves breaking over our silent beach. Just south from here, dozens of weekending Sydneysiders have moored their ego-cruisers at Coasters Retreat and are chucking back the beers with their trophy girls, screaming at spoilt kids for fiddling with the onboard sound system, and charcoaling steaks on their halogen barbecues. Hundreds more have invaded the Basin with tents and eskies and volleyballs. But we're spared the world here, alone on this dark fringe of the park.

We're going to spend the night on the veranda. We're going to make love here, sleep here, drink coffee together in the early morning here. We're not moving from this spot.

For the first time in my life, I wonder what it would be like to conceive a child.

'What colour is your suit?' I murmur.

'Grey.'

'Oh, very good.' I run my fingers through his curls. 'I'm glad they didn't make you cut your hair.'

'They did, but only a little. Tabitha was very strict with the guy. Warned him you'd rip his nuts off if he cut too much.'

'Good for her. They give you a desk?'

'A whole office.'

'No way! What do you have to do?'

'I'm a Senior Executive Marketing Manager.'

'That means something?'

'Guess I'll find out Monday.'

'Was Kirsten there?'

'Came by in the afternoon. She was in sailing gear but she looked so businesslike! Never seen her like that before. Kind of impressive.'

'Really?'

'Sharp, efficient, totally focused.'

'I bet.'

'You see her talk to her staff, you really get that she's running the show.'

'Don't be too impressed.'

He laughs in the darkness. 'Give me a hot coastguard any day,' he says, drawing me in.

•

Billy and I wake with the dawn on the old couch. Pretty soon I'll have to head out in the SilverBird. A lot of people try to drown themselves on Sundays. But we've got another hour of delicious sleepiness under the big patchwork quilt. Time to doze, to chat about nothing, to laugh at everything. Time to remind ourselves that we're getting married. Time to smile.

And I guess we're probably doing something more than that, because when Moses pokes his head out the door, utters a sharp exclamation and backs away all upset, my first reaction is guilt that he's witnessed something so adult. Not that we're full on – just fooling around, the usual slow, sleepy morning thing. Most of it's under the covers, and whatever our hands may be doing is definitely out of sight. But maybe Moses never saw a man and a woman together, and I'm already feeling sorry it was us that spoilt his innocence.

'Whoops,' murmurs Billy. 'Forgot we had a prophet in our midst.'

'A kid, anyway. I'd better check he's OK.'

But when I wander along the beach to see how he's doing, there's Moses quite calm and relaxed, squatting with shoulders rounded and splayed toes turned inwards on one of the sandstone boulders at the far end. So I ask him, 'What's up?' and he says, 'Nothing.' I ask again and this little frown appears. Now Billy's come to join us, a towel around his waist, and he's giving Moses that lovely warm smile of his and saying, 'All right, mate?'

It must be the sight of us together again that gets Moses going, because suddenly he's shivering and staring at the ground, and refusing to answer us. I'm starting to wonder if we've done something terrible, scarred him psychologically with our fooling around.

Then Moses looks up at us with those sad eyes and delivers his horrible verdict. He says, 'I wish you could be happy, but God makes Fate and we cannot change it. That is why you both cannot stay together.'

That's it. That's what the little snake says.

There's no need for questions – I understand exactly what he's telling us. I don't challenge him or contradict him. I don't even look at him more than two seconds longer. Instead, my eyes go to Billy's face and find dismay and shock there.

'It's not real, Billy.' I say it fast, with force.

He's still staring at Moses. I grab his arm and pull him, hard, away from the boy.

'It's not real. He can't see the future.'

'What *was* that?'

'It's not important. He's a fourteen-year-old from the back of beyond who doesn't have a clue about you and me. His imagination is going to get him into a lot of trouble, because that's all it is, Billy, a stupid, ludicrous imagination.'

'Yeah . . .' Billy tugs free, stares back down the beach. Moses looks very small, squatting alone, gazing out across Pittwater. 'He reckons we're going to break up?' The man I love turns to me. 'That's what he's saying?'

And I'm shaking my head, forming the denial, though I can't utter it because it's a lie. Somehow, there are tears in my eyes. 'But he's wrong. He's absolutely wrong. And the only way he could possibly become right is if we believe him.'

•

The whole of my watch, I'm furious at Moses. There are no distress calls, nothing to take my mind off his senseless, destructive words. All the boats from Broken Bay to Long Reef are well fuelled, stable, skippered by experts. We cruise slowly up and down our Area of Responsibility, longing for the radio to come alive. After my fourth call to Billy, Stuart takes away my mobile and tells me I need to concentrate on saving lives, even though there aren't any lives to save just now.

To complicate matters, we have a volunteer with us. Dan Worrell is one of the Associate Coastguards, unpaid individuals with basic boat and rescue training who are available to supplement Inshore crews in emergency. The SilverBirds require a minimum of two staff for operational duties, and in bad weather we prefer to have three. Associates don't do patrol work, nor do they have to know how to direct a rescue operation or resuscitate a casualty. But if we need an extra pair of hands in rough seas, there's usually a dozen ACs ready to leap out of bed and join the crew.

When their jobs permit, usually at the weekend, Associates can join a regular crew on patrol to build up experience. But there's not a lot of best practice for Dan to learn from while no one obliges us with a distress call, so we end up running an impromptu training session in the calm seas off Whale Beach. Stuart, for once, makes the wrong call on the toss, and we put a lifejacket on him and dump him in the water. Dan gets two minutes to look over the MOB drill sheet. Then I drive back and forth, and have him practise all the different methods of recovery – casting a float line, directing entry via boarding ladder or transom, the corkscrew lift, the recovery strap, the immobilisation litter for serious injury, as well as the crude but fast hauling over the gunwale necessary when an unconscious casualty is face-down and urgency is everything.

After Stuart's been recovered a dozen times, a Whale Beach surf lifesaver wearing a Santa hat paddles out in a kayak to check what's going on. 'Need some help?' he offers amiably, as Stuart falls back into the sea once more. Ten minutes later, once he's come on board *Giselle* and tried a two-man lift with Dan, we sign him up as an Associate trainee. Stuart goes on strike then, demands a towel and his sunnies, and we resume our patrol.

When I get back home it's already time to take Moses into town for Daran's show, and I'm in no mood to be pleasant with him. I make him carry a bag of garbage on the surf rescue board; he's puzzled by our cargo, but since he never asks questions and I'm not inclined right now to explain the complications of living out of reach of Pittwater Council services, he remains unenlightened. In the SilverBird, Moses keeps a careful grip on the garbage bag until I tell him to leave it alone.

Billy offered in the morning to stay at Saaremaa, to look after Moses while I was on patrol. But no way did I want the two of them discussing the end of my engagement. I know Billy so well: he would have had to probe for more information, however much he told himself it wasn't true, lodging the break-up prediction deeper in his mind. I told him to go dune biking with Buzz instead. I'm hoping a lot of action and noise and risk will knock this nonsense clean out of his mind.

Moses and I don't speak more than absolutely necessary on the way to Spring Cove, where he solemnly watches me separate the garbage into the various recycling receptacles. Carole gets him kitted out in the fancy clothes he wore for the *Sentinel* party, while I busy myself with a review of the current SilverBird deployment. Truth is, I'm waiting for Moses to apologise, which is stupid because he thinks he's just telling it how it is. He can see I'm upset, he's emotionally aware enough to understand he's caused it, but other than telling me that Fate is often cruel and that two of his sisters died of disease before they were four years old, he doesn't see any need to respond.

I leave him with Carole and shut myself in my office until it's time to go.

•

RTV's studios look grand enough from the outside, but the corridors and rooms we're led through are a mess. At Spring Cove it's a rule that every doorway and passage is kept clear, every surface left empty when not in use. No clutter means no accidents and no delays in reaching sinkers. The stakes aren't so high in television, but all the same the piles of hardboard, electrical cables, tools and discarded overalls strike me as amateur and sloppy.

We're kept hanging about in an uncomfortable waiting room, no refreshments offered, for over an hour. When I ask to speak to Daran, a production assistant curtly declares that Mr Sacs doesn't see anyone but his courage counsellor and make-up artist in the three hours preceding his show. It's becoming clear that no one's taking Moses seriously. Not that he minds: there's an excitement about him, a lust for this new experience. The lowliest clipboard girl draws his fascinated gaze. When a sheet of scenery painted as the interior of a very ordinary bathroom is carried by the window, Moses rushes over to watch until it disappears behind another building.

Eventually, they come for him: a producer, a performance coach and a make-up guy. All three exude the air of professionals who have better things to do. With the minimum of courtesy, the producer points me toward a cubicle, empty except for a screen and a couple of hard plastic chairs, then leads Moses away. Obediently, I take one of the chairs and face the screen. There's no remote, no button to change the channel. I can't even see a way to switch it off.

I sit in front of RTV's Sunday afternoon *FoodFun* slot and wait for five o'clock.

•

'G'day,' says Daran Sacs, his hair perfect, his grin locked in place. As applause fills the tinsel-festooned studio, he gives us his famous wink. 'And a big, big merry Christmas to you all. We've got a great line-up for you today, bucks, a real triple whammy. The last show of the year, the best of the best, a feast of fun. Please welcome internationally renowned sculptor, Daniela Windsor . . .'

Enthusiastic applause as Daniela walks on, followed by two assistants carrying a complicated mess of matchsticks, glue, thread, cigarette packets and drinking straws. Gingerly, the 'sculpture' is set down on the table in front of the guests' seats.

'. . . ground-breaking dog-opera director, Hexley Hughes . . .'

Still louder applause as Hexley enters, a Pekingese close on his heels. He takes his seat and the dog leaps onto his lap.

'. . . and is-he-isn't-he South African prophet, Moses Lukoto.'

Confusion dampens the applause. But still, Moses is greeted by a barrage of sound and light which elicits an awestruck expression on his face. In close-up those elevated eyebrows, given new definition by the make-up guy, are creased into exaggerated curves; the tip of his pink tongue rests feebly on his lower incisors. Two anonymous hands are briefly seen pushing him forward.

'Come on, come on,' cries Daran, 'don't be shy. What's the matter, buck? Wasn't what you were expecting?' With a twirl to the audience, Daran roars his unique laugh. 'Get the gag?'

It's hard to define the emotions that pass across Moses's face during those opening seconds. At first he appears lost, blinded by the lights and the novelty of it all, and my heart can't help but rush out to him: the young African boy, ignorant of our strange world, stranded in the barbarians' circus. But then, a transformation. He's caught a glimpse of the crowd beyond the lights. He has seen the studio audience, registered their enthusiasm, and he's understood that he is the focus of their attention. His eyes widen, his lips fold inward, his neck cranes. It isn't quite excitement, but neither is it fear or nervousness. It is a kind of appetite that emerges, until –

'Moses, Moses, we're live here, please!'

The curious expression disappears as Moses hurries obediently to the last remaining seat.

'That's the way, buck, that's the way. Now, Daniela, welcome to the show. How about you begin by telling us what inspired this heap of sticks.'

'See, Daran, that's just the kind of cultural philistinism that gives our country a bad name. I am a serious artist, and my *Transcendence of Earthly Delights* is a serious statement of moral outrage in the face of this government's continued illegal participation in the bombing of innocent Muslims in . . .'

What Moses thinks of the experience is difficult to tell. Occasionally the camera gives us glimpses of his face, but his expression is too rigid, too uncertain to betray his inner self. How much does he understand of Daniela's confused ideas on the convergence of art and politics? What does he make of the bizarre Hexley Hughes and his Pekingese diva?

'Honestly, Mr Sacs, she's singing *The Barber of Seville*. Can't you hear? *Io sono docile, son rispettosa, sono obbediente* . . . Can't you hear the words?'

'She's whining, Hexley! What did you put in her food?'

'No, no, Mr Sacs, listen carefully. Hear it? Pom-pi-pom. Louder, Maria! *Cento trappole . . .* You hear?'

'My God, you're pinching her!'

Most of the time Moses gives an impression of polite bewilderment. But every now and then, he turns and gazes searchingly towards the audience. What is he looking for? Has that single burst of applause sown a desire for more? Does the celebrity virus work that fast?

'And now, bucks, let's give a big Aussie welcome to a newcomer to our shores. Put your hands together for – Moses Lukoto!'

Because there it is. The applause starts and Moses straightens, turns, beams – it's undeniable. No one has a clue who he is yet, but already it's in his blood. He's hooked.

'So, Moses, you reckon you can see the future?'

'Yes.'

'Like, you can tell us what's going to happen tomorrow?'

'Sometimes, yes.'

'So what is going to happen tomorrow?'

'I will have breakfast and watch television.'

'Come off it, buck! Call that a prediction? Give us something more interesting. What's going to happen to me tomorrow?'

Moses frowns. 'I don't know.'

'Well, is it going to rain?'

'I don't know.'

'Dear oh dear, leave your crystal ball behind?'

Puzzlement stirs his gaze. 'I haven't got a crystal ball.'

'Who's going to be First Citizen?'

'Mr Nathan Partridge.'

'Do you actually know anything about this election?'

'Mr Nathan Partridge will win, and Mr Rodrigo Valance will come second. He will be very angry. He will shout at people who ask him questions.'

The ring of truth makes Daran falter. 'Will he now?' he mutters.

In my little cubicle, I find myself feeling proud of Moses, with his quiet, straightforward responses. He's picked up enough sense of the First Citizen contest to sound credible, despite his incredible claims. It almost gets me wondering. He's not impressed by Daran's inflated ego, perhaps not even aware of it. Although his eyes occasionally swing towards the studio audience, he remains dignified, immune to the ridicule that has left Daniela irate and Hexley squirming.

'So you can predict an election result that's over a week away, but you can't say what the weather will be twenty-four hours from now?'

'Yes.'

Beside Moses, Hexley is face-to-face with the Pekingese, whispering desperate threats to his canine star.

'Not too reliable, your forecasting, is it?'

'God does not show me everything.'

'Sing, Maria, sing!' mutters Hexley.

Daran turns to Daniela Windsor. 'How about you? Any questions for the oracle?'

Still scowling, she says, 'Yes, I do have a question. Seeing as Mr Sacs doesn't appreciate my art, perhaps you can tell him how much I'm going to sell this sculpture for?'

'No.'

'My, my, buck, your god really doesn't want you to know much, does he?'

'Maria, love, sing a tiny bit of *O mio babbino caro* for Daddy.'

'Excuse me, Mr Sacs, I mean the . . .' Unsure what to call the construction on the table before them, Moses simply points, and continues, 'It will not be sold.'

'Ah-ha!' cries Daran Sacs. '*Now* you're making sense. Hexley, stop pinching that dog!'

Moses leans toward Daniela with compassionate eyes. 'I am sorry for you. I know you love this . . .' And again he can only point at the sculpture. 'It will be broken very soon.'

'*What?*'

'I'm sorry, Mrs Daniela, yes, it will be broken.'

'Please, Maria . . .'

'Is he threatening to vandalise my art? Is that bloody boy about to take a swipe at —'

'Now calm down, Daniela. That's not what he said. All he said was —'

At which moment, on live TV before an audience of three and a half million, something extraordinary occurs:

A sudden outraged yelp; a guilty look on Hexley's face, his finger and thumb caught in the action of pinching; the Pekingese leaping from his knee and ploughing into *Transcendence of Earthly Desires*, scattering cigarette packets and matchsticks all over the studio.

The camera catches all their faces. There is realisation, revelation. And there is deep shock. For everyone except Moses.

He hasn't taken his eyes off Daniela. Now, he reaches out his hand and touches her arm. 'I am sorry for you,' he repeats.

'Holy fucking crap!' roars Daran. The producers are too dazed to bleep that one. They make no attempt to change camera angle, nor zoom in on the wreckage, nor follow Hexley Hughes on his pursuit of the Pekingese around the studio. Even Daniela has to shake herself before she can speak. And it's not her ruined sculpture that has her stunned. Hers is that same impossible question they all ask: '*How the hell did he know?*'

That's the problem with this whole prophecy madness. Even though it's obvious to me that no one can look into a pool of water or bird intestine or tea cup and see the future, it's very hard to answer that simple objection. How else could he know?

I sit quietly in my cubicle trying to silence the screams in my head. *It isn't true*, I remind myself over and over again. *He can't see the future*. But I'm plagued by the memory of that vision out on the ocean. The ships dying. The waves like hills, the wind that sings and shouts.

And something else: I have to accept that this trivial chat-show miracle, this ludicrous coincidence, was almost certainly witnessed by Billy.

CHAPTER 5

There's a thing I do in any really serious emergency at sea: I compartmentalise my fears, my thoughts, my hopes, my imagination. Professional
rescue workers can't function if they let the anticipation of disaster muddy
their planning or disrupt the procedures they've practised a hundred
times over. If there's a dozen small boats caught in bad weather, and you
let yourself worry that you're not going to reach them all in time, then
important parts of your brain start shutting down. I've seen an experienced
water police officer flat on the deck with his face in his hands, when he
should have been responding to a distress call, because he'd convinced
himself that a little girl – reported speared by a spinnaker pole – was going
to die. And here's the thing: I understand exactly why he did it. I've felt
that urge. And the way I fight it is to compartmentalise.

The problem with compartments in your mind is this: they don't
always make sense together. They can be contradictory. Above all else, I'm
out at sea to save lives. So even if the guy in the water is a rapist I'd love
to watch drown, that feeling gets locked away in its own compartment
while I get on with the job of rescuing the bastard. And if reaching someone in a dicey situation means I might get killed before I'm able to help

the other five people in the water, I just have to ignore that calculation, lock it away, and get on with doing what I do.

It becomes a way of life after a while, compartmentalising. This is how I apply it now.

In the first compartment is my world view, my bedrock of understanding of how the universe works. Dad brought me up in his Christian faith, but it didn't take long to work out that there is no God holding us in the palm of his protective hand. My mother's death was the final confirmation; by then I'd already seen enough of life's random cruelty to reject the Church's lame explanations of evil as a product of free will. The world is an indifferent, dangerous place, and it's up to us to help each other survive. No one else is going to step in. To believe is to defer responsibility, to make critical judgements based on false premises, to hamper the common sense and huge intellectual potential of every one of us. Belief becomes a substitute for proper precautions and the protection of life. And just as there is no God, so too there is no witchcraft, telekinesis, psychic healing, prophecy, nothing. Moses is a boy with a strong imagination. That's all.

Then there's the second compartment, the one where I protect people at sea. Where I respond to any threat, any hoax call, any slight chance of danger, however unlikely. In this compartment, I place my professionalism, my training, my instinct, my absolute dedication to the preservation of life. And it's in this compartment that I now revisit what Moses said in the SilverBird. Because although I absolutely don't believe in any of this soothsayer nonsense, that certainty belongs in the first compartment, not here. In my professional capacity, I have to take seriously any threat to human life at sea. And Moses, who's just demonstrated on the face of it a startling piece of foresight, has given me clear warning of a catastrophe.

I have no choice, in this compartment, but to respond. However much I doubt Moses's supposed powers, I have a responsibility as a coastguard to consider the remote yet dreadful possibility that he might be right.

Finally, there's the third compartment, and this is where I place my heart. This is where I hold Billy, and imagine what it would be like to lose him. This is the compartment in which I lock my biggest fear. And I deal with that fear by refusing to believe. I say it to myself: *I refuse to believe*. Here, scepticism is not enough. It is by force of will that I deny the possibility Moses could be right when he tells Billy and me we cannot stay together. It is by sheer determined obstinacy that I dismiss the accumulating evidence and tell myself that no car crash or blood on Kirsten's hand or bolting Pekingese could possibly prove Moses correct. I refuse to believe. For the sake of our future together, I have to refuse to believe.

•

That evening, I visit my father.

My mental compartments are in contradiction. This is not going to be easy. Apart from everything else, I don't want to be doing this. The Sydney Hobart, for all it has cost my family, is too important. Australia's a bloody wonderful place, but as a nation we don't have much beyond the odd sporting hero to shout about. We didn't give the world Michelangelo, or the Internet, or coffee, or even cricket. However much we love our country and don't give a stuff what anyone else thinks, we can't completely rid ourselves of the suspicion that if Australia vanished tomorrow a lot of people might not notice. So the Sydney Hobart, this race that has sailors travelling round the globe to compete, that attracts the admiration and respect of every seagoing community, well, it matters. It may not be Gallipoli, but it's an emblem of our nation all the same.

Dad lives in a smart modern bungalow in Avalon, which he would never have been able to afford without the generous assistance of the last sinker he rescued. It was just lucky, in a grisly way, that the accident happened while he was saving the life of a multi-millionaire.

He hates the house, as I would if I had to leave Saaremaa. Instead of the sea, he looks out on his neighbours' oppressively neat lines of blue agapanthus, and less neat jumbles of garish plastic toys. The occasional visits by lorikeets and possums are a poor substitute for the riches of Ku-ring-gai Chase. His lifesaver's eye has no waters to scan, no storms to monitor and no boats to see safely back to their moorings. But at least he can move around the house easily, get to the shops and church, and generally look after himself. There are no doorsteps or awkward obstacles; the bathroom's been specially fitted to give him a handhold whatever he's doing; a neat remote-control system in the kitchen allows him to turn kettle, microwave or grill on and off without leaving his seat.

Most of the time, though, Dad likes to be standing. He's determined to fight his disability and I'm really proud of the courage he shows. I always knock on the front door rather than letting myself in with my key. He hates me making things easier for him. He'd always rather limp his way to the latch.

But it's not Dad who opens the door this time, and for a second I'm terrified that the tall and distinguished man in his hallway is a doctor or policeman or mortician. That is, until I recognise him.

'What are you doing here?' I blurt out.

'We were never introduced yesterday.' He's dressed in the kind of informal clothes that leave you in no doubt he's a formal man. Perfectly creased slacks, firm edges to the shirt collar. His brown shoes gleam. 'Forgive me. I was rather weak from the blood loss.' He holds out his hand. He looks anything but weak now. 'David Fowler.'

'*Commodore* Fowler?' Most of the faces I know in the Navy belong to the junior ranks. But there's a few names sea people don't forget, and one of them belongs to the man who led the most distinguished Australian Task Group in the Persian Gulf. He is not the kind of figure you expect to encounter in an Avalon bungalow. Or, for that matter, in the clutch of Snapper 3.

'I know, I know,' he sighs. 'Your father gave me the same lecture about the transceiver batteries you did.'

'You're . . . OK now?'

'Perfectly,' he says, standing aside to let me in. 'A few stitches, a little blood, all fixed. Nothing internal. I was going to have your father pass on my thanks. I owe you a great deal.'

Attempting a nonchalant smile, I say something obnoxious like, 'I'm glad you felt able to trust me in the end.'

'Moment I heard your name,' smiles Fowler. In the living room, Dad sits on an upright wooden chair, a glass of whisky in his hand. He's still in his church clothes – black flannel trousers with a white long-sleeved shirt. 'I've already told Lewis his daughter's as obstinate as him. And an even better seaman.'

Dad snorts at that. 'Is she competent in a boat?' he says. 'I would hope so after everything she's been taught.'

'Of course. Well, I must be getting back to Garden Island. But may I ask a favour of your daughter, Lewis, before I go?'

Dad frowns, but Fowler takes that for assent.

'I'd appreciate your help in testing a new piece of rescue kit. It's a remarkable device: a fully flexible walkway that can link a distressed vessel to a rescue ship. Some kind of innovative polymer. Very elastic. Whatever the movement of the vessels, the walkway remains intact and taut. It can stretch as they draw apart, and contract as they come together again. Might be very helpful in heavy swell.'

'You should speak to Donald Carter. He runs the Offshore Coastguard. I'm sure they could use a piece of kit like that.' Donald's a former merchant seaman who, when he wasn't ploughing the oceans, used to serve in the same volunteer outfit as my father. He was always the one they called if there was an incident out to sea, and when they bought an ageing All-weather Life Boat cheap from the British RNLI, he was given command. Now his four Sentinel-funded, high-spec ALBs roam fifty miles from shore and take on the bigger yachts, fishing trawlers, even cargo ships that get into trouble. They see a lot of swell. SilverBirds don't. *Giselle*'s designed to get to drowning children fast, not suffer gale force punishment.

'We've already got Donald involved,' says Fowler. 'I'm asking you as well because I value your instinct.'

'Seriously? Then – sure.'

'Thank you,' he says. 'Tomorrow, Garden Island. Eleven hundred hours.'

When he's gone, Dad pulls himself up, takes his glass to the kitchen and empties it into the sink.

'Bring the bottle, Petra.'

I pick it up. It's nearly full, a good brand. Expensive Scotch. 'Why not keep it, Dad? For visitors.'

'What visitors? Give it to me.'

He dumps the lot down the drain.

'I didn't know you were friends with a Commodore.'

'He's not my friend. We worked together on Harbour safety regulations, a long time ago. He was only here because of your heroics.'

'Dad, it's my job.'

The bottle goes in the garbage. He turns, steadying himself against the counter. 'Are you obliged to go to the aid of sailors in distress? Of course. Does that mean you should get reckless? Next time think about the crews who will have to rescue you if you aren't so lucky.'

He's never once stopped looking out for me, my father. I know how rare that is from what other girls said at school, how lucky I am to have him as my dad. I probably would have drowned a thousand times over by now if he hadn't done such a great job teaching me about the sea. But he does tend to worry about me too much. And it doesn't take him long to move on to the other thing that bothers him.

'It's becoming too dangerous, Petra. The city's different; women shouldn't live alone in the bush. Think what they did to those hitchhikers. All kinds of criminals around these days. Bad people can hire boats same as good people. Don't think you're safe just because there's no road.'

'Come on, Dad, this is Pittwater.'

'You think those thugs from Redfern can't steal a launch and come rape you in the night?'

'That's not nice.'

'No, it's not nice. You shouldn't be there on your own, no one nearby. There's a spare room here and you can –'

'Dad, I'm not going to be alone.' Until now, I haven't found the right opportunity to tell him. Uncertainty about his reaction has held me back. His favourite water temperature is 14ºC, and sometimes that comes through in his tone. But now all the cautious speeches I've been lining up since South Africa go out the porthole. 'Dad, Billy's asked me to marry him. I'm going to get married!'

My father always likes to think things through before he makes a judgement. It's a sign of wisdom. He takes his time, never makes snap, meaningless statements.

I mean, he's right to think it through.

'Dad?' I say, because even though I know all this, his silence is filling me with dread, and I'm afraid he's going to say something horrible about Billy. 'Dad? Isn't that great? Aren't you pleased?'

He fills the kettle and switches it on. 'Billy Farris, eh?' He takes down two mugs and drops a teabag in each. 'Not a bad fellow. Not bad at all. Is he the smartest man in Sydney? Perhaps not. But is he capable? Will he take care of you? Can I go to my grave confident you'll be looked after?' And now my father surprises me more than anything – with a smile. 'Yes, I think I can.'

Unprepared for his approval, I start gabbling.

'Billy's going to be a wonderful husband, Dad. And he is smart, you'll see. Right now, he's getting ready to go to work – a proper marketing job that'll really make the most of his enthusiasm and energy.'

'Good for him. What company?'

'Sentinel Bank.'

'Kirsten McKenzie?' My good news is quickly forgotten; Dad shakes his head gloomily. 'That girl. I looked over the Hobart boat when they put her in the water. Dangerous, that's the only word for her. The canting keels were bad enough, but this canting hull madness . . . Too many moving parts: something's bound to break. You'd think after all I taught her she'd know better than to build a thing like that.'

'The new *Sentinel*? Everyone's saying she's a genius design. Could average 26 knots in the right conditions.'

'No doubt she's fast. But will she hold when she hits real seas? People forget this race used to be about survival, about simply making it through. This complacency, we've seen it before, whenever there's a few years of easy winds. People throw everything they know about solid boat-building out the window and think of nothing but speed.'

A little whisper of fear settles in my stomach. 'Dad,' I say carefully. This part's going to be much, much harder. 'Dad, actually I wanted to talk to you about the race.'

'Tell her to charter a different boat. That's my advice.'

'She's not the only one I'm worried about. Look, I've been hearing stuff.' I hesitate. 'Talk of bad weather.'

'There's always talk of bad weather. Half the country wants those boats tested. Half the skippers too. It's like hoping the Poms will field a decent side for once.'

'But, I mean, aren't the meteorologists picking up anything?'

He frowns. 'What meteorologists have you been talking to?'

'Well, I haven't exactly been . . . What are they saying on the Safety Committee?'

'The forecast is clear.'

'Right . . . But if there was a warning sign, something that could develop into extreme weather, what would be the process?'

'The process?'

'For, you know, assessing the safety of the race?'

'Petra,' he says heavily, 'what is making you ask me these questions?'

'I'd just like to understand. As a Director of the Coastguard.'

'Inshore Director. You have no responsibility beyond the start of the race.'

'Not formally, but there's a lot of people heading out into Bass Strait, friends of mine, some inexperienced sailors – all potentially at risk.'

'As they are every year.'

'But if this year were different . . .'

'All right, enough. If you know of some cause for concern, Petra, you have a duty to speak up.'

I hesitate. 'It's not something I can explain to you.'

'Try me.'

'You'll dismiss it. You'll say I'm being stupid.'

'Is your vanity more important than lives at risk?'

And so I have to tell him.

It isn't easy explaining about Moses, how he happens to be in Sydney, what he was doing in my boat on Friday night, what exactly he claims to be. Some half-truths creep into my account, but the important points are all there. 'It's not that I believe any of this, see.' And I'm still reasonably sure of that, despite the growing list of validations. 'It's just that if by some chance . . . I want to be able to rule it out definitively.'

He stares at me long and hard then. '"If by some chance"?'

'You know what I mean.'

'No, Petra, tell me what you mean.'

'It is possible, right? Dad, he described waves like houses – like hills! He's never seen a wave. He didn't even use the word – it's not part of his world. But I swear to you, that's what he saw in his mind. Force eight minimum, that's what he described.'

'Tell me,' he repeats doggedly, 'what you *mean*.'

I hesitate. 'Maybe we should think about . . . maybe the Committee should think about . . . being prepared to cancel the race.'

'Hah!' That's how he laughs. This raspy, scornful 'Hah!'

It's fair enough though. Of course it is. But, still. 'Dad, it could happen, right?'

'Could a storm happen? Always. Should the Safety Committee call off a world-famous race because some kid spins you a story about boats "dying"? Are you *out* of your *mind*?'

'What if he really is a prophet? Like John, or Ezekiel?'

Dad grips the tablecloth. 'Petra, you may not have room for God in your busy life, but I'll thank you not to disrespect my faith in my house.'

It would be a relief to concede, to let it go, to forget all about Moses and his crazy predictions. But if there's one thing I'm supposed to do it's protect lives at sea, and I can't walk away from this one. I force myself to think of the blood on Kirsten's hand, force myself to believe for one compartmentalised moment in what it signifies, and in a small voice I mutter, 'What if it's another '98?'

'Don't you dare,' he growls.

'This isn't about Mum.'

'Then don't bring up '98!'

'My friend's going to be out there, in a boat you just said is not seaworthy. How many entrants this year? A hundred and twelve? Donald Carter can't watch over them all.'

'You think I don't consider the possibility of a storm?' he yells. 'You presume to sit there and lecture *me* about the dangers of this race?'

My mother died in that Sydney Hobart – the 1998 one. She sailed on a small yacht called *Blueberry* that got caught in the worst of the storm. At some point they were knocked down and dismasted, and the force of the wave broke Mum's safety harness. When *Blueberry* came upright, the crew spotted Mum two hundred metres off the leeward side, but with the mast dragging in the sea they couldn't sail to her. The engine was flooded with seawater and wouldn't start. The skipper secured a long line to his harness and dived in after her. But the waves carried her away before he could get near. By the time the SAR helicopters reached them, it was dark. They never found her.

We'd heard there was a chance of bad weather on the first evening of the race. I woke up on 27 December 1998 to the news that a weather station on Wilson's Promontory had registered gusts of 92 knots. Dad hadn't been to bed. All morning he was on the radio, calling every marine authority contact he had for news of *Blueberry*. While Dad raged and shouted and demanded action, I went into the kitchen and tried to work out how to make macaroni cheese. It was not successful, the sauce was lumpy and grey, but Dad ate it without noticing. That afternoon, as the reports from Bass Strait got worse and worse, I watched him give in to his frustration and hurtle off in the new Zodiac. I waited for hours by the shoreline, moving only as the tide moved. It was past midnight when he returned to tell me of a search that had been abandoned, of hope that was entirely lost.

That's all there is to say. It's been a tough old nut sitting in the middle of our little family ever since. No one's fault, but Dad was a volunteer coastguard for forty years, and he can't deal with the idea he lost her to the sea. A car accident would have been different. The sea – he thinks he's supposed to be able to handle the sea. He's always taught me it's dangerous, treacherous, unforgiving, all those things. He just never quite believed it for himself.

As for me, I will never forget the sheer sense of impotence in waiting alone, knowing the news would be the worst, guessing she might still be alive though not for much longer, and being able to do not one bloody thing about it.

•

Billy doesn't come to Saaremaa that evening.

He wants an early night before his first day at work, he says when I call him. Wants to make sure his suit is pressed, his shoes clean. Wants to memorise the facts and figures from the Sentinel Bank website. I know none of this is the real reason, but I don't challenge him directly. Instead, with an eye on Moses's door to make sure it's fully closed, I ask if he saw the RTV show.

'Yeah, I saw it.'

'That dog, huh, what were the chances?' I say, in a good light voice.

'I'm putting money on Nathan Partridge.' It's an attempt at a joke, but on my little screen his face looks tired and drawn.

'Honestly, you'll wait up for Santa next.'

No immediate reply. He's looking down, away from his phone camera. His eyelids are drawn in tiny detail on the screen. At last he says, 'Obviously he's wrong about us – there's no reason in the world for us to split up.'

'Got that right,' I say shakily, wishing he hadn't spoken those two awful words. 'Look, we're both tired. Let's talk in the morning. Good luck at the bank, lover.'

He looks up then. 'Yeah. Thanks.'

'I love you, Billy,' I say.

'I love you too,' he answers – with certainty, at least.

•

Commodore Fowler's invitation to Garden Island has meant a last-minute adjustment to Monday's roster, with me and Stuart moving to the afternoon watch. As a result, I've got a lie-in. Or at least I would have if those nagging doubts over the race hadn't brought me awake even before the cockatoos started their screeching. As it is, I have a long morning to kill, and I decide to devote a little time to Moses. My reaction to his break-up prediction was unkind and unfair. There's no more point blaming him for what he thinks he sees than there is blaming Billy for believing him.

He's a fourteen-year-old kid without a friend for six thousand miles, badly confused by the strange world he's landed up in, and I've given him a hard time for long enough.

'How would you like to go across to Palm Beach for a swim?' At his age, I found the ocean side so much more exciting than our placid Pittwater beach. For hours on end, Kirsten and I would toss ourselves into the waves, loving those dangerous moments when the water would flip us right over and fill our hair, noses and bikinis with sand. Even the shore wash was mesmerising: the way opaque, foamy sand-heavy sea would flush up the matt rust beach and then, for just a second before it receded, clear magically to reveal a glistening spread of gold beneath the film of water.

But Moses shows no interest in Palm Beach, and when I unearth a pair of boardies for him, the reason becomes clear: he has never learnt to swim.

'Really? *Never?*' I can't help saying, because although it's fair enough, given the scarcity of swimming pools in rural Vendaland, the idea is so far removed from my own conception of normality.

'Swimming is not important,' declares Moses.

'Uh-huh,' I croak, inwardly traumatised by that assertion. 'All the same, useful to learn.'

'I will never learn it.'

'Never say never.'

'I've seen this,' he says patiently.

'You've seen yourself *not* learning? What does that look like?'

He blinks at me, then decides to laugh. It's a charming sound, quite like the tinkle of a child's bicycle bell. 'You don't believe me,' he chides.

'Not really,' I admit. 'Listen, you don't have to swim, but how about putting these on anyway? Then we can paddle.'

There's a couple of places on our beach that are special to my family, and seeing Moses in those oversized boardshorts I get an urge to share them with him. In the rock pools on the northern side of the cove, where Mum and I pretended to keep a pet whale, Moses tugs at the braid weed and, when a piece comes free, rolls it thoughtfully between his fingers. Standing in the shallows, he watches with fascination a tiny fish darting around him. Four times he tries to catch it, spearing his hand into the water and snatching at the place where it used to be. When he gives up, I commiserate appropriately, then lead him along the beach to Balloon Rock.

We always said it was shaped like a balloon, but it isn't really. It's a large, smooth lump of sandstone whose only distinguishing feature is a concave underside. Two people can just squeeze themselves into the space beneath. It's not dignified, and Moses looks unconvinced when I suggest it, but I promise him a shower to wash off the sand afterwards and he lies down beside me to wriggle under the rock.

The space is so tight, it's hard to move your arms. I have some difficulty getting the torch out of my pocket. As an adult, I've only once brought someone else here, and that was Billy. In the company of Moses, I'm all elbows and grazed knuckles, and it's a bruising, awkward process getting the torch into position. Moses lies quietly beside me, not complaining when I bump his ribs.

'There,' I say, switching on the light.

Above us, a few centimetres from our faces, are the scratched letters of my name.

He sees it, recognises it, cries out with delight. 'Petra,' he says, I think for the first time.

'And here,' I say, pointing to the next name. 'Kirsten, see? She was seven years old when she wrote that. And this one here's my mum.'

Those letters – H A N N A H – are so beautifully carved next to my childish effort, their shapes so rich in associated memories, that I fall suddenly still. Moses touches his fingers to the name, tracing those decades-old lines. He places a forefinger at each end of the word and draws them slowly together, then out again, enjoying the palindromic beauty of my mother's name.

'She said we shouldn't mark any of the other rocks,' I whisper. 'But it was OK under here, where nobody else would see.'

'She is a very wise woman,' declares Moses.

'I suppose, perhaps she was,' I mutter. Shifting the beam, I say, 'And here's Dad's. Well . . . we did it for him.'

Moses's forefinger taps the last name in recognition.

'Billy,' I say, remembering the way he kept his left hand between my thighs while he carved the word. Remembering how hard it was to keep the torch steady. We made love under here, beneath my parents' names. Perhaps that's why I haven't been back since. We did it on our sides, the sandstone scraping at our hips and shoulders, our legs sticking out for any passing angler to see. It was a remarkable experience, intense and concentrated, a flavour of the caged fantasy about it, a dizzying density of lust and love.

It's indecent to think these things while Moses is squashed beside me. It's indecent, but I can't help it. Billy has taken over my thoughts at far worse times – during rescues, in meetings with NSW Maritime, while I'm talking to my father. My lover has a grip on me I would never have imagined possible and wouldn't wish to shake off in a thousand years. The only way to escape it temporarily is to get on with something else, and so I reach back down to my pocket and pull out a small screwdriver.

'You want to write yours?'

'All right,' Moses says. 'I can do that.'

'You don't have to. Not for my sake.'

'It's OK.'

'Moses, it would be nice if you'd say what you actually want. The way you talk, it's like you're just doing me a favour.'

I make as if to return the tool to my pocket, and he says quickly, 'I want to. Please.'

It's a stupid moment of clumsiness: he's reaching for the screwdriver, I'm bringing it back up towards him, our movements are constricted, and somehow I manage to stab his hand with the blade. A small puncture, that's all it is, unlikely to hurt much. And beyond a yelp of surprise, Moses shows no sign of distress while I'm apologising. Instead, he studies his palm in the torchlight, watches a single drop of blood squeeze from the wound. The echo is obvious to both of us, but only he has something unexpected to say about it.

'I didn't see blood on her hand.'

'What? Look, we should go inside, get some antiseptic on that.'

'She said I saw blood on her hand.' He turns to gaze at me. Our faces are too close. 'I never said that.'

And while I stop fussing, fall silent in my surprise, he takes the screwdriver from my fingers and carves, with careful strokes, into the soft stone.

•

Kirsten calls while Moses is in the shower.

'Have you seen what they're writing about him?' she says with excitement.

I bring up the *Herald* site in semi-grey over her face. WHO IS DARAN'S AMAZING PROPHET? the third news item reads.

'All the news sites,' she's saying. 'One leaping dog, and Moses is a star!'

'Why's that a good thing?' I clear the website to get a better look at her expression.

'Honey, I need you to bring him back today, yeah? This is too good. In fact, can you get him to me this morning?'

'What's the hurry?' I say, still confused about that blood prediction. 'What is it you want from him?'

'Me? *Nothing*. What could I want? But now that the media are interested, we need to . . . protect him.'

'Protect him from what?'

'This isn't your world, honey. Don't worry, I've got a whole team interfacing with the media. Bring him over and I'll make sure he's kept secluded.'

'More secluded than at Saaremaa?' I shake my head. 'He's going back to South Africa. I'm sorting the arrangements with the Consulate today.'

'No, you're not,' she laughs, like I'm teasing her. 'Send away our TV star, what are you crazy?'

She's making no sense. But now the pressure of compartment two is building so strong I have to tell her: 'Kirsten, listen. Moses saw something. For the Sydney Hobart. He saw a storm. He saw *Sentinel* – said she went under. Said she "died".'

Kirsten pauses, looks more closely at my image on her screen, blinks twice. 'He said that?'

'Yeah.'

'And you believe it?' she says wonderingly.

'It doesn't matter what I believe. People are saying *Sentinel*'s not robust enough for serious weather.'

But Kirsten has withdrawn, moved on. 'You have a good day, babe. Get Moses over here soon as you can, please.'

'Are you even listening to me?'

'Always, honey, always. Kiss, kiss.'

•

On the way to the Harbour, I bring it up with Stuart. 'She isn't taking Moses's storm forecast seriously, which is fair enough as she doesn't believe he can see the future any more than I do. But it's as if she still thinks he could do something important for her.'

'Well, God, imagine. If he *could* see into the future, she might as well print money.'

'What, spotting the next iPod . . .'

'Sure, but that kind of blockbuster product is fairly rare. Making money in the markets can be far more mundane – a small shift in the perceived value of a canned fruit manufacturer is all it takes. And you only need a slight advantage: I'd be a billionaire if I could call heads or tails correctly even 51 per cent of the time. So if Moses really could predict stock market movements —'

'Which he can't possibly.'

'Still sure about that after the RTV show?'

'Stuart, come on. This is ridiculous. *Prophecy?*'

'Do you know how many people correctly predicted the sinking of the *Titanic* and the assassination of JFK?'

'Stuart!'

'All right, yes, it's ridiculous.'

'So why is Kirsten so keen to keep Moses here?'

He falls silent for a while, watching the mutton-birds skimming the water ahead of us and swerving out of our way. The ocean is clear of boats; we have the whole stretch from Narrabeen to the Harbour to ourselves.

'Strange thing happened last year,' he says thoughtfully. 'A trader I knew started sleeping with the finance director of a publicly quoted IT services company. Everyone assumed he was getting insider information, so when he bought a chunk of her company's stock on his own account, all the other traders piled in. That sent the stock through the roof; he sold out, made a killing. And the joke was, there wasn't any reason to buy – no unexpected profit announcements, no insider information. He just knew they were all watching him, so he made the play and cashed in.'

'Why are you telling me this?'

'Kirsten's a smart woman. She understands how the markets work.' He shrugs. 'If people *think* you can see the future . . . That might be enough.'

We pull a couple of shark biscuits out of the water around ten thirty, then Stuart drops me off at the naval base on Garden Island. Already the temperature's reaching uncomfortable levels; we're in for a hot Christmas. With the Harbour breeze blocked by a lot of berthed military steel, the sweat's running down my back before I've gone twenty paces.

Commodore Fowler has been called to Canberra, but he's detailed a Lieutenant Neil Loak to meet me and escort me to *HMAS Darwin*. The experimental walkway is already set up between the frigate's lower stern deck and a rigid inflatable: a long chain of threads that look a lot like stretched mucus – all translucent and glistening. Donald Carter, standing on the deck with a bunch of technicians, waves to me and says, 'Impressive piece of kit, isn't it, Petra?'

Perhaps I'm looking doubtful, because the Lieutenant urges me straight on to the thing. 'Go on! Try it!' He hands me a lifejacket. 'We'll come and rescue you if you fall in.'

Funny guys, these Navy types.

The walkway has a meshwork of rubbery cords underfoot, and a couple of rubbery ropes at hand level that look like pure slime. I touch one uncertainly, and am surprised to discover a dry, rough texture – easy to grip. I slip on the lifejacket.

'For the moment, it's called the RX582,' says the Lieutenant. 'That's something we need help on.'

I look round. 'You've asked me here to give you a pretty name?'

He takes a step back. 'Course not, Captain. Er . . . if you'd like to go ahead?'

I glance at Donald. As always, he's dressed in neatly ironed knee-length shorts, dock shoes, and a crisp white short-sleeved shirt. There's a gentle, competent older-era maleness about Donald that I love. Hair cut short and combed precisely around a smallish bald patch. Well-tested calves marked by a couple of liver spots and slightly protruding veins. He's the kind of man you know would offer you his seat on a bus. A solid 18ºC man, through and through.

'Keep me company?' I say.

He's about to join me, when the Lieutenant squawks, 'Specifications allow only one person at a time, Captain,' so I shrug and step onto the meshwork by myself.

The steadiness of the structure is awesome. It looks so feeble, but my weight's not making it sag at all. Halfway across, I look back and the

Lieutenant says, 'Now, Captain Woods, if you'll stand there a moment.' He gives a signal to the coxswain of the rigid inflatable.

The RIB starts moving. The coxswain drives forward and back, side to side, and the RX582 does a little aerobics session under my feet. It's a strange sensation being on a bridge that's stretching and shifting and contracting all the time, yet all you can feel is a slight sway in your hips and a shudder in your soles. Even as the RIB gets more aggressive – backing and roaring around like a dirtbike – the RX582 accommodates every movement with ease. When I walk back on board the frigate, I have to admit they've come up with something pretty special.

'Needs to be tested with vertical displacement as well,' I say. 'Get the full effect of the swell.'

'Yes, Captain Carter's also made that point,' agrees the Lieutenant.

Donald smiles lightly when I catch his eye.

'And it needs colour,' I add. 'All that foam and water splashing around, low light levels, heavy rain – no one will be able to see this thing in a storm.'

'Good point,' nods Donald.

He's a very experienced mariner, so a little praise from him goes a long way, even though we now hold equal rank within the Coastguard. Once, as a volunteer apprentice, I joined his crew for a rescue on a foundering trawler, at night, in heavy seas. While he was manoeuvring our ALB to keep it alongside the trawler, I jumped across to help the guys off. But when I jumped back, the waves bounced the ALB away and I found myself falling between two steel hulls. Next moment, the ALB should have rolled back against the trawler and I should have been crushed, but Donald was so deft in his handling of that cumbersome vessel I got to live another few years. Not many skippers would have had the skill for that sea dance.

The Lieutenant confers briefly with the technicians.

'Shouldn't be difficult,' they admit finally. 'Pink fluorescent dye in the polymer.'

'Maybe something luminous.'

'Couple of months, we could have it ready.'

Lieutenant Loak offers us an early lunch in the mess, but I want some time alone with Donald and I drag him off to the Harbour Hazard café.

There's Christmas carols playing, the bubbly American kind. We're regulars here, and we manage to get the music turned right down. After we've worked our way through the usual catch-up chat about Coastguard staffing and equipment shortages, I ask casually, 'So what's the forecast looking like for the Sydney Hobart?'

A trio of teen girls, barefoot with lazy, rolling hips, wander past our table. They're wearing impish smiles and the flimsiest of sarongs, tucked carelessly to leave a little buttock on show. They remind me of Kirsten and myself, years ago, sauntering around Palm Beach like we owned the place.

'Pretty straightforward.'

'Nothing lurking?'

'Not to my knowledge.'

He's ordered a small and very thick black coffee. He stirs in a tiny quantity of sugar, then drinks the whole thing in one go.

'So we can be sure, can't we, about the race?'

'I would never go that far,' he says, mildly bemused.

'But if there was going to be, say, a huge storm, we would see some meteorological sign of it by now, right?'

Donald's married, with four kids. The big All-weather Life Boats he skippers are practically indestructible. They can turn over without any problem. Wind, waves, lightning strikes – nothing is so bad they can't just batten down the hatches. When he sets off with the race fleet to Hobart, he should be all right, whatever the weather. But still, he understands what it would be for his children to lose their parent to a storm. He understands me.

Laying his hand on my arm, he says kindly, 'I don't think you've any cause to worry this year.'

•

Nolan is not expecting me. Like all the best sailing masters, he is protective of his charge and suspicious of all non-crew trespassers. He suffers with mostly concealed irritation the journalists and photographers who want a guided tour of the favourite. He answers their questions, however lame, and explains the hydraulic machinery which so fascinates all those land-hugging types who can't recognise the greater technological achievements in the construction of the hull and the computer-moulded curve of the mainsail. But he draws the line at friends and bed partners of the crew – even best friends of the skipper.

'Nolan, this is Coastguard business,' I say, storing up all manner of guilt in my mind.

'We've been inspected already. Why does the *Inshore* Coastguard need to see inside my boat?'

Noting the robustness of both emphasis and possessive, I fall back quickly on a less heinous lie. 'I lost a precious earring on Friday night, and I can't concentrate in my work until I find it. Lives are being put at risk, Nolan!'

He sighs incredulously. 'Women!' Holding out a hand, he helps me aboard. 'Be quick then. We're testing the engines in ten minutes.'

'Thanks.' I hurry down the steps.

'We sweep all the time,' he warns. 'You won't find it!'

Inside the main cabin, the essence of an ocean-going vessel has been restored. The long sailbags are back on board, obliterating the walkways either side of the engine block. Plasma screens, removed for the party, have been replaced around the navigator's station. Tools, thongs, kitbags, sunnies, scribbled lists and chocolate bars lie scattered around. The booze, pile carpet, and Sentinel Bank banners are all gone.

As is that one jagged screw.

But it's not the missing screw that concerns me. It's the complete absence of any screws whatsoever in those bunks. Fashioned out of moulded plastic, they are as I should have expected them to be: seamless, joinless, utterly screwless.

All that's left, to prove I didn't dream the entire episode, is a single neat hole.

•

Though we've been friends forever, there are certain parts of Kirsten's life that are closed to me. The Sydney Hobart race is one of them: for some reason she's never invited me to sail with her. Perhaps she thinks I would find it painful, given what happened to my mother. It doesn't bother me. I've had plenty of offers from other skippers, and besides I've never been into that macho big boat stuff. Kirsten gets a rush from ordering twenty-two crew about, but I prefer single-handed sailing. Well, truth is, I really just prefer engines. Anyway, so that's one side of Kirsten I don't see. Another is the bank.

Once or twice I tagged along when Kirsten skipped school to go shopping in the city, calling in on her father for spending money. Lester was always nice to me, asking fondly after my parents, but I found the President's suite a depressing place. It's grand enough, with views over the Harbour and the Opera House, and it's lined with the most expensive art on the market. But there's a hunger about it, like it's got this constant, clawing need for new deals, new money, new people to consume. I once told Kirsten she should replace the potted ferns with carnivorous plants. It was meant as a joke – when she moved in, I wanted to draw some of the stress from her face – but she didn't take it well.

The other thing I don't like about the bank is the lack of colour. As if in defiance of the expensive corporate Christmas decorations, everyone is wearing grey or navy or black. When I wander into the lobby in my yellow Coastguard shirt, trackie daks, yellow baseball cap and runners, I feel like all these suits are curling their lips at me. I mean, who *are* these people? Don't they go to the beach at the weekend? Don't they surf, drink beer, have sex? Do they always look so judgemental? It's particularly dismal today because Billy's now one of them. He's somewhere in this building, being taught how to sound professional, how to write business-speak, how to walk their brisk walk, how to be.

On the forty-fifth floor, I'm met out of the elevator by Tabitha. 'She's very busy.' Her voice is a low monotone. 'I don't know if she can see you. Is it important?'

Around us, seven groomed men – all men – are waiting for their chance to see the CEO. Some are young: nervous or arrogant or both. Their eyes scan the framed photographs of earlier *Sentinels*, captured in peak racing form, with taut sails and frozen sprays of sparkling water slicing crisply off their bows. The older men have tired faces and sallow skin. Too long in this deadening world. But their expectant expressions betray an unmistakeable respect for Kirsten's achievements – the celebrated M&A deals, the rescue consortium for the Fijian sugar industry, the bold redundancy round, the lightning takeover of Britain's favourite pensions provider, the unconventionally upfront advertising campaign targeting those UHNWIs. There is, even to an outsider uninterested in the world of finance, a sense of legend about the place.

'This won't take long,' I promise, and I walk past them all to Kirsten's office.

•

Finding Billy there is a shock. I don't know why it bothers me so much. Seated at her sleek steel desk, Kirsten is running her fingers across a set of papers with a sweeping, curving motion, like she's testing the ink won't smudge. Billy's crouched uncomfortably beside her. The suit looks awful on him – it's the right size, good quality from what little I know, but it doesn't hang right. Something in him is battling to throw it off.

All his attention is focused on the papers. His brow is creased. He doesn't notice me come in.

But Kirsten does. She nudges Billy and smiles.

Billy straightens up fast. At least he's pleased to see me. 'Hey, P, how are ya, gorgeous?'

The suit doesn't look so bad when he's standing. Passable anyway, though I'm finding it tough to see him in it. The tie he's chosen – or was it Tabitha? – is light blue with pink polka dots. I've never seen a scrap of pink on Billy before.

'Hi,' I say, still unsettled.

'Nice to see you,' says Kirsten. 'You've brought Moses?'

'We need to talk,' I say, already discomforted by a business atmosphere that so excludes me.

'I'm taking Billy through the work he'll be doing, but no worries: we can finish this later,' Kirsten offers. Her eyes slide to Billy: 'Can't we, babe?'

'Yeah, course.'

He comes round the desk to give me a hug. 'Sorry about being weird last night,' he whispers in my ear. Then, louder, 'Have fun, girls.' And he's off out the door, whistling like Sentinel Bank's inner sanctum is just another seafront bar.

Kirsten's wearing two silver bangles she picked up years ago in India. Everything else about her is regulation chief exec. Heels not too high, skirt not too short, jacket and top perfectly chosen to give her a presence, but not sledgehammer dominance.

'I really think he might have a talent for this,' she says cheerfully, coming over to kiss me. 'It's going to be a stretch at first, but he's definitely got the smarts. And everyone in Marketing loves him. We'll make a Sentinel Bank man of him in no time.'

'Kirsten, what is it you're doing?'

'Running a public company, honey, when I'm not shooting the breeze with you.'

'I've come from CYCA. Decided to check the rest of the screws in your bunks were safe.'

She looks at me with a long, evaluating expression of interest. 'How clever of you.'

'Yeah, save it, Kirsten. What's going on? Why would you cut yourself deliberately?'

'Hush! You make me sound like a psycho.' She stretches one leg out, arching the foot. 'Simple entertainment. A party trick. Don't you think they were entertained?'

'"They" being, by chance, a bunch of journalists and investors?'

'By chance, yes.'

'Kirsten, don't lie to me.'

When she doesn't answer, I fan open my clutch of news site printouts. 'It's not often I look at the financial media. Amazing what they're saying about Sentinel Bank just now. Have you seen?'

I hold out the pages. Kirsten draws back, vaguely repelled. 'I've seen,' she admits.

'Of course, Sam Drauston started it. But there's all these others since Daran's show, even an editorial here: *Prophet may profit Sentinel Bank*. Catchy. You've really got the message out there.'

'Are you honestly suggesting I want people to think this bank is run by a seer?' She laughs dismissively. 'You're the one who put Moses on TV.'

'Don't treat me like an idiot.'

'Market makers are not gullible people. They're not going to believe this prophecy shit.'

'Maybe they don't have to. Maybe they just have to believe someone else might believe it. You told me once they all knew the Internet boom was hot air, but bought anyway because they reckoned there were enough mugs out there to push the prices sky high. How's your share price doing today?'

'Petra, you're trying to understand a world that's too complex. This stuff happens all the time in the markets. We suggest, we imply . . .'

'Mislead? Deceive?'

She frowns at my black expression. 'Jesus, will you get off your high horse? You know how badly we need this stock issue to work. So many people depend on Sentinel Bank – for their jobs, their savings, their pensions. This is not about me. The whole Australian economy would be hurt if the bank went under. I *have* to get that money in.'

'By exploiting a child to con your investors. How can you possibly think it's going to work?'

'It's already working,' she says coldly. 'The trading floor is reporting a lot of copycat action: other traders following where our guys lead. Do you have any idea what that means? We buy, so others buy, so the price goes up and the Bank makes a lot of money. We're moving markets! Which just strengthens the perception we've got a precognitive edge.'

'Perception is everything, huh?'

'Anyone calls, we deny the story: it hooks them all the more. And it's going to keep building. A buzz like this, no trader can resist it. Combine it with a strong win in the Hobart, Sentinel Bank is going to look at the top of its game for the sixth of January. We'll be oversubscribed, however high the price goes.'

'Then what? You ditch Moses?'

Kirsten unfolds from her tautly defensive posture. 'Honey, listen, my promise to Moses was completely sincere. He gets two years of top-quality education, a nice home, fun holidays, then a chance to work at the Bank for as long as he likes. This doesn't mean I don't genuinely want to help him. Who in his village ever had this opportunity? All it'll cost him is a couple of weeks of media attention.'

'He's going home.'

'You need to stay out of this.'

'Do you know how much I've been worrying about that storm? About . . .' I stop myself, get control of my anger. 'I've already spoken to the South African Deputy Consul. She's coming over to Spring Cove this evening to arrange the flight back.'

'OK, enough,' snaps Kirsten. Her persuasive reasoning gives way to that sudden blitzing resolve which comes to the surface only when a sailing trophy or desired man is nearly, but not quite, within reach. 'Do that, and you can forget about Coastguard funding from now on. I'm serious, Petra. This is too important to fuck around.'

My shoulders stiffen as the anger floods back. 'You're threatening me?'

'No, shit, no,' she sighs, already regretting that tone. 'All I mean is, if the Bank goes down, obviously the funding ends. We're in this together! Sailors' lives depend on the new issue succeeding, depend on Moses. Don't you see that?' She lifts her watch. 'Look, I've got to take a meeting. Ten minutes late already. Petra, please, don't do anything today, OK? Sleep on it. Stall the Consulate. Let's talk later.'

CHAPTER 6

It's past six o'clock, and I'm expecting Grace Cadey at any minute, when the first weather alerts come in from ALB-3. There's a lot of after-work boats heading out; we have to move fast to get every channel transmitting the same warning. What makes it harder is the unexpectedness of the squall. Nothing was forecast for this evening, so we're getting requests for confirmation from everyone: Marine Area Command and NSW Maritime, CYCA, Surf Life Saving, even the Navy. According to the Bureau of Meteorology, the seas should be calm, the sun shining. But ALB-3 is forty miles out on exercise, and they have a visual on the rough stuff that none of the satellites or modelling systems have picked up.

'They can see it,' I'm having to repeat for the seventh time. 'Gale-force, moving west at eighteen knots. Estimating Sydney environs, twenty-one hundred. We're not making this up. Send the message!'

The alert is finally transmitted. All channels, all authorities. Red flags are raised from Gosford to Botany Bay. The twelve SilverBird crews are scrambled, and for a couple of hours we rocket back and forth around the Harbour and the ocean beaches, taking the message to any boats not radio-equipped.

By eight, the sea is empty. I send the order to stand down all Inshore crews. Carole confirms that Grace Cadey has been and gone. 'She totally understood,' promises Carole over the radio. 'I showed her the alerts, and she told us we were doing a brilliant job. She'll be back tomorrow morning, OK?' It's a relief to have had a genuine excuse for missing the Deputy Consul's visit. Kirsten's line about Coastguard funding is too serious to ignore completely. I don't think she would really turn off the tap, but a little more time to think it through is very welcome.

In the dark, it's hard to see much evidence of the approaching squall. The wind has picked up, a few waves are forming, but so far there's no sign of the trouble ALB-3 has forecast. Impossible to miss, however, are the port and starboard lights of a large sailing vessel heading out to sea.

'What are they thinking?' I mutter to Stuart. Racing across the black sea, we recognise the shape of the yacht long before we reach it. 'Coastguard two-one to *Sentinel*, imminent severe weather. Recommend immediate return to Harbour.'

Kirsten's voice comes back good and cheerful. 'Evening, Petra. What are you doing out so late?'

Beating to windward, she executes a textbook tack. Actually, it's better than that: the kind of tack that inspires textbooks, her bow swinging onto the perfect course to maximise headway, her sails thundering round so efficiently that barely any speed is lost in the manoeuvre. My father may have taught her the fundamentals of sailing, but since then she's developed her skills to an extraordinary level. Through constant practice and relentless determination, she's left the rest of our little Pittwater sailing class far behind.

'We've got a nasty squall coming this way. Didn't you receive the warning?'

'That's why we're here, honey. Perfect training conditions for that storm Moses is promising us.' She says it with a chuckle. Then, more seriously: 'Crew need the rough-water practice, boat and equipment need testing. I don't know why no one else is out.'

We're close enough now to see her at the helm. One hand on the windward wheel, the other holding a radio and giving me a wave. The whole crew is dressed in foul weather gear, working nicely in unison to keep the boat trimmed. Even from a distance I can sense the anticipation, the nerves. They know they're about to get walloped, and they're looking forward to it.

'Be sensible, Kirsten. This is beyond a training exercise. The estimate we have is force seven gusting to force nine.'

'You saying we shouldn't prepare for gales in Bass Strait?' she replies, and I don't answer because I know she's thinking, like me, about my mother on *Blueberry*. At the funeral, Kirsten sat beside me and held my hand the whole time. Her own mother died three days after she was born, from complications in the delivery. That, perhaps, has become our strongest bond.

'You shouldn't be out here, anyway,' continues Kirsten in a gentler voice. 'Your SilverBird isn't designed for gale force conditions.'

'I know that,' I snap, but I don't press the transmit button. Only Stuart hears it. Instead, I turn *Giselle* about, touch the button and say, 'Be ready to run for shelter if it gets bad.'

'Sweet dreams, Captain. Don't forget to bring Moses over first thing.'

●

The bad weather hits at 21:43. Later than expected, but it has all the mean force we feared. At least we cleared the sea. In the summer, lots of guys like to take boats out until late. Things could have been messy without the warning.

I'm trying not to think too much about *Sentinel*. But I do have the volume on my wrist transceiver set loud.

Moses has been watching soaps and chat shows all day. I make a point of turning off the TV once I've cooked us a mushroom and cheese omelette.

'You missing your family?' I ask. 'Do you want to call them, check they're OK?'

Rain batters the windows. The roof timbers creak in the wind.

'They are fine,' he shrugs. 'They will all live a long time.'

'You've seen their future?'

'You don't believe my predictions,' he scolds lightly.

'Um . . . No.'

'You should believe.' There's a hint of a smile there, as if he's winding me up.

'Convince me. Give me some predictions and we'll see if they come true.'

'Your brother will have four children,' he offers.

'I don't have a brother, Moses. Or a sister.'

He puffs out his cheeks. 'That wasn't a real prediction.'

'Fine, so give me a real prediction.'

Drawing back, he stares at me. His eyes narrow and lose focus, his lips tighten. He lays both hands flat on the table. His gaze turns remote. 'When you have more money,' he declares, as if from a slight remove, 'you will build a new house, high up the hill.'

'Well, that's unlikely,' I laugh, 'seeing as it's illegal to build in the Park.'

Dropping his hands into his lap, he gives a fractious snort. 'It could happen,' he mutters.

Somehow I've gone and killed the cheerful mood. It's often like that, I find, when you cross someone's belief. One moment they're loftily telling you why they have all the answers, then you point out a flaw in their creed and they go all morose.

'Have you decided what you want to do when you're older?' I ask, to get him back. 'You're a bright guy. We might be able to sort you out with a training programme in South Africa if you'd like it.'

'I won't get older,' he says defiantly. 'I'm going to die.'

'Moses, please!'

As if to illustrate his point, he glances upwards. The old tin roof always makes a racket in a downpour, and tonight's a heavy one. It doesn't worry me any more than the groaning of the great ship's timbers that form the frame of the house. Saaremaa's been standing a long time, and sailing even longer before that. Going to take more than a squall to do any real damage.

'It won't fall down, I promise.'

'Strong wind.'

'Wind that sings and shouts?' I suggest playfully.

'No.' He meets my smile with a humourless stare. 'That will be much stronger.'

In the face of his grim certainty, I'm actually relieved when my phone rings. It's Donald Carter.

'Petra, good evening. Look, this weather got me thinking about your question this morning. I've just had a look at the latest satellite pictures, and there is something. Not major, but you did ask.'

A sense of dread unfolds around my consciousness. 'What is it, Donald?'

'A rather unusual low forming below the 50th. About 55 degrees east of Auckland. Shouldn't come this way, of course.'

'You don't sound sure.'

'You never know, these days, do you?' he sighs. 'Chaos in the stratosphere. Global warming messing with the old patterns. Prevailing winds reversed. Uncertainty in every raindrop. The Met Bureau can only predict so much.'

'Why's the low unusual?'

A slight hesitation. 'It's concentrated, dangerously so. Liable to shatter a few icebergs if it deepens.'

'Are you serious?'

'But like I said, it should stay well south of the race.'

•

The distress call comes at 22:08.

'Mayday, Mayday, Mayday, this is *Sentinel Sentinel Sentinel*, super-maxi nine miles off Whale Beach, man overboard, man overboard, man overboard, visual contact lost, search in progress, request assistance Offshore Coastguard, Marine Area Command, and any vessels in the vicinity.'

At night, in bad weather, it's one of the worst things that could happen. Locating an MOB in these conditions is going to be a nightmare. And it's hard not to think of my mother, struggling to stay conscious as that relentless storm tossed her about, praying in vain that one of the helicopters roaring past overhead might catch her in its spotlight.

I'm a little touchy about man-overboard calls.

Moses is back in front of the television and I'm waiting for Billy to get here. He's had to stay late in the office, which is a bit extreme on his first day. But Tabitha's offered to give him a crash course in banking terminology so that he makes a strong first impression when he meets the Marketing Director tomorrow, and I guess that's important. He's promised to be here by ten, and even though I'm nervous about him riding his motorbike in this weather and kayaking across the choppy black Pittwater, I really feel it's important we have the night together, to put Moses's unnerving prediction firmly in the past.

But he hasn't arrived yet, and now there's a guy in the water, and I'm pacing up and down the veranda waiting for the Night Duty Officer at Spring Cove to reassure me there's an ALB on its way to *Sentinel*.

'Oliver? Talk to me, Oliver.'

The radio's getting a lot of static tonight. 'Stand by.'

Rain drives in under the veranda roof, drenching the couch, reaching to the front door. Lightning forks overhead. The waves in sheltered Pittwater are a good metre high. Beyond the Palm Beach peninsula, out in the ocean where the serious wind is, they'll be closer to five metres. Somewhere amongst those waves someone's coughing on seawater, alone in the dark, carried south by the current, wondering if anyone is going to come and get him. I really hope he's wearing a lifejacket.

'Oliver, what is the status on ALB-3?'

'Stand by.'

'I've *been* standing by! Have they fixed the engine yet?'

'Negative. We're scrambling ALB-4.'

'Time to MOB?'

'Donald's here, but he's still two crew short.'

My mobile rings then. It's Stuart. In the pounding rain, I can't hear the speaker, so I turn off the video link and press the mobile to my ear. 'Are we going or what?' he says.

'The SilverBird's not rated for this weather, you know that.'

'I also know it's going to take that ALB twenty minutes minimum to deploy, another hour to reach Whale Beach from the Harbour. We're already here.'

'It's too dangerous, Stuart.'

'Ah, bollocks to that. Shall I try Dan Worrell for our third?'

I give myself thirty seconds to make the decision. It's what I want to do, after all. Stuart knows that. He also knows the only thing holding me back was an unwillingness to ask it of the guys. 'Tell Dan it's completely voluntary. No pressure, no shame, OK? I'll pick you up in ten.'

•

It's never a good idea to be out alone in a boat in rough seas. One unexpected wave could knock you cold or have you over the side, tether or no tether, with no one to help. Even the short Pittwater crossing to Seaplane Wharf looks hairy, and I pull on my drysuit and helmet, and clip on, before I even start the engine. Doing all this while *Giselle* is tossed about like driftwood is a miserable experience, and it's a relief to get moving and reach the relative shelter of the sand spit.

Flashing headlights in Governor Phillip Park tell me Stuart and Dan are already there. Impressively fast, given that Dan lives in Mona Vale. There's been some speeding on the roads tonight.

Stuart's already wearing his drysuit and helmet; Dan has his bundled in his arms, and he pulls them on as we head out into the violent waters of

Broken Bay. Onshore gales clash ferociously with the heavy Hawkesbury River here, and a lot of old ships litter the seabed. I hand out personal locator beacons and satisfy myself that the guys have got them strapped on right and set for separation activation: the beacons will start transmitting in the event they move more than five metres from the base station on board *Giselle*. It's a great system, and one I've repeatedly recommended to Kirsten. Our job tonight would be a lot easier if she'd listened to me.

The conditions beyond Barrenjoey Head are something horrible. Heavy rain obliterates everything; even the lights of Palm Beach are faint. The prevailing wave pattern is directly towards the shore, so driving out to sea is hard work. Intense winds buffet *Giselle*, catching her bows whenever we rise up a wave, and threatening to spin her round or topple her. The only way to deal with big seas in a SilverBird is to dance her all over the place, keeping clear of breakers, riding the backs of waves or weaving through the troughs, with always enough power kept in reserve in case an emergency manoeuvre becomes necessary. At night, it's that much harder, because even with the searchlight we can't see every wave coming. It's exhausting work, and once we're a few miles offshore Stuart takes the helm to give me a break.

Approaching *Sentinel*'s original position, I call them up to get a full sitrep on the Man Overboard. Stuart's doing a great job of dodging the worst waves and riding the best, helped by Dan's deft handling of the searchlight. Despite the conditions, I feel complete confidence in these guys.

'*Sentinel*, Coastguard-two-one, any visual on your MOB?'

'Negative.' It's the navigator, Ryan. 'We have a strobe-lit dan buoy in the water, dropped within a few hundred metres of MOB. Last known position: nine miles east Whale Beach, sixty-five minutes ago. Our datum point is the dan buoy, currently a little over two miles south-west of original position, suggesting drift of three knots.' He gives the coordinates of both points. 'Thanks for getting here so quick.'

Up ahead, *Sentinel*'s searchlight comes visible through the downpour.

'Offshore should be along soon.' I feed the coordinates into the onboard computer. The screen brings up the two points. 'What's your search area?' I ask.

'Circle, two mile radius, centred on datum.'

'Search pattern?'

'Sector search.'

A sensible first choice. They've been ploughing *Sentinel* back and forth across the circle, passing regularly through the datum – the most probable position of the MOB – changing their bearing by 120° each time. But when the search object still wasn't found after 45 minutes and eight turns, the search should really have been declared ineffective and a new approach attempted.

The information goes into our computer, and an image of their search area comes up on the screen. I check it against our own GPS-sourced position, then set it to drift south-west at three knots.

A double blast of *Sentinel*'s horn.

'Who is it, Ryan?'

'A student, Martha Salford. She's nineteen, won some kind of Sentinel Bank award for endeavour.'

'From the coast?'

'Negative. Little outback town.'

The poor girl. Out of her depth in every way. 'She can swim?'

'More or less. She's in a jacket.'

'Would hope so.' We're getting close now. The red and green navigation lights are clear, as is the strobe at the top of *Sentinel*'s mast. 'Give me the skipper will you, Ryan?'

'Sure, Petra. Good luck.'

A wave lifts us high, offering us a better look at the search area. There's the dan buoy, its bright white strobe raised nearly two metres above the surface. There's *Sentinel* ploughing towards it on a westerly heading. So far Kirsten's done everything by the book other than recognise when her search pattern wasn't working. Her engine is just about audible over our own. The sails have all been lowered: no one's going to tack a search pattern in these conditions, although I bet Kirsten was pissed off having to change to motor power. It's like a sign of defeat for her, that's how serious she is about sailing.

'Petra,' she says over the radio. 'Nice to have you back. You sure your vessel can take these waves?'

'I'll look after her,' I promise. 'What can you tell me about the MOB?'

'Strong enough. She'll be scared but hanging on.'

'How many times have you passed datum?'

'Too many. Clear enough she isn't there. I'm expanding the radius to three miles.'

Another couple of blasts on the horn. The outback girl is not going to have any problem working out where the yacht is. Or the dan buoy, if she's got her eyes open.

'She conscious?'

'Crew heard a cry as she went in. Another shortly after. Certainly should be.'

She's been in the water just over an hour. No way is she fainting from the cold yet. Which means she should be able to see everything. Yet she hasn't swum to the strobe. Why not? The dan buoy was dropped close by her. Even an outback girl should be able to manage that.

'What's your breakdown of the drift?' I ask.

'Wind's strong, but leeway's minimal for small objects in these waves. Wind-driven current's the bigger factor – maybe two knots, 265 degrees. Sea current is two knots, 190 degrees. So even if we don't find her, she'll hit the shore around Long Reef somewhere.'

'Not a nice shore to hit,' I mutter distractedly, testing some variables on the computer. Kirsten's sea current estimate sounds low to me. It can be hard to measure in bad weather. And the current may have a greater pull on an adult human body than on a small buoy being tossed about on the waves. 'We're going to try a parallel pattern to your south. Keep this channel open, please.'

'Whatever you say. No offence, but have we got any bigger boats coming out? I don't rate your chances of seeing our girl from down there.'

'ALB-4 just cleared the Heads. Water police have a cruiser abeam Curl Curl. Coastguard helicopter's ready to go, but waiting for the weather to pass.'

'All right for some,' she says. There's a gallows humour in her voice that I can't help admiring. I find it very hard to laugh at times like this. And it's not as if Kirsten doesn't care; even if Martha Salford herself means nothing to her, she's the kind of skipper for whom losing crew is the worst possible failure. The right kind of skipper, in other words. 'Do what you can anyway.'

It's not necessary to give the order. Stuart's heard my decision and already has the SilverBird heading south. I use the touchpen on the computer screen to draw up a rectangular search area, four miles by three, directly south of *Sentinel*'s three-mile radius circle. As we reach it, Stuart says, 'Start parallel tracks?'

'No, take us to the southern boundary. We'll work north to intercept the MOB drifting south.'

Our east–west tracks are going to set us against the prevailing wave pattern. It'll be slow, uncomfortable work. The temptation to take a creeping line pattern, north–south, is strong, but I know we'll see nothing at all if we just drive up and down the troughs between the waves. The MOB could pass a few metres from us the wrong side of a wave and we'd never spot her. And if the current's as strong as I think it is, she could drift right through our search area while we're still halfway across it. At least if we work against the current, we should catch her.

That said, our sweep width is miserably small. The darkness, the heavy rain, the mishmash of waves and the tiny size of our search object mean that we're having to follow tracks less than eighty metres apart. At precise five-second intervals, Dan shifts the searchlight, giving our eyes just long enough to scour each sector of tumbling water for that little yellow hood and yellow lifejacket before moving on to the next. His job's all the harder because of *Giselle*'s instability. Every time we climb a wave, we get buffeted. And there's still a strong risk of the wind catching our bottom and flipping us over. Stuart's getting tired, making mistakes in his approach to waves. He's starting to yell at Dan whenever the searchlight catches the white edge of *Giselle*'s gunwale, reflecting back into our eyes and blinding us.

'Want me to take over for a while?' I say quietly.

'I'm fine,' he snaps.

'Listening search,' I call. We do this every two minutes or so. Stuart cuts the engines at the top of the next wave, we call her name, blow a whistle, and then all three of us strain to hear something over the crash of the waves and the bellow of the wind. But there's no cry, no human sound at all. As Stuart reaches for the throttle at the bottom of the wave, I touch his arm and say, 'I have the helm.'

He doesn't like it, doesn't want to be withdrawn, but it's a clear enough captain's order and he responds rightly, stepping away from the helmsman's seat the moment he's checked my grip on the wheel.

'Three minutes' rest, Stuart,' I say, as I bring up the throttle. 'Then I want you on the light.'

'Sure,' he says, a little mollified.

Following a search pattern in ugly conditions at sea is a difficult trick. I've chatted with Search & Rescue professionals from the Air Force and the Army, even with salvage divers who have to scour the bottom of the sea, and I can say for sure they all have it easy. The desert doesn't move, nor does the seabed. Those guys always have fixed points of reference. If they wanted to, they could put down markers to show where they'd been. And if the search object is a downed plane, or a chest of gold, or a truck that's run out of fuel, that's not moving either. What a simple life that must be.

For us, it's a whole different story. Our search area is a moving rectangle of anonymous sea. The search object is also in constant motion. There's nothing to distinguish one patch of water from another. All we can do is steer an east–west heading, then move eighty metres north and follow the reciprocal course. On a turbulent sea, it's not an exact science: even with the best computers and compass work, it's easy to leave too much water between tracks – two hundred metres, not eighty – and scared little Martha Salford could be somewhere in the middle of it.

'Listening search,' I call, earlier than I should, because I can't get that worry properly compartmentalised away.

'Martha!' roars Dan, who has the loudest voice. 'Martha!'

He goes quiet and I make the same call. Sometimes a female voice carries better. After my call, three sharp whistle blasts, then we all remain strictly silent.

Still nothing.

Nausea, which usually isn't a problem for me, gets to my stomach around then. These are foul conditions. Perhaps I judged Stuart too harshly – I'm not doing much better myself. *Giselle* is shuddering with each heavy drop from a wave crest, and I'm starting to wonder if we're doing her any serious structural damage. As if to underline my fears, Donald comes on the Coastguard channel.

'Coastguard two-one, this is Coastguard zero-four, we're reaching your search area and request you stand down. Conditions too severe for Inshore craft.'

'Negative stand down. We're doing fine. You going to join the same pattern?'

'Petra, you shouldn't be doing this. There's a reason we call these boats "All-weather".'

'MOB is Martha Salford. Nineteen years.' I've already transmitted the data on the two search areas to ALB-4's onboard computer. 'Suggest you take our rectangle one further mile south and commence parallels on southern boundary. Police have western zone covered.'

'Roger that. Petra, please activate your personal locator beacons now as a precaution. We'll let AMSA know we're monitoring them.'

'If you insist, Donald.' I pass the message on to Dan and Stuart. Three signals should now be bouncing off a satellite and bringing up alerts at the Australian Maritime Safety Authority in Canberra.

'Thank you, Coastguard two-one. We have your signals four point three miles north-west of us. Please be careful, Petra.'

'Always. Thanks, Donald. Out.'

By now, we'd hoped the worst of the weather would have passed, but the wind is getting stronger. The spray on my visor is so bad I'm struggling to see anything, let alone a tiny head poking out of the waves, fifty metres away. The roll and tumble is also worsening, and I'm getting to the point where I'm going to have to give the helm to Dan and empty my guts over the side. Not something I want to do in front of my guys. Happens to everyone, but I could do without the jokes going round Spring Cove for the next two weeks.

The sense of encroaching physical weakness gives me an extra dose of mental strength. This squall is not going to get the better of me. At the top of the next wave, I summon up my brightest voice and call, 'Listening search,' as I throttle back.

'Martha!' goes Dan. 'Martha!'

The searchlight stretches out across the water. 'Martha!' I try. 'Martha!'

The whistle blasts, then silence. Then –

A voice.

It's a wail, an exhausted half-scream. No clear word, just a back-of-the-throat gurgle. But we hear it. And we place it.

Stuart swings the searchlight round. 'Martha! Again! Shout again!'

And there she is. A second wail, and Stuart's able to catch that telltale splash of yellow in his beam. 'Visual!' he cries, holding the light steady against the buck of the wave. 'Visual!'

I'm on the radio and opening the throttle simultaneously. 'All stations, Coastguard two-one has visual on MOB. Repeat, we have visual. Estimating two miles south-south-east of *Sentinel*. Visual MOB.'

After fifty minutes of painstaking search, it's almost an anticlimax to reach her now. In seconds we're beside her, can see her ashen, exhausted face. 'It's OK, Martha, you're safe now. Just swim towards us if you can.' Her hands are reaching out for us, then dropping back into the water as she understands there's a little further to go, splashing through the swell, thrashing more than swimming. But she's getting there. Stuart has turned the blinding searchlight away from her and is holding a torch to guide her, while Dan uses another torch to keep her visual at all times. Now that we're stationary, the roll of the SilverBird is more unpleasant than ever. We have to endure a few more moments of it, just long enough to pull her aboard, then we can get out of here.

'Thank you!' she stutters. Her whole jaw is shivering so badly the words are chewed to nothing. 'Thank you!'

'Shh! Save your strength. We're going to pull you by your lifejacket, Martha. You don't need to do anything. OK? Ready?'

'Ready,' she says, her fragile smile collapsing under a torrent of tears.

We so nearly make it. Dan and Stuart actually have a hold on her when I spot the wave. Without the searchlight, my field of vision is cut right down, but all the same I see that destructive profile a couple of seconds before it hits. And in any other circumstance I could have driven us hard away from it. Only, as things stand, we have a girl in the water right where I'd need to drive us.

'Wave!' I yell. 'Protect her!'

There's not the slightest hesitation from Stuart. He rolls forward, drops flat over Martha, so that when the wave hits *Giselle*, sends her tumbling over, it's his body that takes the impact of the gunwale, not the girl's neck and head. He has the lifesaver's instinct through and through, and in that awful moment I feel immensely proud of him.

Everything's black. Underwater, disorientated, but only for a second. Air comes rushing out of my neck seal as the water presses in on my drysuit, pinching around my groin and armpits. My lifejacket throws me back up to the surface at the same time my shoulder strobe activates. I'm under the upturned boat, looking up at the dark console, and now two more patches of flashing light come visible. Two more illuminated shoulders, one a water-diffused flicker. Dan is already up beside me, but Stuart and the girl are wedged under the starboard gunwale. There's no need to say anything: we both reach down and grab them simultaneously, pulling them free so that their lifejackets bob them straight up into our air pocket.

It's calmer under here. Away from the elements, it's much quieter. Just a few muffled waves against the hull and the splashing of arms reaching for handholds. It takes a moment to match my breathing to the rise and fall of the water, and inevitably I swallow a couple of mouthfuls before I'm settled and ready to work.

Martha whimpers and coughs, but she's not my priority just now. 'Stuart?' I slip the pen torch out of my sleeve pocket, pull back the visor on his helmet and shine the beam directly into his eyes. The pupils contract immediately. 'You with us?'

His hand bats the torch away. 'More or less.'

'Your head?'

'Fine. My ribs took the blow.'

'How's your breathing?'

He gives me a couple of deep ones, in and out. 'OK. Hurts a bit. Maybe a couple cracked, nothing worse.'

'OK, Dan's going to take you now.' I vent his drysuit for him and unclip his harness from the tether. 'No trying to act tough, all right? Let him do the work.'

He gives a nod, and I turn to the girl. 'Martha, listen to me. This is quite normal, understand? You've been located. You're safe now.'

'We're upside down!'

'It's OK, Martha. What is it you won? A prize for endeavour? You're a strong girl. You've made it through the worst bit. We're going to get you on board the big lifeboat, OK? Take you home, give you a hot shower, warm clothes, something good to eat.'

She nods faintly. I run the torch over her face to reassure myself she's all there.

'Good. OK, I need you to move up to the bow. You know which end is the bow?'

She may be an outback girl but that sparks some little flame of defiance in her. Several weeks of training on *Sentinel*, and her basic knowledge of boats is being questioned? Without a word, she pulls herself forward. Dan has already got Stuart up front, and now he's helping him push under the gunwale and out. It's pretty hard, fighting the buoyancy of a lifejacket and a drysuit, and I'm guessing the process is taking its toll on Stuart's ribs. But they're both out and that's the important thing.

'See what they did?' I say to Martha.

She nods, more resolutely this time. Grabbing the gunwale with both hands, she ducks down and disappears. I vent my drysuit, unclip my harness, and follow straight after.

It's not pleasant floating in this swell, and Martha's doing all right considering how long she's been out here. No one's going to feel great when the boat that's supposed to be rescuing them is upside down beside them.

'I keep thinking about the sharks,' Martha cries through the renewed noise of wind and water, as I lead her to the stern. 'All the time, I imagine them circling beneath me.'

'You'll be out of the water in no time,' I promise her, reaching under the transom.

'Will Ms McKenzie come and rescue us?'

I can't help laughing as I pull out the swim line and hand it to Dan. He makes sure Stuart has a firm hold, then indicates for Martha to grab on, while I reach for the airbag cable. 'Watch out now.'

One small tug is all it takes. I slip back from the boat, the swim line running through my fingers until there's a comfortable gap between us and *Giselle*. Already there's a shaking of the frame as the airbag fills. Beside me, Martha watches in wonder as *Giselle*'s hull rears up and topples sideways. A moment more and she's upright, the great orange airbag held high above the stern on its self-raising struts.

'That's amazing!' she cries. It's the first time she's sounded whole.

'This way. Quickly now.'

Pulling her back along the swimline, I show her how to climb up the transom. Dan goes next, and I hold Stuart close until Dan's ready to reach down and lift him up. Once we're all aboard, I have Dan do the structural checks while I get the hydrosparks going again.

It's feeling a bit crowded all of a sudden, in this part of the ocean. *Sentinel*'s approaching from one side, ALB-4 from the other. Even the lights of the police cruiser are coming into sight. Lots of radio calls we've missed, no doubt, and I hook up my helmet again and set their minds at rest. 'Coastguard two-one. All fine. MOB unhurt.'

'Good job, Petra,' comes Donald's reply. 'We'll take her from here, get her warmed up.' He's not going to comment now on me putting my crew in a situation that required deployment of the airbag. Some point tomorrow, he'll drop by for a quiet chat. It won't change the way I work, though. We got the MOB, that's what counts.

'The best,' says Kirsten simply, over the radio. 'Petra, you're the best.'

It's at times like this that I remember exactly why we're friends.

•

CYCA keep the bar open late for Kirsten. Dan's taken charge of Stuart, escorting him to Manly Hospital for the X-ray and check-over, so I'm free to join her for a couple of vodka tonics. Dermott, Ryan, Nolan and the rest of the crew celebrate with the beers like they've just made it through an important initiation rite. The conditions tested them all, even before the MOB, and they're rightly pleased with their performance. The *Sentinel* baseball hats are back on; foul weather gear lies in trampled, dripping heaps along the wall. Dermott tells a joke he picked up from Billy in Africa, raising a great collective laugh, and I feel oddly proud at the unconscious reach of my fiancé's rough wit. Even Nolan, famous for his lack of humour when near any vessel in his charge, cracks a smile.

Ryan proposes a toast to Martha, in her absence, and the whole crew throw up a cheer loud enough to reach her in Manly. She'll have to stay in hospital for a night while the doctors check her for hypothermia and secondary drowning. It's unlikely she's suffered a serious core temperature decrease, but a little seawater in her lungs could cause all kinds of problems.

'She'll be all right?' I ask.

'Yeah, she's a tough one.' Kirsten and I are sat a little way off from the others. The stutter of straining lines, the squeak of rubber fenders and the gentle shudder of the floating docks against their concrete pilings are the only hints left of the recent weather.

'Will you let her sail to Hobart?'

'Why not? She's not going to forget to clip on ever again, is she?'

With a discreet hand signal, a patrician gesture she'd mastered long before she was old enough to use it in bars, Kirsten has another round of drinks sent to the ALB crew. They're huddled around Donald, at the far end of the terrace, listening attentively to his measured voice. Not all of them have been exposed to such severe conditions before, and Donald's eager to use the night as a training opportunity. It's also a way of showing it wasn't a wasted outing, what with Inshore snapping up the search object before Offshore had really got started on their pattern. It's a different type of coastguard who opts for the Offshore life. They're mostly older and coarser, the ancient mariner type. The kind of men and women who'd lose patience if they had to rescue a kid on a windsurfer, or some angler in a tinny who's forgotten to check his fuel. They like to be out of sight of land, like to sleep aboard and wrestle with the monsters of the deep. Sound people, all of them, if not always that much fun.

'Be honest,' says Kirsten. 'Do you think I made the wrong call tonight?'

'You set up a good search pattern. The current was stronger than you estimated, that's all.'

'I mean, putting to sea in those conditions.'

'You're probably the best maxi skipper in town,' I hedge. 'If you reckon it's safe, that's all there is to it.'

'Because of my decision, one of your guys is in hospital.'

'He used to be your guy.'

'Petra, why are you avoiding the question?'

A suggestion of jeopardy hovers somewhere between us. 'Because the answer's yes,' I sigh, 'and right now, after what we've been through, I don't want a fight.'

She fiddles with her glass a while. 'At least we proved the boat's up to weather. Canting hull worked a dream.'

'Weather can get a lot worse than that.'

'We'll handle it.'

'Some storms no one can handle.'

Kirsten meets my gaze, and says, 'You don't believe his predictions any more than I do.'

'There's an area of intense low pressure south-east of New Zealand. Real weather.'

'Nowhere near the race.'

'We should be taking precautions. Assessing the risk.'

'We have a Safety Committee for that.'

'I don't believe they fully appreciate the danger this year.'

She sits back, stares at me in wonder. 'You *do* believe him.'

'I believe not every MOB is as lucky as Martha Salford.' It takes a couple of breaths to calm the tremors in my voice. 'Kirsten, I'm going to apply for special audience at the Committee.'

There's a long silence. Kirsten lifts her glass but doesn't quite drink from it.

'It's a potential cyclone, could easily shift northward. With so many lives at risk –'

'Petra, honey, there's no fucking way we're going to cancel the Hobart.'

'The Committee should at least consider the warning.'

'*He's not real!*'

'I hope he isn't. Most of the time, I'm sure he isn't. But, Kirsten, what if he is?'

'Do you know how much *Sentinel* cost to build? Can you even guess the amounts of money the Bank is putting into the promotion campaign centred on this race? Our Hobart party alone is three million. Commercial slots are ten times that. If we don't cross that finish line first, we've flushed the best part of a hundred million dollars down the drain at a time when we can least afford it. I am not going to let that happen.'

'As a professional coastguard, I have to —'

'Petra, I respect what you're doing, but this is not the time to encourage ungrounded fear. You could really screw things up for me. You're not on the Safety Committee: it's not your problem. Stay out of it.'

I draw a breath. 'As a professional coastguard it's my duty to make the Safety Committee aware of potential risks to race participants. Including you.'

There is a moment in the silence that follows when I can almost see the fault line cracking open between us. A splitting of the air, dividing us one from the other. Kirsten clicks her teeth, twice – a double tattoo. She begins to speak, then turns the first word into a brisk, brutish exhalation. 'Fine,' she says, abandoning her drink and getting up from the table. 'Then I'll see you there.'

•

It's late. The sea is flat now, the air fresh and still. Mine is the only boat moving in the Harbour. Apart from the water police.

'Captain Woods, stop your vessel.'

It's the greatest feeling, after a stressful operation, to race across a calm sea in a perfect speedboat. The rush of air against your face. Nothing beats it. Specially when you've had a few.

'Captain Woods, this is the New South Wales Police Marine Area Command. You are ordered to stop your vessel!'

Behind us, the Harbour Bridge still lit up, the Opera House sails gleaming with indecent beauty beyond the heavy industrial glare of Garden Island. On the bow, the dark outlines of the Heads. And through it all I race across sleek water, alone but for –

'Petra, look, just slow down, will you? We won't make you blow in the bag.'

How easy it is to lean on the throttle. The SilverBird lifts out of the water and skims away towards the ocean at a speed no police tub could match.

A friendly wave.

And then I'm gone.

•

Billy's waiting for me on the beach at Saaremaa. I know he's there because of the fire he's built against the chill in the squall-fresh air. Because however many times I tell him not to light a fire near the hydrofuel tank, he always goes and does it. And I love the reckless bastard for it. I love hearing him swat away my recriminations, telling me there's no way that little fire's going to reach the tank, feeling him tickle me and kiss me until I'm the one chucking wood on the flames and building us a blaze that sends magical flickers of orange and pink out over Pittwater.

Billy's naked body is spread across the sand in front of the fire – a sleeping silhouette. I come out of the water close enough to hear his soft snore. He's on his back, his hips tilted a little so that left calf rests on right ankle and his left hand falls across his tight stomach. The firelight sets his body gleaming and turns the hair around his cock a reddish gold. As I pass him, I let a few drops of the Tasman Sea patter against his cheek. Just enough to wake him.

The lights are still on in the house. Crossing the veranda, I step out of my wet clothes, laying shorts and T-shirt over a chair to dry. In the kitchen, an open packet of crackers and an empty tub of peanut butter suggest Billy hasn't been told about the late-night meal service Sentinel Bank offers its employees. The door to Dad's room is shut. A gentle whistling comes from within: Moses is fast asleep.

I switch off the generator, leaving the house in darkness, and step noiselessly across the beach. Billy's sleeping again, his breathing even and quiet now. For a while, I crouch beside him and watch his face twitch out these little half-smiles, wondering to myself what impossible mountain he's conquering in his dreams. Then I lie back onto him, bringing my head to rest against his shoulder. No way are we staying outside to risk another mind twister from Moses in the morning. But a couple of hours together, naked by the fire, we can give ourselves that.

'You're a heavy gull,' Billy murmurs sleepily.

I don't reply, just shift a fraction every now and then to keep him awake. To get him sensing. My legs creep up onto his, so that every piece of me is supported by his body.

Still I say nothing, knowing my smile can't be seen, as his cock rises between my thighs.

'Now look what you've done,' he says, like he's complaining.

I roll my head so that my lips are against his cheek, and close my legs around his cock.

Beneath me, Billy catches his breath, stretches suddenly, and falls silent.

•

The next morning, as I'm leaving for work, Moses tells me he's glad the woman in the water was OK.

A shadow passes across the new day. 'How'd you know it was a woman?' I demand.

Moses shrugs and goes back to eating spaghetti.

Already late, I have to hurry off to Spring Cove without getting an answer.

CHAPTER 7

The Sydney Hobart Race Safety Committee was set up three years ago by the Federal Government as the independent body responsible for green-lighting the event. Previously, CYCA had taken the brave stance that the race would never be cancelled. Whatever severe weather the boats might face, it was up to the skippers to decide if it was safe to sail. Then two fatalities in successive bad-weather years scared the government into imposing new regulatory controls on the nation's iconic high-risk contest. If conditions were deemed to be too dangerous, the cancellation option was now on the table. So far, it has never been exercised.

December 24 is the last formal meeting of the Safety Committee. Extraordinary developments can trigger extraordinary meetings on Christmas Day or even the morning of the race. But in practice the final go-ahead is given two days before, so that CYCA can go through their pre-race operations without worrying about a last-minute cancellation.

The Safety Committee is made up of representatives from all the main marine authorities. My father, selected for his decades of volunteer coastguard work, has chaired the Committee from its inception. Donald, as Offshore Coastguard Director, is one of its members. So is Kirsten, as last year's winning skipper. I'm not.

Only by special invitation from Donald am I able to attend.

•

The backlog of paperwork is piling up at Spring Cove, and some of it can't wait beyond Christmas Eve. In particular, the admin for our Offshore support of the Sydney Hobart has to be completed today, and although Donald's taken care of most of it, there's a load of countersigning and verification that falls to me as the other Operational Director of the Coastguard. Then there's the Incident Report on the tumble we took in *Giselle*, and the medical insurance claim for Stuart. Going by the book, I should also submit a note to CYCA on *Sentinel*'s MOB, even though no one's going to bother to read it in this frantic period.

And sometime before two o'clock, on a day that's surely the hottest so far this summer, I need to work out how to explain to the Safety Committee why I've requested special audience.

It's crazy: I have to try to persuade them of something I don't want to believe myself. But I've been unable to dismiss that terrible lurking fear: *what if he's right?* Kirsten was not pleased this morning when she heard I was going ahead with the advisory. That was after she'd sent over a case of champagne for the MOB rescue, then called to find out why I still hadn't brought Moses back to her. Grace Cadey's visit, though brief and good-natured, compounded my sense of chaos. Her instructions for Moses's return were simple; it's the likely consequences, particularly Kirsten's reaction, that worry me. Way too distracted at Spring Cove to plan for the Committee meeting, I look in on Comms, check all is calm, then take myself off to the State Reference Library.

Libraries aren't my natural environment. I'm happy enough reading important stuff, and a lot of textbook study goes into making a good coastguard. But I'd always rather pore over the manuals on a rock above Pittwater, with the scent of the sea giving meaning to the words. Something about a wall of books puts me right off.

It's not a universal problem evidently. Sam Drauston, for example, looks right at home. His table, beside the glass wall that frames a jungle of hothouse foliage beneath Macquarie Street, is awash with scribbled notes. Four stacks of books mark off his territory. There's even a mini-scanner connected to his laptop.

'Hi again,' I say, when the librarian points him out.

'Petra . . . hello.' He gets up to shake hands, a gesture that minutely surprises me. His tie is loosened, but still he looks the financial part in his tailored suit and ivory shirt.

'You're a long way from the Business section.'

'I'm diversifying,' he smiles. 'What are you after?'

'Same book as you, apparently. *Prophecy, Divination and Foresight*.'

He finds the title, holds it out. 'I'm done with that one.'

'Thank you. You're still looking into Moses?'

'Can't get him out of my head. I've been writing business pieces for eight years and to be honest I'm sick of it. This story is fresh, exciting – exhilarating.'

'I thought it *was* a business story.'

'Before the RTV interview, perhaps. But now I think we have to ask ourselves: *could this possibly be genuine*? If so – and it's a very big if – we can forget Sentinel Bank. He'd be front page news the world over.'

'I guess it is pretty unusual,' I concede.

'Actually, not really. Unusual in Australia, but the weight of world history is against us.' He waves a hand towards the stacks of books. 'Prophecies are everywhere, drawn from the stars, from dreams and visions, from tea leaves, entrails, puddles and birth defects, even from handwriting. Shakespeare loved them, so did the ancient Greeks. Think of Macbeth and Oedipus. The Chinese would roast turtle shells, then interpret the cracks that formed. Tibetan *mopas* still make predictions drawn from the flames of butter lamps. Precognition seems to hold a very powerful psychological resonance for all humans.'

'Doesn't mean it's real.'

'No,' smiles Sam. 'Look, I need a coffee. Want to join me?'

He makes the invitation sound so casual, like we're old colleagues.

'What's your ideal water temperature?' I ask.

'To drink?'

'To swim.'

'Not something I've thought about. At a guess, twenty-four degrees.'

Close. Surely I can justify a quick coffee break if it will accelerate my research.

'You really believe in the supernatural?' I say, as he leads the way upstairs and through the bookshop to the library café.

'Absolutely not. But precognition doesn't have to be supernatural.' He chooses a nudie juice, not coffee, and insists on paying for my iced tea. Like him, I'm feeling the heat. 'Back in the 1970s, the Stanford Research Institute ran experiments which they claimed "provide unequivocal evidence of a human capacity to access events remote in space and time".'

'Clairvoyance.'

'Exactly. Since then, the hunt has been on for a scientific explanation.

You know much about the physics of time?' He throws a quick glance at his reflection in the mirrored wall behind the counter, and I find myself doing the same. Both of us straighten slightly.

'I can read a clock.'

Something about him makes me want to be playful, and I like the rich warmth of his laughter. I like being the cause of it. He carries our drinks to a table outside. A yellow umbrella casts a solid square of shade. From one side comes the birdsong of the Botanic Gardens, from the other the roar of traffic on Macquarie.

'I'm no expert, but this is what I've found out so far,' he says. 'Time is not absolute. That's the starting point. Two perfect clocks: one is sent up in a space ship, the other remains on earth. The first will advance faster than the second because gravity slows time. Speed has an impact too, as does atomic energy. Time can be distorted, like a sheet of rubber, bending and twisting, maybe even reversing.'

'What does this have to do with Moses?'

'Theoretical physics can get pretty crazy. To some cosmologists, the movement of time is an illusion. They would say all events that have ever happened and will ever happen exist now in a permanent state, although we animals can only perceive that tiny fraction of events we designate "the present". We're blind to the rest, but they're out there, always, spread along the dimension called Time. Now, if that dimension can bend, if it can fold up like an accordion, then what happens when one fold of time rubs against another? Is it conceivable that an unusually sensitive viewer in the earlier fold could observe events in the later one?'

'Everything's predetermined, and time folds?' I can't help the teasing grin.

'As I said, it's crazy. And frankly unlikely, in my view. But it would

171

explain a phenomenon that millions down the ages have claimed to witness, without recourse to gods or spirits.'

We talk on longer than either of us can probably afford. There is something luxurious about nursing a cold drink while office workers desperate for exercise sacrifice their lunch break to jog past us in the full punishing glare of the midday sun. When, eventually, we return to the library, Sam scoops up a pile of his books and lays them on a neighbouring table for me. 'Check out the pages I've marked. Lots of good examples.'

'Thanks.'

'No worries. It's been a pleasure, Petra.'

'Likewise.'

He smiles shyly. 'Then perhaps we should do it again sometime.'

•

The Sydney Hobart Race Safety Committee meets in the boardroom at CYCA. The Club, with just two days to go, is a sun-baked swarm of activity. Every race boat has at least two or three crew working round the clock to repair broken equipment, clean and reassemble winches, load stores or coax troublesome radios into life. On the super-maxis, sailing masters walk a tense line between panic and despair, dispatching crew to source spare parts or repack sails, while simultaneously entertaining sponsors and meeting the demands of the media. Up and down the lines of yachts, sweating figures can be seen aloft, lifted on a halyard into the rigging to adjust the deflection of the spreaders. Scuba divers drop below the boats, scrubbing the hulls clean of any creature that has managed to gain a hold on their smooth surfaces. Sunburnt crew wives in big pearls and tight white linen trousers gather on the terraces beneath the line of sponsors' pennants, talking too loudly, drinking too much, celebrating before the race has even been officially sanctioned.

The CEO of the Yacht Club, Martin Allways, opens the boardroom doors to my father and the Race Director, Tessa Irie, at half past one. Across the way, a riotous corporate Christmas lunch is in progress in the function rooms. By the time I get there with Moses, the club staff are already panicking that the party won't be finished in time to clean the rooms properly for the Skippers' Briefing at three.

The rest of the Committee begins to arrive ten minutes before two o'clock. First in is Sid Morrison of the Bureau of Meteorology, accompanied by Donald Carter. Two officers from the Australian Maritime Safety Authority, AMSA, and one from NSW Maritime follow them in. The Navy Search & Rescue Unit Commander arrives with the water police Superintendent, and both of them make a point of congratulating me on Martha's rescue before asking what the bloody hell I'm doing here.

Kirsten arrives two minutes late. She's smiling, even though she must be irritated as hell with me. Withholding Moses, casting doubt on the safety of the race – I haven't been a great friend to her today. Nevertheless, she makes a point of kissing me before she sits down. A hint of caramel lingers on her breath.

The meeting kicks off with a report from the Race Director on the seaworthiness of the competing yachts. All are declared sound, and this is confirmed by Superintendent Jason Swift on the basis of random checks by his officers.

'What about these canting hulls?' asks my father, without looking at Kirsten.

'Only *Sentinel* has one, and she performed well during recent rough weather,' says Tessa. 'We're confident she's safe in the right hands.' An obsequious smile to Kirsten.

The Navy man delivers an assessment of shipping and obstruction threats along the 628-mile course; in the past, yachts have collided with unlit Filipino trawlers, cargo containers, even sunfish and whales. Then it's time for the weather review. Sid directs his laptop's projection beam to a patch of white wall. Neat digital outlines of Eastern Australia and New Zealand appear.

'There's still very little going on in the Tasman Sea,' he says, bringing up a cascade of satellite images. 'The current is shifting direction, according to the rigs in Bass Strait. By the 27th, we expect it to come from the south, at two knots, meaning the water will be colder than usual. But if winds remain sou'-easterly, we'll be spared the clash of current and wind that has created such difficult waves in the past. The biggest problem will be lack of wind. Could be as low as three knots, with very little change expected before the 29th. This is going to be a slow, dull race, I'm afraid.'

'Dull's good,' laughs the Navy SAR Commander. Tessa Irie's tight smile makes it clear she doesn't agree. For the Race Director, media excitement is paramount.

'The only conceivable threat remains this area of low depression here, now designated Juno.' Sid points south-east of New Zealand. 'As you can see, Juno is deepening; she's likely to develop into a vicious little cyclone. But although she is moving westward, her course remains constant along the 53rd parallel with no northerly aspirations whatsoever. She's going to give the roofs on Auckland Island quite a rattle, but she should pass well south of Hobart.'

'Thank you,' says Dad. I do admire his ability to chair this meeting so calmly. Everyone in the room knows what happened to his wife, but

Dad has never looked for sympathy from anyone. Nor has he run away from the ocean or the business of assessing risk for adventurous sailors. For him, it is a lifelong duty, neither strengthened nor diminished by his own loss, to protect lives at sea. 'And now,' he adds, consulting his notes with impatience, 'a contrary view from the Inshore Coastguard.'

'That's right,' I say, standing up. 'G'day. Thanks for having me along.'

Kirsten sits closest to me, arms crossed and chair turned so that only I can see her unreadable smile.

'Guys, I wouldn't even be here if it wasn't for that depression – Juno, right? But the fact is, we have a potential storm out there. Sure, it's not supposed to come our way, but we've heard that before, haven't we? It *could* veer north, we *could* have a major problem. I've done the calculations: the rate of progress needed for Juno to reach Bass Strait during the race is high but not outside observed limits. And that's reason enough for me to bring this other thing to your attention.'

My laptop's all prepared, the RTV download cued to the right point. It's only a few seconds long, and it captures the Committee's attention straightaway.

'That's not real?' says Tessa. 'Surely it's staged.'

'Computer-generated?' suggests Sid.

'It's all live,' I assure them. 'And witnessed by a studio audience.'

Already faces are turning from the screen to the boy at the back of the room.

'I heard about this show,' says Jason Swift. He looks at Moses. 'My daughter thinks you're some kind of wizard.'

'Petra, what's this about?' asks Sid. 'He's said something about the weather?'

'He saw the Sydney Hobart boats caught in a major storm,' I say quietly. 'He described the yachts "dying" and "going underwater".' I look around, not quite able to meet any of their incredulous stares. 'That's it. That's why I'm here.'

Kirsten shakes her head slowly, raises her eyes to the ceiling. Disapproval sours my father's gaze.

Tessa breaks the silence: 'I'm sorry but, with respect, this is bullshit. We're not here to make decisions based on a fortune-teller's scare-mongering.'

'Well, let's not be hasty,' says Jason. 'The kid did something pretty remarkable on TV. We shouldn't dismiss him out of hand. At least let's look into this.'

'I've got to agree with Tessa,' says Martin Allways. 'Petra, think about what you're asking us to accept. Don't you think it's a little . . . inappropriate?'

'I just reckon maybe there's some more we can do to be sure those boats are safe.'

'Look, I'm not saying I believe this stuff, but I would feel more comfortable if we checked this out,' says the Navy Commander. 'What other tests could we conduct? Are there any other weather diagnostics we could use to assess this risk?'

'The Bureau's run every available model,' says Sid. 'I promise you we don't come here with anything less than our fullest possible forecast.'

'You're asking for what?' says Tessa sharply. 'Extra precautions? More lifejackets? A naval presence in Bass Strait?'

'Maybe,' I stammer, 'or . . .'

'Because I know you wouldn't suggest we should cancel on this basis.'

Donald comes to the rescue. 'I'd like to ask Moses a question, if that's OK?'

'Of course,' I say gratefully.

Moses jumps up at my signal and comes to the front of the room.

'Hello,' says Donald. 'Thank you for helping us here.'

Moses smiles warmly.

'I hope you don't mind me asking, but have you ever made a prediction that didn't come true? Have you ever doubted your ability?'

Moses, gazing solemnly around his audience, looks as if he's about to stall from nerves. But it's not that; he's waiting to ensure he has their attention. 'God shows me the future,' he says. 'So I cannot doubt it.'

'What god is this?' demands Dad.

'He is a big snake. He lives in Lake Fundudzi.'

Dad snorts, but Jason leans forward and asks, 'He can show you stuff here? Across the world?'

Moses gives him a pitying look. 'Gods are very powerful.'

'Of course,' smiles Jason.

'I don't believe we're having this discussion,' says Tessa. 'Gods? *Snakes?* We're trying to run a modern sailing race here.'

'Without wanting to rush anyone,' murmurs Martin, 'may I remind the Committee the Skippers' Briefing starts at three.'

Now Kirsten leans forward. 'Perhaps I can resolve this.' She smiles at Moses, greets him warmly. 'Remind me, Moses, can you induce . . . can you choose to see the future?'

Moses nods.

'How do you do that?' she asks innocently.

'I look at what is here, then look through it at what will come.'

'You *look through* the present?' Kirsten turns to Dad. 'I have a way to test this. May I?' She takes a pad and scribbles a picture on it, using her hand to keep it hidden from Moses. 'I'm drawing a common object. In a moment, I'm going to show it to you,' she says, turning the pad upside down. 'Can you look into the future and tell me what it is you're going to see?'

Moses blinks.

'Wait a minute, you can't expect him to do that on the spot,' I say. 'It's not a fair test.' I remember the coin flick Daran tried on *Sentinel*, as no doubt Kirsten does too. Moses had fifty-fifty odds then and flunked it. He's got no chance now.

'Seems fair to me,' says Tessa. Martin Allways nods in agreement.

'Prophets don't get a continuous read-out on the future,' I insist. 'They see isolated incidents, flashes of foresight. Nostradamus predicted the execution of Charles I, but not the civil war that preceded it. Cassandra foresaw the sack of Troy without knowing how it would come about. You can't assess a prophet with a parlour trick.'

'Just do the test,' orders Dad.

'Well?' Kirsten asks, fingers toying with the pad. 'What do you see, Moses?'

There's a moment when it seems like he might actually try it. He stares at Kirsten; his eyes narrow and lose focus. *Looking through the present*. His lips open, ready to deliver. But then he shakes his head.

'I see nothing.'

Around the table, the tiny flame of possibility stutters and goes out. Faces, momentarily open and curious, turn cynical. 'Wait a minute,' I urge. 'Moses described a storm wrecking *Sentinel* and a whole lot of other yachts. He talked about waves like hills, wind that "sings and shouts". He's never seen anything like that! He's never been to sea, experienced an ocean storm. How would he know that stuff?'

A heavy silence. Impossible to tell what's behind it. Have I made an impression at last? Then Kirsten says, 'Actually, Petra, I might be able to help you with that one.' She reaches for her bag and pulls out a DVD. 'Moses did watch a lot of movies while he was staying with me. Including this one.'

She passes the DVD to Dad, who reads out the label with distaste: '*Killer Ocean.*'

'An American action adventure set in some pretty stormy conditions. A bunch of cruising yachts take a pounding off Florida. Terrible dialogue, but the special effects are very impressive. Frightening stuff. I really shouldn't have let Moses watch it.'

I snatch the DVD from my father's hand, march across to Moses and thrust the label in his face. 'Did you watch this? Did you?'

Moses stares back, motionless.

'A film, Moses! Did you see a film with lots of boats "dying"?'

Slowly, brow creased at my anger, he nods.

Dad, watching with a grey, dismal expression, says, 'I think we should leave it there.'

But the horrendous possibility, diminished as it is, hasn't gone away. Juno is still out there. My mother is still dead because no one fought to stop the '98 race. 'Just consider it, at least! A serious storm in Bass Strait could wipe out half the fleet. There's over a thousand lives at stake.'

Dad closes his file. 'There's also a multi-million-dollar race at stake.'

'Since when has money mattered more than protecting lives?' I shout at him.

A dreadful stillness comes over the room. Dad looks up at me with tired regret. 'Let me ask you this, Petra. Tell the truth now: do you yourself believe Moses can see the future?'

'Dad, please, think of the people who died last time.'

'Answer the question.'

'If you'd had a warning, would you have let Mum go?'

'*Answer the question!* On whatever it is you hold sacred, do you truly believe Moses can see the future?'

I've failed. It's over. Looking at my father, I see a fragment of pity in his eyes. And he's right to pity me, because although my mind contains several compartments, none of them can help me here.

I drop my gaze. 'No,' I admit. 'I don't.'

•

The Sydney Hobart Race Safety Committee gives Tessa Irie her final authorisation at 2.35 p.m.

The signature on the document is my father's.

•

There's not a lot anyone can find to say to me afterwards. Half the Committee manage to leave without catching my eye. The Race Director dashes off with the AMSA and Met guys to prepare for the Skippers' Briefing. Jason gives me a sympathetic shrug and Donald squeezes my shoulder in support. For a couple of minutes, waiting for his taxi outside the Club, I try to mend some bridges with my father. It's while I'm doing this that Kirsten shamelessly tempts Moses towards her car.

She has this sweet Maserati, low-slung with dragon's eye headlights. What boy wouldn't want to get into it?

'You could have told me about that movie,' I say to Kirsten as I grab

Moses by the wrist and hold him firmly back from the car. 'Instead of torpedoing me in front of everybody.'

'Honey, it just occurred to me this morning. But I did say you shouldn't take this nonsense to the Committee, didn't I?'

'It could still happen.'

'A storm? Of course it could,' she smiles. 'Moses, would you like to come with me? See some more movies? I've got a new games console – latest kit.'

She gives Moses a warm, inviting look. My grip on his arm tightens.

'As you like,' she says to me. 'No more trading this year, anyway. But I want him back straight after the race. We're going to engineer a big media splash a week before the issue, Moses looking omniscient in front of the bank. So no hiding him away then, please.'

'Too late,' I tell her, with no satisfaction. 'He's booked to fly home on the 27th.' Grace had the ticket reservation in her hand when she arrived at Spring Cove this morning. While charming as before, she made it clear the arrangement was not negotiable.

'*What?* Why did you do that?' Kirsten sighs. 'Shit, Petra, I'm trying to be patient here, but you're really . . . Look, when the time comes, I'll arrange the flight. First class, with a bag full of cash for his family. But he's not going anywhere before our new issue.'

'It's not up to me.'

'Don't make me start talking about Coastguard sponsorship again. We shouldn't need to be like this with each other.'

'The South African Consulate organised it. With the dry police,' I add, because Kirsten's look is worrying me. There's too much rapid calculation going on behind those so-familiar eyes. Too much concealment.

'Kirsten? He's going, OK? That's the end of it. You should be worrying about the race, not Moses.'

She says nothing. Jaw set rigid, she gets in the car. The engine hums alive. Suddenly, I have to get through to her. I have to make her understand.

'Listen to me, will you? There's a cyclone out there! Why risk everything?'

She pauses, hand on the door, staring hard at me. 'Because that's what you have to do to win,' she says.

The door closes, and she's gone.

•

On the way back to Spring Cove, Moses says, 'I didn't want to go with her.'

A dozen race yachts are out, several with spinnakers set despite the imminent southerly buster. The sky to the south is grey. Any moment, a mass of ripples will spread over the water, the air temperature will drop several degrees, and any large rigs still up are going to take a beating. It occurs to me that these same yachts may be in for far more serious weather in three or four days' time. How well would they cope? Which of them would be strong enough to withstand force nine or ten?

'I told you it was the same,' Moses is saying. 'Her house, your house.'

'I remember.'

He shuffles over from the gunwale and takes the jump seat next to me. 'It's not true,' he says. His fingers trace an inquisitive path across the radios, the depth sounder, the radar. 'It's better with you.'

I have to stop the boat and look at him, to make sure he's not paying me out. But no – he means it. So then I have to get *Giselle* going again fast to cover my reaction. 'Thank you, Moses. That's sweet.' My tongue catches. 'That's really sweet.'

'Her house has a bigger television,' he says wistfully.

It occurs to me later that Kirsten never did show Moses that picture she drew. It's a small point, and I don't believe it makes any difference, but there was no future event for him to see.

CHAPTER 8

That night, Billy and I meet up at a Christmas Eve party in Potts Point. By the time I get there, Billy and Buzz have somehow got a full keg up the heavy-limbed angophora in the garden, and are securing it with ropes in the uppermost fork. Around forty thirsty partygoers watch from below. When the job is done, Billy tugs the keg a couple of times to test the knots, then the two of them drop back down to earth.

'Roll up, roll up,' Billy laughs. 'Take your marks.'

And with an imitation gunshot he sends a dozen men tearing up the tree, shoving and fighting, determined to reach the keg first. A young Asian guy is the quickest, flicking the tap and opening up his throat under the stream of beer. But he's soon knocked aside by a tattooed surfer. The girl beside me screeches, 'You got it, Foozy!' and then turns livid when her boyfriend is hauled away from the keg by a red-haired guy with glasses. 'Foul!' she screams. The surfer's already struggling back up the tree, but there's at least four others between him and the prize. And the guy with the glasses is holding his position under the tap surprisingly well.

Billy's arms fold around my shoulders. 'You want a go? I reckon you could take them all.'

'It's dangerous,' I say, because I have to. 'Someone could get hurt.'

And Billy just laughs, which is what I want him to do, because otherwise he wouldn't be Billy.

'Maybe I'll race you up there sometime,' I say, turning in his arms. His kiss is warming, but not so tender as usual. There's a determination about it that unsettles me.

'Say the word and I'll clear all these people out. Just you and me and a keg.'

'Wouldn't be a party without the people,' I smile. 'It's good to see you on form.'

For a fraction of a second, he looks uncertain. Then he grabs an ancient surfboard from a pile against the fence. 'That's me: always on form,' he laughs, snapping off the tail fin. 'Buzz! Give us some music, mate!' And with that he springs up the tree, surfboard clutched under one arm.

The contest for the keg is waning, and seeing Billy the guys in the branches clear aside. Billy opens his mouth under the keg for a good long soak and then, as his favourite metal anthem starts up below, he slams the tap shut, balances the surfboard on top of the keg, and climbs aboard.

'Oh, no,' I'm whispering. Then, at a shout, 'Billy, no!'

But in these situations, there's never any stopping him. The surfboard rocks precariously on the keg. Billy strikes a wave-rider pose. And with a wild, joyous whoop he's off down the tree, flying the surfboard from branch to branch, shooting over the heads of the roaring crowd below, bracing himself against each impact, yelling the lyrics of 'Bronze Boarder', conquering the world.

Any moment he might fall, but I can't look away. The surfboard slips and slides from branch to branch. Billy ducks and twists, he crouches low, he rocks about to keep his balance. And when the inevitable comes and the next branch angles the wrong way, he throws himself clear of the doomed board, snatches at a lower branch to break his fall, and tumbles into a neat landing at the centre of the crowd.

They love him for it. *I* love him for it. Though it floors me to think I'm going to have to worry about him breaking his neck for the next thirty years, the joy of seeing Billy be Billy more than compensates. Shaking off his fans, he comes charging through the crowd and wraps his electric body around me.

We're the centre of attention. Inspiration for dozens.

'A toast,' yells Buzz. 'To the happy couple!'

'To the happy couple,' comes back the cry.

'May their marriage last longer than Billy's surfboards,' Buzz adds.

'All right, mate, steady,' says Billy. 'We're not married yet.'

'What's the matter? Getting cold feet?' grins Buzz.

Billy's face drains of colour but Buzz doesn't see it.

'Going to bail?' he jokes. 'Run off and desert poor Petra?'

'Drop it,' growls Billy.

The warning signs make no impression on Buzz. He's always been the last guy to pick up on the sensitive stuff. 'Guess what, Petra? If Billy bails, the best man gets to marry you.'

None of it's anything more than the usual banter between these two, but for once Billy doesn't see it that way. First thing Buzz knows about the change of rules is Billy's hand about his throat.

'I am *not* going to bail!' roars Billy.

The humour snaps out in Buzz's face. 'What the fuck . . . ?'

'Billy, take it easy,' I cry, stepping up close and laying a hand against his taut forearm. 'It was just a joke.'

The anger quickly fades. Billy looks around at the expressions of shock on our friends' faces. His fingers loosen and his arm drops. 'Wow, listen to me,' he mutters. 'Sorry, mate.'

'Let's go find something to eat,' I suggest quietly.

•

We pick a Chinese BYO in King's Cross. Our order placed, we fall silent. The room is full of noisy backpackers enthusing about Thailand and New Zealand. Their tables are cluttered with cheap wine and beer from the bottlo across the road. Two boys from Ireland dare two Swedish girls at another table to kiss them. One girl agrees, kissing both. Her friend films it all on her mobile, then messages the videoclip – so she says – to the other's boyfriend back home. We find it easier to watch them than face each other. After twenty minutes, when the food has come and we've both eaten what we can, Billy rocks forward and says, 'I'm sorry, P. I'm such an idiot.'

'You're not.' I take his hand. 'But you're still worrying about this break-up prediction, aren't you?'

'I can't help it. I don't want to, you know that. I keep telling myself it's bullshit. But that dog on TV —'

'Don't you think if Moses had really foreseen that, he would have mentioned the dog? All he said was that rickety sculpture would be broken. Anyone could guess that.'

'Maybe.'

I could cry at the irony: the Committee wouldn't believe in Moses, while Billy won't stop believing. 'He can't foresee a thing, I promise you. I watch him at home: he drifts from moment to moment – never has a clue what's about to happen. Billy, seriously, you've got to drop this crazy idea, or it's really going to screw us up.'

'And the storm?' he says quietly. 'What if that happens? Should we believe him then?'

'Don't even say things like that.'

Across the room, a British group start chanting football anthems. The Irish boys look up in disgust. We call for the bill.

That might have been the end of it, but on our way out Billy stops a waiter and asks, 'You have any toothpicks?'

The Billy I know doesn't use toothpicks. He just sticks his fingernail in there and hauls whatever's bugging him clean out. I'm already at the door, but I turn around and say, 'What d'you want a toothpick for?'

He says, 'That sweet and sour beef,' and I go, 'Yeah, what about it?' and he says, 'It's stuck in my teeth, stupid.'

'So dig it out with your nail, stupid,' I say, and he comes back, real quick, 'That's not polite.'

I know immediately where he's got that from.

'Since when did you think that?' He shrugs, so I say it for him. 'That's Kirsten, isn't it?'

'So what?'

'When did she get you using toothpicks?'

'I guess . . . at lunch.'

'Today?' I think back to Kirsten arriving late to the Safety Committee, that hint of caramel, and I try to imagine why she might have had lunch with my fiancé and not told me about it.

It's not that there's anything wrong with Billy and Kirsten eating together. But I'm pretty disturbed that neither has mentioned it to me until now. When I ask if it was just the two of them, he doesn't deny it: 'It was a business lunch,' he says airily. 'We had to discuss bank stuff.' And I can't help thinking of her possessive hand on his cheek, or how she had him crouched beside her desk. How she could tell him to do the stupidest thing now that he works for her, and he would just say, 'Yeah, sure, Kirsten.'

•

Moses and I spend Christmas morning at Dad's house.

The first couple of years after Dad had to leave Saaremaa, I would take him to church and then bring him home with me for a good festive lunch. But getting in and out of the boat hurt his leg too much, and after that we pulled the crackers and opened the presents at his bungalow in Avalon. Sad, really. Christmas isn't the same there.

Dad's still pretty wound up about the day before. We both are. He reckons I made a fool of myself – and him – which I guess is true. He's also angry about the email I sent all the race skippers, telling them what Moses had said. I had to do it, just in case. None of the skippers took any notice, but Dad thinks I've undermined the authority of the Safety Committee. He's not inclined to indulge in much good cheer.

The business of pulling crackers is new to Moses. He says he knows what they are when presented with one, even grips the end with a fair amount of confidence, but at the bang he shoots backwards, nearly upsetting the table. The scattering of goodies that falls from his half mystifies him. The paper crown, when I unwrap it for him, is purple and he adores it. He is less impressed by the little plastic whistle, blowing it once and then discarding it. But the crown holds his attention; twice he rushes off to inspect it in the bathroom mirror. And when he returns, he insists on pulling another cracker with Dad. Again, he ends up with the larger half, but he brushes aside any suggestion that he has won another haul.

'I have a crown,' he says firmly. 'This is for you.'

'No, thank you,' says Dad.

Moses unwraps the crown, holds it out. For a dreadful moment, I imagine he might try to plant it straight on my father's head.

'Go on, Dad,' I urge. 'Take it.'

'He won it. He can keep it.'

'Dad, please.'

'Petra, what do you want from me?' he snaps. 'On the Lord's birthday, isn't it enough that I invite your witchdoctor friend into my house?'

'Dad!' I look at Moses, crown still extended, but cheerful smile now slipping. 'That's rude.'

'Rude,' he scoffs. 'I'm not allowed to say what I think now?'

'We have a guest. Whatever you feel about —'

But Moses interrupts me with a gentle hand on my arm. 'You are both very kind,' he says.

There's a long silence.

With slow, careful movements, my father takes the rustling paper crown and slips it over his thin grey hair. He doesn't look at either of us when he's done it, but gets painfully to his feet and makes his way to the kitchen. When he comes back, holding a tray steady with much effort, he unloads biscuits and orange juice onto the table. I help him fill three glasses.

Moses declares, 'Your daughter is very clever.'

Dad finally looks him in the eye. He doesn't say anything, but his expression has become more gentle.

'And she will have many children.'

'Moses!' I laugh. 'Enough of that.' I can't help wondering, though, at the little surge of pleasure that daft prediction brings me. Where did that alien feeling come from?

Delighted, Moses leaps up and takes both my hands. 'We are friends,' he says, squeezing my fingers.

For a short while, we stand there, holding hands. Then Moses turns to Dad. Before my father has a chance to evade him, Moses has both his hands in a tight grip.

'All right, yes, friends,' mutters Dad, pulling free.

'And now, you both,' says Moses, bracketing my father and me together with flattened palms.

Sighing, Dad takes my hands.

'No, no!' cries Moses. 'This is for friends. You are a family.' And he mimes a generous embrace.

All this standing must be killing Dad's leg, and he could easily use it as an excuse to sit down. But he doesn't; instead he meets my gaze and nods. When I go to hug him, I'm surprised by the strength of his arms around my shoulders, undiminished despite the years of inactivity. That's when I realise I haven't felt him hug me since school. All of a sudden, I get very shaky.

'Thank you,' I whisper.

Dad says nothing, but his arms twitch – a last, strong embrace before we separate.

'We should watch that race report,' he says gruffly, limping back to his chair. 'Already missed ten minutes.'

Moses, as the television comes on, beams his approval. He knows, I'm sure, that my thanks were intended for him.

The first person to appear on screen is Daran Sacs, balanced on the foredeck of an RTV launch in the Harbour. His team is filming the yachts on their final training runs. *Sentinel* glides by, then feathers into the wind with Kirsten signalling to the RTV launch to come on over.

She does this neat, sexy jump onto the launch foredeck, nearly toppling Daran into the water, and she greets us with a big friendly wave. 'Merry Christmas, everyone,' she says, all smiles, to the camera.

Daran's going to fall in, I'm convinced, and then the morning Coastguard watch will have to perform a rescue in front of the cameras. Without realising I'm doing it right away, I notch up the volume on my wrist transceiver. The Coastguard chatter doesn't bother Dad – he barely notices it any more. It's part of the air for both of us. Sometimes at night I can't sleep when the radio's silent.

'Well, well, Kirsten McKenzie, you look like the cat that got the cream,' simpers Daran.

'I'm just here to compete.'

'That's a beautiful boat you've built. Is the race in the bag?'

'Certainly not, Daran. Of all the great ocean races, the Sydney Hobart is the most unpredictable. Anything could happen out there.'

'*Sentinel*'s tipped to take line honours. Have you bet anything on yourself?'

'More than you could imagine,' smiles Kirsten.

'What's it going to take to win this race?'

'Nerve, stamina, and a little help from God.'

'God? I didn't know you're religious.'

'We all have a spiritual side. Even bankers,' she says, raising a jovial Daran laugh. 'Seriously, though, you remember my new friend from South Africa, Moses Lukoto?'

'That kid's something else, huh?' Daran turns to the camera. 'Remember him, bucks? Just about gave me a heart attack.' He looks back to Kirsten. 'So what's the deal with Moses?'

'Well, Daran, he was telling me how in Africa anything important gets blessed before it's used. And although I don't suppose my crew will care one way or another, I thought it'd be nice for Moses to come down to CYCA tomorrow and bless our boat.'

I stare in disbelief at the screen. 'You're bloody kidding,' I mutter.

'That girl's in a strange place,' says my father. 'And don't swear, Petra.'

Moses watches attentively, missing nothing.

'Did you say "bless" *Sentinel*?'

'Why not?' she smiles knowingly, as if to make clear it's all just a bit of fun. 'It can't hurt. Maybe his blessing will see us safe all the way to the Derwent River.'

My father switches off the TV. 'I never heard such horse manure.'

Moses contemplates the blank screen. He frowns, steeples his fingers, arches his back.

As his eyes settle on some faraway point, I wonder exactly what he's going to believe about himself by the time we've finished with him.

•

Aside from the crackers, Moses didn't get much of a Christmas at Dad's house, and I was on duty all afternoon. So when I make it back to Saaremaa that evening, I'm glad to see Billy already there.

He runs into the water. 'Happy Christmas, Happy Christmas, Happy Christmas!'

High tide. The water's up to our chests. I cling to him and kiss him, and for a moment it feels like everything's normal again. He's salty, even where his skin is still dry, and I love the fact he hasn't shaved today. A precious day off work, away from the bank, back into our world.

Moses comes out of the house and stands on the beach, watching us. Although I can't see his face in the dark, I sense the pessimism in his stare. It chills the moment.

I let go of Billy, walk up the beach. 'Did you get the stuff?'

'Yeah,' says Billy, perplexed by my sudden change of mood.

'Come on, then.'

He's brought everything I asked for: streamers, glo-in-the-dark party hats, a big Christmas pudding and enough brandy to set it alight ten times over. He's also thought to add some mini-fireworks, and he lets these off at the waterline while Moses watches wide-eyed the flashes and sparkling explosions overhead.

Afterwards, we sit around a fire and Moses has a wild time flicking streamers over us while I set light to the pudding. Some of the streamers go in the fire, others in the burning brandy, until there are little lines of flaming paper crisscrossing the sand. He loves that.

'Here, Moses, mate,' says Billy, producing a small package. 'Humble offering for the wise prophet. Merry Christmas.'

Moses has already had his presents from me – two new shirts and a pair of sunnies. But he seems twice as pleased to get something from Billy. 'Thank you,' he says graciously. There's something rather grand in his manner that wasn't there before Kirsten addressed him on national TV.

He removes the shiny paper with great care. Inside is a chrome-coloured watch that pulses with blue and yellow lights.

'Billy, that's a brilliant present,' I whisper.

Moses is thrilled. He straps on the watch and waves it through the darkness, leaving blue and yellow traces on our retinas.

'There's one more,' Billy says, retrieving another package from his bag. 'This is from Kirsten.'

Even before the paper's come off I know it's going to be something expensive and flash, and I'm irritated with Billy for bringing it. But he doesn't see my expression; already I'm realising how bad I'd look resenting Kirsten's generosity. It's Christmas, after all. Why shouldn't she send Moses a present?

She's given him a mobile.

It's not just any mobile, either. It's the latest satellite Motorola, with more functions and data memory than any of us would ever know what to do with. Its casing is speckled amber. Worth at least a couple of thousand dollars. Trust Kirsten to dazzle him with her generosity.

'So, look, Moses,' says Billy, when we've helped him enter our numbers. 'Did you see Kirsten on TV this morning?"

'Oh, Billy, no . . .' I start, as Moses nods.

'What do you reckon, mate? You think you might like to bless her boat?'

'Yes. I will,' says Moses with a certain condescension, like it's what he does every day.

'Moses, would you be an angel and fetch me some water?' I say.

He gets up and slopes off to the house, his new mobile clasped in his right hand.

'Damn, Billy, did she send you to do this?'

'What's wrong? I thought it was a nice idea. Show the human side of the bank. Supporting Africans. All he has to do is go and say something in his own language, maybe wave his hand over *Sentinel*. It'll be a laugh,' he smiles.

'He's not a performing monkey.'

'It's just a PR thing. No one's taking it seriously. But loads of media will be there – could be great publicity, especially after that RTV show. Kirsten needs you to agree to this, P.'

'Well, she's certainly got you wrapped round her little finger.'

'That isn't fair. I work for her.'

'Is this in your job description? Recruiting children for religious charades?'

'How could I refuse to do something so straightforward?' he demands. 'Be reasonable. I'm new to the company. I have to make a good impression.'

'Or what? You think she's going to fire you? Bullshit! She loves you working for her. The only precious things I have, the Coastguard and you: now she's got her claws into both.' The shock of voicing it forces me to acknowledge the ignominious suspicion that's been growing in me ever since Kirsten marked my engagement by snaring Billy with an unbeatable job offer. Whether her motive was jealousy or control is unclear to me. But the fact is, I've begun to distrust my oldest friend.

'Petra, what are you talking about?' Billy looks aghast. 'Kirsten's done us a big favour giving me that job.'

'Hasn't done me any bloody favour.'

Moses ambles back out, and for a while I glower in silence. The sea is unnaturally still. Apart from the occasional swish of a bat wing, no sounds come from the park. Moses gives me a glass, and I have to drink water I don't want. He settles back down into the sand between us.

'I can bless all the boats,' he offers loftily.

'That won't be necessary,' I snap.

Then Billy says, 'Look, P, I don't know where you're coming from with that stuff. It's not like you. But even if you don't want to do this for Kirsten . . . I need you to do it for me. Kirsten's given me shore-side responsibility for the start tomorrow, and it's a great opportunity for me to prove my stuff. The truth is I'm finding the job tough, the financial part anyways. But this is what I'm good at – talking to people, getting all the balls in line. It's important it goes well. Please, I need you to let Moses do this.'

•

By morning, I've agreed to it. But something has changed between us. I won't admit it yet, but I can't see Billy the same way any more. The man I found halfway up a cliff, wrist broken but spirit unscathed, would never have made that plea.

CHAPTER 9

My 08:00 Boxing Day briefing kicks off at 07:58. Not one member of the Inshore staff misses the start.

'For those of you who have joined us since last year, the Sydney Hobart is this city's most spectacular annual event. It is also, for the water police, for Maritime, and therefore for us, the biggest annual headache. People come from all over the world to see these yachts up close. Many of those who take boats out have forgotten how to operate them safely; some never learnt. At least half will leave their radios switched off. Most of their passengers will be drinking heavily. Hardly anyone will bother with lifejackets.

'Within the Harbour, there is generally a reasonable level of order. Most skippers respect the exclusion zone. If you see an infringement, inform Maritime. It's not your job to enforce the exclusion.' On the large wall map, I position markers for seven of the Inshore crews between Bradley's Head and the ocean. 'Watch for danger signs before the race – excessive boozing, unsound vessels, arguments. With crowded waters and drunken spectators, it's easy for a man overboard to go unnoticed.'

Stuart gives me a cheery smile from the back. He's on sick leave for three weeks: he didn't need to get up this early. But he's come in to lend support – to the crews, to the dispatchers, to me. Dan Worrell has taken his place in *Giselle* and is doing OK, but I miss Stuart. He steadies me; he provides a sense check to all my decisions on and off the water.

'There are rarely incidents in the Harbour, but once the race fleet reaches the Heads and the exclusion zone comes to an end, all kinds of trouble kicks off. The ocean is calm right now. It won't be like that at quarter past one. If you've never seen the chaos outside the Heads on Boxing Day, you need to prepare yourself. This is where the thrillseekers wait – in launches, yachts, dinghies, even canoes. Hundreds of vessels, right in the path of the fleet. The larger cruisers and media boats have professional skippers who understand the dangers. Assume the rest are driven by drunken amateurs.

'The moment the leading super-maxis reach them, they'll be revving their engines and turning a calm sea into boiling froth. Most of you have experienced difficult conditions, but this is different. In a squall like the other evening, the waves are spaced out and come mostly from one direction. Not how it'll be today. All that motor energy churns and whips the water into something entirely unnatural and dangerous. Any swell or shore break just compounds the problem. Waves come from all directions, at three times the normal speed: steep, choppy waves; freakish waves that explode upwards; violent waves that deliver a vicious punch.'

Dan's looking nervous. He's been with us less than five months, part time, and the squall was a stretch for him. Unlike the other Inshore staff, he'll have to wait around Spring Cove all morning, tension building, until I bring Moses back from CYCA. We won't be doing any patrolling before the race: it'll be straight out to the thick of the action for us.

'Understand, you *will not* always be able to ride these waves. Even a SilverBird hasn't the agility to take evasive action. It's going to be uncomfortable and wet. If you're not wearing goggles, you'll be blinded. If you're not clipped on, you could end up over the side. About twenty-five helicopters will be roaring past you at terrifyingly low altitude. All around you, launches driven by intoxicated idiots will be rolling out of control. Everyone will be crisscrossing each other's path, fighting for space, while ninety per cent of their attention is on the race yachts. These people will be desperate to get close to *Sentinel* and *Alfa Romeo* and the other super-maxis. They'll have glamorous chicks clinging to their foredecks, and they'll take all kinds of risks to impress them. This is the busiest, most anarchic scrap of ocean you'll ever see. It's going to be hard enough keeping clear of other vessels, never mind the job you're there to do.

'But the job is crucial. In these conditions, there's a good chance someone will fall off a deck, or a dinghy will capsize. The race yachts have to plough through foaming white water, helicopters hovering close by their masts; their focus is beating the competition and looking good for the media boats: none of them will want to change course suddenly if some idiot spectator doesn't get out of the way. And you'll see how close it gets. Guys on jet skis sit right in the path of the lead yacht until the very last minute. If their engine fails them, twenty-five tonnes of super-maxi are going to make mincemeat of them.'

Moving back to the map, I place the remaining four markers outside the Heads.

'Four crews will be stationed with the ocean spectators from eleven onwards. The rest of you, except one-four and one-seven who will remain on Harbour patrol, follow the fleet leaders as far as Bondi – grid formation, three hundred metre separation – then work your way back in a sweep line, checking for casualties as you return. Lowest priority are the out-of-fuels and the engine failures. They can wait till the end for their tow. We're there for the capsized dinghies and MOBs. And, if we're unlucky, we're there to patch up the casualties when some moron turns the wrong way down a wave and causes a multiple pile-up.'

I scan the faces of the new hires. They look suitably scared, which means I've got the right message across. The old hands have that tense, expectant look which signifies a proper level of readiness. As much as it's possible to be before an event like this, I feel satisfied.

'Have fun today. It's an incredible experience. But be ready for anything to happen.'

•

During the ninety minutes it has taken me to brief the Inshore crews, oversee the radio tests, check on the dispatchers, and confirm final arrangements with NSW Maritime, Moses has been waiting in my office. Already dressed in his smart party clothes, ready to dispense his blessings to anyone who asks, he's spent the time in a studious rearrangement of the papers on my desk. Met briefings, technical logs, performance reviews, AMSA rulings – all have been ordered by colour, with the majority whites in the centre of the desk, the blues and greens to the left, and the pinks, reds and yellows to the right. In most cases, this coordination has brought documents of the same category together. But it's also generated some surreal couplings: Christmas party catering bills with an application for leave to recover from a duodenal ulcer; a letter from a Hawkesbury children's sailing club requesting safety training with a notice from Canberra concerning the rise of amphetamine smuggling in dinghy yachts.

The television is showing live coverage from CYCA, where final preparations are being made for the race. Despite the flat, dead air and the unexciting weather forecasts, RTV's warm-up interviewers are managing to extract the usual bullish quotes from the skippers.

'This is a race of attrition. How are we going to beat the super-maxis? We'll tail them to Bass Strait, then watch those over-engineered nancies fall apart.'

'Look, mate, pay no attention to the forecast. I'm telling my crew we're going to be whacked by the weather. And I *want* to be whacked.'

'It's all about the unexpected in this race. Expect the unexpected. And we do.'

But even the super-maxi crews are glumly conceding that no records are going to be broken with these feeble winds. When asked if they'll make it to Constitution Dock in time for the big Sentinel Bank party on the 28th, the skippers of Kirsten's two main rivals, *Gardens of Suzhou* and *Alpha Romeo*, both swear they'll be there. Even if, they wickedly add, the host isn't. It's all good fighting talk, but the notion of a Sentinel Bank party with no *Sentinel* in dock leaves me further unsettled.

Moses stands at the edge of the desk, one hand on his waist, the other spread possessively over the red end of his colour spectrum. 'You're worried,' he frowns.

'Well, it's a big day.' I pull out the CYCA Order of Start and sit down to memorise the timings.

He considers that excuse, and quickly dismisses it. 'Please,' he says, 'don't worry.'

'OK. I won't.'

'I don't mind dying.'

'Oh, Moses, honestly!'

RTV has switched to library footage, reeling off statistics and trivia from previous races. Maps of the New South Wales coastline and the island of Tasmania flash up, while the fledgling commentator gleefully talks through the hazards of each leg of the course.

'It's the dangers of this blue water classic that attract top-class sailors from all over the world,' he announces. 'Since the first race in 1945, when a storm battered the pioneering fleet, competitors have always anticipated "extreme conditions". Here, on the first leg along the coast, there's a good chance they can find a safe harbour if things get bad. But once into Bass Strait, they're at the mercy of the weather for over 150 nautical miles. And in these unusually shallow waters, just fifty metres in places, the wind can stir up fearsome waves. Bass Strait is where things get hot.'

The usual cases are dredged up from recent years: the two maxis that collided in fog, the French boat that ended up in New Zealand, the defective canting keel that wrecked a super-maxi, the dismastings and sinkings during various gales. 'In the last nine years,' says the commentator with extra solemnity in his voice, 'sixteen boats have been lost, along with three lives.' There's the inevitable pause, then: 'But the worst year of all was 1998, when —'

Grabbing the remote, I switch off the television.

11.15–12.15 Radio Checks. Scheduled position reports (skeds) are a mandatory requirement of this race, and every participant MUST confirm contact with the Radio Relay Vessel on 6516 kHz before . . .

12:30 End of Storm Sail and Safety Equipment Checks. All participants must have satisfied the inspectors on the Start Boat by this time.

12:50 10-minute cannon . . .

'You're not relaxed,' Moses observes cheerfully.

'Look, I need to concentrate a moment, OK?'

He considers this. Lifting up both arms, his face glowing with generosity, he says, 'If you want, I will bless your office.'

'No, of course I don't want . . .' My flustered rejection peters out. His cheeky grin leaves me feeling foolish. 'You're teasing me.'

'It's good when you smile.'

I drop the Order of Start. 'It's good when *you* smile.'

•

Being honest, this is all procrastination. Rereading a CYCA document I know by heart, chatting with Moses, revisiting Comms and irritating the dispatchers with unnecessary questions. Moses has stopped smiling now. He senses the approaching deadline. He sits quietly, expectantly. He's looking forward to his big moment. By contrast, I feel queasy at the thought of assisting in this farce.

But I've promised Billy. I have to do it.

Eventually, at ten thirty, I know I can't put it off any longer.

•

Already the Harbour's busy. With marker buoys in place around the wide exclusion zone, NSW Maritime's small launches speed up and down the boundary, searching for transgressors. The early-bird spectator craft are concentrated just above the northern start line, for perfect camera shots of the super-maxis. Two media helicopters circle overhead; a skywriting plane spells white smoke letters at a tantalisingly slow pace. Another helo, dragging an advertising banner, appears over Rose Bay. Crowds have already gathered on all the best vantage points, from Middle Head to Shark Island. A black RIB crosses my bows, its black-uniformed crew bearing automatic weapons and scanning the Harbour for terrorists. Their bullet-proof vests read 'Water Police', but those hardened faces don't look like any of the boys I know from the force. Impervious to all this activity, the Manly ferry ploughs resolutely through the empty zone.

The Coastguard SilverBirds are all in position, patrolling slowly amongst the spectators, but so far not a single incident has been reported. Mostly, the spectators are behaving themselves; occasionally, a dinghy driven by an idiot will plough off into the zone, but the Maritime launches are quick to intercept, and in any case there are hardly any race yachts out yet. The first four are currently parading past the Start Boat, their tiny orange storm sails set to prove they're equipped for bad weather. Behind them, the super-maxi *Atomic* is testing her canting keel: on a still sea, the bare mast rolls slowly but impossibly – thirty degrees to port, thirty degrees to starboard, as the keel is shifted from side to side. On 6516 kHz, the race frequency, the skippers are reporting numbers on board and confirming all safety equipment checked. The orderly process soothes me somewhat.

It's eleven o'clock by the time we reach CYCA, and quite a few race yachts are casting off. I suppose I've been hoping *Sentinel* might be among them, but as we draw in to the docks I spot the outline of her mast high above the others and resign myself to seeing this through.

We moor at the northern end of the docks, away from the crowds, and I lead Moses at a slow, reluctant pace to the shore and through the packed car park to the Club. The southern docks are more congested than ever: concession stands at key junctures block the flow of people on the already narrow walkways; journalists from foreign sailing magazines conduct interviews in the path of the crowds; tearful mothers hug the younger participants and refuse to let them go, even when the weight of spectators struggling past threatens to overwhelm them. Last-minute supplies – sacks of baguettes, bags of ice, sweating slabs of cold beer – are still being loaded. A grand old lady, carrying an umbrella against the sun, parades along the dock, expecting all to make way for her.

Some of the sailors are already in seaboots, others clamber unwisely about the decks in thongs. A couple of older skippers are wearing faded Fastnet shirts to intimidate the competition. Several crews have started on the beers. One feisty little yacht has *Highway to Hell* blasting out of four speakers. Immaculate long-legged girlfriends, distraught to be ordered out of their heels, perch awkwardly on cases of mineral water. Having invited them aboard, their guys ignore them to show off obscure knots to each other: 'Ah, yeah, mate, but d'you know this one?' The same line is being called up and down the dock: 'See you in Hobart.'

Moses's newfound celebrity delays us further, with RTV viewers recognising him and insisting on a handshake or a photograph, so that it's 11:20 before we're even close to *Sentinel*. The media are gathered in force around the super-maxi, led by Daran Sacs and his RTV team. Neglected heaps of camera equipment and tripods are scattered about the dock. As each crew member climbs aboard, Daran is there, gleaning a last quote, looking for something sexy, someone scared, anything to pull the image of this race out of the background blur. Overhead, two news helos hold position, adding their alarmist roar to the shouts and whistles and cheers of the crowd.

We're still fifty paces back when Daran calls up to Kirsten, 'No sign, yet?'

She's walking around the cockpit with Nolan, examining every piece of equipment, satisfying herself of the boat's readiness to race. 'He'll be here.'

'The media boats are leaving,' grumbles a photographer from *The Australian*. 'We've got to go in, like, two minutes.'

'No rush, Kirsten,' says Daran, one smug eye on the dedicated RTV launch waiting just beyond *Sentinel*. 'Take your time.'

Two crew haul Dermott up the mast on a halyard, to make final checks of the mainsail track. Forward of the mast, another halyard lifts a spinnaker out of a deck hatch, a metre at a time, while Martha Salford ties little strands of wool around it. Nolan interrupts his inspection to correct her technique, then rejoins Kirsten to look over the rigging. Other crew are still loading fresh food aboard from a wheelbarrow. The two senior watch captains, Sue and Scott, field all the questions from the media.

On the dock below, Billy squeezes his way through the crowd, offering Sentinel Bank gift bags to the most important of the journalists and celebrities. He looks stressed, as several are bluntly refusing the bags. 'They've got tickets to the ski dome,' he promises. 'And chocolates from Italy.' He's the only man I can see wearing a suit.

The moment she spots us, Kirsten gives a triumphant cry, and commands her shore team to clear a way through the spectators. The media pack, hearing the commotion, wheel round and bear down on Moses.

'What good will this do?'

'How much do you charge for a blessing?'

'Did you have an agreement with Hexley Hughes to wreck that sculpture?'

'Who's gonna be First Citizen?'

Kirsten, meanwhile, is busy issuing orders to her minions, and I notice one squinty type climb off the yacht and push through the crowds. Passing us, he keeps his eyes averted, and I can't help thinking that's strange when everyone else is fascinated by us. I watch him uneasily until Tabitha calls my name. Reluctantly, I turn round to say hello. But now Kirsten's launched into a speech.

'Ladies and gentlemen,' she's saying into a microphone, 'I'd like you all to welcome my new friend, Moses Lukoto. He's from South Africa, he's a bright kid, and Sentinel Bank will be sponsoring him to study here for two years. We hope that people like Moses will in the future help drive development in Africa, and we're all very proud at the Bank to have the opportunity to help him maximise his potential.'

'What about his predictions?' cries one journalist. 'Is it true he's picking stocks for you?'

'Please!' laughs Kirsten. 'Moses is here to go to school. We have quite enough professional analysts of our own, thank you.'

'Then why is he spending time at the bank?' cries another.

'OK, this isn't an interview. We're here to race, guys! Moses has been kind enough to come along today to give *Sentinel* a traditional Vendaland blessing. We're not looking for any divine edge here.' A dutiful laugh from the crowd. 'We just want to get there safely. Moses?'

She holds out both hands to us, arms outstretched – very angelic. Grudgingly, I lead Moses to the dock steps and help him climb aboard. I'm about to follow when a security man holds up a discreet hand. Moses keeps going, oblivious, completely psyched on the buzz of the crowd. The hand has become a definite barrier. Puzzled, I look up at Kirsten, but she's busy smiling at the cameras.

The security man mutters, 'She's asked you to wait here.'

'Why?'

'Looks better on TV, I guess.'

I'm tempted to push past him, but now Billy's beside me, and I step back, leaving Moses to greet Kirsten alone.

'Hi, P,' says Billy, kissing my cheek only. 'Thanks for bringing him.'

'How's it all going?'

'Oh, good,' he mutters. One finger tugs at his collar. It's too tight for him. 'Yeah, going well.'

Whatever anyone expected from Moses, the blessing must be an anti-climax. All he does is kneel down to press his hands against *Sentinel's* deck and mumble some stuff no one can hear. Then he stands up, walks a couple of metres along the deck, and does it again. And again. I still can't understand why Kirsten is going through this charade. For a psychological edge in the race? For a little more publicity to boost her investment prophet fiction? I can't see her game at all.

Pretty quickly, the media become restless. It's approaching midday. The CYCA media boats were due to leave at 11.30, and only the most influential of the journalists are confident they'll wait much longer. One by one, the cameras are lowered, and reporters and photographers begin the difficult scramble through the crowds on the dock, back to the hard-stand where their allocated boats are moored. Even Daran stifles a yawn, shrugs apologetically to Kirsten, and signals for his launch.

'They'd better get a move on,' Billy observes, after fifteen minutes of kneeling and mumbling. All remaining yachts are casting off now, steering out of Rushcutters Bay on their engines, running up their storm sails for inspection. The sponsors, yacht-spotters, families and friends who have been watching Moses's blessing with diminishing enthusiasm transfer their attention to the departing yachts.

Kirsten looks unconcerned by the erosion of her audience. With less than an hour to the start, she waits patiently until Moses finally stands. She shakes his hand with unnecessary formality, and says, 'Thank you, Moses. Thank you so much. Can I offer you some Coke and cookies?'

When he nods eagerly, she smiles at the remaining spectators and says, 'Thank you, everyone. See you in Hobart.'

•

Right away, I'm suspicious. Somewhere in my subconscious I'm already seeing what's about to happen. A dreadful unease comes over me as Kirsten leads Moses below decks for his reward.

'That was all right, wasn't it?' says Billy.

'Yeah,' I answer vaguely.

Again, I approach the dock steps, and again I'm turned away by the security man. 'Only crew aboard,' he says in a raised, irritated tone. I'm about to insist, when Billy starts talking about some surfing champion who turned up, and how embarrassing it was meeting him in a suit, with a clutch of Sentinel Bank gift bags in his hands.

'Billy, it's your choice to work for Kirsten. If you don't like it, resign.'

'I'm doing it for us both,' he says, hurt.

'You're having cosy lunches with rich women for my sake?'

Billy draws back like I've stung him. 'What's happening with you, Petra? You're changing.'

'*I'm* changing? Look at you! Crawling up to celebrities and trying to bribe them with chocolate!'

Somehow I've ended up with my arms tightly crossed and my mouth screwed into an ugly grimace. A flash of anger crosses Billy's face, and he stoops to put down his gift bags. I don't know what to expect from him when he straightens up. Is he freeing his hands to hug me or hit me? It really does seem possible, in this ghastly moment, that the man I've loved and trusted beyond everything could knock me down for what I just said.

The bags are on the dock; he's still crouched, face turned downwards; my heart is full of the terror of what he might choose, when something else, something outside our little world, pulls at my attention.

It's a boat hook, scraping the edge of the dock.

We've been so caught up in our argument that neither of us noticed *Sentinel* start to move. Her engine has been running the whole time, and in the chatter and clatter of all these people, the slight increase in revs made no impression. Only the sound of that boat hook alerts me.

'What?' I mutter in disbelief. 'Where's . . . ?'

The boat is a metre off the dock now, and the noise of the engine suddenly builds. In unison, the spectators turn back to *Sentinel*. Kirsten's at the starboard wheel, her attention entirely on the delicate task of navigating her great yacht out of the crowded bay.

'Wait!' I cry. 'Where's Moses?'

But the whistles and applause from the docks drown out everything.

Desperately, I search *Sentinel*'s deck. Nothing but crew stowing mooring lines and fenders, readying halyards, running through the drills they've practised a thousand times.

I turn back to Billy. He hasn't hit me, hasn't hugged me either. His empty hands hang limp by his side. He's watching me in bewilderment.

'Is Moses still on board?'

Billy frowns. 'He can't be.'

'Did you see him come off?'

'God, not even Kirsten would have . . .'

The way he trails off, his voice filled with doubt, turns me cold. It seems to presage terrible suffering and fear for Moses: a boy who can't swim, trapped aboard a boat destined for destruction.

Next moment, I'm forcing my way through the crowd, knocking over the racer chasers in their high heels and lipstick, yelling, 'She's taken Moses!' And they're not understanding, or worse, they're just laughing. Broad daylight, and no one saw a thing. They watched him go on board, then they turned away and talked about something else.

The narrow dock is so crowded with dawdling spectators that it's almost impossible to break through. Well-wishers who have watched their yacht motor out into the Harbour now stand around drinking coffees, posing for photographs, commiserating with each other on missing that last airline seat to Hobart, marvelling at the price of bottled water. My haste and alarm only make things worse. Drinks are spilled, tempers roused. Two guys, hard bastards from the wrong side of town, grab hold of me and won't let go until I've apologised to their satisfaction. Neither my Coastguard shirt nor my dreadful fears for Moses move them to release me, and though I try to spit out the apology they want, their hands remain locked around my arms.

'Guys, what's going on?'

It's Billy. Whatever he thinks of me after that bribing celebrities comment, he's standing by me for now. At first I worry he's going to hit one of the men, maybe both of them. But instead he uses diplomacy to secure my release.

'She's a good one, mate, best let her go. Here – have a gift bag. Your girlfriend will love the bath oil.'

He comes the rest of the way with me along the dock. By the time we make it to the shore, *Sentinel* is out of sight.

Grabbing my hand, Billy says, 'Don't do anything stupid, P. Kirsten's under a lot of pressure right now.' He kisses me on the lips. 'But make sure you get him off that boat.'

'I will.'

I run through the car park, up the northern dock to *Giselle*, and cast off fast. The hydrosparks growl under my throttle. Even though Kirsten's got a long head start, I can stop this madness. There's still thirty-five minutes to the cannon, and not even a super-maxi can outrun a SilverBird on flat water.

Roaring out into the Harbour, many things become visible at once: the massively expanded ranks of spectator boats, the Maritime launches and Coastguard SilverBirds zipping back and forth, small whitecaps emerging in a strengthening wind, twenty helicopters circling above, a hundred yachts tacking across the exclusion zone, three vast pleasure boats flying zone permit flags in amongst them. But all I really see is *Sentinel*, her storm sails set, passing at that exact moment in front of the Start Boat.

She's the last yacht to complete the safety procedure. By the time I'm into the exclusion zone, *Sentinel*'s crew have packed away the storm sails and hauled up the mainsail and genoa. Already, Nolan's intensively trained team has the rig perfectly trimmed and shaped, like *Sentinel*'s been out here preparing for hours. As I draw alongside and reach for the loudhailer microphone, I can't help that tiny wrench of admiration at the effortless precision on display.

'Pull into the wind,' I order. 'Pull into the wind or I'll block you.'

Kirsten calls the tack and spins the wheel, turning away from me. Her crew are all too busy with the sails to do more than glance in my direction.

'Kirsten!' I circle round after her. 'Stop the damn boat.'

Still no acknowledgement.

'Last time I'm asking, Kirsten. Come on! You know there's no way you can outrun a SilverBird.'

Except, just at that moment, I discover there is a way.

It's a sound I've never heard before, the sound of hydrosparks dying. A coughing, painful sound. Then silence. In confusion, I try to restart each engine. Nothing.

Only then do I look at the fuel gauge.

I don't know how it was done, when it was done, who did it. But someone screwed me, and my suspicions fall firmly on Kirsten's man with the averted eyes. I refuelled *Giselle* that morning from the tank at my house. Filled her to the top, saw the hydrofuel wet the rim before the cap went back on. Someone has drained her.

There are so many reasons to be outraged. Kirsten has deliberately disabled the lead Coastguard vessel on our busiest day of the year. She's had an unqualified guy handle highly flammable hydrofuel, probably without any understanding of the risks involved. And now she's removed all doubt as to her intentions: she really is planning to risk Moses's life in Bass Strait.

I call her mobile immediately. 'What are you doing? You can't take him out to sea.'

'I wouldn't have to, if you'd been more cooperative,' she says.

'He's never been on a yacht before! He can't swim. What if you get into trouble?'

'I'll look after him, don't worry. He's in a life preserver, tucked safely away in the forward cabin. He's too valuable to lose.'

'He'll be terrified!'

'Why? He's blessed us,' she mocks.

'Kirsten, he's meant to be flying to South Africa tomorrow.'

'Why else do you think I'm taking him to Hobart?' she says before she hangs up.

I call the water police. This has gone beyond the point where I'll cover for her. Sergeant Philip Lawson answers. I tell him in short angry sentences what Kirsten's done. When I've finished, he says, 'Stand by.'

There's a swishing rush of water behind me, and I turn to see one of the older maxis tacking upwind towards me. They're expecting me to get out of the way, and when I throw on my strobes, the helm has to reach fast to avoid *Giselle*.

The correction puts the maxi on a collision course with a Cookson 50 which, being on port tack, is forced to bear away. Two more yachts closing from the other side on parallel tacks expedite immediate gybes to clear the Cookson 50, only just missing each other. A third appears unexpectedly from behind a pleasure cruiser, blocking the wind of a fourth, while a fifth tacks at exactly the wrong moment, as a sixth comes barrelling downwind into her path, and suddenly I'm at the centre of a horrendous mess.

With so many large and fast-moving vessels scrabbling for breathing space behind the start lines, *Giselle* is horribly vulnerable. More and more yachts are piling into this tiny scrap of the Harbour, none of them expecting a motorboat – particularly a Coastguard – to sit unmoving in their midst.

'Port!' roars the bowman of a Reichel/Pugh 60. His vessel has tacked with a thundering of sails to escape a collision, only to come straight at me. 'To port!'

I feel as useless and stupid as a kid washed out to sea in a rubber ring. The helmsman rams the tiller over just in time, and eighteen metres of sleek yacht scrape past my stern, a spoonful of air between us.

'Dumb fucking woman!' screams the helmsman.

I pick up my radio with trembling hand, and call on the race frequency, 'Attention all yachts between Clarke Island and Bradley's Head, Coastguard two-one stranded in exclusion zone, unable to take evasive action. Proceed with caution. Repeat, proceed with caution.'

A silence on the airwaves, then, 'What's wrong, Petra? Forget your rudder?' Some bastard I can't place.

Containing my anger a moment longer, I repeat the alert, then switch to the Coastguard channel. 'Will someone bloody come and get me?' I snap. A cannon shot signals ten minutes to go.

Philip comes back on the line. A dozen more yachts have sliced past me, some deliberately close, the crew of each pointing me out with laughing grins. I would care if I wasn't so frightened for Moses. 'Yeah, Petra, I spoke to Kirsten. She says the boy's back at CYCA.'

'She's lying.'

'. . . OK. What do you want me to do?'

'Go on board, search the cabin, get him out of there.'

'Petra, the race is about to start.'

'Hold her back!'

'I don't have grounds.'

'He's under the minimum age for the race, he's not certified AYF crew, and he hasn't registered with CYCA. He's an illegal participant on three counts.'

A hesitation. Then, a second cannon shot. Five minutes. The smaller race yachts are jostling for position behind the southern start line. It's a horribly tense time, the possibility of collision is very real, and every skipper is trying to judge the perfect tack that will take their yacht over the start line at exactly 13:00, not a moment sooner. The last thing they need is a powerboat drifting out of control amongst them.

'Stand by,' says Philip.

That's when another call flashes up: a number I don't recognise. But I know immediately who it must be.

I tap the screen, and Moses's face appears.

'She's taking me to the ocean.' He says it hurriedly, and I know that crumbling tone too well from all those stranded kids trying to be brave. But this is so different: when I hear Moses's terror I feel like my stomach is turning inside out. It scalds me.

'It's all right,' I tell him. 'Don't worry, OK? It's going to be all right.'

'There will be a storm. I told you this.'

Sentinel is tacking back and forth across the northern start line, as if challenging the other super-maxis to match her agility. Two media helos are hovering close by, well below the height of her mast. Another helo appears directly above me. The downwash from the rotor sets *Giselle* rocking.

'You're safe, Moses,' I shout above the thundering roar of the helo. 'I'm coming. We're going to stop the boat and get you —'

But the picture disappears and Kirsten's voice cuts me off. 'Bye, Petra,' she says, and kills the call. When I ring back, the number is unreachable.

The yachts around me are all streaming in the same direction, all heading for the start. Beyond, the maxis and super-maxis are hurtling towards the northern line. Beyond them, the media boats are revving their engines, photographers hanging over their sterns in readiness for that lucrative start shot. A line of twelve helicopters – media, sponsors, billionaire spectators – has formed directly above, all facing the oncoming fleet. The mood of tension and anticipation is overwhelming.

The police lines are all engaged. I get through to Philip's mobile, as an alert comes over the Coastguard channel: some cruiser passenger gone overboard.

'I just spoke to the boy, Philip. He's terrified.' A part of my brain stays with the Coastguard channel, waiting for a response.

'I'm sorry, Petra. The Superintendent won't allow a search at this time.'

Three Coastguard crews rush to assist the MOB. Mentally, I let that one go.

'Philip, I swear she's got him on board!'

The cannon. Third and final shot.

'Well, I guess it's too late now,' says Philip.

At that exact moment, perfectly judging her approach, *Sentinel* crosses the northern start line and begins the race to Tasmania. One hundred and eleven yachts follow in her wake.

I cut the call and ring one more number. 'Donald, it's Petra.'

'Hey, Petra, I heard you made a distress call.'

'I'm fine,' I say sharply. 'Where are you?'

'Off Clovelly. Waiting for you to send us some yachts to look after.'

'Donald, you have to stop *Sentinel*.'

'Say again?'

'Stop *Sentinel*. Kirsten McKenzie's boat. Metallic silver hull, with "Sentinel" in big blue letters on the —'

'I know what *Sentinel* looks like, Petra.'

'She's taken Moses. She's got him on board.'

Silence.

'Donald?'

'Look, Petra, I know you're unhappy about the Committee's decision, but —'

'She's kidnapped Moses, and she's sailing into a fucking cyclone with him!'

The silky roar of SilverBird hydrosparks emerges out of the background din. The crew toss me a line.

'I think you should take a rest,' Donald says finally. 'You've done so much for us, especially with the funding. You're carrying the Coastguard on your shoulders. Take a break. Have some fun with Billy.'

'He's fourteen!' Suddenly, to me, he seems so much younger than that. A desperately vulnerable fledgling who needs me as I have never been needed before. We can't just let this happen!'

'I have to go. We've got to run through our checklists before the fleet gets here.'

The SilverBird carves a wide circle around *Giselle* and sets a course for Middle Head, following slowly in the fleet's wake. Frustrated beyond words, I slump down in the stern and let them pull me back to Spring Cove.

•

Dan's waiting patiently on the docks, wide-brimmed hat on his head, sunscreen, water bottle and goggles clutched in his hands. He knows he's missed the start and it's clear enough he's disappointed. There's no time to explain the situation. He takes charge of the fuelling while I head to my office and begin making calls.

First on my list is CYCA. The lines are permanently engaged, so I assign Matthew the task of pressing the redial button while I call up Jason Swift at Marine Area Command. He listens patiently to my explanation, then gives me the same line Philip used. It's a frustrating conversation. They've already contacted *Sentinel*, he says. They've spoken to the navigator and he has assured them there's no minor on board. It shocks me that Kirsten's making her crew lie for her. What does she think is going to happen in Hobart when Moses walks off the boat in front of spectators, race officials and police? If they ever get to Hobart, that is.

'I spoke to him, Jason. He called me from a mobile, five minutes before the race started. He's on that boat.'

'We'll ask the Tassie police to check at the other end,' promises Jason. 'But I can't interfere in the race without solid proof of an illegal act.'

'Isn't my word as Director of the Coastguard enough?'

'You could say the same about the President of Sentinel Bank.'

'There is proof!' I say, wondering why I haven't thought of this before. 'The phone records. You can check my incoming calls, can't you?'

'We can't get the actual conversation. The phone companies don't usually record them.'

'But you can see Moses called me at 12.55, right? That's something, at least. And then . . . and then, aren't you able to track the location of his mobile from its signal? You can prove he's out at sea.'

'Possibly. The mobile is registered in his name, is it?'

'No, but —'

'Whose name is it in? Yours?'

My frail new hope collapses. 'Kirsten bought it for him.'

A timid knock on my open door. Matthew gives a thumbs up. He's got through at last.

'As I say, we'll liaise with Hobart, but —'

'Forget it, Jason. I'm going to try CYCA now.'

But there's no more help to be had from Martin Allways. 'Do you realise what it would look like for us to make the race favourite withdraw? There are eleven media helos out there right now. Think what they'll say if *Sentinel* has to turn around.'

The screen in the corner of my office shows the feed from one of those helos. Already *Sentinel* is drawing ahead, using what little northerly wind there is to fill her snow-white spinnaker. The commentator is wildly praising Kirsten's skill and leadership.

'And anyway,' Martin continues, 'what makes you think Kirsten would obey an order from me? She wants this race, Petra, you know that. Even if we disqualified her, she'd still want to be seen to win it. She'll keep on sailing till she crosses the finish line or that boat sinks under her.'

'Don't say that!'

'Look, I'm sorry. Kirsten's just too important to CYCA for us to get in the way of what's important to her.'

There's only one more call to make. And it's going to be the hardest of all.

'Dad?'

'So they got off then?'

I know he's at home, the television switched off. Each year, I offer to take him to North Head for the start, but he always refuses. Since 1998, he's contributed in every way to the smooth and safe running of the race, but he's never wanted to see it again.

'Yeah, they got off.'

'And the blessing?' he says with heavy irony.

'Dad, she took him. She's got him on board. She's taking Moses to sea.'

'But he's underage.'

'The police won't stop her, nor will CYCA. Dad, I need your help with this.'

'What am I supposed to do about it?'

'You have authority. Your contacts in the Navy and —'

'You want them to fire across her bows?'

'This isn't a joke. He could be killed!'

Dad doesn't answer immediately. 'Is this about that weather prediction?'

'She can't do this to him. You can't let her do this to him.'

'I wonder,' he says slowly, 'if you are fully in control of yourself.'

He hangs up, but by then I've run out of pleas. When Matthew knocks again to say there's a journalist outside, I'm already resigned to the fact that Moses is going into Bass Strait.

'I've heard a rumour you think there's going to be a storm,' says Sam Drauston when Matthew shows him in. 'Two independent CYCA sources mentioned an email to all the race skippers. Is that right?'

Alarm bells sound. 'What I think is irrelevant. There was an unconfirmed warning. I considered it my responsibility to pass it on.'

'A warning from Moses?'

'What makes you think that?' Nowhere in my email was there any mention of Moses. I ascribed the warning to 'secondary weather forecasts'.

'You were researching precognition. From what I hear, you're pretty much totally focused on coastguard work. Seemed likely your research was inspired by something he said about a danger at sea.'

'You're clever,' I say uneasily.

'I am.' He smiles to soften the arrogance into something quite appealing. 'So, he did say there'll be a storm?'

For a moment, I'm tempted to confide in him. The warmth in his eyes, the sense of intelligence coupled with a readiness to accept anything makes me want to share some of my anxiety. But then I remember what he is, and I have to say, 'I can't talk about this.'

'That's not a denial.'

'No comment.'

'Did he predict casualties?'

'Look, Sam, I really can't talk about this. Please. Give me some space here.'

'Where is Moses now?'

'I don't know.'

'He's not staying with you, while Kirsten's away?'

'I just told you —'

'Because I'd really like to ask him some questions about his predictions.'

'They're not real,' I snap. 'When are you going to get that?'

Suddenly, I'm crying. What exactly kicks it off I don't know, but everything's racing through my mind – my fears for Moses, for the whole fleet, for my life together with Billy – and I can't get a grip on myself. Sam's instinctive step back is followed by a quick step forward and he puts his arms around me, resting his cheek against mine.

'It's OK,' he whispers. 'It's OK.'

'I'm sorry. That was rude.' I pull back a fraction. 'But I can't discuss this with a journalist.'

'Then talk to me as a friend. It sounds like you really need one.'

I go a little weak at that. He's not much taller than I am, his body's thin and wiry, but there is a solid comfort to his cheek and I let myself rest back against it. Just for a second.

Maybe a little longer.

I become aware that his face has shifted only when his lips touch the corner of mine.

'Hey . . .'

He kisses me again, this time on my open mouth.

'Sam, no!' Forcing him away, I glare at him in disbelief. 'This is my office. What are you thinking?'

'I'm sorry,' he says immediately.

'I'm getting married! Don't you know that?'

'I'm sorry.'

'Why do you have to be such a typical guy? There's thirteen hundred sailors heading towards a cyclone and you're trying to crack onto me?'

He opens his mouth, and I'm waiting for a third apology. But he doesn't say anything, just considers me a moment longer, then gives a little smile.

Too late, I realise what I've said. 'Sam, I'm not telling you there's definitely going to be a —'

'Goodbye, Petra. I hope you'll let me make this up to you some time, but right now we're both busy.' He smiles again, then hurries away.

There's going to be a piece in the *Business Times* about this. All I can do is remind myself that words are irrelevant when there are lives at risk on the ocean. Blocking Sam Drauston out, I pull up the latest satellite images. Juno is still sitting well below the 52nd parallel. It's absurd to worry about such a far-off threat. In two or three days, most of the crews will be safely up the Derwent River in Tasmania. How could Juno possibly swing right up to Bass Strait before that?

Dan's waiting in the crew training room. 'So,' I say, pulling on my sunnies and summoning up a smile. 'A hundred and twelve yachts just set out on one of the most hazardous courses in ocean racing.' He looks up, worried. 'How about you and me find ourselves a drunken pensioner with an outboard that won't start and rescue him from whatever millpond he's drifting in?'

•

By the end of our watch, we haven't even had that much excitement. We've avoided discussing the race, although I've made occasional checks on the satellite pictures and we've been receiving regular updates from Donald on the fleet's progress. There hasn't been much. What little wind there was died around four o'clock, leaving the fleet becalmed off Wollongong. I drop Dan off in the still shallows at Bungan Beach, and head back to Pittwater, gloomily wondering whether Billy will turn up as he promised.

The house feels cold and empty without Moses. His few possessions are neatly arranged in Dad's room. I wonder how he's getting on in that strange and frightening environment. Kirsten had better have brought along some extra clothes for him. She planned everything else; it's not asking much. Will he be able to sleep in the boat, with the noise of the sails, the hydraulics, the winches, and the constant comings and goings of twenty-two crew? What will he think when the wind picks up? I just hope that Kirsten has the consideration to talk him through the different sensations he'll encounter, reassure him when the yacht heels over, when the crash of water against the bows becomes alarming.

Two hours late, but thankfully without his suit and gift bags, Billy paddles out of the darkness and beaches beside me.

I'm standing at that point on the shore where a still sea just covers the arches of my feet. I've been standing there a long time, watching the lighthouse on Barrenjoey Head run through its familiar sequence: four pulses – pause – four pulses – pause. The alternative is my computer, and the obsessive checks I can't help making on the state of Juno. The storm is building, no question, but it's still a long way south-east of New Zealand. That would be reassuring if the fleet were speedily racing towards safety. As it is, with the wind barely a whisper along the New South Wales coast, even *Sentinel* is still flailing around Nowra. Juno's got plenty of time to move north.

Billy rolls out of his kayak, tosses the paddle up the beach, and stands beside me looking out over Pittwater. We haven't touched.

'I'm sorry about this morning. What I said to you.'

'You reckon they'll be OK?' he asks, not hearing me.

'Course!' I reply. 'Calm as anything out there.'

'No storms on the radar?'

'None.'

'Not even any —'

'None,' I repeat loudly.

He's silent for a while. But I know Billy so well, and I can sense when he's gearing up to something – some statement he's been planning. 'Because that would be proof,' he says.

'Oh, Billy,' I cry, 'do you *want* us to break up?'

That's when we touch at last. His hands go to my face, mine to his. 'Not ever,' he says with such strength in his voice.

'Then we won't,' I whisper. 'We won't! There won't be a storm, Moses won't die. Listen to me! I can see it. I can see us. We're going to be fine, Billy Farris, just wait and see.'

•

Sam Drauston's piece gets front page billing in the *Business Times* next morning. THE BIG TEST FOR SENTINEL BANK'S STORM PROPHET, it reads. I scan it once for my name, to discover what new trouble I've brought on myself and the Coastguard. To my amazement, I find I'm not mentioned at all. From what I know of journalistic practices,

Sam has been extraordinarily restrained. He could easily have used my last outburst about the storm, could have given his piece more edge with a direct quote from a harried Coastguard Director. But for some reason he's chosen to spare me the media spotlight.

He hasn't spared Moses though: *There could be no more dramatic test of this young man's claim to precognition. The Bureau of Meteorology say there won't be a storm, Moses Lukoto says there will. In the unhappy event that he is proved right, what conclusion are we to draw?*

Chapter 10

'You're taking your crazy ideas to the newspapers now?' demands my father.

The weather on the morning of the 27th remains calm and unthreatening. It's a sunny, pleasant summer day, and until Dad called I was almost enjoying it. To help his development, I've put Dan on the helm for the whole watch, and declared him skipper until further notice. So far he's handling the radio well and looking nicely in control, and I'm taking the opportunity to ride up front in the bows where the sense of the sea is greater. I'm wearing my favourite cobalt-blue shades, we're listening to Michel Mistry at full volume, and *Giselle*'s moving like an angel on rails. If I could only get the race out of my head, I'd feel great.

'You read the *Business Times*?' I ask in surprise.

'It's on all the news sites, Petra. I'm getting calls from a dozen journalists wanting to know why the Safety Committee allowed the race to go ahead. I do not expect to have to defend myself against the theories of delusional psychics, particularly not to *Woman's Day*!'

'I'm sorry, Dad.'

'Are you now? I ask myself, does my daughter really regret causing this circus, or is this her way of getting back at the grown-ups?'

'Dad, I didn't say anything to the media.'

'You sent the email, didn't you? Are you telling me you didn't anticipate this?'

Afterwards, Dan turns the music back up, but I shake my head and
he switches it off. The mood's gone now. Moving aft, I pull up the latest
weather satellite images. Nothing much has changed. Juno is continuing
its westward track, with no shift to the north. It's certain to pass well south
of New Zealand. But the slow progress of the race bothers me. The fleet
leaders have only reached as far as Jervis Bay. At this rate they won't leave
the shelter of the Australian mainland and venture out into Bass Strait
until tomorrow. So much could happen in that time.

'Heads up, Petra, I said we've got a canoe stranded at Bungan Head.
I need the chart up on that screen with all submerged rocks that might
be a threat on this tide red-flagged.'

'Hang on, I'm just checking one more satellite feed . . .'

'Negative, Petra. That was an order from your captain. Stop wasting
time on weather in Antarctica and focus on your job. I asked you to bring
up the Bungan Head large-scale. Do it now.'

When I look up at him, surprised, there's the slightest nervousness in
his eyes. Other than that, he's rock steady. 'Very good, Dan,' I murmur.
Then, more loudly, 'Of course, Captain. Chart coming up.'

·

My veranda table is sagging under a pile of marketing textbooks. It's not
a happy sight, but at least Billy's chosen to stay at my place.

'Do you really need to study that stuff over the holiday?' I ask lightly when I get back from work. 'Your boss is out sailing. Hardly seems fair.'

'Yeah, but what she's doing is Promotion. There's four marketing Ps, and Promotion is everything to do with advertising and PR and getting people excited about Sentinel as a brand.'

'Uh-huh?' This doesn't sound like my Billy, but in order to avoid those recent choppy waters I feign interest. 'And what are the other three Ps?'

'Price . . . and two I haven't got to yet.' He gives an approximation of his old easy smile. 'But there's some good stuff in here. It's giving me ideas for how to bring in more punters for the canyoning.'

'So you're definitely going to go back to that?' I say hesitantly. 'Not . . . stay at the bank?'

'Are you serious? Moment I get the money together, I'm away to Queenstown to leap those ravines!'

Kneeling over him on the couch, suffused with relief, I let my hair fall loose across his face and draw in close to kiss him. 'I thought I was your only P,' I whisper.

That magical light-of-the-world smile revives, swatting away in an instant all my anxieties for him, for the fleet, for Moses.

'You so are,' he agrees, letting the textbook fall.

•

Without Moses around, we're free to play the way we used to, and there's no more talk of Promotion and Price that afternoon. Both of us make a big effort to empty our minds and concentrate on our bodies. It helps a lot that the sun is shining and the prognosis for the race is still good. Threats of storms seem very remote, even surreal, in this peaceful Pittwater refuge. As I look up at Billy from my burrow in the old veranda couch, I can't help marvelling that this scarred, tanned body, this naked creature I love so much, is the same one that only the day before was trapped in a grey suit and laden down with corporate gift bags. Arched now above me, he seems a primeval being, the incarnation of an ancient hero. He feels untamed inside me, a vigorous force that lifts me, trembling and exhilarated, into a new and beautiful world.

'We've been neglecting ourselves, gorgeous,' he laughs through his groans. 'This is what it's all about. This is us!'

And I can't form the words to reply, can only shiver harder, open my mouth further, smile wider, gasp louder.

•

That evening, Billy and I watch the race highlights. *Sentinel* has slipped into third place behind *Atomic* and *Alpha Romeo*. The fleet is opening up, spreading out. Some are hugging the coast, others are seeking better winds and currents forty miles offshore. Brief mention is made of the storm prophecy rumour. The Bureau of Meteorology confirms it still has no grounds to issue an alert.

Our sunny mood has deteriorated and we find ourselves arguing about the washing-up. Grace Cadey has left five messages, demanding to know why I failed to get Moses to the airport. As yet, I haven't called her back. The house feels dead. We're on a downer following our lovely afternoon. We go to bed early but don't sleep much. I pull up the weather satellite images a couple more times, at 23:15 and 00:40. Billy goes for a walk on the beach and spends a long time brushing the sand off his feet when he comes back in.

I wake at 02:40 to find Billy has thrown off the sheets and is sweating badly in his sleep. With the bedroom door closed behind me, I turn on the TV. Juno has hit South Island, and the race leaders have reached Bass Strait. The pictures from New Zealand show whole barns blown away around Invercargill. Cyclone damage is reported as far north as Dunedin. I pull up the satellite feed: Juno looks a whole lot closer to the 50th parallel. Something about the devastation on South Island compresses my lungs.

I just know Juno's turning north.

The Night Duty Officer at Spring Cove takes a while to answer my call.

'It's Petra. What's the latest from AMSA?'

'No new developments.'

'Have you seen what's happened in New Zealand?'

'The Bureau's got the same advice up as before. Nothing for us to worry about.'

'Are you sure? Can you check again?'

'I'm sure,' he laughs. 'Petra, you should be asleep.'

'Just check again, please. Refresh everything.'

The Duty Officer sighs, but he does what I ask, crossing to the weather desk and running the refresh. On my screen, I can just see the edge of his back, but it's enough to know immediately. His body stiffens, and already I'm calling to him, 'Oliver, what is it? What are they saying?'

He comes back to the phone, face pale. 'I swear, Petra, it's only just gone out. Stamped three minutes ago.'

'OK, listen, I don't care. What are they saying?'

He blinks and looks away from the camera. 'It's the works. All Stations alert. Force nine building to force eleven cyclone in Bass Strait from 07:00.'

'Juno?' I demand.

'Yes. Juno. Turning north, swinging up to Taz and on towards Melbourne.'

'The leading yachts?'

'Already thirty miles across.' They'll be right in the middle of the strait when Juno hits.

It's horrific. It's everything Moses said. For a moment I just stand there, dazed. There's a whole lot of pressure building behind my temples. 'You know what to do,' I say curtly. 'I'll be there in an hour.'

Even before I've cut the call, I can sense Billy behind me. He's staring at the images from New Zealand on TV; he's heard the Duty Officer's news. I have to turn round and face him, even though my head feels like it's about to shut down.

'It's happening?' he whispers.

'It's happening.'

Right now I need him to be strong. I need him to be the man I met up a cliff with a broken wrist and an attitude like a bulldozer.

'Then he's right, isn't he?' says my death-defying hero.

'Get a grip, Billy,' I snap, dialling Kirsten's number.

She answers after five long rings. She's in the main cabin, by the navigator's station, looking dishevelled but calm.

'Kirsten, turn around. You could still make it to Eden. At least get close to land.'

'Petra. Sweet of you to call. Moses says hi.'

'The cyclone's coming straight for you. It's happening, Kirsten. It's really happening.'

'I know it's happening. I've got a dozen email alerts from AMSA and your crowd right here. The radio's not giving us any peace either.'

'So you're turning round?'

Kirsten laughs, and although it's a bad line and I can hear all sorts of clatter behind her I still make out the rasp of tension in that sound. 'We're going to win this race. Don't you know that?'

'You're going to kill yourself!'

'That's always the risk,' she says quietly. 'Got to go, honey. Lot of prep work to get done this end.'

Steeling myself against that terrible sense of impotence, I close the phone.

Billy presses his fists against the table until the veins bulge. 'That poor kid,' he whispers.

'Listen to me, Billy,' I say fiercely, gripping his arm and forcing him to meet my glare. 'Storms happen all the time. I can't do anything about the storm. But Moses is not going to die, hear me? I promise you, Moses is not going to die. You'll see he's not real, that he doesn't know shit. When he's standing here in front of you, whole and well, you'll have to admit he hasn't got a clue about us, right? You've got to believe me, Billy. *I am not going to let him die.*'

•

I'd better try to explain why Moses's storm prediction, at least, turned out to be right, against all professional meteorological expectation.

The area of low pressure known as Juno was not the only significant weather feature in the South Sea on 26 December. To the north, centred at that time somewhere south of the Cook Islands – but also drifting westward – was a much larger and more stable depression, designated simply 284.

No one was too bothered by what Depression 284 might do to Brisbane and Sydney when it finally reached the Australian coast. The pressure differential around it was spread over a large area – in technical speak, its isobars were well spaced out – so no major weather shocks were likely. However, 284 was doing what all depressions do: sucking air in from surrounding areas. Such was the scale of 284, it was even sucking in little Juno.

This is where it gets complicated. The sucking of air, for reasons best understood by physicists, does not happen in a straight line. Instead, like the water draining from a bath, it moves in a spiral fashion known as the Coriolis Effect around the depression. And as the air moves, it creates winds. This being the southern hemisphere, the winds move clockwise around the depression. To the south of the depression, the winds are heading west; to the north, they're going east. Depression Juno was located directly south of Depression 284, so at that point 284's winds were carrying Juno due west. And because 284 was also travelling west in parallel, Juno remained directly south of its big cousin. So long as that was true, Juno kept heading west – well clear of Tasmania.

Unfortunately, 284 stopped moving somewhere between Fiji and New Zealand. As the weathermen say, it stalled. Juno kept moving west, until it reached a point where it was no longer due south of 284. And that was when, like a hungry croc caught in a whirlpool, it started moving clockwise around 284. The Coriolis Effect was pulling it north.

The meteorologists didn't see the change at first. They were expecting the southern tip of New Zealand to take a beating from Juno's extremities, so they thought little of the more extensive damage done there. It was only when Juno was well into the Tasman Sea that they spotted the new, curving trajectory on the satellite pics. By 03:00 the depression was accelerating, and the experts gave it just three hours to reach Tasmania. The Australian Maritime Safety Authority issued emergency alerts, and these were immediately broadcast and transmitted to every boat. To be fair to the forecasters, they gave the crews just about enough time to get out of the way of the cyclone. But it's never easy to persuade an experienced skipper to abandon the race of the year without giving it a couple of hours to, well, see which way the wind blows.

Of the 112 yachts competing, only five retire. By the time the rest have understood for themselves that the meteorologists aren't kidding, Cyclone Juno has them firmly in its grip.

If only they'd had good winds early on, most of the boats would have reached Tasmania before Juno struck. Instead, they're strung out across Bass Strait. Sitting ducks.

•

Reaching Spring Cove at 04:10, I first satisfy myself that all four ALBs have received the latest weather and are confident of their own seaworthiness. I check on the fleet status, and receive with dismay but little surprise the news that so few yachts are taking evasive action. Only then do I realise what must come next. For Moses. For my promise to Billy. 'I've got to get down there,' I say, more to myself than to the Duty Officer.

'Petra, this is AusSAR business,' he objects. The Search & Rescue division of AMSA can call on any civilian or military asset available if the situation is serious enough. Inshore coastguards will never be top of their wish list for an ocean storm.

But like a talking doll, all I can say, over and over, is, 'I've got to get down there.'

It's not just Moses. All those lives, any one of them would be reason enough. No way am I standing on a beach waiting uselessly for news this time. I fire up a spare console and run a GPS search on our assets. Donald's four ALBs are scattered about the fleet, ten to thirty miles south of Gabo Island. Our helo is already stationed at Merimbula. By road, that's over 450 kilometres from here.

I call Garden Island. After six long minutes of waiting, they put me through to the Watch Officer. 'This is Captain Petra Woods, Sydney New Coastguard. I need a ride to Bass Strait. Any of your helos heading that way?'

There's silence from the Navy. 'Hello?' I try.

'Stand by, Captain.'

The Duty Officer eyes me uneasily. He has nothing more to do. Nobody's out boating around Sydney at four in the morning. All the action's a long way off.

'Captain Woods?' I recognise the voice, but can't immediately place it. 'This is Commodore Fowler.'

I sit up at that. 'Good morning, Sir.'

'No. It isn't.' He has an entirely different voice now. 'We're in for a shit storm.'

'Yes, Sir. I meant —'

'What's this about wanting to go down there? You're Inshore Coastguard.'

'I can swim just as well in blue water, Commodore.'

'Anyone goes swimming in Juno, they aren't coming home.'

'I have skills that would be helpful.'

'Go back to bed, Captain. You don't have the first idea what an ocean storm is like.'

'If there's a helo heading that way, I'd —'

'Only available Seahawk departed fifteen minutes ago. Go home.'

'Thank you, Sir.' It feels a lot like insubordination and I have to remind myself he's not my boss. 'I guess I'll be driving then.'

'For God's sake, Petra! They're spinning up *Darwin* as we speak. Do you understand how bad it has to be for me to give that order?'

'That's why I've got to go.'

'Please. I'm asking you to think of your father.'

'I'm thinking of my mother, Sir.'

He breathes a heavy sigh down the line. 'You're a fool,' he mutters, and hangs up.

The Duty Officer does his best to slow me down, without actually blocking my way. He hesitates when I ask him to load extra thermal blankets and lifejackets into the fastest of the Coastguard jeeps, and he stalls for ten minutes on an order to call ahead to Merimbula. Finally, when I'm in the jeep and making a last equipment check, he comes running out of the building.

'What now?'

'That presenter guy's on the phone. Says he's a friend of yours and could he borrow some gear?'

'What? Who are you talking about?'

'The one with the hair. Daran Sacs. He's worried his helo might go down in the storm. He wants to stop by and borrow a liferaft and survival pack.'

I switch off the jeep engine and surprise him with a broad smile.

•

The RTV helo is one of the new 'environmentally friendly' Bells. Very sexy paintjob, great fuel endurance and relatively quiet. Ideal for hovering over sporting events, but not the fastest bird in the sky. Four camera lenses protrude from various parts of its anatomy. On board is a cameraman, a producer, a lot of high-tech TV kit, and an ashen Daran Sacs.

The Bell touches down on our helipad at 06:13. I have a stack of equipment waiting to be loaded. One item I'm already wearing. It was delivered by a Navy adjutant just minutes before, accompanied by a note: *Petra, if you must be stupid, at least take this. It will help us find you. Fowler.* It's a tiny radio beacon. Looking it over, I reckon the Navy have got their hands on a technology a hundred times more powerful than our personal locator beacons. The adjutant had orders to strap it to my ankle himself.

'This is going to be all right, right?' shouts Daran over the noise of the rotor. 'I mean, helicopters *can* fly in storms, can't they?'

'It's going to be horrendous, Daran,' I tell him sincerely. His face turns paler still. I load the remaining kit aboard and jump on.

We lift off at 06:21.

•

It takes the RTV helo 98 minutes to reach Merimbula, where we land to refuel. The proximity of the storm is already apparent: leaves race across the runway in a strong westerly; the helo is clamped to the ground during fuelling; our pilot is given a formal caution against proceeding by the airport authority.

The Sydney New Coastguard HH-65 Dolphin is already in the air, as are the three available Navy Seahawks and the two Victoria Police

Eurocopters. I have no choice but to stick with Daran. While he disappears with his make-up case to the bathroom, I pull on my drysuit, then visit the AusSAR Rescue Coordination Centre, hastily assembled in the cafeteria. The Search Mission Coordinator gives me a speedy briefing. His screens show six EPIRBs – Emergency Position Indicating Radiobeacons – and a bunch of personal locator beacons already activated. Four race maydays have come in, with an unconfirmed fifth relayed by a Chilean cargo vessel. They're appealing for every civilian and military aircraft they can get.

According to Donald's reports, the cyclone struck the fleet around 07:20. In the north-east quadrant of the storm, nor'-westerly force eight winds clashed with a strong opposing current in shallow waters, throwing up waves the size of two-storey buildings. The EPIRBs started lighting up soon after. High winds had been causing crews difficulty since 06:15, but the waves didn't become violently unmanageable until an hour later. The best of the boats enjoyed a period of high-speed reaches before gale force winds obliged them to reef their mainsails. By then the skippers all knew the cyclone was coming, even the ones who hadn't been willing to accept the first flashes from AMSA. They may not have been able to avoid it, but they were at least ready to see it out.

That's what they believed, anyway.

My mobile rings as we're climbing back into the helicopter. It's Sam Drauston.

'I have a Sydney water police source claiming Moses Lukoto is on board *Sentinel*,' he says. 'Can you confirm it?'

Now the police believe it? 'I'm working, Sam.'

'Me too. Where are you?' he asks. 'Are you down there?'

The pilot gestures for us to hurry up. Gusts tug at the helo, making it rock alarmingly.

'Got to go.'

'For God's sake, be careful, Petra.'

I cut the call and leap aboard.

We're moving again by 08:07. The moment we're clear of the ground, the wind carries us thirty metres laterally before the pilot can angle to compensate. The weather deteriorates fast as we head out into Bass Strait. Heavy rain hits us soon after. Visibility is low enough to make the cameraman swear and the pilot switch on every nav light and strobe available.

We spot the first yachts six miles south of Gabo Island. They're the ones heading back, in a race to escape the cyclone, hoping to reach the protection of Eden. I count seven that will definitely make it. Four smaller boats are lagging about five miles behind. They're likely to be caught short, but at least they'll be close to shore if they need helicopter assistance. The ocean's looking meaner. Waves are around half the height of the masts, although their slopes are still shallow enough for the boats to ride them without difficulty. The cloud base is just 600 feet, swirling grey, fat with rain. We skim low over the yachts, 200 feet above the wave crests, and head for the black fury to the south.

•

The first victim of Cyclone Juno presented live on RTV to Australia's breakfast viewers is *Galloping Goliath*. She's an 18-metre beauty, and she's lost her mast. The remains of her sails and rigging are spread half across the deck and half in the water, dragging the port side down and giving the boat an added tilt that she really doesn't need. Her crew sit huddled in the cockpit, likely berating each other for not reefing in the mainsail sooner. They haven't managed to get the engine going, probably because the boat's half swamped. Each new wave sinks them a little lower in the water. At the moment they're facing eight-metre seas. From our vantage point, we can see far worse heading their way.

But the crew are in luck. A Navy Seahawk is already hovering overhead. As we watch, a rescue swimmer on a wire is lowered into the sea behind the boat. The crew lash a rope around their oldest member and he leaps overboard. Within four minutes, the rescue swimmer has him in the horse collar, being winched up into the helo.

Daran, looking queasy, steadies himself in the open doorway and speaks as best he can to the millions watching. It can't be easy in this turbulence. Every few moments, the aircraft drops twenty feet or rocks viciously sideways. The cameraman is braced against the back of the cabin. Twice Daran's safety harness is tested by a sudden jerk of the helo, but he manages a good two minutes of commentary before the producer cuts back to the fuselage cameras.

'We can leave these guys to the Navy,' I shout into my head mike. 'They're going to be fine. Let's move south.'

'Are you kidding?' the producer says. 'This is live-action heroics! Pure gold.'

'There'll be plenty more,' I tell him blackly.

He doesn't pay any attention to me, but after a while he comes to realise one winch lift is much like another, and he signals for the pilot to continue south. Daran looks relieved – hovering in this gale is not a comfortable experience. Better to be driving forward.

I'm starting to wonder what good I can do on board a TV helo. Search & Rescue is not RTV's priority, and wasting valuable minutes filming a Navy operation got me seriously wound up. I'm pretty sure, looking ahead, that our pilot's going to throw in the towel before we reach the worst of it. Coastguard and Navy pilots have the training and the motivation to plunge into a cyclone – it's always worth risking your life to save a life. But you've got to be pretty dumb to do it for money and ratings.

The waves are reaching ten metres. They're getting steeper, closing up so it's harder for boats to ride them. The only two yachts in view are still racing, as far as we can tell. They're both on the same reach, both with a single reef in the mainsail and a midsized jib. The crews are dashing about on their jackwires, working the grinders, calling the bigger waves – showing real determination. It's a heartening sight. The first boat I don't know; the second I recognise as *Midwinter*, a seasoned Hobart player with a skipper I'd expect to make it through most weather. As we fly low towards him, he waves once, then clamps both hands back on the wheel.

'Lovely shots,' says Daran faintly, eyeing the monitors. The wind rushing through the cabin has flattened his hair, giving him a strangely aged appearance. 'Lovely, lovely.'

The producer keeps us circling over *Midwinter*. I don't know what he's hoping for – maybe a killer wave to knock them down on live TV – but I'm getting pretty frustrated. Since we left Merimbula, five more EPIRBs have been activated. All the data are coming through on my laptop. Factoring in the maydays, AusSAR now reckon seventeen yachts to be in distress. Everyone's expecting that number to increase. To complicate matters, a swamped Canadian trawler is floundering forty miles east of Gabo Island, and one of our ALBs has had to divert to pull her crew off.

There's perhaps six helos and four fixed-wing planes in the area now. HMAS *Darwin* won't get here for hours. A cruiser from the Tasmanian Police Marine Division is somewhere north of Flinders Island. Two Air Force Orions and a handful of civilian aircraft are on their way, but there still won't be enough eyes in the air to locate all the endangered boats. And even when the GPS interface on its EPIRB is functioning correctly, locating a stricken yacht in these conditions is the hardest part. We could be doing so much more than babysitting a healthy vessel on the edge of the storm.

It's while I'm stressing about this that the pilot turns and throws me this look, points to his intercom jack and holds up two fingers. The producer is completely focused on his screens. Daran is hunched over, feeling sorry for himself, and the cameraman is cleaning the spray off his lens. No one else sees the gesture. I look to my own intercom jack, see a small knob, and turn it to Channel 2.

'Let's keep this between ourselves,' says the pilot, 'but what can I do to help?'

I'm so surprised it takes me a moment to reply. Turning to hide my face from the others, I say, 'The EPIRBs are all south-west of here. That's where we need to be. The more sea we can cover, the more chance we'll have of spotting them.'

'I'll do my best,' he says, switching back to Channel 1.

He gives it a couple more minutes, then taps the producer on his shoulder.

'Sorry, mate. Engines are heating up. We're getting salt in the vents. I have to take her high and stretch her legs some, or we'll be risking engine failure.'

The producer looks irritated, but Daran perks up and says quickly, 'Safety first, yes definitely, buck. You're in charge.'

And next moment we're climbing to the cloud base and circling away from *Midwinter*, setting course for the eye of the storm.

•

It's not long before we spot the first flare. I tap the pilot's shoulder and point. He sees it just before it dies, and banks towards it. The sea below is empty, foul, fearsome. The wind is still building, stretching out the crests of the waves and blowing great dollops of foam across the water. Rain drives hard against the glass. The ocean is turning from warning-black to spittle-white: we've reached Force Ten.

To the south-east, Donald's ALB is battling through the waves. Switching my headset jack from the helo intercom to my HF radio, I select the Offshore Coastguard frequency. 'Coastguard zero-four, this is Petra Woods on RTV-aerial.'

Donald's voice comes back immediately. 'Coastguard zero-four. Where are you, Petra?'

'RTV-aerial currently six hundred feet, two miles north-west of zero-four.'

A pause. 'Zero-four. I have you visual. We're responding to a Mayday in your vicinity. *The Merry Widow*, broken rudder, twelve on board. Do you have her?'

'RTV-aerial. I think we're about to. Stand by, zero-four.'

The pilot is already reducing speed and height, bringing us low over the yacht. Its mast and rigging are bare – not even a storm jib. There's no one on deck. The companionway hatch is closed. As we look on, a washboard slides back and a figure appears, clutching a flare. He raises it, then, hearing our engine, turns and signals urgently in our direction.

The yacht is broadside on to the waves; with no forward motion it's taking a horrendous battering. The crew inside must be suffering horribly at each knock-down. Waves taller than the mast pound against the deck every fifteen to twenty seconds, ramming the boat sideways and down. Despite the onslaught, the figure in the companionway holds his position, determined to keep waving until help arrives.

'RTV-aerial. Yacht in distress below. Negative confirmation of identity. Do you still have visual?'

'Zero-four. We have you visual. Proceeding towards you now.'

I switch back to the helo intercom to tell the pilot what's happening. 'Can you hold this position until they reach us?'

'Affirmative,' says the pilot, real calm. Never mind that we're being knocked around like a fly in a Dyson. I like this guy a lot.

'We can only guess what's going through that buck's mind,' Daran is saying to the camera. 'Clinging on for dear life, praying that someone will come to his rescue . . .' The cameraman struggles through to the end of Daran's piece before thrusting the camera aside and vomiting hard over the floor of the cabin.

They film the arrival of zero-four, and I have to confess to thinking – just for a second or two – about the great PR Sydney New Coastguard's getting from these images. Kirsten ought to be benefiting too, but the Sentinel Bank logo along the side of the ALB isn't so visible from above. Right now, I don't feel too bad about that.

'Zero-four, RTV-aerial. You got them?'

'Zero-four. Affirmative. Thanks, Petra. Let us know if you see any more.'

'Good luck, Donald. Out.'

We hang about long enough for RTV to get their fill of this little disaster. They film the ALB rolling violently in the same waves that are pounding the yacht. A couple more sailors appear, and clamber across the sliding deck. They hang on to the lifelines, shivering, while zero-four manoeuvres around them. Then two of our guys come to the side of zero-four and fling a line to the yacht. Amazingly, the crew catch it first time.

Daran summons up a brave smile for his last words as the ALB tows the stricken yacht east, away from the storm. Already his producer is congratulating him, ecstatic at the great TV they've made.

'I think we might go back now,' says Daran weakly.

'There's a lot more yachts out here,' I say. 'Don't you want to check on the others?'

He cringes. 'Not right now.'

'Daran, Kirsten's out here somewhere. Probably in trouble. Shouldn't we find her?'

'We don't know she's in trouble.'

'Wait. I'm going to call her. OK, Daran?'

He nods miserably while I switch to the satellite link on my mobile and plug the lead into my headphones. Her phone rings and rings, but there's no answer.

I cut the call and get my face in order. I think of my mother's funeral. 'She's in trouble,' I say.

He fidgets hopelessly. 'OK . . .' he says at last.

On his signal, the pilot turns south-west once more.

•

It's carnage. We've only seen the periphery, so far. Climbing to just below the cloud base and pushing deeper into the cyclone, we start to make out the full extent of the destruction.

We count eight yachts in trouble in the space of six minutes, and I call in position reports on each of them to AusSAR. Most still have some control – a triple-reefed mainsail, an engine, even just a storm jib – and they're doing their best to keep the waves on their stern or bows. But these seas are murderous. There's an ALB in amongst the yachts, and even she's struggling. The two super-maxis down there, so enormous from *Giselle*, look as frail as paper junks against the vast expanse of writhing, roaring ocean.

Powered only by a small jib, the super-maxi *Gardens of Suzhou* comes tearing over a wave and narrowly avoids colliding with *Sunkist*. Another wave curls over her and dumps a few tonnes of seawater on her poor crew. She's just about recovered, trying to run with the wind, when she's lifted twenty metres in the air by a bastard of a wave. It holds her up there a second longer, and then she starts sliding forward.

I can't watch.

The wave is so steep, it might as well be a precipice. *Gardens of Suzhou* plunges forwards, her bows fall away, her deck turns vertical and she drops. At first I think she's going to make it – going to land with a bang, but come out all right. Then, when it looks like she can't tip any further forward, her stern tumbles away from the wave and she pitchpoles.

I've never seen it happen to a big yacht. Even the old boys who talk about it so vividly in the Harbour Hazard Bar have probably never witnessed it. But this is real. This is live to the nation. I want to be sick.

The whole yacht cartwheels forward off the wave, landing on her great mast which just snaps. Even from half a mile away, with the noise of the engine and the howl of the wind, I'm convinced I hear the thud of her deck against the sea.

'Get over there,' I'm yelling to the pilot. 'Quick!'

The producer's in shock. He can't believe the pictures he just got. Daran's collapsed back into his seat, breathing like an asthmatic.

By the time we reach *Gardens of Suzhou*, fourteen of the crew have emerged from under her. The keel points straight up to the sky – a token of defeat. Another man pops up by the aft rudder.

I'm already sending HF distress calls to both Navy and Coastguard, and I'm even debating going down there myself. There should be another eight crew at least. Very likely they're trapped by their own safety harnesses under the boat.

Back on the helo intercom, I ask, 'Can you get us closer?' But now another great wave bears down on the upturned yacht. The super-maxi's crew, clutching the edges of the hull, look up at it in terror. One man tries to swim away from the boat, to get clear of the anvil he's trapped against.

The wave does two things. It picks up the crew and flings them sixty metres from *Gardens of Suzhou*. And it piles into the yacht's keel and rudders with enough force to turn her back upright. When the mass of foaming water clears from the deck, we see three more crew, still clipped to the jackwires, gasping and choking but alive.

The mast is not completely detached; its jib-heavy bulk, trailing in the sea, does a useful job of stalling the yacht while the rest of the crew try to swim back to it. Eight of them make it by the time the Coastguard helo arrives. Four others cluster together, some way off. We drop life-rings and a strobe radio beacon to them. The other two, despite a careful search of the surrounding water, we don't see again.

The RTV producer silently gives the signal to move away before the first sailor is winched to safety.

•

'We've got thirty minutes before we need to turn back for fuel,' says the pilot, after a patch of fruitless searching.

Daran nods vigorously. 'Yes,' he says. 'Fuel, yes. Important. Very important.'

I know I should be focused on every single life down there, but my mind keeps coming back to Moses. In the circumstances, we can't use the main radio channels for anything less than urgent communication, so I call up Donald on my mobile. The satellite link takes precious seconds to connect. 'Do you know where *Sentinel* is?'

'Negative. Last known position thirty-eight miles south-south-west of Gabo Island. They've been off the air for two hours. GPS reporting ended the same time, which is worrying. But no EPIRB yet.'

'Where are you?'

'Still towing *The Merry Widow*. Going to be at least another hour before we can get them clear.'

We've moved into an area of completely empty sea. Not a yacht or helo in sight. The pilot is flying an impressive search pattern that makes me wonder if he's had professional SAR training.

'We're going to have a last look for *Sentinel*, then head back to Merimbula.'

'All right,' says Donald. 'Then please stay on the ground, Petra.'

I hang up and go back to searching the sea.

•

When the flare erupts in the sky ahead of us, I understand immediately why the Stellar series was banned in Australia. It's a fireball on a rocket. Brighter than the sun – that's how it seems in those grey and stormy skies. All flares are dangerous if handled incorrectly, but they're unlikely to be life-threatening. The Stellar is something else altogether. The upper casing is steel, to protect the parachute from the searing heat. AMSA reckoned the explosive potential of the charge was enough to punch through a concrete wall. If a helo was overhead, the damage one of those flares could do to the rotor or fuel tank is unthinkable.

But there's no question it helps us locate *Sentinel*.

CHAPTER 11

She's sailing on the mainsail, only single-reefed, like the wind's just kidding around. It doesn't make sense. You don't fire distress flares when you're cruising along on a single reef. OK, there's some problem signs: a drogue slung out on a long line behind to slow her down on the bigger waves; no foresail; collapsed stanchions and a gash along the leeward deck. But still, this boat is roaring ahead, with at least twelve crew spread along the weather-side for balance. They've missed a sked, and maybe their radios are out, but they haven't activated the EPIRB or called in via SatCom. So why the flare?

As we draw closer, however, the state of the crew becomes clear. Their weight's in the right place; they're just about managing, with the keel at full stretch, to stop the super-maxi broaching under all that sail. But their postures don't read well. These are exhausted, injured people, clinging to an uncertain refuge. They respond slowly and clumsily to shifts in balance, enduring the waves that break over them as wretched survivors, not competitors. Only Kirsten, at the helm, looks OK. From the way she handles the wheel, there seems to be a problem with her left shoulder, but she's standing proud, feet firmly planted in the cockpit, placing the boat perfectly to ride each wave.

What a sailor. I have to give her that credit.

There's one other person in the cockpit. I can't see his face because he's lying, huddled and motionless, on the sole.

They've spotted us now, and their reaction just adds to my confusion. One of the guys on deck staggers to his feet: Dermott, clutching the flare. He's waving frantically at us, screaming something we can't possibly hear, like he's afraid we haven't noticed the boat. For a moment I'm nervous he might launch another Stellar towards us. But now Kirsten is turning to us and flicking her hand like she's dismissing us. As we fly lower and closer, I begin to make out that Kirsten is yelling at Dermott, really furious with him. A couple of others are pulling themselves up, facing off against Kirsten through the spray and the rain. And her damaged left arm is jabbing angrily at each of them, underlining whatever it is she's telling them. A savage gust knocks *Sentinel* down – a terrifying action in a boat that size – sending everyone sliding down the deck to the limits of their tethers. When the boat rights itself, the argument just keeps on going like nothing happened.

That's when I get there's a kind of mutiny in progress: Kirsten's still going for those line honours, but her crew have had enough. For a crazy moment, I actually wonder if Kirsten hasn't deliberately disabled the radios and EPIRB, to force the others to keep going.

All of this is hard to take in, and I'm still making sense of it when Dermott gets up again and yells something at Kirsten. Whatever he's said must really anger her, because she takes her eye off the sea and doesn't spot the ugly wave that sneaks under the stern and spins the yacht through the wind like a toy gyroscope, so that the boom comes thundering around and smacks into Dermott's skull.

He goes straight down. He lands face-first on the deck, rolls to the leeward side and hangs there, suspended by his tether. Completely limp. His body bounces and shudders with the boat, while Kirsten struggles to regain control, but otherwise he doesn't move at all.

'Did you get that?' mutters Daran in a deathly voice.

The producer just nods.

'Oh, God,' says Daran. 'Oh, God.'

Sentinel crests a high wave and surfs down the back of it. Two of the crew on the windward side start to edge their way towards Dermott. Then a wave swamps the deck, flattening everyone, and the two men retreat on their stomachs to the windward lifelines. They slump down like broken dolls. No one else moves.

'Why aren't they helping him?' cries Daran uselessly. 'Fuck's wrong with them?'

What I decide to do in that moment is not supposed to be heroic. You don't think like that if saving lives is your job, you really don't. All I'm thinking is there's a guy lying unconscious on *Sentinel*'s deck, and no one's doing anything to help him. I don't really blame Kirsten for that. She's at the helm, and it's not like you can engage autopilot on the side of an eighteen-metre wave. On the other hand, she is the skipper, and I can't see her ordering anyone else to help.

Before I take off the helo headset and replace it with my helmet, I fire off a few brief instructions to the pilot. Low, I insist, as low as possible. And as close to the stern as we can get without risking the rotor on the mainsail and mast. Be ready to adjust power to compensate for the reduction in weight. Immediate protest comes from everyone, but I'm already strapping on my equipment belt, and checking my drysuit is properly sealed and my lifejacket half-inflated.

At the open door, I steady myself against the aircraft frame and try to get a feel for the pattern of the waves, counting the sets to time my jump. We're too high: the impact would be like hitting concrete. Turning to indicate this to the pilot, I see Daran greenly clutching his microphone in front of the cameraman.

'Bucks, you're about to witness an extraordinary act of bravery. This beautiful young lady is going to the rescue of that poor buck down —'

By which time I've pushed the camera away and told Daran to grow up. The image on the little broadcast monitor switches to *Sentinel* once more. Dermott's body lies alone on the deck, a halo of crimson around his head. If they knew for sure he was dead, I find myself wondering, would they still broadcast this?

The pilot brings us closer in and holds a difficult hover almost directly above *Sentinel's* stern. The mast is right in front of us, rising well above the helo. Foam and spray whirl about the boat in the downdraft. We're still too high, but now *Sentinel's* approaching the next great wave. It lifts her fast, bucking with the momentum, towards us. The mast tips backwards and the pilot has to veer away to escape it. A hundred and twenty metres behind the yacht, the drogue is still lagging in the trough, about to be yanked up the wall of water. The pilot rolls us back behind the stern and as the crest of the wave comes towards us, I jump.

Despite the pilot's skill, despite the wave, the drop is still more than twelve metres. Plummeting through spume-filled air behind *Sentinel*, I see the drogue begin its climb up the wave, coursing through the water in wild pursuit of the yacht. It's a large white bag, on the end of a red-striped rope. It seems too close, skimming up the wave faster even than I'm falling.

The impact hurts more than I anticipate, sending a jarring shudder through my pelvis and spine. I'm underwater for crucial seconds, and by the time I surface the drogue is already approaching the wave crest. Furiously, I swim to intercept it. The white bag, a few centimetres underwater, still seems a mile away as it passes me. In desperation I lunge for it.

My fingers find the corner of a strap, scrabble for purchase, and then I'm flying off down the back of the wave after *Sentinel*.

•

It wasn't smart, what I did. High chance I'd miss the drogue, and then AusSAR would have had to waste time looking for me when they should have been rescuing crews. But sometimes you just go with your instinct, and I really didn't feel like I had any choice. Not with Dermott lying there, dead or not dead, unaided by anyone.

The water is so cold. That Antarctic current. I'm skimming along after *Sentinel*, trying to get a better grip on the drogue, and an icy layer is wrapping itself about my neck and head. At least the seals on my drysuit are holding, but I have to focus all my concentration on my fingers to keep them working.

All about me is just this big roar. The crash and bellow of waves larger than I ever want to see again. So much louder than we appreciated in the helo. Like having jet turbines on full whack all around you. Only there's another sound too: the hideous screaming of the wind. Easy to imagine it's this live swarm of creatures, smacking through the air above you, hissing hatred. For the first time, I really understand what my mother must have gone through.

Up ahead, through the stinging horizontal spray, I spot Kirsten waving commands at her crew. It's too far to see her face, but I know already she's furious with me, and I'm briefly afraid she's going to have them cut the drogue loose. I'm not saying she's murderous, but she mightn't mind leaving me treading water a few hours until someone picks me up.

But then two of the crew, young guys from Melbourne that I met briefly at the launch party, make their way to the flat stern and take a hold of the drogue line. They haul it onto a winch and set to reeling me in. The pull of the waves is so violent, it's all I can do just to hold on to the drogue. I'm cursing myself for not bringing gloves, and between the anger of that and the pain in my frozen fingers, I've got just about enough blood curdling in my brain to keep my grip solid until they get me on board. While I'm clambering over the liferaft canisters Kirsten's voice finally becomes audible.

'What the *fuck* are you doing here? You had to go and bring the media, didn't you?' She's yelling back over her shoulder, her eyes always fixed on the mainsail and waves. 'I've been rolled six times, four of my crew are concussed, nine have serious injuries, the rest have freaked out – and you put it all on TV!'

'Dermott needs help,' I stutter.

'The sail that just clubbed him has "Sentinel" written across it in three-metre-high letters. Do you understand what that looked like to the biggest live audience of the year?'

Numb, shivering from the shock of her venom and the cold water trapped in my helmet, I can only say, 'Where's Moses?'

'Is that why you're here?' she demands. One of the crew huddled on the weather side yells a wave angle, and she responds with a neat course correction. 'He's fine. Not a hair out of place in any of the knockdowns. Try worrying about the people who are hurt, first.'

She gestures at the man on the cockpit sole. It's Nolan, the sailing master. His arm lies at an unnatural angle, there's blood on his forehead, and his eyes are closed. Kirsten's criticism hits a nerve in me, and I want to remind her she's talking about PR ahead of a boyfriend with a cracked skull. But my training kicks in and I swallow the bitterness, wipe my visor clear, and check Nolan's pulse. Slow but regular. His breathing is solid – he'll live.

Without another word to Kirsten, I get up there on deck. I clip the tether of my safety harness to the leeward jackwire and then, with the sea throwing us all over the place, I work my way up to Dermott.

He's beyond help. I see that straightaway. It's not surprising, given the size of the boom that took him down. Maybe Kirsten always knew it. Maybe the whole crew did. That's why they didn't go to him. I'd like to think that, although truth is most of them look too shocked, frozen or seasick to do anything.

The side of Dermott's head is just broken. That's the simplest way to say it. There's a lot of blood coming from the mess above his ear, his left eye is gone, and it's clear enough he's dead. But all the same, I do what has to be done – I check for life, initiate CPR, keep hold of hope. When after all there is no life, no hope, I unclip his harness and haul the body towards the cockpit.

'What are you doing that for?' shouts Kirsten, a shrill madness to her voice. 'He's dead, isn't he?'

I ignore her. The effort of hoisting that weight across a rolling deck doesn't leave me any breath for conversation. Every few moments, seawater floods the deck, wrenching at my grip on boat and corpse. Kirsten is doing a good job of keeping our bows into the waves, but occasionally a big one smacks us hard.

At the companionway, I unclip myself, draw back the upper washboard and set about tipping the dead man into the main cabin. I've lowered him most of the way through the hatch before the stench hits me. The long sailbags on either side of the engine block are spattered with vomit. Each bunk in the main cabin holds an injured crew member, strapped down against the next roll. Sue's in the nearest, her knee in a brace and her left thumb bound. The other watch officer, Scott, is unconscious. A large bandage covers most of his head. Of the senior crew only Ryan, the navigator, is still fit for duties. Among the other injuries, he mutters hurriedly, are broken fingers and ribs, a fractured leg, a suspected ruptured spleen, three twisted ankles, a crushed testicle, deep internal bruising, serious lacerations and a detached retina. Raising my visor, I try to imagine the violence of the capsizing necessary to inflict that level of injury on the crew. These people have been tossed about mercilessly. It's not surprising the crew on deck aren't up to much.

Ryan helps me stow Dermott's corpse in the aft quarters. The battery of waves is terrifying below decks, a kraken smashing against the side of our eggshell sanctuary. I ask him about the EPIRB, which he says is broken. When I look unconvinced he swears it's true. Everything got flooded or smashed in an early roll, he says. SatCom, VHF, even the HF. With crew and gear hurled about the cabin, it's not surprising the comms equipment didn't survive. I believe him; you don't mess about once there's a death on board.

Just before I go back on deck, I catch sight of an anxious face in the forward cabin: Moses. Unharmed, as Kirsten said. I throw him a quick smile and climb up into the cockpit.

The howl of the wind is louder than ever. Spume and spray blind me. I pull my visor back down and assess the situation. The cockpit wind speed indicator reads a staggering 68 knots. Kirsten has sensibly locked the canting hull in its neutral position: it's just too dangerous, with the possibility of a gybe at any moment, to commit the yacht to a single tack. But as a result, *Sentinel* is heeled right over, nearly on her side. We're horribly vulnerable to the larger waves.

'This blow is way too strong for the mainsail,' I tell Kirsten. 'We have to take it down.'

'What a brilliant idea,' she scowls. 'Why didn't I think of that?'

I gaze through the spray at the straining sail. 'It's jammed, isn't it?' I say miserably.

'The halyard's snapped. We can't disengage the locking mechanism on the mainsail track without raising the sail to take the strain off the slide. But don't bother suggesting we replace the halyard. Nolan went up there, tried to do it. No one else is volunteering.'

Nolan is still unconscious. The broken arm says it all. Understandable why none of the junior crew wanted to follow him up the towering mast. They must be exhausted, scared, perhaps hypothermic, most likely paralysed by seasickness. The kind of deep gut nausea that lays you flat on the deck, weak as a beached dogfish, barely able to lift your head to vomit.

'I'll do it,' I offer quietly. My words are lost to the storm, but Kirsten knows what I'm saying. She doesn't try to stop me. I'm already clipping on to the jackwire and making my way forward. 'I need some help,' I tell the crew.

Four of them are still able enough: the two Melbourne guys, a Chinese student Kirsten's brought along to help Sentinel Bank's international image, and the outback girl, Martha.

'Are you sure you're up to this?' I ask her, voice strained against the roar of the sea.

She nods. There's this tough survivor's glower in her eyes. She's scared to death, but she's determined to make it.

Martha and the student go forward to ready the storm jib, currently still in its bag and lashed to the rail. The Melbourne guys brace themselves as best they can against the shrouds, then each take hold of a spare halyard.

'Don't drop me,' I say, when there's a slight lull in the wind and the boat comes somewhere close to upright. I clip both halyards to my harness, unclip my tether, and before I can think again I'm soaring up the mast.

They're good sailors, those Melbourne boys, and once they've hoisted me up they make fast one halyard so at least I'm secure, even if the top of a super-maxi mast in a horrendous storm is not a place I'd ever choose to be. The spray's not so bad, although there's more spume, flooding off the wave tops and splattering in great gobs over my visor. But worst is the movement. The wave motion was punishing enough on deck; at the end of a 44-metre lever, every twitch becomes a whiplash. When *Sentinel* is hit by a sudden gust and heels over, I'm torn through the sky and brought to a sudden, agonising halt just above the sea. Clinging to a spreader, my elbows and shoulders are horribly wrenched. A wall of water hammers into me, then I'm racing back upward. No chance to recover before we shoot up the side of a wave and crash down into the trough beyond. *Sentinel* drops four metres through empty air, and the impact when she hits bottom makes the whole mast vibrate. I'm actually stunned. My body feels cracked apart. The harness has bruised and torn at my waist. It's very easy to convince myself Kirsten's steering a deliberately violent course.

Still in place, still breathing. The RTV helo is close by, the pilot making supportive gestures, wishing me courage. That helps a lot. It gives me the strength to reach for the head of the mainsail and unclip the torn halyard before we get knocked down again. This time, the mast goes underwater, taking me with it. I have a moment's nightmare that we're going to capsize completely, and I wonder if I'll have time to free myself from the halyards before I'm 45 metres deep.

But we come right again, and somehow I get the second halyard unclipped from my harness and onto the mainsail. The hard part is over. The Melbourne guys waste no time getting me back on deck, and when Kirsten brings us into the wind they tug on the second halyard to free the mainsail. They give this exhilarating, whooping cheer when the track lock disengages. That encourages a couple more of the crew onto their feet to help. Kirsten activates the mainsheet winch to make the boom fast but even so, facing into wind, the enormous sail is flapping about with frightening force. Pulling it down takes five of us, and it's not easy work. Kevlar fabric whips our faces; our arms disappear in great mountains of the stuff; our footing is constantly tested by the bucking of the deck. But eventually we get it lashed to the boom.

Finally, with the Chinese student hoisting the tiny storm jib, we've got a sensible rig for these conditions. We can bear away from the wind and sail a controlled path through the maelstrom. The wave calls come with more authority now. Martha and the Melbourne boys tidy away the lines and help the sickest crew members back into the cockpit. Kirsten keeps on steering as good a course as anyone could. The boat starts to feel like it has a serious crew again. I give a wave to the RTV helo, grateful to them for sticking around so long, and they head straight off to refuel.

Now and then, we all have to grip something and brace ourselves against a new onslaught. At one point, the whole bow plunges straight into a watery cliff, submerging us for longer than I like to remember. But mostly, we seem to be winning. I glance at Kirsten, who for once is looking moderately satisfied, and we even share a smile, confident that we can sail this boat clear of the cyclone.

That's pretty much the moment when the wave under our bow falls away, spinning us around and leaving us broadside on to the biggest mountain of water I've ever seen.

It towers over us. It rears up; it turns vertical. It chooses that exact instant to break.

And it smashes down on us, a thundering, curling avalanche of steel-hard water that blasts us sideways and over, forcing the mast down until the deck is vertical and we're hanging from our tethers, watching the torrent pour over us, feeling the deck roll further, further, until I notice I can't hear the wave any more and I understand at last that we've turned over.

Tied in place. Trapped by a lifesaving tether. The water's a dark, murky green, completely silent, colder than ever. The reason for the coldness dawns on me: my drysuit is filling with water. A tear in the rubber has rendered the whole thing useless. At least I'm not gasping for air. Somehow I managed to fill my lungs before we capsized. But it takes another ten seconds of waiting, of dazed uncertainty, before I accept that we're not going to roll back upright. The wave is passed, yet the deck is solidly flat above. The only sensation beyond the icy cold seeping into my drysuit is the tug of the harness.

Running my hands around my waist, I locate the harness release mechanism and unclip the tether.

I come to the surface and see the stretch-keel – that magnificent piece of engineering – twisted backward at its blade-thin base. The twelve-tonne bulb has punched straight through the hull, embedding itself in the stern and pulling it downward. Seconds later, the stern has sunk beneath the surface and water has begun to flood the ruptured hull.

There's no way *Sentinel* is turning upright any more.

I draw in a lungful of new air, and drop down under the deck again.

·

We're clustered together in one of the life rafts: Kirsten, unconscious Scott and Nolan, Ryan, four of the injured crew from the cabin, Martha, myself and the Chinese student. On two dives under the boat, I managed to release three people from their tethers. The first two were still alive. The third I tried to resuscitate in the water and then in the life raft. His body now lies beside me, proof of my failure.

Others made huge efforts too. Kirsten unclipped Nolan, got him to the surface and kept his head above water until the Melbourne guys had managed to release and inflate the two life rafts. Martha freed two trapped crew from the jackwires. Ryan brought Scott and the other unconscious crewmember with him when he came out of the upturned cabin. Sue ignored the shattering pain in her knee and thumb to help three more out before she abandoned ship. Even the man with the detached retina risked his life to get the boy with the broken leg to safety. They were heroes. Truly. They did more than could be expected of anyone.

But working on instinct, saving their crew-mates, not one of them remembered there was an extra person on board.

So now I'm leaning out of the hatch of the life raft and clinging to *Sentinel*'s forward rail. 'He's still in there!' I shout at Kirsten. 'We have to get him.'

'Petra, the next wave that hits us will slam us against *Sentinel* and collapse the raft. Then we're all dead, understand? Let go!'

'You brought him here, Kirsten. You're responsible for him.'

'There's no way he's alive. Even if the roll didn't kill him, that cabin will be flooded by now.'

I turn to Ryan. 'Is it flooded?' I demand.

He's busy assembling the antenna of the life raft's emergency radio, totally focused on sending our mayday. 'It was filling fast.'

'But the bow's still above water. He's in the forward cabin, right?' Ryan nods and I look back at Kirsten. 'If he's in an air pocket up front, he's still alive.'

It couldn't be worse timing. A new wave thuds into the hull and we all hear the creaking rip of carbon fibre. Still clinging to the rail, my arms are wrenched as the wave tugs at the raft. When the water clears, the crack in the hull has extended two metres forward. The whole yacht has tilted: the stern is now a metre underwater.

Kirsten shakes her head. 'Petra, this is my raft. Let go before you kill us all.'

I stare at her in simple amazement. Still, after all these years, I don't know her. Sadly, I let go of the rail.

'Thank you,' she says unsteadily. 'Now, let's all —'

And I roll back over the side.

•

I don't look back. There's no time, with *Sentinel* breaking up and filling with water, and besides I can't think about Kirsten and the others now. The only way to get through this is to concentrate on the task, locking all other mental compartments tightly shut. I fill my lungs before hitting the water, then keep going down, feeling my way under the deck, into the cockpit and through the companionway.

It's dark in the water, but that's nothing to the inside of the main cabin. The moment I enter it, I'm completely disorientated. All the lighting has failed, which it shouldn't have done even underwater, but perhaps the crack ripped the electrics apart. I can't see anything, can only feel the painful bumps of my hands and elbows against the infrastructure. My fingers are so numb from the cold I hardly dare reach for my torch. But I'm starting to panic now – stuck underwater, barely knowing which way is up, cutting and bruising myself whenever I move, bumping against the great sailbags suspended all around me. I have to have light.

The first thing my torch beam shows me is the floating body of Dermott. His head wound has turned the water around him, around me, bright red. The shock of the corpse so close up makes me spit out breath I desperately need. But I keep hold of the torch. Pushing myself away from him, using the edge of the navigator's table for leverage, I get my face clear of the blood and work out my situation.

The main cabin is full of water. I pull myself upwards to the sole, searching for air pockets, but find none. Feeling giddy from the pressure at the back of my throat, the need for air, the horror of drowning, my head is close to cracking with the cold. I push my way through the snaking sailbags, and swim fast through that long, long cabin, past the bunks where Kirsten cut her hand and Daran Sacs couldn't remember my name, past the galley where a cloud of coffee granules muddies the water, past the heads and the streaming white strands of toilet paper. Finally, with lungs close to rebellion, longing to inhale anything – even seawater mixed with vomit and blood – I make it through the hatchway into the forward cabin and find air.

It's a tiny quantity, a few litres, but it tastes better than the freshest Pittwater breeze. I raise my visor and suck air in. Droplets of water drip onto my cheek. It's a comforting sensation, which goes some way to relieving the foul headache the freezing water has given me. What doesn't help is the frightening proof that *Sentinel* is sinking. There should be more air in this cabin. For the water level to be so high, *Sentinel*'s hull must be nearly all submerged. I don't want to imagine what it will feel like if she goes to the bottom while I'm still inside.

Moses is not in the forward cabin. I sink my face back into the water and run the torch beam over the crew lockers and medical station. No sign of life. That leaves the wedged-shaped forward buoyancy compartment, normally sealed by a watertight hatch but just now wide open and full of water. Did one of the crew, exhausted and nauseous, leave it unsealed after a routine inspection? Did Moses, terrified by the inflow of water, figure out how to open the hatch in a misguided attempt to escape the flooding hull?

I'm starting to shiver badly now. The first stages of hypothermia aren't far off.

The hatch to the buoyancy compartment is barely large enough to fit through. It's a struggle just to get my shoulders past the bulkhead. To haul the rest of my body into that steeple-like space, I clamp the torch between my teeth, lay my hands flat against the bulkhead and push. The manoeuvre works, but my entry into the compartment is clumsy and unbalancing. My mouth jerks open and I drop the torch. It sounds so stupid. But I've lost a lot of feeling, my body is shaking violently, I'm desperate for air, and it just happens.

It's only as the torch falls away – down through the hatch, through the forward cabin, down into the main cabin – that I realise the boat has completely shifted her position. Gravity shows me what my own sense of orientation has missed: *Sentinel*'s stern has dropped right down. She's hanging almost vertically. Perhaps sinking fast, I briefly imagine, until I remember I'd feel the pressure build. Somehow we seem to be staying afloat. For the time being.

But the main exit is now twenty metres underwater.

Everything is black again. I kick upwards and erupt into air. Lots of air. Enough air to accommodate my head, my neck, even my upward stretched arms. I'm gasping and heaving in that narrow knife-blade of space, making so much noise that it takes me a moment to settle down enough to hear the quiet sobs behind me.

'Moses?' I turn around. He falls silent.

Yellow and blue pinpricks of light pulse underwater. The watch, Billy's Christmas present, is all I can see of Moses. Not even bright enough to illuminate his arm. Something in me goes off the rails for just a moment. That boy's invisible presence in this terrible place – it turns me molten inside.

'Moses, it's me. Petra.'

The sobbing begins again and I feel my way towards him. Not wanting to scare him more by accidentally hitting him, I move slowly, edging my hand through the water to locate him. My fingers brush a polystyrene life preserver.

'Are you hurt?' I work my hand up his life preserver to his neck and then around his head. There's nothing out of place. He might be bleeding a little, but there's no major wound. 'Don't be scared, Moses, I'm here now.'

I reach underwater for the yellow and blue pulses, and find his hand gripping a frame. I ease his tight fingers loose. He's a whole lot colder than me. He hasn't been moving about, hasn't got even the insulation of a compromised drysuit – his body temperature must be dangerously low. By concentrating on these physical essentials, the fundamentals of my profession, I'm just about managing to keep my emotions under control.

I rub his fingers with mine and the sobbing diminishes.

'You poor thing. You must have been so scared.' I put my helmet on his head to slow the heat loss.

'I'm going to die,' he whispers.

'No, you're not. We'll be out of here in a second. There's a hatch just below. It leads straight onto the deck, remember? The crew put the sails through it. We're going to get out that way, OK?' My speech is slurred from the cold. I shake my head to clear it, but that only makes the headache worse.

I can't see him at all, can't read his face, can't detect any body language. 'Moses, you have to answer. Do you understand what we're about to do?'

More silence. A wave thuds hard against the bow, making our little watery cell reverberate.

'Moses! Yes or no?'

'Yes.' It's a feeble sound. I'm not so sure he gets it. I'm going to have to force him out.

'OK, good. Now wait here while I open the hatch.'

He doesn't answer. Giving his arm a squeeze, I take a breath and dive down. Getting through the buoyancy compartment hatch is no easier the second time, especially without the torch. There's no longer any air in the forward cabin, and it scares me to think that this narrow hatch I can't see stands between me and the nearest oxygen.

Pushing that fear aside, I feel my way down to the forward deck hatch and search for the release mechanism. Usually it's a lever of some kind, sometimes a button, sometimes a simple catch. I run my hands across the underside of the deck hatch, feeling for any kind of protuberance.

There is nothing. The hatch is flat, smooth, bare.

Quickly I move my fingers around the edges of the hatch. How do they open it? I've never seen the crew use the hatch. Is there an indented mechanism? A remote lever? What stupid new design has Kirsten used?

My air is running out. I'm starting to get anxious. I have to get back inside the buoyancy compartment within a minute at most. My arm gets caught in the funnel mouth of the spinnaker packer, losing me precious seconds. When it's free again, I search blindly for a toggle, a cable, anything that might be connected to the hatch. There's nothing. The roof around the deck hatch is entirely smooth. Losing all remaining calm, I try hitting the hatch with the heel of my palm, with my elbow, with my knee. I brace myself against a frame and kick it as hard as the water will allow. No movement. The blackness, the cold, the sense of failure and imprisonment, of claustrophobia, they all suddenly crowd in on me and I scream. Underwater, I scream until the sea pours into my mouth and throat.

Horrified at my weakness, I claw back just enough control to fight my way up through the hatch into the buoyancy compartment, scramble to the surface and cough up the water in desperate gasps.

Only when I'm breathing normally once more, when I've stopped acting like a drowning baby, does Moses say again, 'I'm going to die.'

With immense effort, I pull myself together for him. 'No, Moses, that isn't true.' With deadened fingers, I open a pouch on my equipment belt and fish out my mobile. It's waterproof – it should still work, if only I can find a signal.

'It is true,' he says solemnly, while I'm fumbling to redial Kirsten's number. The meagre light from the mobile's screen illuminates his drawn face a little. 'I saw it. You know this. I'm going to die.'

Shuddering, I press the call button.

A huge wave crashes into the bow, making the whole hull vibrate. The balance between *Sentinel* floating and sinking is so precarious, each movement terrifies me. On one side of the scales, twelve tonnes of keel are pulling us down; on the other, the inherent buoyancy of the hull and a tiny pocket of air are keeping us at the surface. The slightest shift in that balance will carry us straight to the seabed. Any further crack in the carbon fibre could be disastrous.

There's no reception.

I wait thirty seconds and try again, but it's still dead. We're a long way from land, and the satellite back-up system rarely works without a clear line of sight. I switch on my wrist transceiver and tune it to the emergency frequency, hoping that Ryan has got the life raft radio working.

'*Sentinel* raft, this is Petra Woods.'

No reply. I force myself to take this slowly. With exaggerated care, I pack away my mobile, then try again.

'*Sentinel* raft, this is Petra Woods.'

This time, an answer: '*Petra?*'

'Kirsten! Kirsten, listen to me. I'm stuck in the forward buoyancy compartment with Moses. The boat's hanging vertical. You've got to come and open the forward deck hatch so we can get out.'

There's no reply at first. I'm suddenly afraid she's lost the radio overboard. But then she says, in this slow, appalled tone, 'We can't even see *Sentinel* any more. She went underwater. How can you still be alive?'

'The bow's not underwater,' I tell her furiously. 'It can't be. You must be able to see the bowsprit at least. Dive down and open the hatch.'

'Petra, we're nowhere near.'

'Come back then! Bloody come back and get us!'

A dreadful silence follows. Then Kirsten says, 'You know that's not possible. Not in this sea. We'll be lucky to stay upright.'

I realise then that I'm choking again. Only this time it's not seawater in my throat; it's desperation. 'Kirsten, how do I open the forward deck hatch? What's the mechanism?'

'Can't you see the red release button on the side?'

'It's pitch black in here,' I scream. 'I can't see a bloody thing!'

A pause. 'There's no lighting?'

'No!'

'Petra, if there's no lighting, there's no power.'

'So what?'

'So the hatch won't open.'

I clutch my wrist tight with my left hand. 'You're telling me you put an electric hatch in your boat with no manual fall-back?'

'Petra . . .'

Another buffet, as one more wave smacks against the bow. This one seems weaker than before, and I start to wonder if we aren't completely beneath the surface now. At the top of a very long, dead boat, hanging down towards the seabed. That final crack that will tip the balance between floating and sinking must come at any moment.

'What about the aft deck hatch. Is that the same?'

'We didn't plan for this eventuality. God, Petra, why did you have to go in there?'

I hear a ripping from below, and I have to force myself not to panic at the sound.

'I've got to go, Kirsten. Good luck with your raft.'

My arm, with the radio on it, sinks back under the surface. I give myself a moment, treading water, then feel for Moses's hand once more.

'Listen, it's going to be harder than I thought,' I tell him. 'The two hatches forward of the mast are locked closed, so we've got to get out through the companionway.'

'I think,' he murmurs, his voice so weak I can hear the hypothermia bite, 'I will die now.'

'No, Moses! Neither of us is going to die.'

'You, maybe not,' he says vaguely. 'Me. God has shown me this. I must die.'

'You're wrong, Moses, you're wrong! You said you would die in Australia.'

'Yes. I will die now.'

'No! We're not in Australia now. These are international waters.' I'm clutching at straws. 'You can't die here! You saw it, Moses. You have to die in Australia. Your god won't let you die here. Say it, Moses! Your god won't let you die here.'

Our narrow watery cell is so black, so silent.

'Say it, Moses!'

Very faintly then: 'I have to die in Australia.'

'Right!'

'God . . .' He's still hesitant. Still letting the icy water numb him into acceptance of imminent death.

'He won't let you die here.'

'He won't let me die here.'

'That's it, Moses. That's good. That's very good. We're going to get out, all right? You with me?'

'Yes,' he falters.

'That's great, Moses.' But my voice trails away, because now I'm think-ing ahead and trying to imagine how the hell we're going to do it. The super-maxi is thirty metres long, and she's hanging more or less vertically. The cockpit covers a third of the yacht, from stern to companionway. We're floating perhaps one and a half metres from the bow. All of which means we have to dive without weights, fins or breathing apparatus nearly two thirds of the length of the boat to reach the companionway. Or more precisely, I have to get an almost full-grown man – who can't swim – to a depth of eighteen metres, in the dark, then drag him back up to the surface before either of us runs out of oxygen.

It's just impossible.

I suck in air that's turning dangerously stale. Then I struggle out of my lifejacket.

Taking it off in this situation is a psychological wrench. Every ele-ment of my training reacts against it. *Never remove your lifejacket. It is Life itself.*

'OK, Moses, are you with me?'

'Yes.'

'Good. We have to get that life preserver off you.'

Silence.

'Moses? Do you understand? We have to swim down to get out, and we can't do it with a lump of polystyrene strapped to you.'

'I can't swim.'

'I know that. Don't worry. I won't let you drown.' My right hand is already tugging at the catches on the front of his life preserver. All three spring open. I thread my lifejacket over my left arm, take hold of a hull frame with my left hand, and grip his shirt front with my right.

'Slip your arms out. I've got you.'

Reluctantly, he does it. As the yellow and blue pulses weave through the blackness, I hear the scrape of his sleeves through the arm holes, the swish of the life preserver against the water. Suddenly, I'm holding him up. It's not easy.

'Try kicking a bit, Moses. It'll warm you up.'

He makes a desultory effort, but the weight doesn't get any less. I'm just too exhausted to support him for long. Pulling him towards me, I let go of the frame to free my left hand. We both start sinking and Moses gasps with panic, but pretty quickly I've grabbed his hand and transferred it to the frame. The moment he feels it he pulls himself up, and we both relax a little again.

'Good. I need to put this lifejacket on you. It's not inflated, so it won't help you float. Just stay still while I do up the straps.'

Now that he has hold of the frame he's ready to obey. He lets me fit my most treasured piece of equipment over his head, and zip up the front. Once I've pulled the straps as tight as they'll go on his too thin frame, I grab hold of his discarded life preserver to give myself a moment's break, then say, 'That's it, Moses. We're all ready.'

'Yes,' he says.

I have to rest just to get the strength to speak. 'In a moment, we're going to swim very hard down through the cabins until we're clear of the boat. Try to kick as much as you can – it will help us get there faster. If your ears start to hurt, pretend to swallow something. The most important thing is you don't hold on to anything, OK?'

'OK.'

'Good. Take a deep breath.' He does. I try to work out how much less time a lungful of this depleted air will give us before we black out.

'Breathe it right out. Now breathe in again. And out. And now, for the last time: take a big breath and hold it.'

He does it loudly. 'Here we go.' Wrapping my left arm around his back, I take in my own last lungful, and pull him down into the dark, dismal water.

Just getting Moses through the compartment hatch is hard enough. I go first, leading with my feet, keeping a firm grip on his arm. When I pull him down, the lifejacket gets caught, and we both use up precious oxygen getting him free. In the first cabin, he bumps into the forward rudder stock, and the unexpected collision has him writhing in my grip. Down below is a faint shimmer of light: my torch is still on, although its beam is getting lost in the sailbags. All the same, it's a useful direction aid and I kick hard towards it, dragging Moses beside me.

He's kicking sporadically. Now I'm wishing I hadn't given him that instruction, because most of the time he just kicks me. He doesn't mean to, but my ankles and shins take a battering at a time when I really can't afford any more weakness.

We plough on down into the long main cabin, and my ears start complaining. I clear them, and hope Moses is managing to do the same. Something gashes my arm. Something else catches around Moses's shoulder, and he wriggles wildly to free himself of it. His thrashing dislodges the helmet, which disappears into the gloom. The long sailbags crowd around us, demanding further effort to push past them. Sometimes they give way, sometimes they don't. It's impossible to know, in this blackness, which path to take through them.

By now, there's a clamping pressure on my chest. I can't help thinking what this depth is doing to us. Twenty metres down, our lungs will be compressed to a third of their natural volume. In some people, the tissue starts ripping well before that point.

I have to just not think about this stuff. We're still only halfway down the main cabin.

It gets harder and harder to kick. The pressure, the depletion of oxygen in my bloodstream. The carbon dioxide, the cold, the exhaustion. I can't even feel pain from Moses's shoes any more. Just dull sensations around my ankles. The light seems dimmer. My brain has slowed right down and I crash into the corpse before I've even remembered it's there. My face collides with Dermott's chest, and in my appalled shock I start back and lose my grip on Moses.

The corpse must have been snagged on a bunk, because now it drifts slowly upwards. The dark shape slides past my face as I try to locate Moses. I feel a current on my neck and turn just in time to take a direct hit in the mouth from Moses's thrashing fist. His terror propels him back upwards. Dazed from his blow, still reeling from the collision with the corpse, it takes me a moment to react. When I do, I can barely see him, but I reach out and catch hold of his leg.

So exhausted, so gone, I've barely enough strength to grip a bunk and pull him back down. My chest feels awful – like it's cracking along a thousand tiny fault lines. I need to breathe so badly. Strange grunting sounds are coming from my throat. My head, racked by the cold, is turning liquid, soupy, primordial.

I feel strangely irresponsible.

'Come on, Moses,' I think I say. And I imagine a friendly response from him. He smiles at me – a clear smile that dazzles me through the darkness – and settles back happily in my arm.

'Come on, then,' I smile back at him. 'Time to go on deck.'

It's strange, that brief hallucination, because I also remember very

277

clearly those last three metres down to the companionway. How they tore at my chest. How Moses fought to get away from me. I remember seeing my torch caught on the navigator's station, feeling that its light was the only thing keeping me going. And then the paleness around the companionway, the different shade of darkness, the open sea.

And as we made it into the companionway, I remember most of all Moses gripping the steps with both hands and clinging on. His face was just visible now. I could see the horror and anguish and ear-pain in the open mouth, the noiseless scream. As my foot stamped on each of his hands, I even imagined the words I would use to explain later why there wasn't the time to negotiate, to prise off his fingers in a more gentle way, why this brutality was necessary.

Then I pulled the tag on the lifejacket air canister, and hugged him close as he flew up to the light.

•

We cling to each other with the bowsprit between us. Moses is balanced on *Sentinel*'s knife-edge bow; my feet have found a kind of hold on the rail. The larger waves threaten to knock us off, and sometimes they batter us against the bowsprit, but they never succeed in breaking our grip on each other. I will hold this boy safe until the end of the world.

There's no sign of the two life rafts, nor any other vessel, aircraft or person. Only the continuing storm. The vicious breakers. Both of us are close to the edge with hypothermia and sheer exhaustion. Moses has progressed to a level of shivering so violent I'm in actual pain from his shuddering grip. His speech is slurred, his reactions sluggish. One by one, the smoke flares from my equipment belt have been ignited and depleted with no result. Our situation might seem desperate, but it doesn't feel that way to us because we never once stop thinking of how we were, so recently, trapped in that horrendous sinking cage we now have beneath our feet.

Sentinel may still go down. We may lose our last foothold. But even floating on the Tasman Sea like my mother is a thousand times better than being stuck in that lightless watery cell. We're bruised, frozen, exposed, thirsty, lost. But we're pretty relaxed about all that.

And, of course, we have Commodore Fowler's miraculous beacon.

When *HMAS Darwin* makes her grand, wave-chewing entrance, we just smile at each other and say nothing.

•

They're using a loudhailer to communicate with us, but their words are getting lost in the shrieking wind. It doesn't matter what they're trying to say. They're here.

The ship has manoeuvred to protect us from the worst of the waves. At first it took them broadside on, but even a frigate has a hard time in these conditions, and they had to turn their bows into the wind, keeping us to stern. The huge waves that have been pounding us for the last ninety minutes now break apart on the frigate's prow. There's still a lot of choppy water, spray, foam, but at least we've got some respite until they can pick us up.

That operation is not going to be easy. There's no helo on deck, so the easiest option, winching, is out. The storm is still generating waves twelve metres high: they can't just send a RIB out to us. And there's no way, in this turbulent ocean, they can come any closer than they already are. Even with clear sea between us, I'm worried the next big wave could lift four thousand tonnes of military hardware right onto our heads.

As it turns out, they've come up with an easier way to get us aboard.

A light flares on the lower stern deck and a single orange rope shoots over our heads. Caught by the wind, it doesn't fall quite close enough, and I have to go swimming once again to retrieve it. More loudhailer instructions. All still lost to the elements. Back on *Sentinel*'s bow, I find it hard to keep my balance as I haul in the rope. The solution is to lean against the bowsprit, relying on Moses to hold us both in place while I pull.

By now we can hear the added growl of the returning, refuelled RTV helo over the noise of warship and weather. Moses waves to them while I lash the rope to the bowsprit; it takes a pinch on his arm to regain his attention.

'We have to go one at a time,' I instruct, my words distorted by my shivering jaw. 'Don't worry, it won't break. Just hold on and keep moving – you'll be fine. Don't look at the helicopter. Concentrate on the ship. And don't look back at me, OK? Hold on tight, and keep moving.'

Moses nods. His shivering seems to fade away. Briefly, I fret that his body has passed to the next, more dangerous level of hypothermia, where the muscles give up warming themselves and turn rigid with cold. But then he smiles the confident smile of the saved. His head ducks towards mine as if he's going to kiss my cheek. Instead he sort of rubs his nose against my forehead. I feel, for a second, as if it is him who has rescued me.

Well, then, that's it. That's when it happens.

Moses turns, with remarkable agility given his condition, and faces the warship. He straightens his back and raises his chin. Then, as if nothing could be more natural, he does the thing that astounds a nation.

Arms spread wide, he steps out and walks over the sea.

I'm allowed just six seconds to witness the miracle, before a sudden blast of vengeful water from behind is followed by unconsciousness.

•

I didn't see the wave that knocked me out. Too busy watching Moses, like everyone else. I have only this vague impression of rushing, tumbling water. It must have whacked my head against the bowsprit, then flung me deep down.

When I come to and find myself caught underwater, all I can think is, I shouldn't have taken off my lifejacket. The depleted buoyancy of my torn drysuit isn't enough to pull me out of whatever current has a hold on me. Now here I am, ten metres down, and I'm going to die because I didn't follow the most basic of rules.

My mind is all over the place. Maybe it's the exhaustion, maybe it's the stun. The idea of swimming, of saving myself, never comes. I look up and see the waves – so angry and violent, yet so silent from down here. This is the second time I've been stuck deep underwater, and I convince myself that this must be the way I'm supposed to go. If it happens twice in one day there's obviously no point resisting Fate. Besides, down below there are welcoming lights – two sets of lights growing brighter by the second. They make me smile.

It is only as a Navy diver grabs hold of me, thrusting a mouthpiece between my teeth, that I realise what the lights are.

•

They lead me, still coughing up water, still retching, still blinking with wonder, from the submersible dock to the bridge.

'Get a message to Captain Woods' father,' orders Commodore Fowler. 'No doubt he's watching whatever those idiots up there are broadcasting. Let him know she's safe.' He turns his granite face towards me. Already, one of his officers is kneeling with a switchblade, removing in a single neat slash the radio beacon from my ankle. 'Petra, I think we'll call this quits.' The slightest hint of a smile is quickly suppressed. 'Well, for goodness' sake, is someone going to take her to the sick bay before she dies of hypothermia?'

CHAPTER 12

Not until much later do the *Darwin* crew allow me to watch the RTV broadcast that has snatched the breath of the nation.

The focus of the media's attention lies asleep in a temperature-controlled cot, an IV drip in his arm, a facemask delivering warmed, humidified oxygen into his lungs. Moses has hypothermia, but beyond that he is simply exhausted, the Medical Officer assures me. Once I'm satisfied there is nothing more serious wrong with him, I let the M.O. strip me and dry me and wrap me in a thermal blanket.

'I'm afraid, with suspected hypothermia, we have to take a rectal temp—'

'I know, I know. Just get on with it.'

While he's examining the bump on my head and shining light beams in my eyes, the divers who picked me up stop by to report the final sinking of the yacht. They'd been dispatched to check for bodies still tethered to the *Sentinel* deck, only to see me come tumbling unconscious off the prow. They're on a high from having saved a life when all they'd been expecting to do was recover the dead.

After I've been checked over and patched up, the crew feed me hot stewed apple and try to make me rest. When they accept that I'm not going to sleep, a warrant officer lends me a pair of grey jeans and her favourite sweater, and they attempt to explain what everyone has just seen. But none of them can get a grip on the story, and they give up and refer me to the RTV download.

Daran's team caught the whole struggle with the mainsail, and it makes awesome viewing. Close-ups of Kirsten, myself, even Martha, give a real sense of what we went through. Then, while the RTV helo heads off to refuel, the feed changes to interviews at Merimbula with a handful of rescued sailors. They talk a lot about family and brave Navy rescue swimmers, and how they're not going to let this put them off doing something equally dangerous next year. I hate hearing survivors celebrating their escape when there are dead bodies still floating out there, and I skip forward ninety minutes to the reappearance of Daran Sacs, back in the air, excited as never before.

'Bucks, it's been confirmed, *Sentinel* is gone. But we've just heard from *HMAS Darwin*: they've found Petra Woods alive! We're going to bring it to you *right now*!'

This is where it gets confusing. Because, when they reach us, something's missing from the picture. The frigate's off to one side, and there's Moses and me clutching the bowsprit, visibly shattered. Nothing else but spray and foam and angry grey water.

'Goodness, bucks, do you see who that is?' comes Daran's voiceover. 'That's young Moses Lukoto, our very own prophet. Did you know he predicted this storm? And he still sailed right into it, the brave little buck!'

In a moment, I'm thinking, the crew on *Darwin* will fire the orange rope over our heads and I'll go swimming to retrieve it. But now I see the rope is already there, lashed to the bowsprit. And I'm struggling to make sense of the picture, because I can't see anything attached to the rope.

'Look, he's kissing Petra on the forehead. He's turning around now. Doesn't he look calm, bucks? Wait, what's he doing? Hard to see with all this spray. He's . . . He's just stepping out . . . He can't be . . . Holy shit, what the *hell*?'

Because, to the unsuspecting eye, it's incomprehensible. It's extraordinary. It's impossible –

With waves breaking and foam billowing all about him, Moses is stepping out onto nothing, is walking across the sea toward the frigate. Is *walking*.

'Jesus Christ!' exclaims the cameraman.

'Well – *exactly*,' cries Daran.

I was there when it happened. I pulled the prototype RX582 in myself, lashed it to the bowsprit, watched the guys on *Darwin* draw it taut and adjust its height to give us a steady, flat walk to safety. I felt the tug of it against *Sentinel*'s submerged bulk as the waves tested its extraordinary flexibility to the limit. I *know* there was a bridge. But even I can't help blinking at this visual trick, this apparent – transparent – miracle.

•

'The Press will be all over him,' warns Commodore Fowler from the cabin door. 'We've issued a statement explaining the plastic bridge, but that image will play and play. Every disaster needs a feel-good story. It's going to be tough for you.'

I freeze the download on an image of empty, chaotic water, left behind when the bowsprit finally slipped beneath the surface. The same wave that knocked me down tipped the balance for *Sentinel*, exacerbating the hull damage just enough to take the great yacht to the bottom of Bass Strait. RTV's camera, redeployed to search for me, failed to capture Moses boarding the frigate or the crew hurriedly severing the RX582 ropes tethering *Darwin* to the plummeting yacht: to the nationwide audience, the Galilee illusion is maintained.

'Tough? Do you know what I've just been through?' The exhaustion of it all shivers through me then. 'A little media attention – I think I can handle that.'

A quick, slight gesture sends the warrant officer away. Fowler approaches with an uncertainty that makes no sense. He takes the chair beside me, dusts the rim of his collar with an unconscious finger. 'Your father's had a stroke,' he says abruptly.

I actually laugh. We're in the middle of Bass Strait, facing the worst storm I've ever known. My father is hundreds of kilometres away, safe on land, and for a couple of seconds in my confused mind radio communications and satellite telephones do not exist. 'What are you talking about?'

His face carries a solemnity more vulnerable than the professional mask of command. 'We called to let him know you were safe. A nurse answered his mobile. It was the shock of seeing you jump into the sea. Into danger. He's going to be all right, Petra.'

'He's . . . he's conscious?'

Fowler nods. 'He's in Mona Vale hospital. They're taking good care of him.'

Something breaks. 'How?' I cry. 'How can you possibly know he's going to be all right?'

'There's only one helo,' he says, not answering. 'In normal circumstances we would fly you back to Sydney . . .'

Though I'm close to lashing out, that incomplete sentence activates some neural pathway which overrides all else: 'No, of course, it must keep searching.'

'We'll put you on board next time it touches down. We can't divert for you, but the helo will likely call at Merimbula at some point to drop off survivors and refuel. You'll be able to get a plane from there.'

'It's my fault? I did this to him?'

'Petra, you saved that boy's life today. Quite possibly *Sentinel*'s whole crew would have perished if you hadn't intervened. Your father's strong. He's lost some movement in his right side, but often that's reversible.'

'It's my fault,' I whisper.

'You couldn't have made him prouder.' Fowler stands. 'Be ready to leave at five minutes' notice. And don't worry about the boy. We'll get him back to Sydney, soon as he's ready to travel.'

I look up at him, at his weary, always-ready eyes. 'Would you have done it? Would you have jumped?'

He turns away before responding. 'You and I aren't in the same business.'

•

The messages start coming.

I'm back in the air, skimming low over those same waves. The storm has passed and the force has gone out of them, but darkness gives them added menace. The Seahawk crew are exhausted; they work doggedly with searchlight and winch to recover whomever they can. They thank me politely for my offer of help and then order me out of the way. They have their procedures, in which a civilian can play no part other than rescue subject. I crouch at the rear of the cabin, pressed between the thermal blankets of two shattered, shivering, incredibly fortunate race sailors.

On behalf of everyone at ABC, may I be the first to congratulate you on your courageous actions this morning. We would very much like to interview yourself and your remarkable young friend Moses, who . . .

One of the sailors asks me for a cigarette. Over the roar of the engines, I tell him it's unlikely the Navy permits smoking on board their helicopters. He clutches his thermal blanket tight around his neck and frowns in the reddish glow of the single illuminated bulb. He has spent six hours in a half-flooded life raft. He can be excused a frown.

You mad woman! How dare you go off to Bass Strait without me? Just because I bust my ribs doesn't mean you get to leave me behind! Darling Petra, we're all so glad to hear you're OK, but please never scare us like that again. There's a nice safe desk waiting for you at Spring Cove, so hurry back.

They've found a sailor everyone believed drowned. His personal locator beacon has saved his life. From the back of the cabin, we watch the rescue swimmer clip on to the wire and then disappear into the night. It takes him just over three minutes to recover the man. Conditions are calm enough to make the hover comfortable. When the sailor is brought aboard, he's unconscious. I flout military rules briefly to help strip him of his wet clothes, steady his breathing and insert a drip.

Congratulations on the rescue of Moses. Would have been a shame to see him die the day he was proved right. Sam.

At Merimbula, an ambulance is waiting by the helipad for the unconscious sailor. The other two survivors are introduced by the AMSA team to local residents who welcome them and promise them a hearty meal and a warm bed. Mobile phones are proffered, calls are made to wives and mothers; once away from the hastily requisitioned fuel bowsers, cigarettes are handed out and lit.

Big, big well done, darling. We got fabulous footage of you. Even if you did make me quite sick. Of course we'll need you back, and particularly that extraordinary boy. Going to be the interview of the century. Big, big fame, I promise.

'There's a Lear headed to Sydney in twenty minutes. Belongs to a hedge fund manager named Grant Wilson, who right now is feeling particularly grateful to the sea-rescue community. We'll tell him what you did out there: I'm sure he'll be glad to have you along.'

We didn't know you were still alive. How could we? She went under-water! Petra, thank God you're alive. But everything else, what a disaster. You shouldn't have come. Bringing the cameras – you ruined everything. I don't mean that. Oh, it's so wonderful you made it. I would have saved him. If you hadn't played the hero, I would have got Moses out of there. Oh, God, God. I just spoke to Dermott's family. The poor guy, he didn't deserve that. His mother's hysterical because the body's gone. You've got to come to the funeral with me, hold me together. We were doing so well, we were flying! Remember it was me who helmed that boat for three hours through the storm before you swanned in and stole the show. Look, babe, you're the best, OK? I love you so much. But I lost four crew. I feel frozen when I say that. I lost four crew. Call me. I don't mean any of this, you know that. Except about loving you. I love you, sweetie.

Though it brings me close to vomiting, I listen to her message again, and then a third time, desperate to find the hint of contrition that simply isn't there. She doesn't seem even to recognise what she's done.

Grant Wilson swears he is never getting in a boat again. Throughout the flight, he remains huddled in his cream leather seat, clutching a lifejacket despite having given the pilots strict orders not to fly over the sea. Four times already, he has called the cockpit to demand assurances that the storm is nowhere near our flight path. Now he stares blearily at me and says, 'You do it for a living? You must be insane. Come work for me. We need a facilities manager. You won't ever have to go near the sea.'

Captain Woods, on behalf of everyone at the Consulate I'd like to thank you for your brave actions in aid of a South African citizen. I look forward to seeing you and making new arrangements for Moses's return home when you're both recovered.

Grant's shoulder is bandaged. His cheek trembles sporadically. The five members of his race crew fit to travel are seated around us. None of them unfasten their seatbelts at any point in the flight. It is possibly the smoothest, calmest journey of my life.

I'm so proud of you. And I'm waiting for you. However long it takes you to get back, I'm right here at Saaremaa, waiting for you. I love you.

•

My father has been given a private room. He doesn't know it, but the reason for this privilege is clinical isolation. It's not the transmission of disease that the doctors fear, but knowledge.

'It was shock that induced the stroke,' I'm told in a small office on the third floor of Mona Vale hospital. 'We've told him you're fine, but beyond that we've kept him in the dark. This stuff the media are saying about him could easily aggravate his condition.'

'What stuff?' It's a strain just to keep standing, let alone interpret this new factor. I feel a millimetre away from collapse.

The two junior doctors eye me uneasily. 'You don't —' begins one.

'Go and see him first,' interrupts the other.

It's still early. The night has receded, but sunrise is a few minutes off.

•

My father's room faces the ocean. The blinds are up: bright light will soon pour in. The wall-mounted bracket that should hold a TV is empty.

'They won't even let me have a radio,' complains my father. His words are slurred by the paralysis in his right cheek. The distortion reminds me of hypothermic Moses. 'They're treating me like a child.'

He is, in that pre-dawn light, the colour of bleached seaweed long dead. His navy blue pyjamas are buttoned to the top of his chest. The air is hot, and he has cast off all the bedding apart from one sheet.

'You need the rest, Dad. You've had a serious episode, and you need to be calm.'

'Is it over?'

'The storm? Yes. It's over.'

'There were deaths?'

'Dad, you don't need to worry about —'

'Petra, you can gloat all you like, but you won't patronise me!'

Gripping the end of the bed, I whisper, '*Gloat?*'

His breathing is heavy, uneven. 'I saw that man hit by the boom. He died, didn't he?'

I nod slowly.

'And before that. The super-maxi that pitchpoled. There were fatalities?'

'We don't know.'

'So there were,' he says bleakly.

'No, Dad. We honestly don't know yet. The Navy and the Coastguard have done a great job finding people. You don't need to worry.'

The first shard of sunlight spears the back wall. Outside, the new day is obscenely calm.

'I will not accept that child is the Lord's prophet.'

'Please, Dad, don't talk like that. It doesn't matter now.'

'It doesn't matter?' His right hand claws uselessly at the sheet. 'I sent those yachts into a storm and it *doesn't matter?*'

'You didn't send them. They chose to go. Look, we shouldn't talk about this now. You need to rest. Please, it's over, get some sleep.'

'How many died?'

'It was not your fault, Dad. Any grounded person would have dismissed Moses in the exact same way.'

'Tell me the number.'

'There is no number! Maybe two . . . three even . . .'

'Not more?'

I look him in the eyes as the sun lifts above the horizon and blinds us both. 'Not more,' I say.

•

'They're not quite calling him a murderer, but the tone is vicious. Every reporter wants to know why the Safety Committee under your father's leadership failed to heed a clear warning.'

I've already heard the essence of the media's attack on my father from the hospital doctors, but it is not until I reach Spring Cove that I'm able to extract the full story from Stuart.

'That's absurd! Why should a responsible committee cancel a race because a kid claims to have prophesied a disaster?'

'Doesn't look so absurd now.'

Matthew comes in. 'Ms McKenzie is on the line.'

I shake my head. 'I can't. Not right now.' Stuart raises an eyebrow. 'Possibly never. She left him, Stuart. Just abandoned him.' I hesitate. 'I don't know what we'll do about funding.'

Waving Matthew away, Stuart goes to the windows and closes the blinds.

'What are you doing?'

'When did you last sleep?'

'There are too many things to deal with,' I say, starting towards my desk. 'Donald's still out there and —'

'The ALBs are fine.'

'The media . . .'

'Will wait. Petra, get some rest.' He leads me to the couch. His gentle voice seems to offer a peace I can't resist.

'Just twenty minutes,' I concede.

The room fades.

•

Moses is standing over me.

The dryness in my mouth, the stiffness in my side — I already know I've slept far too long. Moses's presence here, in Sydney, only confirms it. Focusing with difficulty on the wall clock, I see it is already 16:28.

'You're tired,' Moses observes cheerfully. He's wearing blue overalls, far too big for him.

'You're conscious,' I mumble. My throat feels like brick dust. Then

I'm upright and hugging the life out of him. 'When did you get back?'

A uniformed arm comes into view. Lieutenant Neil Loak hands me a glass of water. The taste of Spring Cove plumbing is familiar and reassuring.

'Thank you.'

'You're welcome, Captain.' He smiles. 'Moses was delivered by air to Garden Island two hours and forty minutes ago. In that time he has undergone a full medical examination and scan. The M.O. is happy to release him to you, on condition that he does nothing arduous for at least a week. No sports, no travel. Is that acceptable?'

I step back from Moses, and look him over. He seems completely untouched by his experience. 'How are you feeling?'

'I'm glad you didn't die,' he says, with big, serious eyes.

'Well, you didn't predict I would, did you?'

He shrugs. 'I'm still glad.'

'Are you hungry?'

'Mr Neil gave me fishcakes.'

'It was my pleasure,' says the Lieutenant. 'I must head back. A lot of balls in the air just now.' A pause precedes his shy laugh. 'I'm sorry you didn't get to use our new bridge.'

•

Matthew offers to take Moses clothes-shopping in Manly, and while they're gone I head down to Comms to find Stuart.

'You should have woken me up.'

'Nothing for you to do. It's all over. The ALBs are on their way home.'

'Casualties?'

'Yes. But none for you to worry about now.' An echo of my own words. 'Something else, though, needs your attention . . .'

He calls Carole, who comes over with a letter in her hand.

'What's this?'

'The answer to our funding problem,' says Stuart. 'Did you know you've become a hero?'

'We've had more money donated by the public since you climbed aboard *Sentinel* than in the whole of the last four years,' says Carole.

'Every TV channel is begging to interview you and Moses.'

'No,' I say immediately.

'They know there was a bridge . . .'

'But he's still the kid who walked on water . . .'

'. . . *and* correctly predicted the storm: he's a major celebrity.'

'It's a fund-raiser. Daran's offering great terms.'

'RTV will match public pledges, cent for cent.'

I stare at them both, overwhelmed by their stereophonic persistence. 'He's a kid who's been to hell and back. I can't believe you're even suggesting this.'

'Two hours, that's all. Right here in this building.'

'Do the show, and we won't even need Kirsten's sponsorship.'

'I am not going to exploit Moses. That's immoral!'

Stuart's eyes turn serious. 'Petra, we save lives. We can't do that without funding. You want to know what immoral is? Immoral is passing up an opportunity to secure a major injection of funds for Sydney New Coastguard.'

'Which is worse?' adds Carole. 'Giving a kid a fun experience in front of a camera, or leaving people to drown because we can't afford to maintain our boats?'

They're becoming quite a team, those two. Odd that I haven't spotted it before. 'Thanks for the image,' I mutter.

'Just trying to put it in perspective.'

●

The generator is running at Saaremaa. The house is a welcoming glow of light. Billy is waiting for me, just as he promised. Seeing him standing on the beach, I want to leave *Giselle* to Moses and dive into the water before we've even reached the mooring. I haven't called him: this has to be a real encounter, our moment of renewal.

I come out of the sea and run up the beach into his arms. 'He's alive!' I cry. My triumph over superstition. My vindication. 'You can feel his solid flesh. You can listen to him breathe. He said he would die but he didn't! He was wrong, Billy, wrong. He's alive, and you and I are going to be together till we're ninety!'

A voice comes from the veranda. 'That's great, honey,' says Kirsten.

She's silhouetted in the doorway. Though Billy is smiling and hugging me, and agreeing with it all, my joyous homecoming disintegrates.

'I have to bring Moses in,' I say dully. Pulling free of Billy, I grab the surf rescue board and run back into the sea.

They're both at the water's edge when I return with Moses. Standing close together, like girlfriend and boyfriend. Kirsten's left arm is in a sling: a torn muscle in her shoulder. It makes her look vulnerable for once, all the more appealing to men like Billy. I steady the board for Moses to get off. Then I don't know where to walk – between them, around them, straight to Billy, straight back into the water. Instead I pick up the board and hold it like a shield so they both have to shift out of the way.

At least they move in different directions.

With my back to them all, I say, 'Can someone give Moses a sandwich?'

'Sure, P.'

'Yes, of course, doll.'

I cry in the shower. I don't know why. It's ridiculous.

•

They've been drinking together. There are empty beer bottles on the kitchen table. It's insanely unreasonable to find fault in that, and yet I half expect to discover my bed rumpled and soiled. I dress in big, shapeless clothes, wrapping my wet hair in a faded scarf. I find an old tub of moisturiser and smear the stuff unevenly across my cheeks. None of this makes sense. It's just what I do.

On the edge of the veranda, I sit with arms locked about my knees. My bare feet feel cold.

Billy crouches beside me and I let him kiss me. More than that: I kiss him. I don't lift my arms or make a sound, but my mouth does everything it can to communicate all the words and hugs and smiles and love I've been saving up for him.

Kirsten squats on the sand in front of me. She has a scary energy about her eyes. Flickering. Too bright. Not surprising after what she's been through – after the people she's seen die. With this big grimacing effort she removes her left arm from the sling. Then she takes my feet in her hands and rubs them. Like she can read my mind. I can't help shivering.

Moses has a smoked chicken sandwich in his hand. He's leaning against the pillar on the other side of the veranda, watching us. 'This is nice, isn't it?' I say, hearing the artificial note ring loud in my voice.

He doesn't answer. He looks out across Pittwater. After Mum died, my father used to stand in that exact spot and stare out with the same melancholic intensity.

'Very nice,' says Kirsten. She straightens up and sits on the decking beside me, massaging her torn shoulder. 'Best friends, back together.' She waits just long enough to pretend she's moved on to a whole new line of thought, then says, 'I'm going to have to take Moses.'

'You're bloody joking.'

Her jaw twitches. 'He is *the* survivor. We need this.'

'Billy, will you take Moses inside, please?'

Billy frowns. 'Sure, P,' he concedes. Somehow, he breaks out a lovely smile for Moses and lures him inside with the promise of an old Playstation game.

When the door's closed, I turn on Kirsten. 'You kidnap him, take him into a cyclone, you leave him for dead, and now you want to *use* him?'

'Please, Petra, you have to understand my position. The brand is in pieces after that race. We were supposed to win, show investors Sentinel Bank always comes first. Instead, all anyone associates with the brand now is a sinking boat and a man being clubbed to death.' Her voice spikes too high. 'Oh, yeah, and you coming to the rescue.'

'I'm sorry you didn't appreciate that.'

'Honey, of course I did. Pay no attention to that stupid message. But you've got to come to the rescue again.' An odd giggle, not at all like her, squelches out. Her right thumb plucks restlessly at her hip. 'Moses is the only one who can get us back on track in time for the stock issue. To a lot of people, the storm proves he's a prophet. If he's in all the media, forecasting huge growth for Sentinel Bank —'

'No way are you using him.'

298

'Investors will throw money at us!'

'Forget it.'

'Petra, we can't sponsor the Coastguard if we go bankrupt.'

'It doesn't matter.'

'No,' she says bitterly. 'Now you're famous, you don't need me any more.'

'Kirsten, you nearly killed him!'

'And I'm sorry, I really am! But you're killing *me* now. Aren't friends supposed to help each other, stand by each other? I never thought you were so cold.'

'Maybe getting trapped in your buoyancy compartment made me cold.'

'And that's just spiteful,' she complains. 'I apologise and still you keep on at me! What else can I say?'

'You can promise you're going to leave that boy alone.'

She stands. 'I could just take him. Any time I like.'

'Do that, and I'll tell the world how the President of Sentinel Bank abandoned a kid to save herself. Think how that'll play on RTV.'

She doesn't reply. Just takes a step back, staring at me like I've turned into some kind of demon. Then she pulls out her phone, summons her boatman and goes to stand at the waterline.

The threat has worked for now. How long it will keep her away from Moses is another matter.

Billy joins me after Kirsten leaves. I'm grateful to him for waiting inside, grateful that he kept out of the argument. A mounting fear haunts me that if forced to declare his loyalty – me or Kirsten – Billy might actually hesitate. Somehow the fact that he remained in my house, among my things, strengthens my confidence. But then he spoils it by saying, 'She's really messed up. I'm worried about her.' He stares out into the darkness. 'We'll need to give her a lot of support after what she's been through.'

I explode. 'Am I the only one who thinks Kirsten should be locked up for what she did to Moses?'

Billy looks at me, immeasurably saddened, but only says, 'She's in trouble enough, P. She needs us.'

I don't reply to that. With those simple, thoughtful words, Billy has just overturned whatever certainty I had. Any answer I give will only hurt us. I feel the corrosion taking root, like a physical disease at the heart of our relationship, leading us inexorably towards that prophesied conclusion.

•

There's a crowd outside our headquarters. I don't like it: crowds make for confusion and accidents, impede urgent action. But somehow, without any real discussion or consideration, Sydney New Coastguard has moved into the publicity game and success here is measured in crowd size.

RTV has been kind enough to send ahead an honour guard of over-muscled men in creaseless T-shirts to 'control' the fans. They talk importantly into radios that are probably going to interfere with our comms. What exactly do they need radios for anyway? They're barely two metres apart. Perhaps none of it is anything more than theatre, to warm up the audience for the star's appearance.

Daran arrives in a midnight-blue Porsche, which he abandons with magnificent recklessness a good two hundred metres short of our gates to go walkabout amongst his fans. The honour guard are ready for this: they surround him entirely, while still managing to lend him an impression of approachability. As Daran grins and quips his way to the gates, hands never leaving the pockets of his gold-buttoned blazer, the honour guard filter out the strange and the strong, letting only the cute and the harmless get within touching distance of their lord's elbows.

Inside the building, RTV has already wreaked havoc with our operational readiness. They bargained hard for use of the Comms room – 'with all those cool screens and shit as background' – but in the end had to settle for Ops with its maps and planning boards. Even that I'm regretting. The chaos of a TV crew is unimaginable; no way will we be able to do anything else in this room as long as they're here.

Peripheral members of the crew have already tried to colonise the corridor outside. 'Petra, would you prefer an evening dress or a business suit?' asks a costume consultant when I step out for a while to escape the punishing lights.

'I'm fine in this, thanks. Look, you can't store that rack here. The passageways must be kept clear at all times.'

Mostly concealing her grimace, the consultant eyes my uniform and says, 'I appreciate you're thinking about publicity, but everyone *knows* you're Coastguard. Wouldn't you rather look pretty on TV?'

It's my turn to grimace. 'Just move your stuff, please. You can use the training room, through there.'

With some reluctance, they allow me to stay in my Coastguard jacket, but I can do nothing to stop them re-clothing Moses. He is enchanted by the white linen suit the producers have chosen. The moment it's on him, he takes to the corridors, running their length with arms spread wide and jacket fluttering behind. By the time he's settled in the make-up chair, his face is beaded with sweat and alive with excitement.

•

'Australia, good afternoon, and welcome to the home of our favourite heroes, Sydney New Coastguard and courageous director, Petra Woods.'

'That's kind, Daran.'

'Petra, darling, big honour, really big, big honour to be here for this first ever live interview with you. Petra is a dear old friend, a lovely home-grown Sydney girl who showed us all on Saturday what it means to be selfless, risking her own life to rescue this lucky boy.' He pauses, turns solemn. 'Moses Lukoto. You've seen him perform wonders on my show, you've watched him escape the jaws of that terrible storm. Before we meet him again, let's view those pictures one more time . . .'

Daran holds the look a second after the camera light goes out. On the monitor by our feet, Moses strides out across tempestuous Bass Strait.

'Five, four, three . . .' goes one of the TV people. The light comes on again.

'Had us all fooled there, Moses. What's it like to walk on water?'

Quietly, respectfully, Moses says, 'I don't know.'

'Right, right, sure, just kidding around. But there is something genuinely extraordinary about this young man. Because while all the experts were telling us the Sydney Hobart would be a safe, quiet race, Moses here knew better: he saw the storm ahead of time. He prophesied the waves, the wind, the sinking boats. He foretold disaster and tried to warn us, but did we listen?'

Daran lowers his head for what is meant to be a grave pause. It's impossible to trust the sentiment. All I see is a showman calculating the gesture of maximum effect. To him, the fourteen people who died in Bass Strait are an abstract concept, never mind that he witnessed several of those deaths with his own eyes.

Today is Dermott's funeral. Kirsten has flown to Brisbane to be there; in the coming days she will have to attend the funerals of the other three crew killed on *Sentinel*. I was saved from accompanying her by the timing of this interview. Billy, who took Dermott's death very hard, went in his grey suit. I picture him sitting close by Kirsten during the service, supporting her, holding her tight while she sobs into his shoulder.

Daran's head lifts – our communal moment of reflection is over. 'So tell us, Petra, what was it like inside that boat? Were you scared?'

My mouth is completely dry. 'You bet,' I say, as brightly as I can. 'I was terrified. But I had a job to do and that kept me going.'

'And what a job it is. Today we're raising big, big funds for the Coastguard, so please go to the RTV website and donate whatever you can to keep these brave people out there saving lives. Petra, you must be delighted by what's come in already. Nearly two million dollars. Should buy a few lifejackets?'

'Yes, Daran. We're really pleased. But the more we can raise, the better chance we have of helping sailors in the future.'

'Big truth. Go to it, bucks.' He winks to the camera, then turns back to me. 'So what are the plans for Moses? There was speculation he was helping Sentinel Bank out with a few stock forecasts.'

'Not at all. He was only ever here to go to school.' It gives me some satisfaction to play back Kirsten's own words.

'Reckon they could use him, with this new issue coming up. Or is he going to join the Coastguard? Handy guy to have around for weather forecasts.'

'He'll be heading back to South Africa as soon as he's fit enough to travel.'

'Are you serious? We love this kid! Why can't he stay here?'

'He's been through a horrible experience. He should be with his family.'

'How about you, Moses? You want to go home?'

Moses shrugs. 'I can't.'

'Why not?'

'I will die here. I've seen this.'

'Awesome,' breathes Daran. 'How do you answer that, Petra?'

It takes me a couple of seconds to speak. Moses's simple words are like a savage kick to me. Didn't we get past this? I'd assumed, after surviving Bass Strait, he would quietly let his death fixation drop. How can he still be saying this!

'I just fished him out of a sinking yacht,' I say grimly. 'I'm not planning to let anything else happen to him.'

'Now, wait a minute. You don't believe his predictions? What about the storm?'

'Not all his predictions come true,' I say, throwing Moses a look. 'I'm really not convinced.'

'Seems to me we've got the perfect test coming up. Moses, last time we met you took a view on the First Citizen election. Do you still stand by it?'

'Mr Nathan Partridge will win.'

'He's trailing a long way behind in the polls. You don't reckon it'll be Rodrigo? Or maybe Elize?'

'Mr Nathan Partridge will win.'

'Well, if he does, I guess even Petra here will have to believe in you. Nathan, if you're watching . . . Of course you're watching – everyone's watching! Nathan Partridge, tomorrow could be your lucky day.'

They want to believe he's a prophet, Stuart said, so let them. We'll save more lives that way. And certainly the money's flooding in at a fierce rate. Superstition, cataclysm and chatshow TV rolled together: what better combination to crack open the nation's wallets? By the end, there's more money in our bank account than I ever imagined possible. Sydney New Coastguard's future is assured.

All the same, when we finish the interview, I feel dirty, deceitful and sick. And I know that I've exploited Moses just as badly as Kirsten.

•

STORM PROPHET PREDICTS FIRST CITIZEN NATHAN is the headline on most news sites within half an hour of the interview. By the evening, when the five remaining candidates come together for the last time on RTV, all the bookies have reversed their odds.

'He's a charlatan,' declares Suzie Marchdale.

Nathan Partridge smiles contentedly and stays silent.

'No, really, I've met the boy,' says Michael Walters. 'Well-mannered, but plainly deluded.'

'I'll fucking crucify the little shit,' snarls Rodrigo Valance.

'Oh, for heaven's sake!' cries Elize Price, speaking not only for her own candidature, but on behalf of all the nation's bewildered civil servants, intellectuals, commentators and politicians. 'You can't *seriously* be suggesting the Australian people will cast their vote according to some African kid's speculation?'

New opinion polls released that evening put Nathan Partridge sixteen points ahead.

•

'So he's too delicate to fly, but he can go on TV and interfere in another nation's political process?'

It is difficult to read Grace Cadey's expression on my screen, and I start apologising straightaway.

'Don't sweat it,' she laughs. 'You saved his life. If the Coastguard can benefit from this Moses madness, I'm glad. But please, keep him out of trouble now? Pretoria's uncomfortable with this attention. And I dare say Moses will recover faster away from the glare of TV lights.'

'I'll keep him hidden, don't worry. Do we have a flight yet?'

'From when he's fit to travel, they're very booked up. The earliest available is the 12th, but if that's too distant we can take him off your hands, house him at the Consulate.'

'It's fine,' I say, although I wish he was flying sooner. It's hard not to feel a superstitious fear for him as long as he's on Australian soil. A ridiculous fear, of course. What can possibly harm him now he's back on dry land?

'He knows my place,' I add, more solidly. 'He feels comfortable there. I kind of like having him around.'

'He's all yours,' she says dryly.

By the following morning, however, I'm having doubts. Media fascination builds rapidly on election day, reaching an intensity I hadn't anticipated. Pollsters can't help but ask the Moses question of every voter they interview. Calls to my mobile, to Spring Cove, are endless: requests for photo shoots with Moses, day-in-the-life pieces, celebrity game show appearances, interviews with foreign news agencies. I turn them all down.

Emails flood in from the public, begging favours of Moses; hand-delivered letters request readings, Delphic advice, even healings. A clutch of strange individuals take to loitering around our headquarters, occasionally approaching the gates to ask if Moses is available. When I head out to visit Dad, they crowd around the Coastguard jeep and plague me with questions about Moses. A man with the look of an outback sheep farmer – cotton hat secured under his chin with a double string, heavy khaki shorts, Blundstone boots – tells me it's his constitutional right to meet the Oracle. An overweight woman with glue in her hair tries to bribe me with five dollars. Two brazen girls tell me they're mates of Moses. Another asks if he has a girlfriend. They're all still there when I get back an hour later. I have to summon the security guard to clear them away from the gate.

Having begun the day in high spirits, thanks to our new financial independence, I find myself lurching towards a state of exasperated stress. This is not a pressure I'm used to handling. Winds and seas, that's what I know, not incessant public attention. When Kirsten rings, pleading with me to reconsider for her father's sake, I lose all patience. I tell her the next time she asks for Moses I'm giving Sam Drauston the full story from Bass Strait. Then, in an attempt to calm myself down, I ignore Carole's recuperation orders and go back on patrol.

A distress call comes in around three o'clock. Dan and I are covering the Manly AOR when we're directed to a launch that's suffered engine failure off Freshwater Beach. I've given Dan the captaincy again, as much to allow myself some space as to help him learn. When he spots the launch and gives me the order to stand by with a line, I comply without thinking.

The guy in the launch is grinning broadly. A brand new red lifejacket is strapped too tightly around his heavy bulk. It looks uncomfortable, constrictive, but he doesn't seem bothered.

'G'day!' he calls out, as Dan brings us to a halt and cuts the engines.

'G'day,' answers Dan. 'Died on you, did she, mate? No worries, we'll give you a tow.'

But the guy in the launch isn't listening to him. His focus is on me alone. 'Get closer, will you?' Brisbane accent. 'So I can jump over.'

'No, mate,' says Dan. 'We're going to tow you.'

He gives me a nod. I toss the line across.

The guy in the launch ignores it. The line falls neatly across his deck, but he makes no move to secure it. Instead, he gets up on the bow and dives into the water.

Dan and I share a bemused look. But people often do strange things at sea, and I get the steps over the side and stand by to help the soaking loon aboard.

'You're Petra Woods, right?' he says before he's halfway into the boat. That grin has become bloated and poisonous. 'I'm with *Stars Hourly*, and I'm authorised to offer you twenty thousand dollars if you'll set up an exclusive interview for us with Moses Lukoto.'

In sheer disbelief, I freeze us both in that posture – him balanced on the gunwale, me holding his arm – and I try to persuade myself it's just coincidence he's here, in distress, on my patch. But a moment longer of that awful grin and I know it's not true.

'You made a false distress call?'

'Petra . . .' warns Dan.

'Hey, come on! My engine's fucked,' gloats the journalist.

A glimpse of Dan's worried face appears in the corner of my vision, but it can do nothing to stop me. One sudden thrust forward, a fist against the guy's chest, and he's cartwheeling backwards, throwing up a king-size splash when he hits the water.

'Petra!' yells Dan. 'What the hell do you think you're doing?'

He rushes to check on the journo, and I simply step around him and take his position at the helm. The engines are humming again before he's even turned back.

'Forty thousand!' splutters the journalist. 'Come on! Think what you could do with it.'

'Turn off the engines, Petra.'

My hand moves to the throttle, but now Dan's palm is against my knuckles, holding the lever down.

'That was an order. Turn off the engines.'

'You're relieved,' I tell him. 'Move your hand.'

'We're in the middle of a rescue!'

'Move your hand, Dan.'

'You're right to be angry, but we have to get this guy to shore at least. We don't leave people in the water.'

Raising my chin, fixing my eyes on the bow, I say, 'Dan, if you ever want to work in my Coastguard again, move your hand *right now*.'

It's enough to make him obey – reluctantly, and with a pointed snort. I don't care. The engines roar magnificently as I bring up the throttle, and that's all that matters to me now. I want that bastard bobbing in my wash for a good few minutes.

Behind me, Dan settles himself down in the stern and says nothing. I feel his glare all the way back to Spring Cove.

•

Donald Carter walks into my office at seven o'clock.

Billy and I have tickets for the Flying Fox Party in Centennial Park tonight. But Billy's just rung to say he has to work, and I've spent the last three minutes ripping the tickets into tiny fragments of gold foil. The new issue, he said: everyone at Sentinel Bank is flat out. Everyone except Kirsten, of course. In token muted colours for Dermott, she'll be hurrying between six exclusive parties tonight, but then she's doing it for the bank, isn't she? It's all about promoting that image, celebrating that non-existent success. Bolstering belief.

'Hi, Donald,' I say tiredly, tossing the scraps of foil into the bin. 'Who'd you vote for?'

'I've just been speaking with Dan Worrell.' He closes the door and takes a seat across the desk from me. 'We need to have a chat, Petra.'

'I went for Suzie Marchdale. I was going to vote for Rodrigo, but in the end I thought, what's the point? We know who's going to win. Moses has told us. So I'm giving my vote to Suzie to make her feel a little bit better about losing. One vote better. Thought it'd mean more to her than Rodrigo.'

There's probably something else I could find to talk about. Eke out a little more time before Donald says his piece. But I'm just too tired to make the effort. Smiling faintly, I flip my palms up and say, 'The bastard made it back, right? Miraculously got his engine going again, didn't he?'

'That's not the point.'

'Fine, so I'm irresponsible, reckless with people's lives, unfit to —'

'No, you're not.' Donald's voice is solidly calm, and I'm reminded how impressive he was in my apprenticeship days, out at sea, with everything happening at once and not a hint of anxiety colouring his steady, reassuring commands. 'You're not irresponsible. You're as devoted to saving lives, to professional coastguard conduct, as anyone I know. You wouldn't have this desk if you weren't, however much money you bring in from friends in business.'

'That's a relief,' I say with a brash laugh. 'Thought for a moment you were trying to suspend me.'

He sighs. 'That is what I have to do, Petra.'

'Excuse me? Didn't you just tell me what a good job I'm doing? Did I miss something?'

'Today, you threw a man requesting assistance off a Coastguard vessel and left him floating in the ocean.'

'Beside a perfectly healthy boat.'

'It was a fundamental abuse of your role.'

'He abused the distress procedure! He transmitted a false appeal, *knowing* I was patrolling the area and would be sent to pick him up.'

'Look, Petra, this won't go on your file. You're exhausted, you're under great pressure from the media, still in shock from the storm, not to mention having personal issues to deal —'

'My personal life is none of your business.'

'It's a temporary suspension until you're rested and recovered. Until your normally excellent judgement is restored. In two weeks, we'll review the situation, OK?'

'Not OK! Since when did you become my superior? You don't get to tell me my judgement needs *restoring*.'

'You want me to pull up the regs? As Operational Directors, either one of us can suspend any crew from sea duties if we believe them to be unfit, physically or psychologically. That includes other Directors.'

'Yeah?' I snap. 'Then I'm suspending you as well.'

'Petra, listen to yourself,' he says mildly. 'Listen to what you're saying and you'll understand why you shouldn't be doing life-critical work just now.'

I do it. I go silent and listen to myself. Mostly it's the strain in my voice rather than the actual words that convinces me. Lowering my head into my hands, I fight hard not to lose it.

'I need the SilverBird to get home,' I mutter. 'Especially while Moses is staying with me.'

'Of course you'll keep *Giselle*.'

'And there's a whole lot of admin to be done.'

'The suspension only covers operational duties,' he says. 'Although . . .'

'Although what?'

'If you took a complete break, the Coastguard might find it easier to breathe. This media circus – I'm absolutely not saying any of it's your fault, but if you were on leave they wouldn't have any reason to jam our lines.'

I nod reluctantly. 'Understood. I'll stay away.'

'Get plenty of rest,' he says, standing up. 'You're essential to us, Petra. We need you back soon.'

•

No Christmas decorations survive in Sentinel Tower. To mark the mourning period for Kirsten's dead crew, the lobby has been stripped of its great Christmas tree, its garlands, its fake snow. The night security people at the front desk know me well enough that there's no problem getting past them, even with a slab of beer under my arm. They understand the idea of a surprise visit, especially on New Year's Eve, and they see no need to alert Billy before they let me up. Two pizzas and a party hat lie on the desk in front of them. That's probably the height of festivity for the unlucky wage slaves still at work in this building.

For some time I stand at the door of Billy's office, watching the man I'm going to marry. His brow is tightly furrowed. His strong, capable fingers are bunched around a tiny pencil, hovering above a sheet of numbers. The muscular flesh of his neck strains against the collar of his shirt. Why is he wearing a tie at this hour, on this day? A little grimace briefly parts his lips as the pencil circles a figure. This kind of struggle is completely alien to Billy, who would think nothing of stripping an engine or keeping a dozen novice surfers safe in perilous waters – tasks that would floor most of the other men working in this building. He is trapped by his conscience in the wrong job, and my heart is close to breaking for him.

'Petra,' he says, noticing me at last. The neon lighting has given his skin the look of old concrete. In this environment, his voice is terse.

'That's me,' I say, closing the stopper on all those feelings, and pulling out an old smile as if this were just another chance encounter at Wango's. 'Thought you could use a drink. It *is* New Year's Eve, right?'

'Ah look, P, I've got so much work to get . . .' He stops, looking at me more closely. 'What's wrong?'

'The love of my life is tied to his desk.'

'No, I mean – with you. What's happened?'

He's standing now, taking the beers and depositing them on the desk, then laying his hands on my shoulders. Waiting for an honest answer. Quietly, I give it. 'Donald's suspended me.'

'*What?*' A flash of anger contorts his face. 'He can't do that.' Snatching up the phone, he demands the number.

'Billy, don't.' My fingers close around his and ease the phone back down. 'I did something stupid today.'

He doesn't ask for the details, doesn't make me embarrass myself. Instead, he takes a long breath and says, 'I'm sorry, P. This stock issue – I've been useless. Your dad in hospital and everything.'

'Have a beer with me,' I smile. 'That'll sort me right out.'

They're good and cold, I've made sure of it, but although Billy accepts a can he doesn't seem to taste it. His eyes, even while we're chatting, keep returning to the figures. At one point he picks up the pencil, unconsciously I think, because he quickly drops it again and forces an unnatural smile.

'You need to work,' I concede.

'I really do, babe. Kirsten wants these marketing projections first thing.'

'First thing, New Year's Day?'

'No one's taking time off around here. Not with the new issue on Monday.'

'Out of interest, did Kirsten know you and I had plans this evening when she set you that little task?'

Billy's too tired, too distracted, to take in what I'm implying. 'She's really busy, P, otherwise I'm sure she'd want to know how you're doing.'

'I mean, did she actually ask you to stay late tonight?'

'She passed me in the lobby today, didn't see me, seemed blind to everything. I had to call her name.'

'Didn't have to.'

Billy is taken aback by my tone. 'This is your friend we're talking about, P.'

A moment of absolute honesty. The urge for it comes out of nowhere. 'Billy, I want you to resign. This place is doing something to you. To us.'

His confusion deepens and takes on a defensive edge. 'It's a job, Petra. We can't blame this . . . friction on a job.'

Friction. His assessment of our problem. In a way, I'm reassured that it's not just my imagination. And yet hearing him give it a label frightens me. It seems to make real something that might otherwise have blown away in the night.

'Then what should we blame it on?' I demand. 'What do we do to sort it out?'

He hesitates. 'Maybe some things are just meant to be.'

His look scares me even more than the words. I grab his arm. 'How can you say that to me? I saved him from the storm! Doesn't that mean anything? He was wrong about dying, he's going to be wrong about us.'

'He only said he'd die in Australia,' says Billy quietly.

'You think I'd let anything happen to him? He's leaving the country in less than two weeks.'

Looking down, he says, 'Let's hope so.'

'Billy, I'm asking you, please: get out of here. Get another job, any job, until you've got the canyoning business together.'

He turns his face back to the numbers. 'You know I can't quit on her now.'

I'm losing him.

I'm losing him to her and I don't know how to stop it.

Long before midnight, I leave Sentinel Tower with my slab of beer nearly intact, and wander slowly back to *Giselle* at CYCA, through the dark Domain, Potts Point, riotous Kings Cross.

Spectator craft lurk around the perimeter of the Harbour exclusion zone. A garbled chorus of broadcast music, laughter, and inaudible chatter drifts from the boats. I skirt south of Clark Island, keeping clear of the zone; technically I no longer have the right to enter it. Passing the anchoring areas off Bradley's Head, keeping to the six-knot no-wash limit, I respond to the greetings from two SilverBird crews with robotic waves.

The fireworks on the Harbour Bridge explode into life soon after. I hear them, I hear the whoops and shouts and fog horns and whistles, and I keep my back to it all, to the celebration that pervades all of Sydney except for Billy and me.

•

That night I dream of burning ships, Billy works until dawn, and a computer in Canberra sorts the nation's votes.

•

PROPHET SWINGS ELECTION reads the headline on the Fox news site, above the serene smile of Nathan Partridge. 'I accept this great honour with humility and resolve, and swear to serve the Australian people to the best of my ability,' he is quoted as saying.

Chapter 13

My mobile rings for the thousandth time since the election news broke. Sam Drauston's number comes up.

It's a grey New Year's morning, Billy is in a different universe, and Moses is sulking because I won't let him watch TV and hear what they're saying about him. I've spent a frustrating hour online confirming what Grace has already told me: there really are no flights earlier than the 12th. Those twelve days now stretch out ahead of me as an unendurable infinity in which anything could happen to Moses. Twelve long days to lose Billy.

In a moment of simple weakness, I tap the screen and take the call.

'Every journalist on the planet is desperate to interview him,' says Sam. 'So I'm not going to pretend this is about anything else. I want to be the one.'

'You're no better than the others,' I say. 'You're worse: you tried to kiss me.'

'Take it as a compliment and give me the interview. The arrangement fee is fifteen grand.'

'Why is *everyone* trying to bribe me!'

Already, those irritating beeps are signalling another call waiting. Perhaps ten other calls.

'Give it to charity. The money's irrelevant. Petra, you're going to have to let someone interview him. He's just altered the course of Australian political history. This is a story that must be told. Resist it much longer and you'll have the whole press corps on your doorstep.'

'He's just a boy,' I cry.

'I can announce the exclusive in seconds. The phone calls will stop. The scramble to locate you will be over. Give me the word, Petra.'

One hour later, a Palm Beach water taxi drops him off at Saaremaa.

•

'You mustn't tell anyone where he is,' I insist. 'They find out about this place, it'll be a nightmare. He'll have to go and stay at the Consulate.'

So far, the media haven't worked out where I live. Saaremaa isn't on any postal, electoral or utility database. Fresh water comes from a park spring, the electricity from solar panels and the generator; no workman has been near the house since the hydrofuel tank was installed three years ago. In this world of interconnectivity, the house effectively doesn't exist. The only people who know about it are my friends and colleagues, none of whom – thankfully – has succumbed to the pleas and bribes of the less ethical journalists. Even Daran has so far kept his mouth shut.

'Are you kidding? You've given me an exclusive. I'm not sharing my prophet with anyone.'

Sam has come to join me on the largest and flattest of the sandstone rocks at the end of the beach. He looks quietly exhilarated after three intense hours with his subject. I didn't want to have any part in the interview;

while Sam coaxed answers from Moses by the water tank above the house, I skimmed pebbles across the lifeless sea.

'You do know he can't really see the future, don't you? That election was self-fulfilling prophecy on an outrageous scale.'

'I might agree, could even write off the storm as coincidence. But I've never quite got over the blood on Kirsten's hand. A very specific prediction which we all saw fulfilled.'

'We all saw it faked.' It's said before I consciously appreciate what I'm doing. Did I mean to let that secret out?

'What?' breathes Sam.

'Nothing.' Whatever Kirsten's done, I'm not going to hurt her deliberately. 'I'm talking nonsense.'

'Kirsten cut herself on purpose? Why? To con me into writing about Moses?'

'What does it matter?' I say quickly. 'Everyone's decided he's genuine.'

Sam leans back, stretching his legs out over the edge of the rock. He's wearing suit trousers and black lace-ups, as he always does. I've never seen anyone wear a suit at Saaremaa before. 'You're right,' he smiles. 'It doesn't matter at all.' The smile is unnerving, like he's planning something. But it's also enticing. It gives Sam an edge, suggests unseen depths.

I lean back next to him, looking at the neat creases in his trousers, and the clutter of scars and bruises on my bare legs. I remember the touch of his lips on mine and wonder whether he'd still like to kiss me.

It's not that I want him to. The only man I will ever kiss now is the one I'm marrying. But Billy hasn't called all day, and I'm close to imagining he's forgotten I exist. Though I know he's swamped with work I'm feeling neglected, that's the bottom line, and it would be nice to think some guy reckons I've still got it.

'You know, Moses remains convinced he's going to die here,' says Sam.

'Well, it's not going to happen.'

'Imagine if he did. What a story that would be.'

'*Sam!* He's not going to die,' I scowl. 'I've kept him alive so far, I'm damn well going to get him on that plane home.'

Sam looks at me for a moment, a half-smile hovering on his lips. 'You're out to save everyone, aren't you? It's truly admirable.'

The judgement unbalances me. 'If he dies,' I say in a small voice, 'then it's like everything will come true.' Hesitating at his obvious puzzlement, I finally admit the selfish motive. 'He's predicted Billy and I will break up.'

'*Oh*. I see.' Sam glances up at Moses, still on the rocks by the water tank.

'I don't believe, I really don't,' I cry, out of sudden, untameable frustration, 'but sometimes it's so hard to keep telling yourself it's bullshit.'

'Jesus, Petra.' I'm expecting some kind of commiseration from him, but what comes out is more like mockery: 'If your relationship is dependent in your head on whether some kid you barely know lives or dies, it can't be worth much.'

'Fuck you!'

'Look, that came out wrong. I just mean, it's a stupid —'

'No, *fuck* you, Sam.' All my dread and anxiety floods out in one tearful rush. I'm already striding back to the house as I shout at him, 'Go write your exclusive article, but don't sit there judging Billy and me!'

•

Sam Drauston holds back his scoop until the following morning – the first working day of the year. His headline is stark: SENTINEL PROPHET FORESEES COLLAPSE FOR BANK.

It comes up on my mobile as I'm leaving Mona Vale Hospital after a gloomy session with my father. Kirsten calls thirty seconds later, and I have no time to prepare any kind of answer to her assault.

'You let Drauston interview him? You let Moses say those things about my bank? Do you have the slightest fucking clue what you've done to me?' Rage drips from every word. Stress and exhaustion flay her voice.

I pull up the rest of Sam's article: *Despite CEO Kirsten McKenzie's claims to the contrary, Moses Lukoto denies he has any continuing connection with Sentinel Bank. When asked what the future holds for the troubled institution, he said he saw no future. Asked to clarify this statement, he said Sentinel Bank would 'finish soon, perhaps within one month'.*

'Kirsten, believe me, I had no idea . . .'

'Do you understand what it means for a bank to go under? How many people could lose all the money they have if Sentinel collapses?'

'It's not real, Kirsten. You of all people know he's not a real prophet.'

'When are you going to get this?' she screams, her voice losing its last shred of control. '*That doesn't matter!*'

·

'You're a bastard,' I tell him over the phone. 'An irresponsible bastard.'

'The truth is the truth. I have the whole interview recorded.'

There is a man watching me shout into my mobile. I recognise the white cotton hat and full beard, even the Blundstone boots, but right now I'm too angry to remember from where.

'You know what this will do to the bank! Just by writing that, in this climate, you have the power to make it come true. Don't you care that you're sabotaging a crucial stock issue?'

'Kirsten McKenzie deliberately misled the financial media. That's playing with fire. She deserves everything she gets.'

'The whole bank will suffer. This is disproportionate revenge. Are you that petty?'

'In this office, I'm a hero today. Like you, I have a job I'm expected to do well. This is how it's done.'

'She's blaming *me* for this. Not only have you hurt the bank, you've probably also destroyed our friendship.'

'Then I've done you a favour.'

'Arrogant prick!'

'Seriously, how can you choose to hang out with a shark like Kirsten McKenzie?'

'You're going to judge my friends now?'

'You could certainly use the help. Your own judgement sucks. You have a conniving predator as best mate, you're set to marry an adrenalin-junkie, from what I've heard you more or less worship a despotic father, and —'

'Yeah, and I *trusted you*!'

'Bullshit. You never trusted me. You gave me the Moses interview because deep down you liked that I came on to you.'

I punch the hospital wall and nearly break my hand. The man with the cotton hat, double strung under his chin, has disappeared.

•

That night, Billy discovers his kayak has been stolen. Rather than call for a lift in the SilverBird, he leaves his clothes on the sand spit and swims

1500 metres across Pittwater to see me.

It's like something from a fairytale, the lover crossing the Bosporus in the middle of the night. His body, when he comes naked out of the water onto moonlit sand the colour of mercury, is glistening and hot with exertion.

'There are sharks,' I whisper into his neck.

'I needed to see you.'

'Me too.'

'You have to help Kirsten.'

I pull away. 'Billy!'

'You're her best mate, she's in trouble, and it's partly your fault. Christ knows why you let that Drauston bastard interview . . . Well, that's the past. The issue's in four days' time and that article has sent our share price through the floor. Clients are asking if their money's safe. The only person who can fix this mess is Moses. You've got to make him support the bank, publicly, on the record.'

'I haven't *got* to do a thing!'

My naked lover steps back and breaks me with his wounded gaze. 'How can you have changed so much since Africa?' he murmurs. 'Don't you care about *anyone* else?'

His arms, cutting through the water, are lost to the darkness before the first tear reaches my lip.

•

I dream, two nights running, of a blazing desert. Unbearable heat. No water for a thousand miles.

•

It is hard to imagine anything could be worse than this uncertain separation from the man I love. But there is always some new thing waiting to strike, even when you don't have the slightest sense of its approach. For me it is a letter, addressed to my father and hand-delivered to Mona Vale hospital by the young widow who wrote it. By dreadful chance, she encountered a nurse just returned from her Christmas break who knew nothing of the isolation prescribed for my father. And by that chance, her needle-sharp arrow plunged through the protective cotton wool and found its target.

Is it true you could have prevented this? Is it true you heard the warning and ignored it? My children have lost a father. And tonight, like every member of every one of those thirteen other families, I will cry and cry with the stupidity and waste of it until my brain feels it must shut down or explode. Maybe you can't understand what it means to lose the most important person in the world. Maybe you think because they knew there was a risk, we should all just accept their deaths. But you had a responsibility to all of us, Mr Woods. You had a responsibility to my children.

•

My father has no life in him.

The machines tell me his heart is beating. His lungs are kept inflated with oxygen-rich air. The doctors assure me he will pull through this second stroke. Scans of his brain show no obvious damage. None of this can counter the impression I have of a being that has fallen apart.

For the first time ever, I see a small, shrivelled man. Voiceless, expressionless, he has so little left to him. His age and exhaustion are suddenly apparent to me. That strong, commanding presence, that reassuring source of firm love, is gone.

Saturday night has drifted into Sunday morning. The Intensive Care Unit at Mona Vale hospital is not busy, and we are left in a kind of peace. I have read and reread a hundred times the letter that did this to him, and although I can't blame the poor woman for writing it, I have come to hate her tightly compressed script and her watery blue ink more than anything in life.

On my father's right hand, a heavy purple vein protrudes above the knuckle of his first finger. Dark freckles mark the skin. His nails need cutting. Once before, I went stealing in a hospital. This time, instead of a scalpel, it is a pair of surgical scissors I pocket. When I return, Sam Drauston is waiting for me. He's standing, despite the three available chairs, as if he knows I'm going to throw him out. My failure to react to his presence confuses him. He watches silently as I take my seat beside my father's right hand and gently straighten out the curled thumb. The surgical scissors are too big, but I manage anyway to cut a reasonable curve in Dad's nail.

The ball of his thumb feels warm, the other fingers colder. Is there better circulation in the thumb? Are the fingers more prone to gangrene? Would you lose more blood through a severed thumb than a finger? These aren't disturbing thoughts for me. They're the stuff of my work. My mind has retreated into familiar professional territory to stave off the pain of the present.

'I'm sorry I said what I did about your father.'

Sam has sat down without my noticing. 'It doesn't matter,' I say. 'You don't know him. It meant nothing.'

He shifts in his seat. He's too close. I don't want him to go, but I don't want him right beside me either. I get up and carry my chair around the bed to cut the nails on Dad's left hand. One of them, on the ring finger, is split. An old split, the edges turned yellow and smoothed off. What heavy work has he been doing, I worry, that might split a nail? These brittle fingers, in their time, have grasped the lifejackets and shirts and arms of countless sailors in distress. They've tugged a thousand halyards, strained under the weight of engines and dinghies, shaped wood and metal, drawn loving patterns down my mother's naked back. They've bruised and broken and bled. Now, I grow foolishly anxious because I suspect Dad of using them to wrestle with a leaking tap or tighten the screws on a cupboard door.

The fingernails are all done now. I lay Dad's left hand close against his thigh. When the nurses came to bathe him this morning, they suggested I might prefer to step outside the curtain while they washed his genitals. I watched them do it, stared attentively, and they probably thought me weird. But I'm preparing myself, that's what they don't know. I'm preparing myself to take care of him, if it turns out he can no longer take care of himself. Those nurses are my teachers. I'm well trained in First Aid and administering injections, I know how to lift a man safely, and now I'm learning how to wash him too.

Sam has been sitting quietly, hands folded in his lap. He has a way of existing peacefully, which I only appreciate when it is interrupted. 'I'm going to leave,' he says. 'You'd probably rather be alone . . .'

'No. I'm glad you're here. So long as you don't expect me to talk.'

'No,' he murmurs. 'No, that's fine.'

He settles back into his chair, and he's still there forty minutes later when Billy walks in.

'What's *he* doing here?' Despite the pallor and exhaustion, his tone is aggressive, and the look he gives Sam is unambiguous.

'I'll wait outside,' offers Sam, standing.

'No need to wait,' says Billy.

Sam accepts this rudeness, makes no attempt to return it, just nods a quick goodbye to me and leaves.

When the ICU doors have closed behind him, I draw the curtain around the bed. 'What's wrong with you?'

'That bastard screwed the bank, and now he's trying to screw you?' For the first time, Billy looks at my father's grey face. 'I'm sorry. I'm . . . Why is that guy hanging around you?'

'He came to give me support. You have a problem with that?'

I sit back down, the bed between us.

'You didn't call me. Why didn't you call me?'

'My father is in a coma. Believe it or not, you aren't the first thing on my mind just now.'

'But Sam Drauston is?'

I stand up. 'Come outside,' I whisper, as controlled as I can manage.

He follows me out. With the curtain closed behind us, I say, 'I don't want you here in that mood.'

'What mood? Can you blame me wanting to know why you called another guy before me?'

'I didn't call him, Billy. He just came. And you know what? I'm grateful to him. He made me feel better, which right now I can't say for you.'

A flicker of resentment crosses his face. 'I'll go then.'

Neither of us moves. He's waiting for me to ask him to stay. I should do – I want to – but the words seem blocked.

Billy rubs his drawn face. 'This really is happening, isn't it? You didn't believe Moses, but look at us.'

'I don't want to talk about that now. My father is sick, and this isn't helping him.'

He kisses me awkwardly on one cheek. 'I'll be at the bank. We're working all weekend, round the clock. The new issue's tomorrow and Kirsten's terrified it's going to fail.' Sighing, he adds, 'I guess that doesn't seem important to you now.'

•

Noise levels build in the hospital as the day progresses. Stuart visits, and drags me downstairs to the terrace for a cup of tea.

'How's he doing, your dad?'

I start crying. 'It's an obvious question, isn't it? You'd think it would occur to anyone who cared about me, wouldn't you?'

He smiles gently, not understanding. A Eurocopter comes in to land on the helipad, making the windsock whip crazily. 'What about Moses? Is he all right on his own?'

'I don't know. I'll have to check on him later.'

'Why don't I stay at your place for a bit? Keep him company?'

I just nod hopelessly.

He pats my arm. 'You take care of your father.'

•

There are visits from a few of Dad's friends, a few of mine. They look at me with kindness and pity. Not much of it gets through. I never have depended on the sympathy of others, and I'm not going to open the door to it now.

For a second night, the ICU staff allow me to draw the curtains around my father's bed and remain with him after visiting hours end.

•

My dreams are full of flickering light and fear.

At some point I wake, a crick in my neck, the edge of the chair digging into my ribs. These are the things that tell me I'm awake, even though my vision is blurred and my sense of balance is screaming that I'm upside down.

My father is looking at me.

'Go back to sleep,' I think he says.

'You're awake,' I cry. 'I was so worried about you.'

'Good girl. You're a good girl.'

His hand strains to reach me. I take it in both of mine, squeeze it tightly.

'That's my girl,' he sighs. 'Sleep now.'

And I do. At least, I don't remember anything else. And I don't dream again.

•

Next time I wake, it is still dark. A throbbing whine comes from the monitors. Running feet sound behind me. I crouch forward over my father's body and press my cheek against his chest. My arms slip under his shoulders and draw him tight against me.

The curtains fly back; white light floods over us. Voices tell me to move quickly, to get out of the way. Their strained semi-politeness carries the same professional urgency I've used a thousand times. 'There's no need,' I tell them, but they pull me clear anyway and try to bring him back. They have to do it, I remind myself. I look away when they pump him and blow their breath into him. I close my ears to their curt orders and calls for emergency equipment.

When it all calms down, goes quiet, I know they're preparing themselves to hurt me. I look back then. 'It's all right,' I say to their practised masks of condolence. 'He's going to a good place. It's fine.'

•

They take his body away and make it clear I can't follow. My father, in common with many rescue workers, has pledged all his organs for donation, and a surgical team is already on its way to extract his corneas and kidneys. The paperwork can wait until the morning, they assure me. They offer me a narrow bed in an administrator's office. For some reason I have no difficulty sleeping. I am still out when the administrator arrives, tells me it is nine o'clock on Monday morning, and asks me without grace for some identification. I break down in the middle of explaining myself, and she backs away through the door to find the nurse responsible for me.

The realisation that Dad is gone forever explodes inside me and I reach fumbling for my mobile to call Billy. My fingers have difficulty bringing up his number. When the call goes through to his voicemail, I can't formulate a coherent message and I hang up without saying anything. Sitting there, numb, I think next of Stuart, of Donald, of Carole. Any of them would be a fine friend to me now. And then I think of Sam Drauston.

•

The first thing he does is lead me to the kiosk and force me to eat. He buys orange juice and wholemeal toast with raspberry jam. Coffee won't help me in this state, he says. When I ask about the work he should be doing, the business stories he should be writing, he waves all that aside with a vague flick of his fingers. Later, I remember the big event of the day: he has given up the chance to cover the Sentinel Bank stock issue to help me through this.

After we've eaten, Sam tells me to wait in the kiosk while he goes to 'find things out'. There are three forms to sign, he explains on his return, and a bag of personal items to collect. He lays the forms in front of me, explains their contents and shows me where the signatures go.

'Do I need to identify . . . the body?'

'No, sweetheart. They know who he is.' He hesitates. 'Did you want to say goodbye to him?'

I shake my head. I don't want to see my father stiff and eyeless. Getting up, I stumble slightly, and Sam cups his left palm around my elbow to steady me. 'Thank you.'

'The personal items, then. One more signature.'

He keeps hold of my arm as we walk back into the hospital. The lift opens on Level 3, and we step out in time to see Kirsten and Billy emerge through the doors of the ICU. It's a shock, the sight of them together, both in business suits like matching dolls sold as a pair. It's a shock, and it's made worse by the animosity that fills Billy's eyes. Sam still has his hand on my arm, but I don't think about that. I only see Kirsten paired with her matching Billy.

The lift doors have closed behind us. Dizzy with grief, I rush down the nearest corridor and hide myself in a ward of senile men. Cackles of curiosity or outrage come from the beds. Someone calls out, 'Sarah! Sarah!' Another demands a glass of gin.

Sam comes after me. 'He's leaving. Would you like me to call him back?'

I press my face against the windows. 'Moses said we would break up,' I find myself whispering.

'Petra!' he says forcefully. 'You don't believe, remember? Don't lose your faith in your disbelief.'

I close my eyes, nod slowly.

'Shall I —' he begins.

'You've been very kind,' I say emptily. 'But you should go now.'

He waits a few moments longer. Perhaps he's expecting me to turn around, to meet his eyes, to offer some sort of last gesture. When I can't, he murmurs, 'All right,' and leaves.

My tears smudge opaque patterns onto the glass.

There's still someone there. Behind me. Drawing close now, a rustle of clothing. Then Kirsten's voice right by my ear. 'I'm so sorry, babe. They just told me. Why didn't you call me? You know how much I loved Lewis. And that's not even the point. Why didn't you call me to be with you?'

She waits. She really seems to want an answer. I can't even turn round, let alone speak.

Her hand caresses my hair. 'When my father died, I . . . Well, you know. You were there. You were there for me. We knew it was coming, but still, his death didn't make sense for months afterwards.' She lays her forehead against my shoulder-blade. 'Petra, honey, I'm so, so sorry.'

A low wail comes from one of the beds. In my traumatised state, I imagine it is my voice, my wail.

'I should have been with you,' she's saying, going on and on. 'This new issue, I was blind to everything else.' She laughs hoarsely. 'It's failing, you know. No one's buying. Our stock has dropped off a fucking precipice.' Her breathing turns irregular. 'There's probably going to be a run on the bank if we don't do something. I actually came to see if you would let Moses . . . ?'

The pause is just too long, too deliberate to deny. But she tries anyway. 'Though obviously now's completely the wrong time. I'm sorry, I didn't mean to bring that up.' She coughs awkwardly. 'Look, honey, I have to get back to the city. Face the music. Are you going to be all right? You want to come with me? Petra?'

Some time after she's given up and gone, a nurse finds me still there, still pressed against the window, and with heartbreaking gentleness she sends me home.

•

The paralysis that lasted a day might have gone on for a month. At Saaremaa, Stuart did his best for me, laid out food and tried to bring my mind back, but even his sympathetic manner was no match for my desolation. Only a sense of massive injustice – that I should lose my fiancé the same day I lost my father – finally pulled me out of that trough of self-pity and sent me searching.

When I found Billy, late that night, he was smashed.

The call came from Buzz; Billy wasn't answering his phone. 'He's in Mona Vale,' Buzz said, naming a bar I've always hated for its sleaze and gloom.

'He's not . . . with Kirsten?'

Buzz snorts. 'Petra, he's never been "with Kirsten". The only reason he's been trying to like that jumped-up princess these last two years is because she's your friend.'

The Pelican is down a back street, flanked by hostels, lit up by two red neon signs. Crates of empties sit right outside the entrance. Billy, stationed at the end of the bar, has thrown his tie over the bottles on the wall opposite. His jacket lies crumpled at his feet.

'Billy, what are you doing?'

His gaze wanders unsteadily across the room. 'Why didn't you call me?' he says, with only a hint of a question about it. Like he already knows the answer. 'Your dad died, and you didn't call me. Why didn't you call me?'

'I did. You were busy.'

'Oh, bullshit.' He turns away. 'Doesn't matter. Clear enough who you wanted.'

'Sam is a friend, that's all. How you can even suggest that, when we're supposed to be —'

'I liked your dad,' he says. A silence follows, into which the despondent chatter of the bar's other three occupants only marginally intrudes. 'Tough old bastard, but I could see you in him.' He taps a finger against the neck of his beer bottle. 'I'm sorry.'

Mentally, I take a step back. 'The funeral is on Thursday. Three o'clock, at St Mark's. Can you get away from work?'

'What work?' he laughs dully.

'Billy, it's important to me that you're there.'

'I'm not the one for you. Moses said it a while ago, and haven't we seen, with all this friction, that he's right? You should be with that journalist.'

His eyes are half-closed, vaguely focused on the bar. Snatching the beer bottle from his grasp, I shout, 'Why are you doing this? Because you think it's what I want? It meant nothing when I turned away from you this morning. My father had just died. And I had this stupid idea about you and Kirsten. Don't break everything we have. It's not what either of us wants!'

'You still think he's not real.' Billy smiles sadly. 'You're supposed to be the sensible one, but you're being irrational. The bank's collapse, the First Citizen, the storm – they've all happened the way he said they would.'

'They were self-fulfilling, don't you see that?' I cry hopelessly. 'Or coincidences at best.'

He shakes his head. 'How many coincidences will you swallow before you have to believe?'

CHAPTER 14

More than sixty people come to Dad's funeral. They are mostly old colleagues rather than friends. Dad didn't make friends easily. Two of the men are in army uniform, comrades from the short tour Dad served in Vietnam. Three of his Avalon neighbours sit next to two regular church-goers who have spent much of the last few years trying to mother him with home-made lasagnes and pies. Commodore Fowler is there in a plain dark suit, along with sailors and nautical administrators from the various committees Dad served on. Donald Carter wanted to come, but his family is on holiday up the coast and I told him to stay with them. Nine former volunteer coastguards sit up front, liver-spotted, gnarled men with salt deep in their veins. Three different people come up and tell me that they owe their lives to my father. It sets me wondering on the hundreds of others who aren't here. There's no reason they would know about the service, but it's comforting to imagine the rows of men and women rescued by my father who might have wished to be present.

Stuart takes charge of Moses, finding a seat for him at the side of the church, so that I can wait outside until the last moment in case Billy comes. He hasn't been in touch since I walked out of that Mona Vale bar in tears. I've left a dozen messages, all unanswered. Tabitha, calling to offer her condolences, let slip he hasn't shown up for work since Monday. Buzz swears he hasn't been back to their flat. It's like he's just dropped off the planet. Twice, outside the church, I seem to hear his motorbike. I even see him across the street, but his smiling face becomes someone quite different. When the minister tactfully touches his watch, I give in and take my place at the front, alone.

The service has already begun when Kirsten arrives and slips into the seat beside me. She's called a hundred times since the new issue failed but I couldn't bring myself to answer. I didn't want to know about the catastrophe that was unfolding at Sentinel Bank, the scramble to regain the confidence of the market. In her hour of need, while I was still reeling from my father's death, I simply couldn't find it in me to stand by her.

But I'm grateful she's here now. The fact that she has come means more to me than any number of apologies. The world is pressing very heavily on Kirsten, and it's a generous act to come out to Avalon in the middle of her bank's frantic last bid for survival. Dad used to say of her that she was the kind of sailor the world needed to remind everyone else where the limits are. She used to say of Dad, simply, 'I wish he was mine.' And if I pointed to her own successful, gregarious and generous father, she'd only reply, 'He doesn't understand the sea.' At times I would become jealous of her respect for my father. Now I'm glad it.

'Lewis Woods was a man of faith,' declares the minister. 'Throughout life he faced challenges to that faith, not least the tragic loss of his wife Hannah, but he never wavered. He understood that though we may be tempted to question God, it was God who gave us the intelligence to pose such questions and in so doing rendered them meaningless.'

The first hymn is Dad's favourite: 'Abide with Me'. Kirsten and I stand close, as we stood close during her own father's funeral. Her presence doesn't make up for Billy's absence, but still it lends me strength, gives me hope. For a few charmed seconds, it feels like we might together, despite all our problems and differences, take on the world.

Then she stops singing and whispers in my ear, 'I want to give you one last chance to do the right thing.'

'What?' With music all around us, I barely make out the words.

'It'd be a miracle, but he can turn it around. After that election result, Moses could say the earth was flat and people would listen.'

I can't believe it. It's not possible: there's no way she would come to my father's funeral to start all this again. But there's nothing else her words could mean. I have to confront that flickering, fanatical energy and whisper, 'Kirsten, stop.'

'I need him, Petra.' She glances across the congregation to where Moses stands beside Stuart. 'It's reached crisis point. We're looking at a takeover, even receivership. Moses could save the bank if we just get the message right.'

'You should go back to the city.'

'I want to give you this chance.' Her voice, uncaringly loud, attracts frowns from the old Coastguards. 'This final chance to do the right thing.'

'Go, please, Kirsten. Just stop talking and go.'

'We'll put him on TV and —'

'You nearly killed him!' The hymn is drawing to a close. 'I'm very sorry about your bank, Kirsten, but there is no way you are ever getting near Moses again. Now will you please leave me alone so I can say goodbye to my father?'

The look she gives me when I step forward to read the psalm is pure hate; I recognise it instinctively, though I've never seen anything like it before. Our lives together, those many years of friendship and shared understanding, become meaningless under that poisonous glare. Though I try to ignore her, my voice grows harsh and taut. I have to pause in the reading, remind myself where I am, remember my father.

He stilled the storm to a whisper
and quieted the waves of the sea.

Other cultures, Dad used to say, have invented sea gods of terrifying wrath and cruelty. But the Lord God guides mariners through the most perilous waters and leads them always to safe harbour. Not always, I wanted to scream at him after Mum died. But I didn't scream; and my father never stopped believing.

Kirsten stands up. Hurriedly, I continue on to the next part of the service. 'I'd like to say something about my father,' I begin.

She picks up her bag and walks to the back of the church. I keep my eyes locked on the lectern.

'My father valued nothing so much as another person's life. It could be a friend, an enemy, a stranger – didn't matter who. Human life was precious to him. I cannot agree with much that the minister said; my father was a committed Christian his whole life, and I have to say now, he died an unhappy man. But I do know this: if there is any kind of just god . . .'

The urge to look up becomes overwhelming. I'm convinced Kirsten's standing at the back, watching me, full of malevolence. I have to interrupt my own words to see.

But Kirsten has gone. Instead there at the entrance, dressed in frayed shorts, his feet bare and his hair all over the place, is Billy.

•

My father once tried to describe the transcendent experience he had whilst still a young man. It took place on Pittwater: a sudden brightening and clearing of the sea to reveal what appeared to be a network of golden cords beneath his boat. His senses sharpened, he heard extraordinary sounds, felt a new energy run through his body, and in that moment became confirmed in his faith.

No such vision has ever challenged my reality, but the closest I have come was walking towards Billy that day, knowing with all certainty that he was mine for ever. It's not that I abandoned the service: I said the words I had planned to say, even sang the final hymn. But I heard none of it, nor for one moment saw anything other than Billy's anxious face waiting for me. And when somehow I became aware the service was over, my feet simply carried me to him without any conscious choice being made.

Leaving the church, walking out into that hot sunshine and Billy's embrace: that was my religious moment.

On his left wrist is an old copper bangle he took off the first day he went to work at Sentinel Bank. I gave him that bangle. I also gave him the shirt he's wearing, faded turquoise and so frayed at the collar it should have been thrown out years ago. But he looks good in it, always has. It goes with his unruly hair, the chafed denims, the weathered tan.

His arms enfold me. His breathing is so familiar I turn to liquid caramel listening to it. People file out of the church and stand in small groups around us. They do not intrude; I have earned my silent communion with Billy. Perhaps they think it is grief for my father that makes me shiver in his embrace. There are tears enough to suggest it. They have no way of knowing how desperately happy this dishevelled, unspeaking man has made me just by turning up.

When finally he does speak, he says, 'I'm sorry. I should have worn my suit.'

'I'm so glad you didn't!'

Those few words open up my senses a little. Still pressed against Billy, I become more aware of the voices around us. The old Coastguards, reminiscing about those rare moments of dangerous excitement that come to define a lifetime of uneventful boating; Stuart, asking after Commodore Fowler's grandson; the minister, trying to chat with Moses, despite mounting theological confusion; two mothers waiting outside the neighbouring preschool, debating cleaning products. And one other voice, barely noticeable at first, it is so polite and soft-spoken.

'Excuse me, please, I want to help him.'

Barely noticeable, yet just strange enough to raise a tremor of unease. With reluctance, I ease myself back from Billy and turn to seek the man whose voice has pricked my world.

'Excuse me, yes, I'm sorry if this is a bad time, but I'd like to help Moses.'

I recognise him immediately, but still I don't see the danger. The same Blundstone boots and khaki shorts, the same cotton hat, double strung under his chin. Only this time his hand is in his pocket and his forearm is piston-tense.

The minister steps back, as it seems the man expects him to, leaving the way clear to Moses.

'Thank you.' His voice has deepened minutely. A slight desperation perhaps, a fleck of uncertainty in a man otherwise utterly sure of his mission. 'You see, there are still people out there who don't believe.'

How fast did I move? In my memory, I leapt through the air quick as a swordfish. But I was slower than the man in the cotton hat, who had fired his first shot by the time I knocked the gun from his hand. And I was slower than Billy, who'd already reached Moses and wrapped his body around the boy, so that the bullet passed instead through his own flesh.

•

Re-entering Mona Vale hospital, so soon after my father's death there, blows the hope out of me. Stuart, leading an uncomprehending Moses by the hand, has to rush forward to catch me. I feel the impact of my own body against his healing ribs and wince for him.

'He's going to be all right,' Stuart murmurs.

'That's what they said about Dad,' I whisper, burning with the unfairness of the world.

'This is different, I promise.'

Already the police are here. They want descriptions from all of us, explanations, some kind of rationalisation of this obscene craziness.

'The boy was the target? You're sure?'

Stuart fields the questions as best he can. 'Moses prophesied he would die here. I guess that lunatic wanted to prove him right.'

Moses huddles with me in the corner of the waiting area. His face is pinched and frozen. Mine, as long as we have to wait for news from the operating theatre, will be the same. As the police start to piece together the story, they eye Moses with an uncomfortable respect. Pittwater isn't normally the kind of place where the mad try to assassinate the famous.

'So how come he got away? Didn't you stop him?'

'Listen, it happened in a second, OK?' Stuart's angry, partly because he's been asking himself this. 'The guy just took off. We were helping Billy – we're *lifesavers*, not cops. The bastard was gone long before we were thinking about chasing.'

When the immediate terror fades, as inevitably it must, a kind of exhaustion overcomes me. This place, this building – I've seen too much of it. I know the taste of its coffee, the smell of its disinfectant, the sound of its floor polishers. Every day for a week I came to see my father, and still he died. I can't do it again. Not when I had Billy in my arms, ready to go with me wherever we wanted, ready to live always for us.

What it must be like to have a brother, a child, a husband, permanently committed to a cancer ward or a life-support machine.

There are things to do, actions that help, as in a sea emergency, to draw the mind a little away from the central crisis. The call must be made to Billy's family in Adelaide. Buzz must be summoned with a few of his things. And Moses must be got away from this country immediately.

'Tomorrow,' says Grace Cadey, when she's had a chance to check with her agent. 'A flight's opened up tomorrow afternoon; 15:40, Emirates to Dubai, connecting with —'

'Not sooner?'

'Petra, that's less than twenty-four hours away. We're talking about a flight to South Africa, not a bus. If you think he's still at risk I'll come and get him. He'll be safe at the Consulate.'

'He's safe with me!' I shout, slamming the phone shut.

Stuart comes over, concerned. He has to leave with the police, help them with their manhunt. They've thrown a cordon across the peninsula, and have officers checking every ferry passenger and boat user along the eastern side of Pittwater. They want me out there identifying too, but there's no way I'm leaving yet. Not before I know whether he's alive or dead.

•

It takes the surgical team two hours to give me the answer.

By the time they come, it is dark and Billy's mother has called a dozen times for news. Occasional messages from Stuart tell of long queues of traffic on the Barrenjoey Road, where he is stationed at a checkpoint alongside two heavily armed officers. The minister, Commodore Fowler, and a few others from the funeral who got a good look at the gunman have also been co-opted. So far there has been no trace.

One very young constable has been detailed to remain with us, against the possibility that the man should be smart enough to track us down. 'He knew about your dad's funeral,' speculates the cop nervously. 'Could easily work out you'd be here, what with your guy having a bullet in his guts and —'

'Thank you,' I snap.

He falls silent. His fingers flicker around his holstered gun.

In fact the bullet, it turns out, passed a little way clear of Billy's guts. It tore through his back muscle, lost a good deal of momentum on the edge of a rib, and tumbled downward into adipose tissue. For a reckless hero, Billy was incredibly lucky.

'He's asking for you.'

'He's awake?' I stutter. 'He's . . . alive?'

'He is,' smiles the surgeon. 'Glad we could give you some better news this time.'

When I walk into the ward, Billy smiles faintly and says, 'This is like where we first kissed.'

My laughter is spattered with tears. 'Are you up to it?'

'Reckon I could survive it, if you do all the work.'

'Fair enough, I suppose.'

'How about Moses? Is he OK?'

'Thanks to you.'

He looks absurdly, shyly pleased at that. 'Always wanted to be a bodyguard.'

'Don't even think about it. I need you to keep clear of bullets for the next sixty years.'

His eyes turn anxious. 'I got so much stuff wrong, the last couple of weeks. Spending all my time thinking about the bank and Kirsten. Not being there for —'

'Please, just . . .' My face falls apart. 'Just be back.'

·

Eventually, I am thrown out. Visiting rules are enforced more strongly in this ward. Anyway, I'm conscious of poor Moses, stuck downstairs with only a jittery cop for company.

'Who's going to be at Saaremaa with you?' demands Billy as I kiss him a sweet, longing goodbye. 'Stuart?'

'Moses will be there. Stuart's still helping the police.'

'What about Donald, or that Coastie you've been training?'

'Billy, I'll be fine.'

He frowns. 'Give me your phone.'

'What?'

'Hand it over.'

I do, mystified. One-handed, he flips through the numbers.

'Billy, who —?'

'Hi, mate, it's Billy.' He's disabled the speaker, pressing the phone to his ear to keep me in the dark. 'Petra's guy? Yeah, right, no worries. Listen, mate? I've just been shot and . . . no, no, it's nothing serious, but could you do me a favour and keep P company tonight? There's this nut-ter wandering around with a gun and I'd feel better if someone was with her. Yeah, you know where the house is? Excellent, thanks, mate. I'll pay you back sometime. Cheers.'

He hands me the phone.

I look at the screen and see that the guardian he has chosen for me tonight is Sam Drauston.

•

Too many terrors and hopes, this afternoon, have crowded my brain for me to recognise how much I briefly hated Moses. When it seemed Billy would die for saving him, would die of a bullet meant for him, I hated the child sitting beside me in the hospital with an intensity made bearable only by my conscious unawareness of it. Now that Billy has been pronounced safe, a great surge of love towards Moses appears from nowhere. It is this which alerts me to the ugly emotion that went before, and in my shame I overwhelm Moses with affection and concern. 'Are you sure you're all right? It's OK to be scared. That was a scary thing that happened.' I've never heard myself speak this way before. 'You're not worried he might come back, are you? Because he won't. Hardly anyone knows about this house, and that guy is probably already halfway to Alice Springs. If the police haven't caught him, I mean, which they almost certainly have.'

Much of it's just the vocalisation of my own worries. The police haven't found the man in the cotton hat and Blundstone boots, this much I know from Stuart's continuing bulletins from the Barrenjoey Road. By now, they've pretty much accepted they're not going to. And yes, if he knew about my dad's funeral, there's a good chance he's got the resources to find out where I live.

But it's not only him I'm worried about. It's the others like him, the two or ten or two hundred people who get the same idea of helping Moses reach his self-declared destiny. How soon before they find the means and the courage to do what that other did? How soon before they arrive at Saaremaa?

It's only one more night, I tell myself. I only have to keep him alive for one more night. Then he's on a plane out of here, and no force on earth can make him die in Australia.

Only one more night. The saddest thought.

The tide is right in. Small waves break a couple of metres from our feeble picnic of canned tuna, canned chick peas, sliced raw onions and old but toasted pita bread.

'Moses,' I say, watching him prod ineffectively at the fire. 'Will you miss this place?'

Will you miss me?

He doesn't answer right. I don't remember what he says, but it's something far off the point. There's no concession to the dismal sense of parting that has turned the already limited taste of our food to cardboard in my mouth.

'I'm going to be sorry to see you go.' I want to hear every day how he's getting on in school. I want to introduce him to new experiences, shield him from heartache. I want to watch him grow up.

He leans over, sensing at last the tone in my voice. 'I won't go,' he offers.

'Moses, that's sweet, but you're on a plane home tomorrow.'

'I will die here.'

'No, not that, not now, please.'

He shrugs, like there's nothing more he can do if I persist in not understanding. He takes the last spoonful of tuna and mashes it into the pita on his plate. Neither of us has touched the onion.

Is there any way he will be able to explain to his family what he has been through here? Will they even begin to comprehend the idea of a great yacht, or the body of water capable of tearing it apart? Perhaps they will understand the shooting – which to me still defies all sense – more easily.

'All I want to say,' I go on, confusedly, 'is that you shouldn't worry about anything. You're safe here.'

And with that I realise I can hear the engine of Sam's boat.

He's got here fast. He must have dropped everything the moment he took Billy's call. I'm touched by his concern, even though I feel foolish to be the cause of such disruption to his busy life.

The engine is louder and more powerful than it should be. A throaty roar, where I'd expected the tinny chatter of a water taxi. He has his own boat now? Surprised, I watch the navigation lights draw closer, and the prow of the launch resolve itself into a familiar profile.

'Oh, no,' I whisper. 'You're not coming here.'

Kirsten slows only minimally on her approach. I've never seen her mistreat a boat before, but now she rams the launch up the beach as carelessly as Daran before her. 'No more talking,' she calls out, killing the engine and abandoning the boat.

'Kirsten . . .' I don't know what else to say. The black clothing, the reckless leap from the deck, the aggressive stance – I don't recognise any of it.

'Don't bother,' she snaps. 'I gave you every chance to help. It's too late.' Striding towards Moses, she reaches for his arm, set to drag him off, and reacts with actual astonishment when my hand deflects hers.

'He's going home,' I say quietly. 'It's all arranged. The flight's tomorrow.'

'Get out of the way, please,' she says. 'I brought him here. I decide when he goes back.'

The exchange provokes only a spectator's casual curiosity in Moses. When I glance his way, expecting fear or distress, he throws me a quizzical smile.

'Do you even know what happened today?' I cry, blocking Kirsten's second reach for Moses, this time with my whole body. 'Someone tried to murder him! Some lunatic watched Moses say he was going to die here, then picked up a gun and decided to make it happen. It was a complete fluke he didn't succeed. If Moses stays in Australia, that man or someone like him will kill him!'

But Kirsten barely seems to register this. Certainly, she gives no sign of understanding the situation. 'I'll tell you what happened today. The Federal Government suspended trading in Sentinel stock and froze all accounts. My bank is dead in the water if I don't do something! So will you please move?'

I can only shake my head.

She lifts her chin, stares down at me in disdain, then abruptly swings round to her boat.

'I'll push you off,' I start to say, until I realise Kirsten has simply reached for something in the launch, and turned back. 'What . . . ?'

In her hand is a Stellar flare. Pointed directly at me.

'Now will you get out of the way?' she says, as if explaining something to a very small child.

349

'You *never* do that with a flare.' I can't credit her threat. I can't. For all the blackness in her face, the alien character shift, the desperation, this is still Kirsten.

'Shall we find out if these are as lethal as they say?' She raises the flare to my face.

'*Kirsten!* Put it down, before this gets serious.'

'Moses,' she says with quiet violence. 'Come here.'

Tearing my gaze away from the flare, I see Moses step forward, as if in a trance. I shout his name, grab his arm.

'Let go of him. Your last warning.'

'You honestly expect me to believe you'd fire that thing at me?'

A second's pause. Kirsten stares emptily into my eyes. I want to offer her a smile, something to remind her of our twenty years together, our shared secrets, our unfailing support for each other. But with that life-preserving, life-threatening flare between us, I can't do it. However sure I feel of her bluff, I can't coax the right expression into place.

Kirsten transfers her aim to Moses.

A jolt of fear threads through me. 'You wouldn't do it. You need him alive. That's why you're here, isn't it? To get him spouting nonsense about the bank?'

A febrile madness disfigures her voice. 'What value is he once he's on a plane to Africa?'

For the first time, I start to wonder if she might actually pull that trigger. 'You could be charged with attempted murder, just pointing that thing at him. How's that going to help the bank? Be sensible! Throw the flare away.'

But Kirsten's attention is somewhere else, and now I hear it too: that so familiar sound of a trusty Pittwater taxi. 'Coming here?' she mutters.

Bursting with relief, I nod. 'Sam Drauston.'

'What the *fuck*?'

'He's coming to keep an eye on me. Make certain nothing happens to Moses,' I add pointedly.

'I'm sure,' she growls. 'Christ, if Billy knew.'

Before I can protest, she's snatched Moses's arm and wrenched him out of my grip. Gasping at the pain in her damaged shoulder, she rushes him towards the house. 'Get rid of him!' she calls back, pressing the flare up against Moses's cheek. 'Don't make me go off the fucking rails here.'

The water taxi takes forever to reach Saaremaa. It heaves into the crescent of faint firelight and comes to a halt by *Giselle* while the boatman, new to the job, quizzes me about submerged rocks.

'I remember a cluster around here,' he mutters, directing a torch at the water.

'That's the next beach,' I say impatiently. 'But look, you don't need to come in. Sam, I'm fine.'

'And hello to you, too,' he laughs.

'Go on, go home. Moses is asleep,' I say, glancing back at the house to check no one's visible. 'We're fine.'

'Think I'm going to pass up on your fiancé's invitation – no, *instruction* – to spend a starlit night with you?' he jokes.

'Sam, no,' I say, too forcefully.

'Petra, I'm kidding. Mate, come on, there's no rocks here. Let's get to the beach.'

'Please, go home, Sam. I'm *fine*.'

'So you keep saying,' he frowns.

'Well, so, go home.'

By now the boatman has overcome his caution and made it to the shore. He casts an inquiring glance at Sam, who considers me a moment longer.

'Go on!' I cry.

'Whose boat is that?' he asks quietly.

'It doesn't matter, please, just go.'

Giving the boatman a couple of notes, Sam steps ashore. 'Thanks,' he mutters to the guy. 'You head off now.'

'Your change, mate.'

'Keep it,' says Sam, his eyes on me the whole time.

He waits until the sound of the water taxi has faded. I can't speak. A terrible stillness hangs over us. A portent of the disaster to come.

Abruptly, Sam starts towards the house.

'Sam, no! She . . . she . . . I think she could really do it.'

He hesitates, backward stare, long enough that by the time he turns once again to the house, Kirsten is standing on the veranda with Moses.

'Are you going to try and stop me, Sam?' she says, almost drowsily.

Slowly she walks Moses down the steps and over the trampled sand to the waterline. Sam holds his position, face devoid of expression.

'Petra says she doesn't believe I'll use this thing.' She flicks the end of the flare back and forth, then returns it to Moses's cheek. 'But I reckon she's not so sure. How about you? Accidents do happen, even in front of members of the press.'

'It'd make a good story.'

'Wouldn't it?' she smiles. 'Your speciality.' A thick snarl develops. 'Slamming Kirsten.'

'Are you all right, Moses?' I call.

'My death is very close,' cries Moses. 'I've seen it. I will die tonight.'

'That's not true! She's not going to hurt you.'

352

Sam lifts a foot, repositions it to give himself a marginally wider stance. Steadier. 'I don't attack you for the sake of it, Kirsten.' He seems oddly nettled. Vexed to be misrepresented. 'I write the story that pays the best dividend. Sentinel Bank in trouble brings the *Times* a lot of readers, and my bonus will reflect that. If you'd employed me, I could have written equally powerful stuff in your favour.'

Kirsten stares sourly at him. 'Perhaps you should have made your venality clear earlier. We might have made a useful arrangement.'

He considers this carefully. His brow lifts. 'You think it's too late?'

'Sam?' I whisper.

Ignoring me, he keeps his gaze on Kirsten's startled face. 'After all, what are you going to do with that kid now that you've got him?'

As if uncertain of her possession, Kirsten grasps Moses still tighter. 'He's going to tell the world Sentinel Bank is a winner. He's going to predict huge profits, and they'll believe him, those people out there, just like they –'

'Wouldn't that story be more powerful coming from the guy who reported the collapse prediction?'

Frozen in stone, Kirsten mutters, 'You'd do that?'

'For the right dividend. You put Moses in front of the cameras, I'll write the script.'

'Sam!' I cry, stricken by his betrayal.

Kirsten lowers the flare, but keeps her grip on Moses. 'How much?'

'Not cash. You haven't got enough. Sentinel stock.'

'It's worthless.'

'I want twenty-five per cent of your holding. It won't be worthless once I've finished writing about it.'

'Chance in hell I'm handing you a quarter of my stock!'

Sam holds up his hands against her indignation, steps back. 'Then all the best to you, Kirsten. Away you go. And good luck getting that boy to say the right thing on TV.'

For the longest moment, Kirsten surveys Sam, while I can only look on in disbelief and despair.

'You'll help us get the suspension lifted? Tell the market we're a good buy?'

'Give me the stock and I'll have the incentive to do a whole lot more than that.'

'Seventeen per cent. We'll have to put it in an anonymous trust. So they can't discredit you.'

Sam inclines his head. 'Twenty.'

'Fine. Yes.' She grimaces. 'Do you have any idea how much money that used to be?'

Sam smiles. 'All right. Let's go,' he says, stepping forward and guiding Moses towards the launch.

'*Sam!*'

He throws an almost weary glance back. 'Sorry, OK, Petra? It's not every day you get handed your whole superannuation plan in one go.'

'If we don't get him out of the country,' I plead, 'some crazed idiot is going to kill him. You put him out there, in the media all the time, he's an easy target. Don't you care about him at all?'

Sam stops, looks across Moses to Kirsten. A tiny expression of thoughtfulness, ridiculously inadequate: 'We should at least take his spare clothes. Anything else he needs.'

Kirsten brings the flare back towards me. 'Go on, Petra. Bring his stuff out.'

'Go to hell.'

'I'll get it.' Sam pulls Moses in the direction of the house.

'I'm not letting you do this,' I tell her.

'Petra, this has always been bigger than you. Sam understands the game; you don't. It's your fault you had to learn the hard way not to interfere.'

'You take him away, I'm calling the police straight after you. Kidnapping charges, threatening behaviour with an illegal pyrotechnic. By dawn you'll have lost him. Probably, you'll be in prison. What can you hope to achieve then?'

'I brought him to Australia, I sponsored him. How is it possible for me to kidnap him?' She's smiling now, sure of her position. 'And if Sam swears there was no flare, what proof do you have?' With the propagandist bought, she's already savouring the miracle recovery of Sentinel Bank.

'Kirsten . . . *please* . . .' I don't know what else to say. I can't fight two of them. 'Don't put him at risk like this.'

But the part of Kirsten that might have responded to a final, desperate plea has succumbed to whatever pitiless psychosis it is that has taken control of my oldest friend. There's just nothing there any more.

The door of the house opens and shuts. I don't want to look round, to lift my eyes from the flare only to see Moses being led away.

Until –

'*Sam?*'

Her voice is newly splintered. Incensed disbelief.

Sam is alone. He is standing in front of the closed front door, arms crossed and legs braced. A forbidding sentry. 'Go home, Kirsten.'

'What are you *doing*? Where's Moses?'

'He's staying inside. Go home, Kirsten. There's nothing anyone can do to help your bank now.'

Her face has turned a dangerous red. 'We have a deal!'

'There'll be takeover offers from a dozen foreign players within a week. Pocket the money, get free of Sentinel. You'll be plenty rich enough.'

'You can't do this, Sam.' Tears are forming. Her shoulders, so rigid and angry, begin to shudder. The horror of defeat, virtually unknown in her life, is suddenly upon her.

'Oh, sweetheart, I'm sorry,' I find myself saying, despite everything. 'I know how desperate you feel right now, but —'

'Don't patronise me,' she screams. 'You do not get to *pity* me!'

'But Sam's right. This could be your big opportunity to get free. Start something new. You're a brilliant business leader. You could achieve so much. Listen to me – I'm your *friend*.'

She falters, lets the flare hang at her side. 'We are friends, aren't we?' She seems genuinely unsure, in need of affirmation. 'I don't have anyone else, Petra. No one real.' Her eyelids flicker. 'Why couldn't you have been a better friend to me when I needed it? Why do you always make things hard for me? I've only ever wanted the best for you. Why couldn't you want the same for me?'

'I do, Kirsten. I really do.'

'Then why didn't you *help* me?'

'I tried to. But I also want the best for Moses.'

It's the wrong thing to say. Kirsten turns glacial. 'Ahead of me?'

'Look, it's not about —'

But she's stopped listening. Kicking the sand furiously, she says, 'Someone really has to teach you a lesson,' and brings the flare back up.

'*Petra!*'

I jerk round to see Sam sprinting towards us. And in that moment

Kirsten pulls the trigger, unleashing a roaring projectile that passes so close by I flinch from its blistering heat.

For a millionth of a second, I look back at her in horror. I just can't accept that she's taken the shot. Then two thousand litres of performance-grade hydrofuel explode, blasting everything around, turning the beach a scalding orange and slamming Kirsten and me into the water.

•

I'm barely conscious. The force of the explosion must have been cataclysmic. All I remember is being in the air, everything bright as day. And I just get that my house, my lovely house, is a mass of flames before screaming pain erupts as a shard of metal embeds itself in my thigh. Then I'm dumped in the sea, skin stinging, lungs heaving, retinas in shock from that acetylene-hot light.

The effort of staying afloat, battered and stunned, seems close to impossible. I'm just about managing it, but I'm not in any state to act professional. Kirsten's out here somewhere; I should be locating her, rescuing her if necessary. And something else is nagging at me which hasn't come clear yet. But all I can do is keep my head above water and wait for my brain to get a grip.

Kirsten appears beside me, takes hold of my arm. 'I'm OK.' I can't hear my own words – can't hear much at all. 'My leg's hurt, but I'm OK.'

Her grip tightens, and I'm thinking that's a strange way to perform a rescue, until I remind myself Kirsten doesn't do this every day and likely she's forgotten half the lifesaving stuff Dad taught us. Then suddenly I'm underwater.

All kinds of instinctive reactions kick in. Muscles that felt vague, remote, burst into life. My legs pound so hard I shoot up out of the water and shake myself free of Kirsten's clutch.

Sucking in air, biting back the pain in my leg, I wipe the seawater from my eyes and stupidly ask, 'Kirsten, what're you doing?'

I try to make out her face in the orange glow from the beach. I need desperately to see her eyes.

She punches me.

I shouldn't be surprised. Not when she's shot off a flare at me. Not when she's just tried to drown me. But I am surprised. I'm incredulous. Nothing in me can reconcile two people struggling to stay afloat with a hostile attack.

Dazed from a blow I wasn't prepared for, I don't have more than a scrap of air in me when I go underwater. Kirsten's fingers find my hair and curl a knot to keep me down. It's so black I can't see her body to fight back. My legs are powering away to get me to the surface, but all they're doing is lifting Kirsten a little higher out the water.

I'm getting horribly scared now.

Strange how the brain goes in a crisis. I just want to talk to Kirsten, explain to her what she's doing, who she's doing it to, like she's not aware of any of this. But unable to communicate, to reason, all I can do is reach up, follow her own arm to her shoulder, her neck, and squeeze hard on her throat.

She lets my hair go. I swim hard and quick away from her, surfacing five metres off.

'Are you out of your mind?' I shout.

She's treading water, rubbing her throat, glaring at me.

Giselle's close by. I swim over and climb aboard. My sense is starting to come back. Just being in the SilverBird steadies me. The shrapnel in my leg doesn't look as bad as it feels: a sliver from the fuel tank, nowhere near the major blood vessels. It's safe enough – if agonising – to pull out.

I switch on the primary radio. The taste of blood lingers in my mouth from Kirsten's punch.

'Sydney Coastguard, this is Petra Woods. We have an emergency situation on Pittwater. Require waterborne Fire Brigade and . . .'

But it's already too late for the fire-fighters. My house is completely collapsed, the side closest to the hydrofuel tank just blown away. Flames sweep across the fallen beams and turn my few possessions to ash. Three posts remain standing, alight like giant candles.

The soft splash of Kirsten's breaststroke reaches the SilverBird. I stoop down and haul her up by her good arm.

'Sydney Coastguard,' comes the Night Duty Officer's voice. 'Pass your message.'

Not until now do I remember. *Pass your message*: lives at risk, location, urgent medical requirements, adverse conditions, hazards. And deaths. At last I see it. The two of them walking through the doorway. Sam shutting him in the safe refuge of the house.

'This is Sydney Coastguard. Pass your message.'

I will die here, he said. He knew it, right back in South Africa. He'd always known it.

I just never wanted to believe him.

•

'Petra, are you there? What's happened? Where's the fire?' Distortion on the radio exaggerates the sense of panic in the Night Duty Officer's voice.

I touch the transmit button. 'This is Petra Woods. Cancel Fire Brigade.

Repeat, cancel Fire Brigade.' I scan the beach for Sam. 'Possible requirement for medical assistance . . .'

But I no longer have the mike in my hand. Kirsten has knocked it
away.

'You've killed him,' I say. My heart is empty. I should feel something,
but there's nothing left.

She hits me again. I stagger back against the foredeck.

'You proved him right. Well done. He's real. Was real, I mean.'

She snatches up the boat hook, groaning at the strain on her injury.
When the hook comes swinging down, I take the blow on my shoulder
and wonder shakily what it would have done to my face. Only instinct
tugged my head aside. A slicing pain runs up my neck.

'Sydney Coastguard to Petra Woods. Transmission interrupted. Repeat
message.'

She lashes out again. I catch hold of the boat hook and tug it out of
her grasp.

Stepping up on the foredeck, I raise the boat hook in defence. But
one look at Kirsten and I know I can't use it against her. I hurl the thing
out into the night.

Kirsten leaps onto the foredeck. Her face, lit by the flames, shows
no hint of the friend I knew. She takes a deep breath, and I do the same.
Then she charges into me, locks her arms around me, and the two of us
crash into the water and sink down, down beneath the boat.

It's strange how peaceful I feel. Remembering the last time I was deep
underwater, in *Sentinel's* companionway with Moses. I know this situation, I'm thinking. It's dark, Kirsten's grip is unyielding, but I know this.
And although I'm surprised we aren't floating back up to the surface with
all that air in our lungs, it doesn't take long to work out that Kirsten has

locked her legs around the mooring chain, and that too seems manageable. Because now she's set the example, and all the annihilating anger I feel over Moses has an outlet.

Her arms are tight around my back, but I'm able to wriggle a little, push, twist myself sideways in her embrace. There are techniques coastguards use to break a panicked grip, sensitive parts of the body to pinch, but I don't try to get free. I've understood that we're staying down here together. To the end. All I do is twist a little further, clear a straight line, form a fist and concentrate all my fury – every drop of it – into that single sledgehammer blow to her gut.

My face is so close to hers I feel the rush of air bubbles spewing from her mouth, emptying her lungs in one fatal burst. It's done now. I no longer twist away. Like her, I twine my legs around the mooring chain. I embrace her. I concentrate on making my own air last as long as possible. I lay my face against hers as she writhes and struggles. I hold her, and I wait.

It is impossible to describe what it was like, as a professional lifesaver, to feel another human being choke, grow faint, and finally lose consciousness in my arms. All I can say is the same thing I told the police.

Kirsten didn't make it.

CHAPTER 15

Throughout the two weeks the police keep my beach sealed off for forensic examination, I eat and sleep in my office at Spring Cove. Many kind people have offered me a place to stay; Billy has left countless messages imploring me to use his flat while he's in hospital; Donald's wife has been in to tell me how much it would mean to her personally if I'd 'join the family' for a while. But my life has been comprehensively shredded – even my belief in the workings of the universe has been overturned by the substantiation of Moses's claims – and I desperately need the bedrock of the Coastguard to keep me steady. It is the one part of me that survives; all other compartments in my mind have been shut down. Though I'm still not in any state to go back on active duty, I feel secure here. I feel part of something.

Mostly, I am left alone. Donald, Carole, Stuart and the rest understand that what I need is a bustle of normality around me, without having to be involved myself. The staff avoid all mention of Moses. As they pass my door, they make a special effort to sound cheerful and busy, discussing knots and barbecues and exaggerated rescue stories. No one comes in, and I'm grateful for that.

From time to time, the police stop by to question me. I'm not under suspicion: Kirsten's body was recovered quickly enough to allow an unambiguous post-mortem verdict of accidental death by drowning. But they are still struggling to accept the story that Sam and I have presented of the crazed actions of a respected Sydney business leader, and the death of the South African minor, Moses Lukoto.

It doesn't help that the forensics team can find no trace of his corpse, beyond the steel fillets of the shoes he was wearing, and the metal components from the watch Billy gave him. Among the forensics community it is accepted, apparently, that human bone tissue can sometimes combust entirely, but no one can understand why his teeth have not been found. There has been gruesome speculation from certain experts as to how the skull might heat up sufficiently to explode and scatter the teeth beyond the search area. As a result, hundreds of kilos of sand are to be sifted from the surrounding beach.

In his eyewitness account of the event for *The Australian*, Sam hinted at an alternative explanation. Isn't it fitting, he suggested, that the boy who saw the future, anointed a king and walked on water should, on his death, have his mortal remains disappear so mysteriously? What may have been a casual joke for Sam, a gentle blasphemy, has sparked intense speculation on blogs and in chatrooms. There are claims now that the Navy's transparent bridge never existed, that something extraordinary has, briefly, passed amongst us.

Sam is doing nothing to dampen the speculation. I'm grateful to him for his intervention with Kirsten, and also for accompanying me to the meeting with Grace Cadey, where he did a lot of the explaining for me. But I've been dismayed by all the lucrative interviews he has given. His appearances on TV are poignant: the burns to his face, arms and hands look raw and painful; his movements are stiff from internal bruising and two shrapnel wounds on the torso; much of his hair was burnt away, and he's shaved the rest off. His unnaturally white skull, streaked with red welts, makes him a fascinating narrator for a rapt nationwide audience. He is a media animal through and through, so perhaps I shouldn't be surprised that he has chosen to exploit a child's death so exhaustively. His latest plan is to write a book about Moses; he wants to interview me for it, before memories fade. In his words, a thirty-year gap may have been a trivial test of recall to Christ's chroniclers, but that's no reason to hang around now.

Like every other journalist or producer who has called since Moses's death, Sam gets nothing from me.

•

I make only one visit to the hospital in Mona Vale, four days after the fire.

A brutal finality thickens the air about me as I push my way through empty streets and hollow corridors to the man who is still my fiancé. His instant delight, the moment he sees me, makes me want to cry.

He tempers it as quickly as he's able. 'I'm really sorry, P. About your house. About Moses.'

'Don't be sorry. It's not your fault.'

Something in my voice confirms for him what he must have already guessed. 'You . . . You aren't worrying about *us*, right?'

There's this titanic struggle in his face. A determination to overcome that inescapable prediction. And I admire it, even as I turn away from it.

'It's not going to work,' I say emptily.

'But . . .' His confusion makes him colour. 'You want this as much as I do, right? We still love each other?'

'What's the point, Billy? You were right. Everything he said came true.'

The flatness of my surrender stuns him. 'It doesn't have to be inevitable,' he says. 'Surely this is in our hands? It's for us to decide, isn't it?'

I stay silent, staring at the floor. I have nothing left to offer him.

'We're going to fight it,' he promises. 'We're going to be strong, hold together.'

'Billy . . .'

'I *love* you! What fucking prediction can stand up against that? We're going to get married and have a boatload of children, and no bloody prophecy is going to stop us.'

I look up at him then through clouded eyes. 'Do you know how hard I fought to keep him alive? In the storm, inside that boat, and again at Saaremaa when Kirsten had a flare pointed at him. And you . . . you took a bullet for him! We fought and fought, Billy, and Fate won. Don't you get it?' Tears trickle into my mouth. The taste of the sea. 'I love you, Billy, you know I do. But he saw our future and there's *nothing* we can do to change it.'

•

I take to camping on the beach at Saaremaa. It heals that part of me I need to get back to work. The distance from Sydney helps. When there's nothing but seawater and pelicans and yachts, it is easier to look beyond what I did to Kirsten, and return to the simple black and white of a stranger's rescue. It becomes possible to remember who I am.

Stuart goes back on operational duties ten days before me. On the strength of my recommendation following the *Sentinel* MOB, the

Promotions Board awards him command of his own SilverBird. He gives it up, when I return, to ride with me. He knows I'm not ready to deal with new crew; it's a deeply generous move.

We don't talk a whole lot during those first few weeks back together. He's picked up some great new music from a guy he met in hospital, and we play the more uplifting tracks over and over. When I feel like nursing my misery and tell him to cut out the happy shit, he just whirls up the volume until I'm laughing through my irritation and the sun's back in our lives.

He watches me carefully when we pick up sinkers, especially if they recognise me and make a big thing about Moses. But I'm calm now. I don't lose it like I did with the Brisbane journalist. Perhaps they don't get all that much sweet talking from me, but I never was so hot in that field. Besides, Stuart's time in bandages has given him an even more sympathetic way with casualties. They don't need me.

What Stuart doesn't do, and I'm grateful for this, is introduce me to new men. Several friends try it, but Stuart never suggests a drink with this 'really great guy', or just happens to have a mate around when I turn up at his place for a quiet chat. He allows me my loneliness, understands it, and won't try to help me out of it until the right time comes.

·

The days cool down; the memories of Moses grow a fraction less acute. Some nights, I don't dream even once about Kirsten underwater.

After a long period of reluctance to take the final step, at dawn one chilly morning I scatter my father's ashes over Pittwater. There is no clearing of the sea, no heavenly appearance of golden lines beneath *Giselle*. Just a smear of dust spreading out and thinning into invisibility.

Improvements are made at Spring Cove, courtesy of the RTV fund-raiser and Kirsten's surprise bequest. A new ALB is launched and the docks are strengthened. Our night-watch capability is enhanced with extra staff. A training module covering rescues from mud is introduced. Overseeing these changes keeps me usefully occupied.

Sam Drauston has received an unprecedented advance for his Moses book. He offers me thirty per cent if I'll contribute my recollections, but again I turn him down. Three other publishing firms have commissioned writers to tell the story of Moses – all of them have plagued me with calls – but Sam's book is expected to reach the shelves first. Pre-sales teasers have already begun appearing on some of the news sites. A copy of his manuscript is delivered to Spring Cove, with a card from him inviting my comments. The pages remain sealed in their 'confidential'-stamped envelope, somewhere under my desk.

People come to Saaremaa, sometimes in groups, to see for themselves the place where Moses died. It has become a mystical site for some. Usually I'm out in the SilverBird, and no one ever touches my stuff, so I don't much mind the many footprints in the sand. When those I encounter ask to see some relic from Moses's short time here, I shrug apologetically. Only when I'm alone do I, from time to time, slide under Balloon Rock and run a torch beam across his scratched name.

Sam visits. Several times. Paradoxically, it's both nice and irritating to see him at Saaremaa. I tell him not to come, but he turns up anyway.

'If you ever want to talk about Kirsten . . .' he offers.

'I don't.'

'It's not a good thing to bottle up. You know I would never repeat any —'

'I said I don't want to talk about it.'

He knows I've no interest in him beyond vague friendship. On one visit, he describes a new girlfriend in such detail I suspect she's been invented for my benefit. And he always asks about Billy.

'I understand it's hard,' he says, 'after what happened to Moses. But you shouldn't let some chance remark from a dead boy ruin your life.'

'There's more to my life than Billy,' I mutter.

'Believe in your disbelief, Petra,' he says firmly. 'Whatever I may have said in the past, whatever I've written in that book, I'm still going to tell you the same: you know he was never real.'

'Go,' I whisper. And he goes, as he always does when I ask.

Sam only ever comes by water taxi. And he only comes in daylight, making sure to leave before any hint of darkness confuses our uncertain friendship. So there is no mistaking the identity of my visitor, one evening, as I'm waiting for the fire to die down and force me towards sleep.

I'm sitting beside my tent, conscious always of the charred Estonian timbers just beyond the firelight, when the familiar old splash of a paddle warns of Billy's approach. He comes ashore with uncharacteristic hesitancy and stands a good ten metres off. He's waiting for me to say something, to invite him over. But I'm unmoving stone beside my fire, completely unprepared for this.

With no encouragement forthcoming, he doesn't venture any closer. Instead, he moves off into the darkness beyond the gutted house and I don't see him again that night. In the morning, I wake early, find the kayak still there, and investigate from a distance. Billy's chosen a patch of sand close up against the house, and he's still asleep. After my exercises, I cook up some coffee on the camping stove, and wait for him to wake.

When he does, he accepts the coffee and drinks it in silence. It's getting late; I have to go to work. But as I'm leaving, he leaps up and says this simple thing.

'Look, P, I know I've lost you and it's my fault, and I'm not going to get you back. But I can't bear to think of you alone here with nothing but a tent. Let me do one last thing.' He glances down, embarrassed. 'Let me rebuild the house.'

And I can't reply. Because I know it's my fault, and I'm not going to get him back, and I've let belief fuck us up as badly as he ever did.

•

It takes Billy three months to rebuild Saaremaa. He's tracked down a ship breaker with a stock of old marine timber, and he reckons the new house should have almost the same character as the old. The materials and tools needed he lists on the backs of old roster sheets, and I have them delivered by barge to the beach. Money is not a problem since the sale of Dad's bungalow; there's nothing else I want to spend it on.

Billy sleeps at the end of the beach, a good distance from my tent. I cook him dinner, which he takes with a quiet thank you and eats by the waterline. In the morning, I leave out bottled water, beer and sandwiches. We don't talk about much, not to begin with, only the progress of the house and any design issues he needs decided. It fascinates me that he is able to mix cement and lay foundations, craft tight joints in timber, build window frames. These are skills I never knew he had. Sometimes I come home early, kill the engines and approach silently with a paddle, so that I can watch him work without being seen.

He listens to a local radio station when he thinks I'm not there. If

I come home the normal way, my engines announcing me, the music is switched off before I moor.

One evening, after nearly two months of this, I serve him his dinner and then, as he's withdrawing to the waterline, I catch his arm and say, 'Why not eat here? It's chilly. Keep me company.'

He sits across the fire from me, and we eat in shy silence.

A group of Korean tourists turns up the following Sunday afternoon. They set to work, with solemn faces, filming every scrap of the beach. Their Australian guide talks them through a hopelessly corrupted version of the last hours of Moses's life. It becomes clear to me, watching this circus, that something must be done. When they've gone, Billy knocks up a large white cross – for want of any more appropriate symbol – and we take it to the neighbouring cove and wedge it firmly in a cluster of rocks at the top of the beach. The boat-hire guys, ferry operators, water taxi drivers and café owners of Palm Beach and Careel Bay enjoy the harmless deception, and pretty soon all pilgrimages are being directed to the new holy site. There's often a group there, these days.

'Moses predicted I was going to build a house up the hill,' I tell Billy during an otherwise silent evening by the fire.

'So he was wrong about something,' shrugs Billy, his eyes not leaving his food.

Work progresses on my new home. It now has walls and a veranda. It's starting to acquire some character. The roof is the hardest part; that takes more than one man. I get back one day to find Buzz heaving a great length of timber up to Billy. He's come to help for a week, and he sleeps next to Billy at the far end of the beach. At meals, Buzz makes us talk, makes us laugh again.

He leaves when the roof structure is complete, but the mood is lighter now. Billy and I can chat without thinking too hard. Without stressing about what it might mean.

'Why don't you listen to the radio when I'm here?' I ask. 'You turn it off. Why is that?'

He doesn't answer. When I return home the next day, the radio is playing.

Billy doesn't stop until the house is finished. He won't take a break, won't acknowledge weekends or public holidays. By the time the weather turns cold, everything but the decoration is complete. It is not quite my grandfather's house, but it's close enough. Standing with Billy in the new kitchen, deciding paint colours and cupboard design, I don't know how to tell him what I feel.

I save that moment until the evening, when I take his empty plate from his lap and wordlessly kiss him for the first time in four months. And even though it is really too cold to be outside, and Billy has been sleeping in the house for some weeks now, we lay our mattresses on the new veranda, in the exact position the replacement couch will go, and we spend the night there.

We make love.

We wait until the foggy dawn to say all the things we've been storing up over the past few months. I tell him about Kirsten, and he wordlessly takes on a part of that burden for me, his fingers against my cheek seeming to draw some of the guilt out of me. Then he tells me the thing he wants most to share with me.

To my profound surprise I find myself joyfully agreeing.

And when I go to pick up Stuart, late, he smiles a little knowingly, and he says only this: that it is time for him to take on his own SilverBird.

CHAPTER 16

After Billy's return, I don't see Sam Drauston for nearly two years. So much has happened in that time, for both of us. His name is everywhere, of course, with the huge success of his book. Some people think of him as a kind of apostle for Moses. They love him on RTV, never tire of hearing him recount anecdotes about Moses. Nathan Partridge, that other beneficiary of Moses's short time here, regularly invites him to dinner. A couple of days a week I have to take *Giselle* past the fancy house Sam's royalties bought him in Seaforth. But I've never accepted the invitations to his media events, nor have I been tempted by the big payments on offer from RTV if only I'd do a show with him.

Billy and I have worked through everything and come out the other side with something unbreakable. In his old generous and untroubled way, Billy even suggested inviting Sam to our wedding. But I wasn't about to risk our happiness. I don't need Sam in my life, and I know Sam's got quite enough people in his to do without me.

So it's a shock, arriving at my office one morning, to find Sam waiting.

His hair has grown back; he looks in perfect health. That confident smile is on proud display. The only trace of his burns is a patch of discoloured skin on the back of his left hand.

'Congratulations,' he says warmly. 'I heard you named her Kirsten. A lovely gesture.'

'She's not a gesture.'

'No, of course. How's Billy's company doing?'

'You want another mansion, there's a seven-month waiting list.'

'That's great,' he smiles. 'Good for him.'

'Sam, what are you doing here?'

'Nice to see you too, Petra.'

When I don't reply, he sighs, 'All right, fair enough.'

He goes to the window, looks out over the three docked SilverBirds. Sunlight glistens on the water of Spring Cove. Another safe boating day.

'Tell me one thing, then I'll leave you in peace,' he says. 'Does it still hurt?'

'What do you mean?'

He turns back, looks steadily at me. 'You know what I mean.'

'No, Sam, I . . .' But I can't finish the denial. Tears are suddenly close. I think about Moses's delight on seeing his first wallaby. I remember so many tiny moments. 'Yes. Every day. It hurts every day.'

He chuckles gently. 'Your wedding present is on your desk. It will help, I promise. You can always tell Billy it's another gift from Daran Sacs.'

He kisses my cheek, and as his lips brush my skin he whispers, 'I did tell you to believe in your disbelief.'

When he's gone, I find it hard to move. The past trespasses into the present and cripples me.

Much later, I open the envelope on my desk. Inside are two air tickets and a hotel reservation.

•

To my surprise, Billy is enthusiastic about the trip. It's where he proposed, he reminds me. Never mind what came after. He brushes aside my anxieties for the little one. If Carole and Stuart can look after one baby, he points out, they'll have no trouble with two. He packs a rugby ball which he plans to kick far into the bush, in memory of Dermott. His gesture seems a little absurd, but it moves me to slip a small photograph that normally sits on my desk into my bag. It is of Kirsten and myself as children, grinning over the stern of a Pacer. While Billy takes the ball off to the game-viewing platform on the first night, I stay alone in our room and spend a little time with my old friend.

We do nothing for the first two days. Both of us are tired. Construction is no less demanding than Coastguard duties, and Billy has been working seven days a week to establish his new firm's reputation. We need the break. Neither of us has spent a night away from our daughter until now. We find the separation difficult and emotional, but we do sleep properly for the first time in eight months.

On the third day, we find a driver to take us to the village. He tells us there once was a witchdoctor in this place. No longer. We nod like interested sightseers. We manage to conceal our deep sense of unease.

The first thing we see on arrival is an elderly man dressed in brown woollen trousers and a faded *Sydney Rocks!* T-shirt.

We stare longer than we should.

The man comes over to us. He taps the image of the Opera House with a questioning smile. We continue staring until he takes my arm in his tiny worn hand. He guides us along a dusty track into a cassava field. He mutters things we don't hear.

And he leads us to Moses.

•

The Storm Prophet has grown up. He must be sixteen, but he looks fully adult. While his gold-grey eyes still hold their beauty, his skin has hardened and dried. His jaw sticks out awkwardly when he opens his mouth. Stubble masks his chin. His hands, clasped around a hoe, have grown callused and scarred.

'What are you doing here?' he asks. The first question I've ever heard him utter. His face is pure surprise. No, he hasn't foreseen our visit.

'Moses?' There's something so different about this familiar figure, I don't blame Billy for voicing our confusion: 'You . . . You are Moses?' A caginess defines him, unthinkable in the boy we knew. Even if he weren't supposed to be dead, I'd have doubts myself.

He lowers the hoe. His T-shirt is worn through. A piece of red plastic string holds up his trousers. I can't help remembering the neatness of his clothes, the care he used to take over his appearance.

'Moses, we thought you were dead,' I mumble.

He unties an old rag from a hoop on his trousers and wipes the sweat from his nose. One side, then the other. Some of the old precision has survived. Across the field, two men stop digging and stare at us.

'The Moses you know is dead,' he says.

'What do you mean? You survived the fire! I can't even begin to think how, but you're alive!'

He shrugs. Another familiar action. 'That Moses was wrong. He believed he would die in Australia.'

'Mate, aren't you glad you were wrong about that?' says Billy.

Moses gives no reply beyond a second, sulkier shrug.

'What about the prophecy?' I ask. 'Do you still see stuff?'

'I see nothing.'

'But what are you doing working in a field? Why aren't you studying? You could do so many things, a smart guy like you. Become a teacher, an engineer. Anything.'

'This is my life,' he says simply.

'Is it money? We can help,' offers Billy. 'College fees or whatever. Can't we, P?'

But Moses has turned away from us to look across at the two men. One of them is coming our way. A threatening gait. 'My brother,' Moses says. 'You should leave now.'

'Moses, what does this mean?' I say, almost desperately. For some reason, I can't quite bear to kill off my unwilling, belated belief. 'You were never right? What about the storm? What about the broken sculpture? Were those just coincidences? Are you saying none of your predictions were real?'

His eyes have grown hooded. 'You are still together,' he observes of us. He seems, if not angry, then a sullen young man. 'I am still alive, and you are still together.'

•

Here is my prediction:

On our return from South Africa, I will first rush to Stuart and Carole's house and hold Kirsten in my arms for about ten hours straight. I will take her home and tell her all about our trip, and put her in the tiny yellow dress we found at Jo'burg airport, and spoil her in every way possible. I will try to explain to her why my chest feels unconstricted for the first time in two years. Then, once Billy has assured himself that his three construction projects are in good shape, I will leave our baby sleeping in his arms and take *Giselle* for a ride.

I will moor at Sam Drauston's private pier, and bang on the door of his luxurious house until he lets me in. I will demand an explanation.

It's not what Sam did that I need to know. That's easy to figure out: sending Moses to hide by the water tank in case Kirsten somehow threatened her way into the house; removing his shoes and colourful flashing watch to minimise the chance of her hearing or seeing him; after the explosion, spotting the opportunity it presented and secreting Moses deeper in the park; picking him up the following morning, via Mackerel Beach perhaps, and then smuggling him out of the country with Grace Cadey's help.

What I can't say with any confidence, because I've never got the full measure of Sam Drauston, is why he did it. The simplest answer must be self-interest: the false death of a false prophet has made him a great deal of money. I've often wondered if he ever believed at all in Moses the prophet, or saw in him only a great news story that might be pumped up by feigning credulity. If so, there is no question that his account would have lacked ninety per cent of its power and consequent revenues if Moses hadn't 'died' as prophesied. When the house went up in flames and only he knew Moses was no longer in it, the possibilities must have been instantly apparent and enormously tempting.

But there is another plausible explanation: that he did it to protect

Moses. In my panic to get him out of the country, I overlooked the fact that simple relocation might not deter a lunatic committed to helping Moses reach his self-declared destiny. After such a dramatic third brush with death, would he really cease to be of interest just because he was no longer in Australia? For a man who is prepared to acquire a gun and risk a life sentence, is it so much trouble to buy a ticket to South Africa? Perhaps Sam did what he did believing Moses would only be truly safe once those obsessed by him thought him already dead.

If that is the reason he gives, I will choose to believe him, and I will forgive him for leaving me in the dark. It is perception that matters, after all. For the sake of authenticity, it was important I was seen to grieve.

But even if he confesses to the first motive, I won't judge him harshly. Because whatever reservations I still have about Sam Drauston, I have come to see I owe him a debt of gratitude. He once said that a relationship dependent on whether Moses lived or died couldn't be worth much. He was right, of course, and if Moses had returned home uneventfully I would always have had the doubt of it scraping at my happiness. That apparent death, though it tore Billy and me apart, also showed us we could only be together. Our marriage, built in defiance of belief, is a thousand times stronger for Sam's deception.

So I will forgive Sam Drauston and keep his awesome secret safe: let his royalties continue to mount up; let the legend evolve as it will. And I'll go home to Billy with a contented heart, glad that not only Moses has survived, but also my simple realist's faith in the way things are.

Acknowledgements

The idea for this book originated in 1998, when I witnessed a sangoma's prophecy come dramatically true. The place was Tswalu Kalahari Reserve, and I owe my inspiration to the staff who allowed me to work there for a while.

I'm very grateful to the Cruising Yacht Club of Australia and CEO Mark Woolf for giving me full run of the club during the busiest time of their year. A big thank you also to the 2005 Rolex Sydney Hobart media team, particularly Nicole Browne and Sam Crichton, for allowing me to hang about their press tent for weeks, and for giving me a place in the media boats at the start of the race – a very special privilege. Also in Sydney, thank you to Peter Campbell, Chris Bolton of NSW Maritime, Lincoln Kirkpatrick of NSW Police Marine Area Command, Murray Spence of *Alpha Romeo*, Will Oxley of *Skandia*, and Colin Booth of *Konica Minolta*.

The wonderful hospitality of Emma Burn, Rick and Clare Garey, and Adrian and Katie Cripps made researching this book a fun, relaxing and gastronomic experience.

The US Coastguard's *Boat Crew Seamanship Manual* and AMSA's

National Search and Rescue Manual were invaluable sources, as were *Fatal Storm* by Rob Mundle (Adlard Coles Nautical, 1999) and *Fastnet, Force 10* by John Rousmaniere (Norton, 1980). *The Book of Prophecy* by Geoffrey Ashe (Orion, 1999) provides a good review of the subject.

For all their feedback and suggestions, thank you to: Caroline Bland, Belinda Byrne, Imogen Cleaver, Paul Cleaver, Paul Denley, Jim Freeman, Alasdair Macdonald, Rosemary Macdonald, Richard Marriott, Alix Percy, Leila Reuter, Bruno Shovelton, Libby Vernon, Andrew Wilson and Kate Wynne. And, grudgingly, Jim Ratzer.

JoJo Mains of the US Coastguard and Jill Hepburn of the RNLI very kindly reviewed the manuscript and steered me away from the worst of my nautical errors. In the interests of narrative drama, I've ignored a small number of their recommendations, so please assume all remaining errors are there by design. If you're trying to kill someone at home, you probably shouldn't rely on a flare.

And lastly, many thanks to my agent, Patrick Walsh, and my editor, Ben Ball, both of whom have expended great effort in drawing the best out of me.